)

THE WEDDING AT PORT-AU-PRINCE

HANS CHRISTOPH BUCH

THE WEDDING AT PORT-AU-PRINCE

TRANSLATED FROM THE GERMAN BY

RALPH MANHEIM

HARCOURT BRACE JOVANOVICH, PUBLISHERS

SAN DIEGO NEW YORK LONDON

Requests for permission to make copies of any
part of the work should be mailed to: Permissions,
Harcourt Brace Jovanovich, Publishers, Orlando,
Florida 32887.

"Ein Fichtenbaum steht einsam," by Heinrich Heine, was
translated for this volume by Richard E. Allen and
Ralph Manheim.

Library of Congress Cataloging-in-Publication Data

Buch, Hans Christoph, 1944–
The wedding at Port-au-Prince.

Translation of: Die Hochzeit von Port-au-Prince.
I. Title.
PT2662.U3H613   1986   833'.914   86-9863
ISBN 0-15-195598-0

Designed by Margaret Wagner
Printed in the United States of America
First edition

A B C D E

A la mémoire de
ma grand-mère Luce Laraque
Morte à Port-au-Prince
le 30 décembre 1969,
je dédie ce livre

Contents

I wish to thank my relatives in Haiti,
Lucienne, without whose friendship,
Toto, without whose library,
and Jeanne, without whose Creole cooking
this book could never have been written.
Like all novels, it tells an imaginary story:
any resemblance to real persons
past or present is fortuitous.

Prologue

THE novel I am setting out to write is shaped like a ruined fortress or castle with three wings—A, B, and C—dating respectively from the eighteenth, nineteenth, and twentieth centuries; its foundations lie buried in the darkest past and its towers are lost in a still-obscure future. This castle stands on a rock in the north of the West Indian island of Hispaniola. It goes by many names—Monrepos, Sans-Souci, La Citadelle du Roi Christophe—but its real name is Fort Dimanche, and it is not really a castle but a prison, a pyramid of skulls. The skulls of defeated enemies lie heaped in the castle yard, to be used as cannonballs in the next war, and in front of the castle walls lie the bleached bones of those who built the castle. The commandant of the castle bears the name of Baron Samedi, lord of the cemeteries; every day, clad in the historical uniform of the black king Christophe, . he inspects every corner of the far-flung edifice; his face is painted black and white, and beneath his moth-eaten uniform he conceals the swelling curves of a woman. Under one arm he carries the collected works of Dr. François Duvalier, known as Papa Doc, an eminent Third World leader; every time he opens the thick tome, which is written in a language no one can understand, a death sentence is meted out. The castle is guarded around the clock by his secret army, whose soldiers wear, instead of uniforms, old-fashioned civilian suits, felt hats, and dark sunglasses. Over the portal is incised an inscription that makes a visitor's blood run cold: THOSE WHO HAVE NOT UNDERSTOOD THE PAST ARE CONDEMNED TO REPEAT IT; inside it hangs a ragged banner with the words VIVE L'AN X DE LA RÉVOLUTION DUVALIÉRISTE! The castle is subject to a terrible curse: its inhabitants are zombies, living corpses, condemned to keep repeating the exact same actions they bungled in their lifetimes.

In the eighteenth-century vestibule of the castle a play is being put on, a dramatic fragment by the German poet Jakob Michael Reinhold Lenz. It is rehearsed day and night. In it a nobleman by the name of Leybold, whose part is played by the French philosopher Voltaire, sits propped on cushions in dressing gown and nightcap, reading a book. His valet, played by the philosopher Rousseau, brings him a cup of hot chocolate. With a grimace of disgust Voltaire pushes the chocolate away.

VOLTAIRE: Take it away, take it away! I'll never touch it again as long as I live.

ROUSSEAU: There isn't any sugar in it.

VOLTAIRE: Simpleton! [*Throws his book on the table*] The sweat of savages clings to it.

ROUSSEAU: [*Stands petrified*]

VOLTAIRE: Don't you understand? Come here. [*Opens the book*] Look at this engraving; it's from the *Voyage de l'Isle de France*. Look, you scoundrels, when you complain of our caprices, look at these blacks. Can the Lord Jesus have suffered more than they? To what end? For the tickling of our palates. As long as I live, you will make me no more chocolate, nor put any more spices on my food; tell the cook.

ROUSSEAU: But even the doctor said you could drink chocolate.

VOLTAIRE: [*Beside himself*] Simpleton! The doctor! The doctor! What about my conscience? Come here, sir. Sit down at the table and drink my chocolate. You made it, it is yours by right. And if I've offended you in any way or have ordered you to do anything unseemly . . . [*Takes Rousseau tenderly by the hand and removes his own nightcap*] Can you forgive me, Jean-Jacques?

ROUSSEAU: [*Exits with the chocolate*] What's come over the old man? I've never seen him so nasty.

Adjoining the vestibule is the marble-paneled reception hall, where the black general Toussaint L'Ouverture is arrested by a French officer named Vincent, while Napoleon Bonaparte, hidden behind a neoclassical column, is secretly kissing his sister Pauline. While being led away, Toussaint keeps repeating the same sentence: "You have felled the tree of black freedom, but its roots will sprout again, for they are deep and widely ramified." Vincent locks him up in a cell along with the German author Heinrich von Kleist, who is here obliged to rewrite his novella *The Betrothal in San Domingo* under the stern supervision of the black general, who rattles his saber as he paces the floor of his cell. Kleist never gets beyond the first sentence: "At Port-au-Prince, on the French part of the island of San Domingo, there lived at the beginning of this century, when blacks were murdering whites . . ." At this point Toussaint, who can neither read nor write, grabs the manuscript out of his hands and tears it up. Poor Kleist, who is fastened to his desk by a heavy chain, wipes the sweat from his forehead and gets back to work.

Next door is the prison kitchen, where my Haitian grandmother sits in a wheelchair, making salad dressing as she was taught to do early in the century at the Lycée de Dames, run by the Ursuline sisters. Meanwhile, black peasant women from the interior of the island set down baskets full of fruit and vegetables on the tiled floor. Holding a rosary in her coffee-brown hand, my grandmother mumbles Latin prayers. A fashionable young man in a sailor suit, with straw hat and cane, looks in through the open kitchen door and recites a line of Baudelaire: *"Bizarre déité, brune comme les nuits"*; it's not quite certain whether this is Marcel Proust, whom she met during the summer holidays at Trouville on the Channel coast, or her stepson Franz, who was a page at the court of the German emperor and later fell at Verdun. Not far off, Aunt Toni sits in a darkened room, watching over and over again the same scene from an old Frankenstein movie: a little girl is picking flowers on the seashore, Boris Karloff bends down to choke her—at this point the film tears. Now shrieks of pain are heard from the adjoining room, where the communist poet Pierre Roumel is being tortured to death by President Duvalier's secret police. In the courtyard of the castle, which is more like a prison yard, my grandfather, an immigrant from Germany, equipped with a tropical helmet, butterfly net, and specimen container, is chasing a brilliantly iridescent hummingbird, which hovers motionless in mid-air in front of him; he murmurs, *"Si les vers con-*

naissaient tes forfaits, ils reculeraient d'épouvante devant ton cadavre."
In a hangar on the other side of the yard my uncle Guillaume is
building an airplane from sailcloth and balsa wood, with which
he is planning to bomb the presidential palace and flee to Switzerland; his plan is betrayed and he escapes on a makeshift raft to
Florida, where he spends the rest of his life making tiny model
airplanes. In the Castle Pharmacy, run by my late grandfather,
my aunt Toni is dissecting a white shark. From its stomach emerges
the perfectly preserved head of her fiancé, a German naval officer.
Meanwhile, on the highest ramparts of the citadel, the black king
Christophe shoots himself with a golden pistol from the Versailles
gunsmithery, given him for outstanding services, while his black
grenadiers march past him through a breach in the wall and disappear into the abyss. In an outbuilding of the castle, a distant
ancestor of mine, a German exporter named Lüders, slaps a black
policeman who is trying to arrest his coachman, thus sparking off
an international crisis, which ends with the bombardment of Port-
au-Prince by a German gunboat; on the road outside the castle
gate, despite Graham Greene's vehement protest, the Tontons
Macoute steal the coffin containing the body of the murdered
communist writer Pierre Roumel out of a taxi cab.

But let me tell the story from the beginning, as it really happened.

BOOK ONE

THE CAYMAN'S
NINE LIVES

*At Port-au-Prince, in the French part of the island
of San Domingo, there lived at the beginning of
this century, when blacks were murdering whites, a
terrible old . . .*

(HEINRICH VON KLEIST,
The Betrothal in San Domingo)

Chapter One

O N the 30th day of January, 1802, a war fleet under the command of Admiral Villaret de Joyeuse, consisting of twenty-two ships of the line, sixteen frigates, four corvettes, and five landing craft, cast anchor in the Bay of Samaná, on the east coast of the island of Hispaniola, which the Spanish called San Domingo and the French Saint Domingue. On board the ships were twenty thousand French grenadiers who had crossed the Rhine, the Alps, and the Nile and, under the supreme command of the Captain General Leclerc and Divisional Generals Rochambeau, Boudet, and Hardy, had won undying fame for the flag at Hohenlinden, Marengo, and Abukir. A second fleet, numbering almost as many ships and men, set sail from Rochefort at the same time. The captain general was accompanied by his wife, Pauline, sister of First Consul Napoleon Bonaparte, who had in person drawn up the campaign plan and supervised the secret preparations in the shipyards of Brest and Le Havre. Also on board were two sons of the black general Toussaint L'Ouverture, who were being brought up in Paris at government expense, and Maître Coisnon, their tutor, who had been instructed to convey the children as well as a letter from the first consul to Toussaint.

The fleet had been delayed by contrary winds. Accustomed to commanding great armies and to defying fate and the elements, the First Consul had plotted the sea route without consulting the minister of the navy and chosen three ill-advised rallying points for the ships. The first was in the Bay of Biscay, where unpredictable currents provoked a collision between two corvettes; one sank with all on board, and the other required time-consuming repairs. The second rallying point was off the Canary Islands, two hundred nautical miles from the direct route. The third was in the Bay of Samaná, where the constant south wind drove the ships westward and forced them to tack endlessly against wind and weather; moreover, this bay is traversed by reefs and shallows, which render a landing extremely difficult even for experienced seamen.

As a result of all this, the transports lost contact with one another and spent days either catching up with the frigates that had sailed on ahead or waiting for other vessels that had fallen behind. Thus the military advantage that might have been expected from the sudden appearance of so vast an armada was forfeited.

From a hilltop surmounting the bay, Toussaint L'Ouverture, whose agents in France had informed him of the imminent arrival of the fleet, looked on impassively as the ships hove in sight. At first he interpreted their piecemeal arrival as a sign of disorder or weakness; as more and more vessels appeared, however, and the entire bay filled with white sails, he was seized with despair and cried out, "We are lost! All France has come to San Domingo to enslave us. France has betrayed us and has resolved to thrust us back into slavery."

Not until December 1801, when the San Domingo expedition was assembling in the harbors of Brest and Rochefort, had reports of its armament, size, and purpose reached the colony, where they provoked an intense ferment among the inhabitants, white, black, and mulatto. For ten years the colony had been laid waste by revolution and civil war. The white colonials, who had returned only recently, feared for their lives and possessions, while the blacks feared for the reintroduction of slavery. There seemed little doubt that every advance of the French armies would be paid for with the blood of white planters. The wealthier left the colony with their movable goods to seek safety for themselves and their families; only a few whites, for the most part soldiers and officials of the colonial administration, remained on the island. Governor Toussaint L'Ouverture was all the more alarmed when one of the highest-ranking officers in Port-au-Prince, Colonel of Engineers Vincent Laraque, came to him requesting passports for himself and his mother. The black general could not conceal his suspicion. He inspected all the entrances to his residence, to make sure they were really alone and that no one could overhear them. Then he returned to his visitor, gave him a penetrating look, questioned him about his reasons for alarm, and tried in vain to placate him. In the end he said:

"If you are determined to return to France I will not stop you, but at least let your departure benefit the colony. I shall give you letters for the First Consul, entreating him to give you a hearing. Teach him to know Toussaint; describe the excellent state of agriculture and commerce in the colony; in short, make him acquainted with my work. I demand to be judged by my achievements. Twenty times I have written to Bonaparte, asking him to send commissioners, competent administrators, agronomists, engineers—he has never replied. Now, taking advantage of the peace with England, which is known to me only through the English newspapers, he is mounting a punitive expedition against me. In its ranks I see my worst enemies, creatures whom I purged from the colony, and whose return threatens it with ruin. Still worse, I have reason to believe that he intends to put pressure on me by treating my innocent children, whom I entrusted to the care of the French government, as hostages—pledges, so to speak—as though I had not offered France security enough.

"Leave as soon as possible; my secretary will provide you with the necessary documents before the day is out. I hope and trust you will get there soon enough to change the First Consul's mind. Make it clear to him that my downfall will spell the ruin of San Domingo and all the Western colonies. I took up arms for the freedom of my race, which France—alone of all nations—has publicly recognized. Our freedom is no longer in France's keeping; it is ours alone. We shall know how to defend it, or we shall die. If Bonaparte is the first man in France, Toussaint is no less a man in the West Indian archipelago."

Those were the last words spoken by the black general to the colonel of engineers. Two hours later Vincent was given a sealed packet and instructed to deliver it to the First Consul immediately after arriving in France. That same night Vincent boarded a frigate, which set sail for France the following morning. On its way through the Bahamas, the frigate was wrecked on a sandbank. By a singular stroke of good fortune, the colonel was saved, but the papers addressed to the First Consul were irretrievably lost. An English merchantman took the shipwrecked colonel on board and, after a roundabout crossing, put him ashore in France, where, despite the loss of his letters, he reported at once to the Tuileries. Perhaps the minister of the navy felt that he was being bypassed and therefore sabotaged Vincent's mission, or perhaps the First Consul was too busy to receive him; in any case, valuable time was lost before Vincent was granted an audience.

When he entered the reception room at the appointed hour, the First Consul was busy with his toilet; seated behind a screen, he was hidden from view except for the tip of his tricorn. His voice sounded strangely muffled, as though he were not really in the room at all; only from time to time a repressed moan could be heard, when his valet brushed his back too violently.

The colonel of engineers did not, however, let these unfavorable omens divert him from his plan of campaign. After the First Consul had inquired where and when he had served—the distinction he had won under Bonaparte's rival General Moreau at the Battle of Hohenlinden did not exactly seem to recommend him in Bonaparte's eyes—Vincent gave a truthful account of his last interview with Toussaint L'Ouverture. Then he could not refrain from referring to the dire fears that had gripped the inhabitants of the colony, regardless of color, when the government's most recent plans became known, and to the ravages which the noxious climate of the West Indies would be sure to inflict on the French army. And, he went on, even if that army succeeded in destroying the enemy, it would remain totally at the mercy of England, which could at any time cut off its supply lines with a blockade. "In the name of the San Domingo colony," the colonel concluded, "I adjure you, Citizen Consul, not to take back the freedom that the French Republic conferred on its colored inhabitants, for so ill-considered a step would result not only in the loss of the colonies and their trade, but also in an unconscionably cruel massacre."

Clad only in his tricorn, the First Consul emerged from behind the screen. As Vincent noted to his astonishment, the soft contours of Bonaparte's body were more suggestive of a woman than of a battle-hardened soldier. "If," said the First Consul, "you had come to Egypt three years ago to preach the emancipation of the blacks, we'd have strung you up on the mast of the nearest ship. I'm white, I'm French, and that's good enough for me. Nature has made it my duty to fight for the predominance of my race. I personally will see to it that no African keeps epaulettes on his shoulders. The black man's friends should hang their heads in shame. I will give you an opportunity to repent your error in a safe place."

The incisive tone in which these words were spoken, even more than their content, told the colonel of engineers that the audience was ended. In leaving the Tuileries, he was given a written order to repair to the island of Elba under police guard, and there to consider himself under arrest until the fleet set sail.

Only a month later the fleet had crossed the Tropic of Cancer and was approaching the Windward Islands, where it lay becalmed for several days. Just as he was due to leave for Elba, Vincent had received a surprising order assigning him to serve as aide-de-camp to General Leclerc, whom he was to join forthwith aboard the frigate *Intrépide*. He walked the deck while waiting for his new commanding officer, who had not yet deigned to receive him. Leclerc tended to cloak himself in morose silence; in emulation of the First Consul, he would pace with his hands clasped behind his back, his cocked hat pulled down over his forehead to give him a look of profound meditation. Sometimes he could be seen standing on the bridge, his collar turned up, searching the horizon through his spyglass, as though hoping by his efforts to raise a wind. The sails hung slack, and not a breeze stirred; the endless sea all around took on a leaden hue in the heat and was slightly ruffled only very occasionally, when a flying fish rose from the water and dived back again. Once a British man-of-war passed in the distance, but it seemed to take no notice of the French fleet.

The men spent the time bathing and fishing; the officers played cards or stood smoking in groups, talking about the prospects for the campaign, which most regarded as an amusing excursion. Some boasted that by drawing their swords and firing a few shots in the air they would drive the rebellious niggers into the sea; as for their leader, Toussaint L'Ouverture, that ape in dress uniform, they would carry him off to Paris in a golden cage and exhibit him for the amusement of the public in the newly opened Jardin des Plantes. Vincent, who had seen the black grenadiers at work and knew what proficient soldiers they were, took no part in these conversations.

During the sultry nights, when sleep was unthinkable, he made friends with Maître Coisnon, an erstwhile Jesuit priest, who with a secret sigh gave himself to be recognized as a Freemason; his republican virtue contrasted pleasantly with the sordid mentality of the soldiers and officers. Though his family owned land in the colony, Maître Coisnon attached no importance whatever to his aristocratic pigmentation, the pure whiteness of which was adulterated with only a few drops of black blood; as secretary to Toussaint L'Ouverture, who had entrusted the schoolmaster with the education of his two sons, he had been well placed to note the absurdity of race prejudice.

One night when Vincent and Maître Coisnon were leaning on the rail, feasting their sleepy eyes on the phosphorescent glow given off by tiny marine organisms, their conversation, inspired by this impressive sight, turned to the immortality of the soul. "We have already died or have yet to die millions of deaths," said the schoolmaster sadly. "Just as the sleep we need for our repose takes up roughly a third of the waking time during which we fatigue ourselves, so, I believe, death will last about a third as long as our lifetime. And the human body requires just that time to rot." Vincent was about to say something in reply when a massive figure detached itself from the shadow of the bridge and, uninvited, joined the two friends. "As for the human soul," said the stranger, whom Vincent recognized by the wavering light of the ship's lantern as Dupuy, the ship's doctor, "while serving as doctor aboard a slave ship, I dissected the dead bodies of several dozen niggers and found no trace of a soul. On the contrary, a surgeon in New Orleans has demonstrated that the brain of a nigger is smaller than that of the bloodhounds used in Louisiana to hunt down escaped slaves." Breathing heavily and supporting himself on the rail, the doctor discharged a cloud of alcohol fumes on the friends. "And, by the way, Citizen Vincent," he went on, "did you know that in the colony of San Domingo there are more than a hundred races of niggers: the Mandingos, who eat human flesh and for that reason file their teeth down to points; the Fulah, who stink so repellently that they can be used only for work in the fields; the Senegalese, powerful and well built, who make excellent coachmen and lackeys; the Ibo, who incline to melancholy and often commit suicide; the Congos, who are always in high spirits and like to dance and sing—to mention only the more important. And did you know, gentlemen, that thanks to constant bastardization these nigger races have split into more than eighty subclasses—mulattoes, mestizos, quadroons, marabous, sacatras—but I don't want to bore you with scientific digressions." With a glance at his watch, the doctor then took his leave: it was time for him to call on the captain general's wife, who was suffering from insomnia brought on by the unaccustomed climate.

The voyage was marked only by one event worth mentioning. Though the crew took it as an evil omen, it provided the superior officers with material for learned discussions. One sunny January morning, when the fleet was still lying becalmed on the twenty-first parallel, a bright-green cloud rose up on the eastern horizon. There was not a breath of wind, yet it passed over the ships, accompanied by a shower of warm rain that drenched the sailors on deck to the skin. Directly above the flagship *Intrépide* the cloud stopped moving; the mizzenmast was struck by lightning, but no thunder followed; a coal-black stone the size of a gull's egg fell on the deck before the eyes of the officers assembled on the bridge. Ship's Doctor Dupuy was the first to examine the stone; because of its glasslike consistency, he identified it as a stray meteorite, whereas Maître Coisnon took it to be a chunk of cooled lava that had been hurled into the air by the eruption of a submarine volcano. Some of the officers supported the one, some the other view, and soon they were divided into two hostile camps. By way of restoring military discipline, Captain General Leclerc issued an order-of-the-day forbidding all further argument about the unusual natural phenomenon, and declared the black stone to be a black cannonball fired by the enemy—a loathsome trick if ever there was one, designed to provoke dissension on shipboard. To get rid of the *corpus delicti*, he ordered the ship's doctor to destroy it in the presence of the entire crew; but when the stone defied all the doctor's attempts to smash it with his geologist's hammer and only gave off a droning sound suggesting a death knell, the captain general, fired by righteous indignation, seized the meteorite and hurled it in a high arc into the ocean. In spite of these countermeasures, the superstitious sailors continued to regard the stone fallen from the sky as a warning from God, which boded no good for the outcome of the expedition.

A frequent and inexhaustible topic of conversation among the men on board was Pauline, the captain general's wife; the wildest rumors were in circulation concerning her. She spent the days bathing on the top deck. A sail had been suspended in such a way as to form a pool, which, despite the shortage of drinking water, had to be filled with fresh water every two hours. To tease the men's imagination, she occasionally let a shapely hand or foot dangle over the edge of the pool. When a sailor was caught taking a forbidden glance at the nude Pauline, the duty officer had him whipped with the cat-o'-nine-tails before the assembled crew; Pauline was said to have looked on with interest through her opera glasses. Still worse was the fate suffered by an inquisitive cabin boy who tried to observe her feminine charms from the top of the mizzenmast; aroused by the unaccustomed sight, he lost his balance and fell to the deck; then, for fear of the punishment that awaited him, he jumped overboard and was torn to pieces by sharks.

One morning when Vincent chanced to be strolling about in the vicinity of Pauline's swimming pool, an envelope fell at his feet; it gave off a bewitching fragrance of Parisian perfume. Suspecting nothing, he picked it up and was about to give it to the officer of the watch when it occurred to him that the envelope might contain a message for him. After a quick look to make sure that no one was watching, he slipped it into the pocket closest to his heart and hurried to his cabin, where he tore it open with trembling fingers. Amid a wave of perfume that made his heart reel, he found a brief, hastily written note bidding him report at midnight to the general's wife's cabin.

Approaching the door of Pauline's cabin at the appointed hour, Vincent, who as Leclerc's aide-de-camp enjoyed unrestricted access to the captain general's private quarters, was no little surprised to see several muffled forms heading in the same direction. In the darkness of the ship's corridor he could distinguish neither faces nor insignia of rank. But before he had time to wonder what this strange gathering might mean, the door opened and a woman's hand pulled him into the cabin. There he saw Leclerc pacing the floor with jangling sword, while his wife, reclining on a Récamier sofa, surveyed the assembled officers with evident curiosity.

"Gentlemen," said the captain general, "I have had you summoned in this unusual way, in order to give you the First Consul's secret instructions for the San Domingo campaign. As there may well be agents of the disloyal nigger Toussaint L'Ouverture aboard our ships, extreme discretion is indispensable. In a decree to be published only after the final victory of our troops, the government has declared its intention of reintroducing slavery in the colony of San Domingo, in accordance with the laws and regulations prevailing prior to 1789. The leaders of the rebel army must be persuaded, by promises of reward and advancement, to surrender voluntarily. They will be transported to France and punished for their crimes. Once the leaders are removed, it will not be difficult to disarm the rebels and restore the tested colonial regime, which made San Domingo France's richest and most productive colony."

The next morning a brisk wind arose, which carried the ships swiftly toward their destination. A few days later they were nearing the coast of Hispaniola, whose eastern, Spanish portion Toussaint L'Ouverture had annexed a year before in the name of the French Republic.

While the ships assembled in the Bay of Samaná, Vincent observed the nearby hills through a spyglass. Even with the naked eye he could see the silver helmets of Toussaint's cuirassiers gleaming in the sunlight. For a few moments he could distinguish the black general's tricorn amid the bright plumes of his guard. This was the moment when Toussaint L'Ouverture turned to his officers and uttered the memorable words "We are lost. All France has come to San Domingo to enslave us."

If Leclerc had ordered an immediate landing, victory would have been certain. Only the day before, Toussaint L'Ouverture had issued a proclamation, calling on the army and the population to welcome the French soldiers as friends and brothers. But by his hesitation Leclerc gave L'Ouverture time to frustrate Bonaparte's plan by alerting his native troops.

Days passed before the vanguard of the fleet finally appeared off Cap Républicain, as Cap Français was called at that time. These ships carried the main body of his fighting force, but even then Leclerc did not order a landing: he preferred to wait for the detachments assigned to the south and west of the colony.

A vital military advantage was thus lost to France. In a stormy interview, Admiral Villaret de Joyeuse reprimanded Leclerc for his blunder, and the captain general's response was to have the veteran officer, who was old enough to be his father, arrested for mutiny. The dissension between the two men was to have fateful consequences for the campaign.

By the time the expected detachments arrived, the wind had shifted, and the reefs with which the bay abounded made a landing impossible. While the captain general was writing a memorandum to the First Consul trying to justify his high-handed procedure, the defenders of the city had time enough to place the fort and the coastal batteries in combat readiness.

By then Leclerc had changed his strategy. Despite the defensive measures being taken, he thought he could take the city without striking a blow. When the weather was right again, he sent his aide-de-camp, Colonel Vincent Laraque, ashore with letters and proclamations that he believed would persuade the black general Christophe, commander of the enemy garrison, to surrender the city.

Vincent was surprised to find the harbor as active as in the days before the revolution. No one seemed to take notice of the war fleet maneuvering offshore. Black longshoremen, bare to the waist and gleaming with sweat, were loading sacks of coffee, kegs of rum, and bales of cotton onto a waiting ship under the supervision of a white planter, who lay comfortably in the shade, smoking a clay pipe. Peasant women from the interior were strolling about, vociferously hawking fruit and vegetables from baskets balanced on their heads. A group of mulatto girls in bright dresses, with motley cotton rags wound around their heads like turbans, were making lascivious gestures in an attempt to attract the attention of some North American sailors, until the menacing looks of a native police officer put them to flight.

Vincent had hardly set foot on shore when he was arrested. No explanation was given. Despite his protests, he spent the day in a prison crawling with filth, suffering torments of heat and thirst. His only comfort was provided by an unknown beauty, who squeezed her breasts swollen with sweet milk through the barred window of his cell. When he begged his mysterious benefactress to lift her veil and, by telling him her name, enable him to show his gratitude on a future occasion, she merely shook her head, but said that if Vincent wished to write his superior officer a letter, reporting his arrest and asking to be freed promptly from his deplorable situation, she would see to it that the letter reached its destination. Shortly thereafter he was released and brought before a black general, who received him in the former official residence of the French governor. Vincent protested his unwarranted arrest and treatment unbefitting an emissary of Captain General Leclerc and official representative of the French Republic.

"Forgive the slight inconvenience, Citizen Vincent," said

Christophe, "but if your skin were the color of mine, I'm sure you would approve my conduct. Treacherous agents, assassins of freedom, have infiltrated our ranks. But they will be foiled—I swear it by our sacred freedom. My devotion to France and the trust shown me by my black compatriots make it my duty to inform you of the crimes being planned and of our oath, which we hereby renew, to die on the ruins of a free country rather than suffer the reinstatement of slavery. No, France will not betray its sacred principles; it will not permit its political morality to be perverted or the admirable decree giving its black children their freedom to be revoked."

The last words were spoken in a loud voice, as though intended not for Vincent's ears alone, but for an invisible third party hidden somewhere.

"*Mon général*," said Vincent, "your misgivings are unfounded. I bring you a proclamation from the First Consul in which he guarantees the freedom of all inhabitants of San Domingo, regardless of skin color. In the name of Captain General Leclerc, I summon you to let the soldiers of the French Republic land and to welcome them as friends and brothers."

Taking the First Consul's proclamation and the captain general's letter, Christophe withdrew to his office to confer with his secretary. Muffled conversation was heard from the next room. Meanwhile, a liveried servant gave the colonel a cooling drink; for fear of poison, he left it untouched.

Christophe soon emerged and handed Vincent his reply to the captain general. At the same time he returned Vincent's sword, which had been confiscated when he was arrested, and also gave him the letter he had written in his cell.

"Forgive my indiscretion," said Christophe while escorting Vincent to the door, "but I am sure you'd have done the same in my position. The unknown beauty who brought you refreshment in your uncomfortable prison was none other than Toussaint L'Ouverture. I hope you will not take his little masquerade amiss."

During the night Vincent returned to the flagship. He reported at once to General Leclerc, acquainted him with the unfortunate outcome of his mission, and stated his suspicion that Toussaint L'Ouverture had been hiding in a cupboard in the adjoining room during his interview with Christophe. The captain general then bade him read the black general's reply aloud, and Vincent made haste to comply:

Cap Républicain, 12 Pluviôse X

Citizen General:

I have the honor to inform you that I cannot surrender the forts and city in my command without an order from Governor General Toussaint L'Ouverture, who appointed me to my post. I am inclined to believe that I am indeed dealing with Frenchmen and that you are indeed the commander of the so-called expeditionary force, but I must await the instructions of the governor, to whom I have sent one of my aides, informing him of your arrival. Should you carry out your threat and resort to force, I shall offer resistance worthy of a general. Should you be favored by the fortunes of war, I shall cause the city to be set on fire and continue to combat you on its smoking ruins.

With respectful salutations,

CHRISTOPHE

During the reading, Leclerc barely kept himself under control. Then, after pacing the floor for some time, turning alternately red and white, he gave orders for all available troops to be put ashore at dawn. This, however, was prevented by another shift in the weather: the boats had just been lowered when a tropical storm broke out. The boats capsized and the sacks of gunpowder piled on deck were wet through and through, rendering the ship's guns useless. After this new misfortune, the captain general sank into a state of listless melancholy and shut himself up in his cabin. There he spent the rest of the day brooding, taking neither food nor drink. Toward evening he ordered the release of Admiral Villaret de Joyeuse, with whom he wished to discuss the new situation. Meanwhile, Vincent observed the streets and squares of the city through a spyglass. Wood was being heaped up outside every dwelling and public building, and trustworthy men stood ready to set it on fire at the first sign of enemy action. After pleading in vain with the black general to spare the city, the mayor distributed buckets among the white population. Christophe had him arrested and marched off to the mountains under guard, along with the rest of the white population, men, women, and children. He then exacted a solemn oath from his soldiers, making them swear to die rather than suffer the restoration of slavery. Upon which they dispersed with torches and set fire to the city at numerous points. Christophe himself offered a heroic example, flinging a lighted torch into his own magnificent, sumptuously furnished mansion, which the British Admiral Maitland had given him on conclusion of the final armistice negotiations. The flames spread quickly, and the roof fell with a crash. At the same moment, flames flared up throughout the city and merged to form a gigantic sea of fire.

The inhabitants who had stayed kept almost superhumanly calm. No screams were to be heard, no lamentations; only the crackling of the flames and the crash of falling roofs. The soldiers on the ships watched the fire with incredulous amazement. Meanwhile, Toussaint L'Ouverture gave spur to his horse and rode out into the night, no one knew whither, and Christophe led his troops in orderly formation to the mountains. At daybreak only glowing ruins bore witness to what had once been a flourishing city, praised by European travelers as the Pearl of the Antilles.

Leclerc, who was convinced that the fire was a deep stratagem and that enemy soldiers must be concealed behind the smoking ruins, ordered the ship's guns to bombard the destroyed city, thus killing countless innocent persons, who were searching the warm ashes for the remains of their belongings. Then, at the head of his army, he marched triumphantly through the blackened ruins, under a blue sky and a radiant February sun. There was nothing more to impede the advance of his troops.

Chapter Two

THE victory was celebrated solemnly in the cathedral, which had been miraculously spared by the flames. Vincent was then entrusted with the honorable mission of conveying the black general Toussaint L'Ouverture's two sons, who had been brought up in Paris at government expense, to their father, along with a letter from the First Consul, calling on the renegade general to surrender. Accompanied by the two black boys, who in their school uniforms trimmed with silver braid looked like pages at the court of Versailles, and by their tutor, Maître Coisnon, as well as Ship's Doctor Dupuy, whose duty it was to make sure that the hostages reached their destination in unimpaired health, Vincent started for the mountains. He was well aware that the news of his delicate mission would precede him, and he felt sure that he had no need of military protection.

The travelers rode through the fertile plain of Cape Samaná, which only a few days before had been resplendent with richest greenery but now lay black and desolate. To the right and left of the road stretched smoking fields, on which half-naked black slaves chanted monotonously as they swung their machetes, lashed by the overseer's whip, while the white plantation owners rested in the half-shade of their verandas, fanned by kneeling bare-bosomed servant girls. "It won't be long," said the doctor, who had joined Vincent during the ride, "before this earth, fertilized by nigger sweat, will bear fruit again. There will be nothing to indicate that this happily industrious country was once a prey to chaos and anarchy." And after a brief pause he continued: "Tropical nature will spread the green cloak of oblivion over the wounds inflicted by fire and sword, and fill the warehouses of the Republic to bursting with sugar and coffee."

Shortly after Limbé, the climb into the mountains began. The

broad military highway narrowed to a path twining between reddish hills; coffee bushes with cherry-red fruit covered the slopes.
Vincent turned in his saddle and cast a final look at the blue bay
receding on the horizon, traversed by the white sails of the fleet
and framed in sheer cliffs, over which somber rain clouds were
gathering. "Captain General Leclerc will have to hurry," said Isaac
L'Ouverture, who along with his brother, Placide, was riding beside Vincent, "if he wants to defeat my father's troops. In a few
weeks the rainy season will flood the colony and turn roads and
trails into bottomless quagmires that will swallow up the French
army, man and beast." Vincent felt that he ought to reprimand
the outspoken boy, but in secret he agreed with him. He won-
dered whether he would ever again see his mother, who had stayed
behind in France. Then his attention was diverted by more pleasant things.

The travelers had entered a subtropical upland forest which in
the prevailing silence reminded Vincent of a Gothic cathedral.
The dense covering of leaves made for a greenish twilight. As
though refracted by stained-glass windows, the falling rays of the
sun painted strange varicolored shapes on the forest floor. Creepers
as thick as a man's arm hung down from giant primeval trees,
whose cleft trunks were so large that four big men with joined
hands could not have encompassed them. Breadfruit and calabash
trees, wild avocados and mangos, prickly agaves and pineapple
trees grew helter-skelter, while slender king palms traversed the
roof of foliage and jutted skyward. Wild ivy and lianas clung to
aerial roots, forming dense hedgelike barriers. When at last the
travelers had fought their way through the evergreen vegetation,
through the mazes of rotting stumps and fallen trees, they beheld
a sight surpassing everything encountered thus far.

Emerging from the cool grotto of the forest into the fiery mid-
day sunlight, they saw on one side a green gully carpeted with
waist-high ferns, its damp bottom swarming with snakes and am-
phibians, and on the other a bristling cactus jungle, which rose
before them like a rampart. The silence all around them was broken only very occasionally by the screeching of a forest bird or

the creaking of a branch. Startled by any such sound, the travelers would reach for their pistols, prepared for the onslaught of a raging tiger or of a black rebel lurking in the underbrush, but in place of the dreaded perils they discovered only a gold-shimmering butterfly, a striped wild boar, or an iridescent hummingbird, held motionless by its buzzing wings while it sucked nectar from the open calyx of an orchid. The children also seemed to sense the magic of the place. Involuntarily, they stood at attention, as though reporting for roll call in a barracks yard or praying in church. Only Maître Coisnon was unmoved by the splendor of the scene. Without so much as a glance at the primeval forest surrounding them, he delivered a scientific lecture to his charges: "On its whole surface," he informed them with upraised forefinger, "our earth is clothed with vegetation, the diversity of which diminishes as we approach the equator or the poles. While in the Northern Hemisphere the vegetation is rather monotonous, often characterized by a single variety of tree, in the Southern countries a varied mixture enhances the panorama and we behold tall trees, resplendent with the colorful blooms of the Malvaceae, Papilionaceae, and Ipomaceae families."

In the next moment he spurred his horse, drew his sword, and gave chase to a butterfly. Some minutes later he fired several pistol shots at a hummingbird that he wished to preserve for his collection. After several unsuccessful attempts, in which he either missed the tiny bird or tore it to pieces with a direct hit, he was inspired to load his pistol with sand. Taking aim at a magnificent broad-tailed hummingbird presenting all the colors of the rainbow, which was feeding nectar to its young in their walnut-sized nest, he actually succeeded in burying hummingbird and brood under a charge of sand. He broke the bird's wings to keep it from escaping and wrapped it in his handkerchief. But when he opened the handkerchief half an hour later, nothing was left but blood-soaked down feathers, which, to make matters worse, had lost all their color. And the doctor had no better luck than the schoolmaster. At noon the travelers stopped to rest in the shade of an overhanging cliff. The reddish coloration of the rock led him to think it contained copper. While testing it with his geologist's hammer, he caught sight of a horned iguana not far away, sunning itself on a flat rock. Approaching on tiptoes, the doctor killed the animal by striking it on the head with his hammer. Unfortunately, the hammer blow shattered the reptile's magnificent horn, which made the iguana worthless; the doctor tossed it aside to be eaten by ants and vultures.

Amid such occupations the day passed. By evening the travelers had crossed the mountains, so completing the arduous part of their journey. Over a wide path cut out of the jungle, they were approaching the Ennery valley, where Toussaint L'Ouverture had his secret headquarters. When they stopped at a pond to water their horses, the doctor sighted a clutch of turtle eggs on a sandy bank. Seating himself on a moss-covered log, which gave off a strong smell of musk, he took his geologist's hammer and broke the hard shells. Inside, to his horror, he found wriggling crocodiles, no larger than the palm of a man's hand, still connected by umbilical cords to small sacs of yolk. He was about to pick up one of the little beasts, intending to preserve it in alcohol, when without warning the tree trunk began to move and glided quick as a flash into the pool, knocking the doctor off his feet with a swish of its tail. Taken completely by surprise, the doctor had barely time to call out to Vincent, "Don't shoot, it would spoil the hide," before powerful jaws seized him and dragged him into the water. The stirred-up mud of the pond revealed no sign of life, only a few opalescent air bubbles, in which the terrified, wide-open eyes of the two boys were reflected. Vincent and the schoolmaster awaited the outcome of the unequal struggle with bated breath. After several minutes, the cayman's eyes, shielded by horny ridges, emerged from the water, and its nostrils spewed small fountains of spray. Vincent picked up his rifle and struck the man-eating monster a stunning blow between the eyes with the butt; Maître Coisnon fired his pistol at point-blank range, but the bullets ricocheted ineffectually from the reptile's armor and came close to hitting the boys, who had escaped up a tree. Vincent's blow seemed to have struck the cayman's most vulnerable spot, however: writhing in pain, it swung its tail about with a splash that left the two men wet to the skin. Then it stretched out its four legs and lay motionless, white belly upward, on the surface of the water.

When they recovered from their fright, the boys took off their uniforms and searched the muddy bottom of the pool for the doctor's body. Maître Coisnon held his pistol in readiness, prepared to defend them if need be, while Vincent searched the reeds on the fringe of the pond. All their efforts were in vain. Apart from a water-filled shoe, in which a flaming-red hermit crab had already made itself at home, not a trace of the doctor came to light. A quarter of an hour later, Vincent pronounced the missing man dead and the search ended. The travelers removed their hats and stood with bowed heads at the edge of the pond in which the doctor had found a watery grave. The schoolmaster leafed through his breviary, looking for a suitable Bible passage, and was just launching into a lengthy sermon when a loud sneeze was heard and the man who had just been pronounced dead emerged from the tall reeds, covered, like a river god, with mud and aquatic vegetation. Apart from a cold resulting from his stay in the water, the doctor was in the best of health; he gave his nose a good blow, then told his companions about his misadventure. The cayman had dragged him into a cave concealed under one of the banks, no doubt planning to make a meal of him at leisure. In a few minutes the doctor had regained consciousness and, once he had recovered from his fright, had waded ashore without further incident. Handshakes were exchanged all around. While the doctor's two companions were congratulating him on his miraculous rescue, the cayman revived and was about to evade punishment by quietly submerging. But now the hunters were on their guard: from two branches overhanging the pond the boys threw a net over the giant reptile. Its teeth and claws were soon caught in the meshes, and in thrashing about with its tail it became more and more hopelessly entangled. Men and boys joined forces to land the dripping prey and bind it so firmly with ropes that the powerful jaws and great heavy tail were no longer a danger to anyone.

But the packhorses showed by their frantic neighing that their minds weren't entirely at rest.

Only then did the travelers find time to examine their catch. The cayman measured six and a half feet from its nose to the tip of its tail and was only half as big as it had seemed to them in their first excitement. Its scaly armor was olive-green with specks of yellow, the underside a dirty white; its eyes, which were wide open in the sunlight, had the dull sheen of amber. The smell of musk that the captive animal gave off was so strong you had to hold your nose to go near it. In its helpless state it inspired more pity than fear. Wishing to preserve the valuable skin, Vincent forbade the two boys to torment the cayman with sticks and stones. He loosened its bonds and tied it to a tree with strong ropes, planning to retrieve it on his return and make a present of it, dead or alive, to Pauline Leclerc, the captain general's wife. The travelers then resumed their journey.

Night was falling when they reached the village of Ennery, where Toussaint L'Ouverture and his staff were quartered in a luxurious country house that before the revolution had belonged to a French planter. Here Vincent, according to Leclerc's secret instructions, was to await the black general's arrival.

The travelers found the village deserted; for fear of being recruited into the army or sold as slaves, the inhabitants had hidden in the surrounding fields. In a hut roofed with palm straw, the friends found a feeble old man, who assured them in a wavering voice that he knew nothing about any black general or his whereabouts; several times crossing himself, the old man swore that he had never in all his life heard the name of Toussaint L'Ouverture. He added that there was no house good enough for them to spend the night in within five miles, but offered them his own tumbledown hut in return for a small fee, which was soon paid. Thereupon the old man bowed repeatedly and, with astonishing dexterity for a man of his age, vanished into a nearby canefield, whose rustling leaves soon hid him from view.

The travelers stilled their hunger with green bananas, though Vincent, for fear of being poisoned, did not touch them. Since every corner of the mud hut swarmed with roaches and scorpions, he preferred to sleep in the open. Rhythmic snores could soon be heard from the dark interior of the hut. Vincent slung his hammock between two stout branches, wrapped himself in his mosquito net, and lay down to sleep under the spreading branches of a calabash tree.

Twilight is short in the tropics; the blinding daylight gives way without transition to pitch-darkness. Though Vincent was very tired and ached in every muscle from the hard ride, it was hours before he could close his eyes. Every moment he expected an invisible enemy to emerge from the darkness. Fireflies darted through the night like the torches of black insurgents and the long-drawn-out howling of a dog barking at the moon, half of which was hidden by inky clouds, seemed an evil omen, presaging a dark future for the French army. Toward midnight a muffled drumming arose in the surrounding cane fields and lulled him to sleep with its monotonous rhythm. The last thing he saw in his half-sleep was the cayman's clouded eye. Deep in a dream it came to him that the wily old man who had lured the travelers into this deadly trap was none other than Toussaint L'Ouverture, the Proteus of San Domingo.

When Vincent awoke the next morning, he found himself in an underground dungeon. Above him he saw the bloodshot eyes of a black savage who was leaning over him, dagger in hand, prepared to murder him. Vincent reached for his pistols, but instead of acrid powder smoke the aroma of freshly roasted coffee beans rose to his nostrils. The sun poured in as a servant opened the blinds and wished him a good morning. To his surprise, Vincent found that far from being in a dark dungeon he was lying in a soft four-poster, whose open curtains revealed an attractively furnished boudoir. While helping him wash and dress, the servant, a young black, informed him that Toussaint L'Ouverture had come to Ennery during the night at the head of his troops, and that when he heard of the Frenchmen's arrival he had given orders to install them in his private rooms. In conclusion, the servant announced that the general was expecting them for breakfast in half an hour.

When Vincent entered the dining room, Toussaint L'Ouver-

ture came to meet him with open arms. The general was wearing
a gala uniform of finest Indian madras and a tricorn with a blue-
white-and-red cockade; on his chest shone the Cross of Saint George
with which the British Admiral Maitland had presented him on
conclusion of the peace negotiations, and in his belt he carried a
brace of silver-trimmed pistols from the Versailles gunsmithery,
which the Directoire had sent him in recognition of his services
to the Republic. "Forgive the slight liberty I have taken, Citizen
Vincent," said the general, "but I could not very well leave the
emissaries of France to be eaten alive by mosquitoes and cockroaches. That is why I moved you into my humble dwelling; I
hope you will not hold it against me." Then, after shaking hands
with the doctor and the schoolmaster, he tenderly kissed his two
sons, Isaac and Placide, who with tears in their eyes embraced
the father they had not seen for so long.

"General," said Vincent, assuming a military stance, "take the
advice of a friend and listen to what your children have to say to
you. I bring you a letter from the First Consul that will dispel
any doubt you may have as to the government's true intentions."
With these words, he handed the general a casket containing a
sealed letter, which at Toussaint L'Ouverture's request Maître
Coisnon read aloud:

BONAPARTE, FIRST CONSUL OF THE FRENCH REPUBLIC, TO TOUSSAINT
L'OUVERTURE, SUPREME COMMANDER OF THE ARMY OF SAN DOMINGO

Citizen General:

The recent peace with England and all European powers has
raised the Republic to the highest pinnacle of greatness. The government is now able to concern itself with the colony of San
Domingo. To that end we have dispatched General Leclerc, our
brother-in-law, to San Domingo and appointed him captain general, the supreme authority over the colony. He is accompanied
by sufficient fighting men to enforce respect of the sovereign power
of the French Republic. Under these circumstances, we hope and
trust that you will prove the sincerity of the sentiments toward

us and toward all France that you have expressed in all your communications to us.

We hold you in true esteem and take pleasure in acknowledging before all the world the great services you have rendered the French nation; if the French flag flies in San Domingo, we owe it to you and to your brave black soldiers.

Raised to the supreme command thanks to your talents and the force of circumstances, you have quelled the civil war, put an end to the persecutions perpetrated by a handful of madmen, restored religion and the worship of God, author of all blessings.

Along with much that is excellent, the constitution you devised contains certain elements that are by no means in keeping with the dignity and sovereign power of the French Republic, of which San Domingo is a part.

The circumstances in which you found yourself, surrounded on all sides by enemies at a time when the mother country could not come to your help or open up new sources of food to the population of San Domingo, justified certain illegal articles of this constitution. But now that circumstances have so fortunately changed, you will be the first to recognize the sovereign power of the nation which, because of your abilities and the strength of character with which nature endowed you, counts you among its most eminent citizens. Any contrary course would be incompatible with our good opinion of you; you would forfeit the many claims you have acquired to the gratitude of the Republic and dig a deep chasm under your feet, which in engulfing you would in all likelihood encompass the ruin of those brave blacks whose courage we so sincerely honor and whom we should be sorely grieved to be obliged to punish as rebels.

We have acquainted your children and their tutor with our sentiments toward you and are sending them back to you. Help the captain general with your advice, your influence, your capabilities. What more could you wish for? The freedom of the blacks? You know that wherever the fortunes of war led us we have brought freedom to peoples who did not yet have it. Esteem, honor, wealth? Can you, in view of the services you have performed for the Republic, services which, especially in the present circumstances, you can still perform, have any doubts about the esteem, the wealth, and the posts of honor that await you?

Endeavor to make it clear to the inhabitants of San Domingo that in time of war France has not always been able to demonstrate the concern it has always felt for their welfare; that the persons who have come from the Continent to incite them and arouse a spirit of partisanship were creatures of those very parties that have torn the mother country apart; that peace and a powerful government will henceforth guarantee the welfare and freedom of the colony's inhabitants. Tell them that if they look upon freedom as the highest good, it is only as French citizens that they can enjoy it, and that any action incompatible with the welfare of the mother country and the obedience they owe its government will be viewed as a crime against the state, will cast a shadow on all their past services and make San Domingo the theater of a disastrous war, in which fathers and sons will destroy one another. And consider in particular, General, that if you are the first man of your color to rise to such great power and distinguish himself so eminently by his bravery and military talents, you are also more than any other man responsible before God for the conduct of your countrymen.

Should any ill-disposed persons attempt to persuade those who have played leading roles in the recent disorders on San Domingo that we have come to investigate their actions during the era of lawlessness, assure them that we take cognizance only of their present conduct and that we shall look back at their past only by way of acknowledging the acts of bravery whereby they distinguished themselves in the wars against the Spaniards and the British, who were then our enemies.

Rest assured of our unlimited esteem and conduct yourself in a manner worthy of one of the first citizens of the greatest nation on earth.

Paris, 27 Brumaire of the Year X

The First Consul
BONAPARTE

Toussaint's facial expression had changed noticeably as he listened. The tender feelings of a father for his sons returned from abroad had given way to the impersonal passion of a statesman determined to penetrate and to foil the intrigues of his enemies. "You must admit, Citizen Vincent," said Toussaint L'Ouverture after Maître Coisnon had finished reading, "that the First Consul's words are in contradiction with General Leclerc's actions. The one offers me freedom, the other makes war on me. General Leclerc has descended on San Domingo like a thunderbolt and has made his mission known to me exclusively by acts of war. In the light of his violent actions, I cannot forget that I too bear arms. Why has he declared war on me in so unjustified and politically unwise a fashion? Because I have rid my country of foreign interference, because I have given all my strength to its welfare and greatness, because I have restored justice and order? If my actions are regarded as crimes, why have my children been returned to me? And why was the First Consul's letter not given me until three months after it was written? If, as you say, Bonaparte sincerely desires peace, he need only order the withdrawal of his troops. I shall write him a letter to this effect, which I shall ask you, Maître Coisnon, as tutor of my children, to deliver."

After these words, the black general arose, strode about the room, his sword jangling at his side, and, undeterred by his sons' heart-rending pleas, dictated the following letter to Maître Coisnon:

TOUSSAINT L'OUVERTURE, SUPREME COMMANDER OF THE ARMY OF SAN DOMINGO, TO BONAPARTE, FIRST CONSUL OF THE FRENCH REPUBLIC

Citizen Consul:

Your communication has been conveyed to me by your brother-in-law, General Leclerc, whom you have appointed captain general of this island, a title not recognized by the law of San Domingo. At the same time he has restored two innocent children to the embraces of a loving father. What a splendid example of

European philanthropy! But dear as these pledges are to me and
hard as it is for me to part with them, I am sending them back to
their jailers, because I have no wish to be indebted to my enemies. The forces sent to assert the supremacy of the French Republic have landed and are spreading death and destruction. Alas,
for what reason? As punishment for what crimes and on whose
authority? Is a crude but unoffending people to be exterminated
by fire and sword? True, we have dared to endow ourselves with
a constitution suited to our needs, which, as you yourself admit,
embodies some good elements, but also certain infringements on
the sovereignty of the French nation! What is the basis of this
sovereignty and how far does it extend? Is it free from all responsibility, without measure or limit? In your letter you say, in effect: "San Domingo, a colony forming an integral part of the French
Republic, is striving for independence." And why should it not?
The United States of America did just that and succeeded, with
the help of monarchical France. But our constitution still has in-
herent flaws and still authorizes certain prejudices. Of that I am
well aware. What human institution is flawless? But, I ask you,
does the system of government that you have imposed on the
Republic you dominate honor individual and general freedom,
freedom of word and action, more than ours? It was not by my
choice that I rose to my present high position; compelling circumstances forced it on me: I did not overthrow a constitutional government; I swore to uphold the constitution. I saw this unhappy
island a prey to dissension and factional strife. My character and
ideas gave me a certain influence on the population and I was
chosen almost unanimously as its supreme leader. I quelled disorders, I stifled rebellion, restored peace, and brought forth order
from the womb of lawlessness. Have you, Citizen Consul, better
claims to the exalted position you occupy? If under the constitution upheld by me the people enjoy less freedom than under other
forms of government, it is because of underdevelopment, because
of the ignorance and barbarism inseparable from slavery. I introduced the only system of government suited to unhappy beings,
barely freed from the yoke of slavery, to their living conditions

and powers of understanding. In certain instances it has failed to prevent violence and despotism; this cannot be denied; but are these wholly absent from the French Republic, that most enlightened of European states? If, as has been claimed, thirty million Frenchmen find their happiness and security in the revolution of 18 Brumaire, shall I be begrudged the love and confidence of the poor blacks, my compatriots?

You offer the blacks freedom and maintain that wherever you have gone you have brought freedom to people who did not have it before. I am not adequately informed of the latest news from Europe; but the reports that have come to my attention do not support this claim. The people of San Domingo would not welcome with a happy heart the freedom that is found in France, Belgium, Switzerland, or in the Batavian, Ligurian, and Cisalpine Republics. Such changes, such freedom are far, very far, from our desires.

You ask me if I desire glory, honors, riches. I do indeed, but not through your intervention. I find my glory in the esteem of my fellow citizens, my honor in their devotion, my riches in their selfless loyalty. Can it be in the hope of tempting me to betray the cause to which I have dedicated my life, that you have conceived the contemptible notion of offering me personal advantages? Learn to judge the ethical principles of others by your own. If the citizen who had not yet renounced his rights to the throne you occupy should call on you to relinquish it, what would your answer be? I have acquired the power I possess as legally as you have yours, and only the express will of the inhabitants of San Domingo can make me relinquish it.

My power has not been bought with blood, nor has it been maintained by the arts of the European politician. The most unbridled villains, whose arm I had often restrained from murder, have been forced to recognize my mercy and forbearance, and I have forgiven the wretches who drew their daggers against me. True, I banished certain persons who had done their utmost to fan the flames of civil war, but their crimes had already been judged by a competent court and they themselves confessed them.

Can anyone come forward and claim to have been condemned without trial? And yet those selfsame monsters have returned from Cuba, bringing bloodhounds to hunt us down and tear us to pieces, and they are led by men who dare to call themselves Christians.

How is it possible that I provoke your astonishment and earn your praise by upholding *religion and the worship of God, author of all blessings*? Ah, that all-bountiful being, veneration for whose holy name has only recently been restored in your country, has always been honored and praised by me. Amid dangers and betrayals, I have always sought safety and comfort in Him, and never has my trust deceived me. I am responsible, as you put it, before Him and before you for the unceasing bloodshed on this island. So be it, let the outcome of this conflict be decided by His holy but terrible justice; let Him be the judge between me and my enemies, between those who infringe on His commandments and who have denied His holy name and a man who has never ceased to revere and worship Him.

Toussaint L'Ouverture

When the black general finished dictating his letter, an embarrassed silence prevailed, interrupted only by the sobbing of the children, who threw themselves at his feet. Even the doctor seemed to sense the historic significance of the moment, for he took out his pocket handkerchief and loudly blew his nose, while Maître Coisnon's eyes filled with tears. With difficulty Vincent maintained the stoical bearing he had developed in years of stern military duty, and asked in a hoarse voice what provision the general wished to make for his sons. "My determination to safeguard the freedom of my black countrymen," said Toussaint L'Ouverture without hesitation, "imposes duties that outweigh nature. Tell General Leclerc that I am sending his hostages back to him, lest he suppose that I feel bound by them. I am sacrificing the happiness of my family to the freedom of my race." With these words Toussaint tore himself from his sons' embraces. Isaac L'Ouverture, the elder of the two, was first to recover his composure: "I am and remain French," he cried, wiping the tears from his eyes.

"I will never take up arms against the Republic that has given my people its freedom." "And I," cried Placide, the younger, "will fight by my father's side against France, which is thrusting us back into slavery."

At this Isaac fell sobbing into the arms of his father, who himself had tears in his eyes, while Placide took sorrowful leave of Maître Coisnon, his tutor, who made no attempt to hold back his tears; even in the doctor's watery blue eyes there was telltale moisture. Only the colonel of engineering kept a cool head. He drew his pistols and pointed them at Toussaint L'Ouverture. "In the name of the Republic," he said, "I arrest you. General Leclerc has ordered me to apprehend you as a traitor. Your house is surrounded, our troops are everywhere; any resistance would be useless. Your sword, Citizen Toussaint! Your time has run out; you are nothing more in San Domingo."

Toussaint surrendered his sword to Vincent with no thought of resistance; he seemed more surprised than angry or grieved. A shot fired by mistake hit Isaac, who was trying to oppose his father's arrest; the boy expired in the arms of his tutor. With his last breath he cursed France, which had betrayed his love. During the night the black general, under military guard, was taken to the frigate *Intrépide*, which lay at anchor in the Bay of Gonaïves and set sail for France at dawn. In boarding the ship, he took a last look at the mountains of San Domingo, which were just becoming visible in the dawning light, then turned to Divisional General Savary, who had been put in command of the ship for the present occasion, and spoke these memorable words: "You have felled the tree of black freedom, but its roots will sprout again, for they are deep and widely ramified."

Chapter Three

O N completion of their secret mission, the three companions, along with the cayman, which stood up well under the trip, returned to Cap Français, where Leclerc received them with military honors. In recognition of his courageous feat of arms, Vincent was promoted to the rank of brigadier general; the doctor was appointed chief medical officer and assigned to the western front, where, after the deportation of Toussaint L'Ouverture, hostilities continued with renewed violence. Maître Coisnon was made chief inspector of schools and left for the south of the colony, with orders to impose racial segregation in the local school system and ultimately to abolish compulsory education for black and mulatto children; this had been done on the island of Guadeloupe, where slavery had been reinstated. Vincent asked to be sent to the front, but instead Leclerc gave him special orders to build Pauline a palace worthy of her station, sparing neither money nor labor power, though by then the army was suffering from increasing shortages of supplies and ammunition. Feeling that the best was none too good for his coddled wife, the favorite sister of the First Consul, the captain general provided Vincent with a work force of several thousand black prisoners of war and a building site near Fort Picolet, overlooking the city. The site offered several advantages. For one thing, thanks to its elevation it was favored by a cool sea breeze, which would contribute to the comfort of future inhabitants and offer protection against tropical diseases; for another, the garrison of the nearby fort would be well placed to ward off any attack by land or sea and if necessary to evacuate the captain and his wife. Since the city was still in ruins and the colony had always been lacking in building materials, Vincent helped himself to the marble walls of the former governor's palace, which had been destroyed in the fire. Day after day, from sunrise to sunset, an endless procession of half-naked blacks, spurred on by whip-brandishing overseers, carried snow-white marble blocks up the winding path from the town—a sight that inspired philosophical reflections in Vincent. Seen from a distance, it looked as though massive stones were climbing the steep hill by their own power.

Six weeks later the shell of the building was complete. While gardeners and decorators were putting the finishing touches to house and grounds, Vincent, at Pauline's request, took up quarters in one wing of the palace, from which he could conveniently supervise operations. Palm and olive groves were planted, straight walks lined with box and cypress were laid out, walls were clothed in begonia and mimosa, and a summerhouse was built with a flowing fountain in the middle, shaded by flowering bougainvilleas; filled with the buzzing of bees and the sound of flowing water, this setting invited the mistress of the house to amorous vagaries. The tropical climate, by promoting rapid growth, contributed to the success of the architect's plans, and exactly six months after his victorious landing in San Domingo, Leclerc was able to move into his fruit- and flower-girt palace, which, in memory of a Ligurian castle where the young couple had spent their honeymoon, they named Monrepos. To celebrate the event, Vincent made the captain general and his wife a present of the tame cayman, which was given a place of honor in a marble-lined fish pool. Each day, despite the food shortage prevailing in the colony, the reptile was fed an ample portion of fresh meat.

Just in time for the solemn inauguration of the palace, which took place in the presence of the entire officers' corps and the most esteemed citizens of the colony, a frigate arrived from France, bringing—instead of urgently needed arms and ammunition—gowns, lingerie, luxurious furniture, and other gifts for the captain general's wife. The captain of the ship handed Leclerc a personal letter from the First Consul, which Leclerc read aloud in the presence of his guests, who, in gala uniforms and *grande toilette*, were assembled in the marble reception hall of the palace.

BONAPARTE, FIRST CONSUL OF THE FRENCH REPUBLIC, TO LECLERC, CAPTAIN GENERAL OF SAN DOMINGO

Citizen General:

It gives me pleasure to announce a happy event, the reunion of the island of Elba with the French mother country. San Domingo will become a second Elba, sending, as it did before the revolution, a stream of sugar and coffee to the seaports of France. As for you, General, you are covering yourself with the highest glory. The Republic will raise you to the summits of greatness; you will crush all its enemies and by your victories show yourself worthy of my unswerving trust. Always remember that difficulties and hardships are nothing when they serve our country and are shared by a beloved spouse.

BONAPARTE

Leclerc, who had several times been interrupted by the applause of those present, had just finished reading the letter when an officer rushed in and, getting his breath with difficulty, announced that England had declared war on the Republic: a British fleet was blockading the colony's ports, a battalion of British soldiers had landed in the bay, and their bayonets could be seen gleaming in the sunlight. Leclerc turned deathly pale and ordered Vincent to negotiate a truce with the commander of the enemy fleet, since the army of San Domingo could not hope to resist the British navy. When Vincent went to the window and looked through a spyglass to estimate the strength of the landing party, he saw, not the red coats of British soldiers, but a flock of pink flamingos, moving toward the beach in straight files like a disciplined army. From a distance their upturned beaks looked like sabers or bayonets.

No sooner had the company recovered from the excitement— Leclerc was quick to demote the officer responsible for the false report—than a new incident aroused further fear: the cayman had escaped its fish pool. Lured by the smell of the banquet, it had hurried to the palace dining room and fallen greedily on the richly garnished tables. Whole rows of ladies fell into a faint at the sight of the scaly monster; officers hid under tables while the black kitchen help, armed with knives and forks, prepared for battle.

Of all the ladies, only Pauline maintained her composure; Vincent shielded her, placing himself between her and the beast, then drew his sword and, executing a dance step worthy of an Italian fencing instructor, chased the cayman out of the palace. While the festively attired guests grouped for the minuet on a dance floor so highly polished that the candlesticks held by lackeys in livery were reflected in it, an orderly dashed in and whispered in the captain general's ear that the city and surrounding forts were being stormed by the black general Christophe. Leclerc took this report for another false alarm, and disregarded it; but then cannon fire was heard and the angry shouts of the black rebels poured in through the open windows. Leclerc hesitated no longer. Ordering Vincent to escort Pauline and her three-year-old son, Dermide, to one of the ships at anchor in the harbor, he himself prepared to defend the palace at the head of his officers.

Vincent found himself surrounded by a bevy of ladies, who pleaded with him to save them from the fury of the savages. When he approached Pauline with a gallant bow and declared his intention of escorting her and her son to safety, he received the proud reply: "Flee if you will, Citizen Vincent. The sister of a Bonaparte does not flee." For Pauline it was permissible to disregard her husband's command, but for Vincent an order was an order. Without further ado, he picked her up, along with her young son. While she entwined Vincent's broad shoulders in her snow-white arms and Dermide played with the rescuer's waving plume, he carried them out of the hall, followed by the frantic ladies, who gathered up their skirts and hurried after them. The palace garden lay in deep darkness; shots were heard in the distance, and the night sky was aflame with the glow of burning houses. Only then did Pauline seem to realize the danger; she pressed closer to Vincent and absently stroked his mustache as he hurried down a secret path to the shore. As he was lifting her into a waiting boat, his mustache inadvertently grazed her lips, parted as though for a kiss. At that very moment a messenger arrived with the order to stop the evacuation: the enemy attack had turned out to be a harmless display of fireworks that had got out of control through an artificer's carelessness. Yawning, Pauline asked Vincent to take her home, where she apologized to the guests for her absence. When he had deposited her on her Récamier sofa with her little Dermide, she whispered in his ear, before dismissing him, that she wished to receive him in her private apartments early in the morning.

Though it had ended harmlessly enough, the second false alarm cast a dark shadow on the festivities, which had begun so happily. Nothing could restore the guests' high spirits; the officers regarded the incidents as proof of their subordinates' poor discipline, and the ladies lamented the jewelry they had lost while running down to the shore.

When Vincent entered Pauline's apartments at the appointed hour, he found her lying in bed under a canopy embroidered with imperial eagles, supported by four exceptionally handsome Senegalese blacks who stood as still as ebony statues. She was wearing a silk negligee, under which her breasts, beaded with cold sweat, rose and fell to the rhythm of her heavy breathing. A black serving woman fanned her with a palm frond, while her kneeling maid tickled the soles of her feet with a peacock feather. Leclerc was standing at the window, his arms folded. "I have sent for you, Citizen Vincent," he said without turning around, "because Madame Leclerc is bored. Boredom, in Latin *melancholia*, is a dangerous tropical ailment that attacks the organs from within and dries out the body like a lingering fever. But it is not too late. Entertain my wife, do everything in your power to cheer her up, to distract her; read her every wish, even the most dissolute and extravagant, from her lips; make yourself the obedient servant of her whims and vices; spare no effort to make her sojourn in the colony as pleasant as possible. The army and the entire fleet are at your disposal; turn San Domingo into a second Paris—that is an order, and I shall hold you personally responsible for its execution."

The captain general turned on his heel and was about to leave the room when one of his pistols, with which little Dermide had been playing at his father's feet, went off. The bullet struck the serving woman who had been fanning Pauline, and she breathed out her life in Vincent's arms. Awakened by the shot, Pauline opened her eyes and asked what had disturbed her slumbers. The dead servant was carried away, the blood wiped off the marble floor; another slave girl was quickly produced, and she began to fan the air while Pauline resumed her interrupted siesta.

Vincent spared no effort in carrying out the captain general's order. He anticipated his distinguished patient's every wish. He sent an expedition into the interior for rare butterflies and orchids and transformed the sickroom into a tropical conservatory, where motley hummingbirds flitted back and forth among open blossoms. To cheer the patient, Dr. Dupuy gave her a tame chameleon, which when set down on a blue-white-and-red flag took on the colors of France, while a parrot instructed by Maître Coisnon sang the "Marseillaise." But all this coaxed no more than a weary smile from the general's wife. Somewhat bored with these offerings, she spent the hottest hours of the day by the fish pool, feeding chunks of bloody meat from the palace kitchen to the cayman, which lay motionless on the bottom. Only when the frigate *Intrépide*, instead of the urgently needed supplies of arms and ammunition, brought ancient art treasures from the Villa Borghese, a gift from the First Consul to his favorite sister, did Pauline's condition show a slight improvement. She had herself carried to the harbor in her litter and personally supervised the unloading of the precious cargo. A Senegalese black knelt in the dust before her, and as her fingertips played over his glistening shoulders, she gazed ecstatically at the nude torso of a Greek god. One afternoon, while Vincent was walking among the statues set up in the palace park, he heard laughter and cries for help from inside the summerhouse. When he went in, Pauline was lying on a bed of roses; her maid was tickling the soles of her feet so vigorously that she was crying aloud for help. Exhausted with laughter, she beckoned Vincent to come closer and asked him to help her loosen her corset. When he applied his teeth to a recalcitrant knot, she grew frantic with excitement. Taking his head in both hands, she pressed it between her thighs, and began to heave so violently that he feared for her health. Afterward she sank back on her couch, exhausted but happy, and fell asleep at once. This treatment, which Vincent repeated regularly at her request, did wonders for her imaginary melancholia. She was soon sufficiently recovered to take part in the social life of the colony by the side of her husband, who, in recognition of Vincent's military accomplishments, put him in for promotion.

Meanwhile, the enemy had not been idle. Despite the brilliant victories of the French army in the north and west of the island, despite its steady advances on all fronts, its overall situation was not improved. Like a hydra, the enemy rebounded with redoubled strength from every blow. Though nowhere to be seen, it still dominated the country. The soldiers of the Republic controlled nothing beyond the range of their rifles; the dispersion of the enemy forces preserved them from a decisive blow. For the French soldiers the war consisted of endless marching under a blazing sun, which wrought more havoc in the ranks than bombs or grenades. The troops were still animated by the same fighting spirit, but they no longer showed it in combat; they showed it by climbing steep cliffs, fording swollen streams, wading up to their waists or necks in swamps, always drenched with rain, sweat, or river water, pursued by clouds of mosquitoes, stung by hungry insects, sleeping on damp ground upholstered with sharp stones or prickly cactuses.

The army no longer pressed forward in massed columns with fixed bayonets, to the accompaniment of drum rolls, and singing the "Marseillaise"; the regular musket fire of an advancing regiment was no longer heard. This war had become a chaotic hunt for an invisible enemy, who lay hidden in the underbrush; seldom did the grenadiers glimpse an organized body of men that could be engaged in battle, but the surprise attacks launched by the enemy when they thought they were in superior numbers exacted greater losses from day to day.

The main enemy of the French army was the rainy season, which brought an outbreak of yellow fever, sometimes known as *le mal de Siam*. It began with a feeling of fatigue, which was followed by headaches and vomiting; more often than not, death came the same day. The superstitious blacks thought the epidemic had been brought about by their leader Toussaint L'Ouverture, to whom they attributed magical powers. The doctor imputed it to the vertical rays of the sun and the pestilential vapors of the mangrove swamps, which were dangerous even for healthy persons but were inevitably fatal to ill-clad, ill-fed soldiers. As countermeasures, the doctor ordered cold compresses and bleeding at regular intervals, but above all body hygiene and a fortifying diet of meat broth and boiled vegetables. Vincent too was infected; taking the doctor's advice, he tied a wet cloth around his head and took walks in the palace garden, where the air was purer than in the sultry city streets. Morning and evening, he rubbed his entire body with cinchona bark. Thanks to these measures, complemented by frequent bleeding, his proved to be a light case. He suffered an attack of fever accompanied by violent pains in his joints, but recovered. The only lasting consequence of his illness was recurrent chills and fever.

The captain general was less fortunate. At the end of October, he complained of slight chills; the doctor advised him to take it easy and to drop his duties for a time—sound advice that the captain general rejected with the proud words "A soldier of the Republic recognizes no sickness other than death." Every morning, as the First Consul had done in Egypt, he visited the overcrowded hospitals, where the sick and dying languished without hope. By distributing medals and promotions he tried to raise the dwindling morale of the troops, and with his waning strength he defended the city walls against the increasing superiority of the besieging blacks. From time to time, as though to hasten the arrival of urgently needed reinforcements, he searched the blue-gray horizon with his telescope, a gift from the First Consul. In a few weeks his exertions and privations had so undermined his resistance that all hope of recovery was lost. Indifferent to the danger, his wife sat by his bedside in the darkened room; the merciless tropical sun penetrated the lowered blinds, marking the marble floor with light stripes that made Pauline think of prison bars.

The couple reminisced about Italy, where Leclerc had won undying fame as a young officer, and yearned for the pine groves of
Liguria, where they had spent their honeymoon, and for Alpine
valleys surmounted by snow-covered peaks. On his deathbed Leclerc dictated a last letter to the First Consul, in which he justified
his military strategy and blamed the government's policy for the
failure of his mission.

I do not believe, Citizen Consul, that I have been guilty of any
fault; and if my situation, which was satisfactory at first, deteri-
orated quickly, it was due largely to disease, which has devastated
my army, and to the premature introduction of slavery on Guadeloupe. Since coming to this island, I have seen nothing but rebellion, arson, and murder, and even the certainty of death cannot
efface from my mind the harrowing scenes I have witnessed. I
have fought here, not only against blacks and the mulattoes allied
with them, but also against hardship, shortages, and the soldiers
of my own army, who have lost courage.

Madame Leclerc and her child are well. Considering how cruel
it must be for her to stay on this island, where she sees nothing
but the dead and dying, I have asked her to go back to France,
but this she refused to do under any circumstances, for she does
not fear death and would rather die by the side of her husband
than live in ignominy.

As for me, Citizen Consul, I have served with devotion. I shall
continue to do so and shall bear witness in the other world to my
high opinion of you. All things earthly are quick to perish, ex-
cepting only the faint traces we leave behind us in history.

On 18 Brumaire of the year XI, three years to the day after
seconding the First Consul in his coup d'état, Charles-Victor-
Emmanuel Leclerc, captain general of San Domingo, died in the
arms of Brigadier General Vincent and Chief Medical Officer Dupuy. He was not yet thirty years of age. The coffin containing
his mortal remains was transferred with military honors to the
frigate *Intrépide*, which set sail for France three days later. In con-

nection with the funeral solemnities, Leclerc's successor, General Rochambeau, arranged for several hundred black prisoners of war, specially imported from Cuba for the purpose, to be torn to pieces by bloodhounds. Pauline, in widow's weeds, attended the hideous spectacle by Vincent's side and was thrown into a state of euphoric excitement. Next morning she expressed a desire to witness more massacres. But the bloodhounds were so sated by the feast of the day before that they would not attack until the overseers ripped open the bellies of the unfortunate victims with bayonets. At the sight of the gushing blood and guts Pauline fell into a faint. Afterward she offered no resistance when Vincent carried her to the ship that would take her back to France; she rested her head on his shoulder, her fingers toyed absently with his gold epaulettes, and a smile of contentment played over her lips, as though she had just experienced the happiest hour of her life.

Chapter Four

VINCENT asked to be sent to the front, wishing to sell his life as dearly as possible, but Commander in Chief Rochambeau could not satisfy his request. Instead he handed him a letter written by the First Consul in person, ordering him to track down Toussaint L'Ouverture's secret treasure of eighty thousand louis d'or, or forty million francs, which Bonaparte needed urgently to replenish the coffers of his army and government. Though Toussaint L'Ouverture had refused to reveal the whereabouts of his treasure, Vincent had reason to believe that it was buried near Toussaint's country villa, perhaps in the pond where the friends had caught the cayman (which in the meantime had escaped from the fish pool and fled to the mountains to join the rebels). The doctor seemed to remember seeing, in the cave where the cayman had dragged him, some gold coins along with a crumbling skeleton, probably belonging to a treasure seeker, who had paid for his discovery with his life. Apart from Dr. Dupuy, who was to accompany him on his dangerous expedition—Maître Coisnon was still in the south of the colony, segregating the schools—no one was informed of the projected expedition, which was code-named Operation Cayman. If questioned, the friends were to represent themselves as cayman hunters, exploring the interior of the island. Since the land route was blocked by the rebel army, they blacked their faces with charcoal and, under cover of darkness, boarded a sloop, which immediately set sail for Gonaïves. The expedition got off to a bad start. The captain was drunk, the ship a waterlogged wreck and hopelessly overloaded; the black passengers made a great fire on deck and grilled fish on it; the acrid smoke brought tears to Vincent's eyes. No sooner had the ship put out to sea than the blacks began to sing; though the discord offended their European ears, Vincent and the doctor felt obliged to join in. The singing went on until shortly before midnight, when the ship ran aground on a reef. The panic-stricken passengers screamed and waved their arms, and glowing coals rolled about on the deck, lighting fires that would have consumed the ship if a tropical shower had not put them out. The captain ordered the passengers below and battened down the hatch to keep out the rain. Our friends spent the rest of the night in total darkness, penned in among the blacks, half suffocated by their effluvia, up to their waists and later up to their necks in the brackish water that streamed in through the leak, surrounded by floating barrels and wet bales of cotton, with squealing rats clinging fast to them. Needless to say, sleep was out of the question. The two whites mumbled prayers, while the blacks sang somber songs of lamentation. By sunrise, when the friends were freed from their floating prison, the rain had washed the charcoal from their faces. Fortunately, their fellow passengers took their change of color as a joke and suspected nothing. A glance at the sea around them made the hunters forget their precarious situation. The water was so clear they could see the bottom; the sloop was suspended over a coral reef as brightly colored as a flower bed. Streaks of dazzling light trembled in the crystal-clear water, which changed so quickly between bright and dark that one seemed to be looking at a garden alive with brilliant-hued fishes, forests of sponges and meadows of sea anemones that swayed in the tide like a wheatfield waving in the breeze. With the help of a long pole Vincent managed to land a splendidly iridescent jellyfish, but its colors faded in the sunlight and nothing remained but a stinking blob, which attracted clouds of flies. By then the captain had more or less mended the leak, the rising tide lifted the sloop off the coral reef, and it reached Gonaïves toward noon.

Vincent went at once to the port commandant, an albino known as Capois La Mort because he looked like a living corpse, and presented a passport issued by General Rochambeau, identifying the travelers as cayman hunters and entrusting them to the protection of the colonial authorities. The commandant quartered them in his own home; a cannonball had made a big hole in the roof, but the house was otherwise undamaged. The town was in ruins; what had not been destroyed by the French in landing had been razed by the rebels before withdrawing to the mountains. People there were few; stray dogs roamed the streets; the only inhabitants of the ruined houses seemed to be rats and bats. Goats were grazing in the reception rooms of the French governor's palace; whenever the bells rang, the vultures perched on the wrecked spire of the cathedral took fright and flew up into the air. The wells were clogged with the bones of innocent women and children who had been butchered by the rebels. The port commandant had distinguished himself by particular cruelty, but his crimes were regarded as covered by the amnesty proclaimed by General Rochambeau.

For lunch the commandant served his guests a dish made with oysters; the doctor ate heartily, but Vincent didn't touch it; only a few days before, the rebels had sunk a ship loaded with French prisoners in the Bay of Gonaïves. After lunch, when the friends lay in their hammocks recovering from the hardships of their sea voyage, they heard excited shouts coming from the harbor and quickly approaching the house. Two ragged soldiers, surrounded by half-naked women and children, were dragging behind them a cayman about six feet long; the commandant insisted on making his guests a present of it. Vincent had the cayman tied to a tree in the courtyard, which was separated from the road by a high board fence. Jeering laughter could be heard from outside, along with these words: *"Portez-li nan caille blanc-là, ça c'est bagaille à li! Blanc-là besoin caiman, ça li veut faire ac caiman nan caille à li?"* ("Take it to the white man's hut. It belongs to him. The white man needs the cayman. What on earth will he do with it in his house?") A crowd formed on the road outside; stones came flying over the fence, the fence trembled, and under the pressure of the crowd the locked door to the courtyard flew open. The assailants poured in, and a hail of sticks and stones descended on the defenseless cayman. The doctor drew his pistols and wanted to resist the mob, but Vincent preferred to alert the commandant and sacrifice the cayman to the popular wrath. Aroused from his siesta, the commandant appeared at the window in his nightshirt and ordered the people to leave the cayman alone and go home peacefully. The reply was curses, laughter, and more stones, one of which hit the commandant in the forehead, knocking him unconscious. Vincent came to his aid with the smelling salts Pauline had given him before leaving the colony. The commandant revived, wiped the blood from his forehead, and ordered his soldiers to disperse the crowd by shooting to kill. A volley of rifle fire rang out; cries of pain went up from the square. Fortunately, a tropical shower put an end to the massacre, washed the blood off the street, and drove the survivors back to their huts. Among the victims was the cayman, which had been so badly injured by rifle fire that the doctor put it out of its misery with a pistol shot.

The next morning, bright and early, the friends started on their cayman hunt. The commandant provided them with his own boat and an escort of two native soldiers, ostensibly to protect them from enemy attack, but in reality to spy on them and discover their true intentions; Vincent suspected that the commandant's real sympathies lay with the rebels. A stray dog, who had been following them around since their arrival in Gonaïves, joined the expedition. He boarded the boat uninvited, and neither blows nor threats could drive him from his place on the oarsman's bench. Muzzle upraised, he sniffed the air and barked loudly at every suspicious movement on the mist-shrouded coast. At daybreak a heavy dew soaked the travelers to the skin; and then the sun, rising over the mountains in the east, shone through the milky vapor. An hour later the travelers reached the mouth of the Artibonite River, which ordinarily was hardly more than a trickle but now, after the rains of the last few weeks, was in full flood. The bank was lined with great uprooted trees carried downstream by the swollen waters and washed ashore. As they drew near, Vincent saw that what from a distance he had taken for trees was in reality a herd of caymans, lying motionless on the sandy banks, basking in the sun. Their terrifying jaws gaped wide; flies swarmed around them and little birds moved fearlessly about among their sharp teeth. As the travelers drew near, the great beasts arose ponderously, submerged, and withdrew into an impenetrable mangrove thicket, leaving a train of bubbles behind them. The narrow boat glided silently in the shade of overhanging trees; whenever it stopped moving, the friends could see a cayman lurking on the bottom. But when they dipped their oars, it shot away as swiftly as a brook trout, stirring up the muddy bottom with its great tail and disappearing. Then it would emerge in midstream, its horny nostrils bursting through the surface and sending up streams of foam that betrayed its position to the hunters. The doctor fired several shots at the reptile, but they missed or rebounded like pebbles from the cayman's armor.

At a bend in the river, the friends went ashore to follow a mountain stream which, according to their black escorts, led to a waterhole known to the natives as Trou Caïman. It was there that Vincent believed the treasure had been hidden. After tying their boat to a great tree, they hacked their way through tall reeds, losing sight of each other and shouting to keep in touch. The reeds were saber-sharp, and the slightest brush left painful cuts, which became inflamed in the heat and attracted swarms of gnats. They waded through a mangrove swamp where aerial roots barred their progress and they sank up to their knees in the muck. Then they climbed a steep hill covered with undergrowth so thick that they had to hack a path through it with machetes. They followed the sound of a waterfall, which sometimes seemed to be near them and sometimes far away. At length Vincent, pushing aside an overhanging branch, glimpsed a pond overgrown with water lilies, fed by the waterfall he had been hearing. At the edge of the pond an enormous cayman, which must have measured at least twelve feet, lay motionless in the blinding sun, its wide-open mouth swarming with maggots and horseflies. To judge by the smell of decay, the beast must have been dead for days. At the sight of this monster, the natives threw down their rifles and started to run, imagining the cayman to be a fabulous beast several hundred years old, an accomplice of Maman Zimbie the water spirit. Even the dog seemed to be superstitious, for, instead of sniffing at the cayman or jumping about barking, it slunk away, whimpering and dragging its tail. Vincent gave no heed to the evil omen; at bayonet point he forced the trembling blacks to go on. Meanwhile, Dr. Dupuy, covering his nose with a handkerchief, bent down over the animal's stinking maw. Thrusting his head between the reptile's jaws, he said to Vincent in a voice that sounded strangely muffled: "Suppose we gut the beast and sell the hide in Paris, where crocodile skin still brings a good price. It's a fine specimen, good for at least two dozen ladies' handbags. We'll go halves; twelve handbags for you and twelve for—" At that point the cayman's jaws closed and the doctor vanished, first to the shoulders, then to the waist. Though he struggled with all his might, the giant reptile would have swallowed him up completely but for Vincent's presence of mind. Once again he struck the cayman a crushing blow between the eyes with his rifle butt, and again the recommended technique proved effective.

The cayman writhed in pain, gave a whisk of its tail that sent the dog, which had ventured too close, flying into the pond, and lay still. Faint cries for help were heard from inside the monster. Vincent threw a lasso around the tail and tugged at it with all his might while the two natives grabbed the doctor's legs, but this haphazard procedure only made matters worse. One of the blacks got a kick in the forehead, and the other found himself holding a shoe rather than a foot. The doctor's cries grew fainter and after a time ceased altogether. Putting his ear to the ground, Vincent could still hear a feeble knocking from inside the cayman. Time was of the essence, and Vincent moved quickly. He immobilized the cayman's tail by fastening the lasso to a stout tree, then tied a rope around the doctor's feet and harnessed the two blacks to the other end. Encouraged by a lash or two of the whip, the blacks went to work with a will and drew the prisoner inch by inch out of the narrow gullet, which, like a greedy eater who had forgotten his table manners, emitted a terrifying belch. One last jolt and the doctor emerged, covered with blood and mucus like a newborn baby, badly shaken but otherwise no worse for wear. Feeling something like a midwife, Vincent held his smelling salts to the doctor's nose and gave him several resounding slaps in the face. The doctor soon recovered, except that his teeth kept chattering. After cleaning himself up as well as he could, he informed Vincent of what he had seen in the monster's belly, along with an assortment of bones: a moss-covered chest brimful of louis d'or—Toussaint L'Ouverture's treasure. It's an ill wind that blows nobody any good. Vincent pledged the doctor to strictest secrecy. The cayman was bound and made fast to a long branch, which sagged under its weight. The guides shouldered the burden and, followed by the dog, who had swum ashore and leapt around them yapping happily, the treasure hunters made their way back to their boat.

Toward evening they arrived safely in Gonaïves, where they paid off their porters and stowed the cayman in a barrel of water sheltered from curious eyes. After taking their leave of the port commandant and thanking him for his help, they boarded the sloop with their precious burden, under cover of darkness.

Though great clouds were gathering, the captain ignored all warnings and put out to sea with his badly overloaded ship. It had barely left harbor when a tropical storm lashed the waves to terrifying heights and sent breakers crashing down on the deck. Frightened by the rolling and pitching of the ship, the cayman burst out of its barrel and spread panic among the passengers, who held it responsible for the storm and wanted to throw it overboard. To save its valuable skin and the treasure hidden in its belly, Vincent decided to kill the cayman, but that was easier said than done. Since none of the passengers dared go near the bound reptile, he fastened the jaws to the mainmast and affixed a heavy cable to its tail. Ten sturdy blacks tugged at the tail cable while Vincent took a run and plunged his bayonet, measuring no less than four feet in length, into the cayman's belly. The cayman thrashed about; a single movement of its tail sent six blacks overboard; five were fished out, but the sixth vanished into the raging sea. Thick black blood poured from the wound; the yellow eye stared implacably at Vincent, and the pupil contracted like a meteor expiring in the night sky and vanished forever. At that very moment the storm died down, as though the elements had wished to confirm the blacks in their superstitious belief. The monster's belly disgorged several pounds of gravel, but no trace of a hidden treasure apart from a handful of Spanish doubloons bearing the effigy of the Emperor Charles V, an indication of the cayman's great age. Separated from the body, the entrails, which still had a life of their own, wriggled about the deck like eels. The doctor threw the bloody guts into the water, where they attracted a school of sharks. He speared a six-foot nurse shark with a boat hook and hove it to the deck, where it expired. Inside it, when he cut it open, he found, quite intact, the head of the black whom the cayman had knocked overboard. As the doctor put the shark's head in alcohol to add it to his zoological collection, Vincent leaned over the rail and vomited; the motion of the boat had made him seasick. After this interlude, the sloop continued on its way without incident.

Chapter Five

WHEN the travelers went ashore on Cap Français, all that remained of the city that had been hastily rebuilt after the fire was smoking ruins. General Rochambeau had withdrawn to the mountains with what troops he had left and was preparing for the decisive battle with General Dessalines' superior forces. Only torn standards and abandoned redoubts bore witness to the proud French army that had invaded the island. The victorious blacks had razed Captain General Leclerc's palace. Vincent and the doctor had hardly set foot on land when they were arrested by a black grenadier and summarily sentenced, by a revolutionary tribunal consisting entirely of blacks, to be shot at sunrise. Their only offense was the color of their skin. While awaiting execution in a pitch-black dungeon crawling with scorpions and cockroaches, they heard a soft gurgling sound. The light of a tallow candle Vincent had obtained by bribing a guard revealed their friend Maître Coisnon, lying on a straw tick in a state of total exhaustion. Luckily the doctor had distilled a phial of oil from the shark's liver. He poured a few drops of this life-giving elixir into Maître Coisnon's mouth and, quickly revived, the schoolmaster opened his eyes. Then, as the flickering candlelight cast fitful shadows on his drawn face, he told his friends what had happened to him since their last meeting. In the following, we shall tell the schoolmaster's story in his own words. Our only license has been to omit repetition and needless digressions, and to fill gaps that would have made the story unintelligible.

"I was on a tour of the south," the schoolmaster began, "inspecting the schools and reinstating racial segregation on the Guadeloupe model. That's where the news of the captain general's death caught up with me. His untimely end shook me—I was very fond of him. And with him gone I feared for my own fate and the future of the colony. By then there were rebels all around me. To escape their knives and machetes, I fled to the mangrove swamps where the runaway slaves used to hide. I spent days and nights in terror, up to my waist in muck, threatened by crocodiles and poisonous snakes, nipped by crabs and snapping turtles, sucked by leeches, eaten alive by mosquitoes. I had to keep moving, deeper and deeper into the swamps, and to make sure that I left no tracks. One night, when sleep caught me off my guard, I sank into the muck up to my ears. My scarf got caught in an aerial root and half strangled me, but that was what saved my life. I lived on wild fruit and roots that I ate raw; I didn't dare to make a fire or shoot game, for fear of being surprised by roving bands of rebels. Once I managed to catch a waterfowl by making a noose of my scarf, but its squawking almost gave me away.

"I can't say how many days or weeks went by. In the end I was so worn out I thought it would be better to be killed by a black rebel than to be devoured by leeches and mosquitoes. My aunt, Madame Lachicote-Desdunes, had a plantation nearby. Over hidden paths I went there. She was a good friend of General Toussaint L'Ouverture, and since she had always been good to her black workers I thought I'd be safe under her protection. I was in for a cruel disappointment. My aunt had died a natural death before the present trouble. She had been spared the misery of seeing her plantation burned down, the white owners massacred, and their children sold as slaves. The plantation, what was left of it, was being run by my 'cousin by marriage.' This was a mulatto bastard, the son of my aunt's husband (who had died young) by a black concubine. He hated everyone with skin lighter than his own. As the rightful heir to the plantation, I stood in the way of his ambitions, so he decided to do away with me, and in the meantime did everything he could to make me miserable. In the days when the whites persecuted the blacks, I had saved his life more than once. But that didn't matter: he was determined to make me die a painful death. He forced me to live in a slave's hut and to wait on him and his cronies, who had made themselves at home in the ruins of the main building. I ran around barefoot, with nothing on but a loincloth, as often as not balancing a gourd full of water on my head. They made me wash their dirty clothes, clean their shoes, and serve their meals. If I was clumsy, if I spilled something, they whipped me and rubbed red pepper in my wounds. I still have the scars of those whippings." Here the schoolmaster interrupted his story to let his friends feel the welts on his back.

After a short pause he went on: "Even so, I'm glad I went through those terrible days. They taught me to be harder on myself and demand less of others. I lived on corn and beans and learned to bear my heavy burden with stoic indifference. At work in the daytime I'd hum monotonous laments, and at night, in my hut, I'd fall into a deep dreamless sleep.

"The black general Dessalines made it his business to restore law and order on the plantations near his sector of the front and encourage the freed slaves to work. When he came to ours on a tour of inspection, I threw myself at his feet and told him about the humiliations and persecutions I had suffered. The magnanimous general took pity on me; he had my false cousin shot on the spot and decreed that I was sole heir to the plantation. But I wasn't destined to benefit by the recovery of my property: under questioning I admitted to a certain knowledge of natural history, and Dessalines appointed me surgeon general of the army. Before I knew it, I was in the field with the rebel army. My medical equipment consisted of a few rusty knives and unlimited quantities of liquor. Luckily I found a medical handbook in the ruins of a razed plantation. I studied for all I was worth, but my newly acquired knowledge didn't do me much good. Most of the time my patients died before I had even completed my diagnosis.

"Dessalines was alarmed by the rising death rate in his army. He began to suspect me of poisoning the wounded entrusted to my care. Holding a pistol to my temple, he forced me to demonstrate my medical skill by amputating the gangrenous leg of a black grenadier. He promised to shoot me on the spot if my patient died. The grenadier, who was full to the gills with rum, was being held by several of his comrades. Suddenly he awoke from his torpor and started bellowing with pain. I fainted in terror. A bucketful of cold water revived me, and under Dessalines' relentless eye I completed my bloody task. True, I couldn't help vomiting at the sight of the sawn-off stump, but my patient recovered: I had qualified as an army surgeon. In the meantime, Madame Dessalines had taken a liking to me, not so much because of my medical skill as because of my white skin. She consulted me regularly for her incurable migraine. One night her husband came home from a battle in which he had incurred heavy losses and found me in his wife's arms. He pulled me out from under the bed by the hair and fired several pistol shots, which luckily missed me. I jumped out the window and started to run, but in the darkness I stumbled over a sleeping sentry, who dragged me in my nightshirt before the infuriated general.

"For a starter, Dessalines practiced bayonet jabs on me. He'd have shot me then and there, but his wife pleaded with him—she didn't want bloodstains on her marriage bed. That gave me a reprieve. I was put in with a group of war prisoners and civilian hostages who were scheduled to be executed at sunrise within view of the French forces. To save ammunition, Dessalines had the innocent victims—including women, children, and old men—buried up to their necks, nailed to boards, or bound and thrown on anthills, to be eaten alive by vultures and termites.

"Again I had a miraculous escape. Aroused from their slumbers by the screams of their comrades, the French army attacked all along the line and drove the rebels back from their positions. Retreating with the main body of his army and the surviving hostages, Dessalines entrenched himself in the mountain fortress of Crête-à-Pierrot, which the French troops proceeded to besiege day and night. More than half the garrison fell victim to the constant artillery fire; the rest were decimated by hunger and disease. The rebel soldiers were beginning to chew lead bullets to relieve their thirst. In this hopeless situation, Dessalines conceived the daring plan of escaping the besieged fort under cover of darkness, breaking through the ring of the besiegers with what troops he had left, and coming back with reinforcements. He decided to blow up the fort along with the prisoners and hostages who were shut up in the powder magazine. Along with other unfortunates, I was lying chained to a barrel of powder. Dessalines came in with a lighted cigar. Smiling amiably, he wished me luck for the future and set fire to the fuse that was to blow us all into the next world. Then he marched out of the fort at the head of his troops. Though my hands and feet were bound, I managed to break loose at literally the last moment—the fuse had already reached the barrel of powder—and to jump through an embrasure. I landed in the ten-foot moat surrounding the fort. At the same moment a deafening explosion was heard and a rain of stones fell on the enemy lines, sealing the fate of the French army. The blast threw me to the ground, but luckily I was spared the murderous hail of stones. I tried to join the fleeing French troops, but ran into Dessalines' advance guard instead. Once again he had me arrested and condemned to death. For three days I've been in this dungeon awaiting execution."

With these words Maître Coisnon concluded his story. The candle had gone out. Huddled together in the darkness, the three friends awaited the dawn of the new day, presumably their last. In the first pale light Vincent looked at his watch. It was five o'clock, and the sun was rising over the mountains in the east. "I do not fear death," he said. "We have already died millions of deaths and we shall die millions more. It's like going from one room to another. Just as the sleep in which we regain our strength takes up about a third of the time we spend awake, so death, I believe, takes up a third or a quarter of our lives. And that is just the time a human body needs to rot."

Just then the doctor caught a scorpion in a chink in the wall, and that gave him an idea. "If a scorpion loses its family," he said, "or finds itself in a hopeless situation, it commits suicide with its poison sting. Who would have thought that under its repellent exterior this insect conceals a strength of character in no way inferior to that of Socrates or Seneca? Once I found a male scorpion under the bark of a rotting tree; the day before I had put its female in alcohol for scientific purposes. The captive insect strug-

gled furiously between my fingers, just like this one here." With
these words the doctor lifted up the scorpion he had just caught.
"It tried in vain to get its sting into me, until I put an end to its
sufferings by pitting it against a bird spider. The spider tore into
the scorpion with its sharp claws, while the scorpion paralyzed
the spider with its poison sting; they fought each other literally
to the death."

In the meantime, the schoolmaster had taken a stylus from his
pocket. With his last strength he scratched on the prison wall a
quatrain, which would be discovered by an archaeologist 150 years
later and painstakingly restored. The stone bearing the inscription
with which Maître Coisnon immortalized himself as a poet is now
to be seen in the historical museum of Port-au-Prince:

> *Humide et froid séjour fait par et pour le crime,*
> *Où le crime en riant immole sa victime!*
> *Que peuvent inspirer les fers et les barreaux*
> *Quand un cœur pur y goûte un innocent repos?*

> [O cold and damp abode of crime and punishment
> Where crime's disciples languish with the innocent!
> What dread, what suffering you hold in store,
> Yet cannot daunt the man whose heart is pure.]

No sooner had Maître Coisnon signed his work with his initials
and the secret emblem of the Freemasons than heavy steps and
loud military commands were heard from outside. The forged
iron door was flung open and the frail schoolmaster, who could
not hope to defend himself with his stylus against the soldiers'
bayonets, was seized by the arms and legs and marched off to the
place of execution. Not so the doctor, who flailed about with his
geologist's hammer, but in the end was sudued by superior numbers and dragged away cursing and swearing. Only Vincent re-
signed himself to the inevitable; bearing himself like a soldier, he
strode past the bayonets of the black grenadiers. Standing at the
edge of a freshly dug pit, the condemned men were blindfolded;
the officer in command of the firing squad, in whom Vincent had

recognized Capois La Mort, the port commandant of Gonaïves, read the sentences and with upraised saber gave the command to fire. The last thing Vincent heard was the bark of twelve rifles.

In a dream he saw the wide-open jaws of the cayman. The head with its gaping jaws was shaped like the French colony of San Domingo, while the body and the serrated tail resembled the Spanish part of the island. The yellowish eye, in which Vincent's past and future were reflected, was located at Trou Caïman, the exact spot where Vincent had captured the cayman. He had no time to think this thought to its conclusion, for at that moment the animal's jaws snapped shut and the world went dark around him. Inside the cayman it was warm and dark as in a jungle at night, but by listening intently Vincent could hear bare feet creeping over the soft forest floor. The sound grew to a rhythmic trotting; hundreds and thousands of bare feet were coming from all directions to a secret meeting place. Vincent was one of them, he was all of them, or, rather, they were all in him, he was the jungle, and he was the ancient cayman hiding in the depths of the forest. Suddenly the date flashed through his mind: it was the night of August 21, 1791. He heard the whispered password: Bois Caïman. He smelled the sweat of naked bodies creeping through the underbrush to the right and left of him. Wet leaves grazed his face; a streak of lightning crossed the night sky. It lit up a clearing where hundreds of ragged black slaves—men, women, and children—were crowding around a gigantic voodoo priest, who was swinging a machete over their heads. A deafening thunderclap unleashed a tropical storm. In a few seconds the ground disappears beneath the water, trees groan in the wind, and stout branches fall crashing to the ground. Vincent is still a child. His mother is holding him by the hand. With gaping terror-stricken eyes he sees the voodoo priest rise slowly to his full height. He spins around, his bare torso quivers. A cry goes through the crowd: "Boukman!" All freeze and hold their breath; all eyes are glued to the priest. A black pig is produced; its squeals are drowned out by the fury of the storm. Swiftly the priest plunges his machete into the pig's throat. The spurting blood is caught in a gourd, which is passed around. All drink of the steaming blood as Boukman intones the solemn oath in a hoarse voice and all repeat it after him, line by line:

Bon Dié qui fait soleil, qui clairé nous en haut
Qui soulevé la mer, qui fait gronder l'orage
Bon Dié là z'autres tendé, caché dans son nuage
Et là li garde nous, li voyé tout ça blancs fait.
Bon Dié blancs mandé crime et pas nous vlé bienfaits
Mais Dié là qui si bon ordonnin nous vengeance
Li va conduit bras nous, li ba nous assistance.
Jeté portrait Dié blancs qui soif d'leau dans yeux nous
Couté la liberté qui parlé cœur à nous tous.

[White God who made the sun and lights the sky,
Who churns the sea with storms and thunders loud.
Make no mistake, He's up there in His cloud
And looks and sees the way the white men treat us.
In fact it's Him that makes them persecute us.
But there's another God who's on our side.
Our hands in bloody vengeance He will guide.
Hark to His voice, for that way freedom lies.
Throw out your pictures of the God who blinds your eyes.]

The drums beat faster and faster, more and more wildly. Vincent can't resist their rhythm, he himself is the drum, the taut hide trembling under the beat of black hands. He jumps up, he stands trembling, he whirls about in a circle, faster and faster, more and more wildly. Foaming at the mouth, he falls, lies still with eyes revulsed. A red glow spreads over the northern plain, thick black smoke rises from burning cane fields and darkens the sun; flaming straw flies into the air and drifts down again, blackened. He hears the baying of bloodhounds as they track fugitive slaves in the mangrove swamps, hears the dull thud of cannonballs crushing black bodies bound to the muzzles of guns, the smacking of whips coming down on bent backs, the squeaking of gallows ropes, the cracking of black bodies being broken on the wheel, the screech of the guillotine blade separating heads from bodies and sending them toppling into waiting baskets, many heads, more and more heads, kinky black heads, yellow heads with smooth pommaded hair, white heads with or without hair or with powdered wigs.

That, too, comes to an end, and Vincent, now in uniform, is crossing the endless blue sea under billowing white sails. The towers of a city rise from the curved horizon. Larger than any city Vincent has ever seen, it is alive with blue-white-and-red cockades and streamers. Every window and balcony, every hat and lapel—all sport tricolor ribbons. Hand in hand with Dr. Dupuy and Maître Coisnon, Vincent enters a hall that is larger than any hall he has ever seen, a theater, an amphitheater; every seat is taken. Over the podium, hanging from the gallery, are banners reading: LA CONVENTION NATIONALE SOUHAITE LA BIENVENUE AUX DÉPUTÉS DES COLONIES! The chairman rises from his place at the center of the podium and announces amid thunderous applause: "Citizens, the commission has examined the credentials of the deputies from San Domingo and found them to be in good order. I move that the new deputies be admitted to the Convention."

Deputy Chamboulas takes the floor. Red in the face, his voice breaking with excitement, he cries: "In 1789 the aristocracy of birth and religion was abolished. But the aristocracy of skin color is still with us. Today its hour has struck: the equality of all men has become reality. A black deputy and a mulatto deputy, representing San Domingo, are about to take their places in the Convention."

[*The new deputies, Laraque a black, Coisnon a mulatto, and Dupuy a white man, are welcomed with long-drawn-out applause. They take their places in the front row.*]

LACROIX [*a deputy*]: The Convention has awaited this moment with impatience. It is proud to receive in its midst members of a race that has been oppressed and humiliated for centuries. I call upon the chairman to welcome them fraternally in the name of the Convention!

[*The new deputies mount the podium. The chairman embraces them and kisses them on both cheeks. The deputies rise from their seats and applaud.*]

LEVASSEUR [*a deputy*]: I propose the following resolution: [*Reads*] When we drafted a constitution for the French nation, we forgot the unfortunate blacks. Posterity will hold it against us. Let us make good our omission by proclaiming the freedom of the black people. Mr. Chairman, do not suffer this assembly to disgrace itself by submitting this point to discussion.

[*Deputy Lavasseur's motion is carried by acclamation.*]

CAMBON [*a deputy, points to the public benches*]: A black citizeness, the mother of Deputy Laraque, has fainted with emotion on hearing us bestow freedom on her people. I move that this incident be recorded in the minutes and that in recognition of her civic comportment the citizeness be given a place on the podium.

[*Amid the applause of all, the woman is seated on the podium. She dries her tears while taking a seat next to Vincent.*]

LACROIX: I move that the minister of the navy inform the colonies immediately of their emancipation, and propose the following decrees: "The National Convention declares slavery to be abolished in all the colonies. It further declares that all persons living in the colonies, without distinction of color, are French citizens, entitled to all the rights guaranteed by the constitution."

[*Thunderous, protracted applause. The deputies rise from their seats.*]

This vision fades into another: Vincent with drawn pistols stepping up to Toussaint L'Ouverture to arrest him. But as he aims his pistols at the bewildered general and disarms him with the words "Give me your sword, General; you are nothing any longer in San Domingo," his hands begin to tremble; looking down, he sees that they have turned black. In the same moment Toussaint L'Ouverture is transformed into First Consul Napoleon Bonaparte, who steps up to Vincent and declares, "I personally will see to it that no African keeps epaulettes on his shoulders." With one hand he then tears off Vincent's epaulettes; with the other he gives him a resounding slap in the face, which awakens Vincent from his agitated dream.

When Vincent opened his eyes, he saw high above him General Dessalines on horseback, flashing sword upraised, and heard him order the firing squad to desist and to remove the blindfolds from the eyes of the condemned men. Drawing a sheaf of papers from his saddlebag, he handed them down to Maître Coisnon, who stepped forward trembling like a leaf. "Translate this document," the general commanded.

"It is a letter from British Commodore Loving," the terrified schoolmaster stammered after leafing through the pages. "The British commodore wishes, in the name of His Majesty the King of England, to seize the French ships anchored in the harbor. To that end he calls on the commander of the Haitian army to send him reliable pilots."

"Your Excellency," said Dr. Dupuy, stepping forward unasked, "send me to the British fleet as your agent; conclude a trade pact with Great Britain, grant England a monopoly on the colony's import and export trade, have yourself crowned king of Haiti and request the protection of the English crown. Your young state needs trustworthy allies to defend it against France." Dessalines frowned, which made his countenance more forbidding than ever. Then, turning to Vincent: "You are an officer. What you would do in my place?"

"As a soldier of the Republic," said Vincent, springing to attention, "I would forbid the British troops to land. The Haitian army has defeated France without foreign help. It and not England is entitled to the fruits of victory. General, do not suffer the foot of European mercenaries to trample the free soil of Haiti!" Dessalines gave spur to his horse and ordered his soldiers to proceed with the interrupted execution. Once again the condemned men were blindfolded. The commanding officer was about to give the command to fire, when again Dessalines turned about and raised his arm to stop the firing squad.

"Citizen Vincent," he said, returning his sword to the colonel of engineers, who had just said good-bye to life, "you are appointed brigadier general of the Haitian army and assigned to the General Staff as my personal aide-de-camp. As for you, Maître Coisnon, you will be my private secretary. Make a note of what your friend and now superior officer just said. You, Dr. Dupuy, will deliver my answer to British Commodore Loving's letter; let the English do with you as they see fit. There is no room for traitors, regardless of color, on the soil of a free republic."

Twenty-four hours later, Vincent found himself on a podium decorated with blue-white-and-red banners, surrounded by the generals of the Haitian army in their resplendent dress uniforms. Off to one side, in the shadow of a fig tree, Maître Coisnon was working feverishly on a manuscript; rivers of sweat were pouring down his face. Opposite the podium an altar covered with purple velvet—the Altar of the Republic—had been erected. On its marble steps knelt the tame lion that Bonaparte had brought back from Egypt as a gift for his sister Pauline. To the right and left stood captured cannon and pyramids of cannonballs. In the foreground, leaning against the pedestal of the altar, the emblems of various trades: drum, anchor, and ax; pen, machete, and trowel; a compass, the secret emblem of the Freemasons; only the geologist's hammer was lacking. Stacks of rifles with planted bayonets and bundles of rods, symbol of the Republic, framed the heroic tableau, over which rose a slender king palm, topped by a fiery-red Phrygian cap.

Gun salutes, cries of command, drum rolls. Clad in a dusty, blood-spattered uniform, Dessalines passes his troops in review. The schoolmaster, breathing a sigh of relief and wiping the sweat from his brow, hands him the declaration of independence that he has just finished drafting; the ink is still wet. Dessalines cannot read. He frowns; Maître Coisnon is so terrified that he falls into a faint. Dessalines stamps his feet, tears the document to shreds, and cries out, "We have already declared our independence, using a white man's skin as parchment, his skull as an inkwell, his blood as ink, and a bayonet for a pen!" Amid thunderous applause, he snatches the tricolor flag from the hand of an officer and with his bare hands rips out the white field, which he tramples in the dust and grinds with the heel of his boot. Then, holding high the blue and red stripes that are left, he baptizes the newly founded republic by its old name of Haiti. Aroused from his faint by the cheering, Maître Coisnon joins in the solemn oath, which all repeat: "We swear to die on the ruins of a free country rather than resume the chains of slavery: LA LIBERTÉ OU LA MORT!

Epilogue

THIS, more or less, is the story as the cayman told it to me, though in other, more crocodilian words. In conclusion he ground his teeth and said "*Krick?*"—his way of calling on Papa Ogoun and Baron Samedi, Maman Zimbie and Erzulie, the goddess of love, to vouch for the truth of his tale. "*Krick?*" And answering his own question: "*Krack!*" Which is Creole, and means "Once upon a time," or "That is the story, all right," or "Well, it may have been something like that," depending on which translation the kind reader prefers. And in return for a piece of cake, the cayman was prepared to tell me the subsequent destinies of the characters of his story. So here goes.

Krick? Krack!

After the founding of the Republic, the friends' ways parted. Dessalines appointed himself governor general of the island and later, taking a leaf out of Napoleon's book, Emperor of Haiti. Vincent served him loyally. After all the French planters had been murdered on Dessalines' order, Vincent was rewarded with a sugar plantation on the Cul-de-Sac Plain; he died on October 17, 1806, while trying to save his emperor's life. Succumbing to one of the bullets intended for Dessalines, he atoned for his treachery in arresting Toussaint L'Ouverture.

After the murder of Dessalines, Maître Coisnon escaped to the south of Haiti, where he became an adviser to President Pétion; it seems to have been Coisnon who advised Pétion to give Simón Bolívar, the liberator of South America, asylum in his capital city of Jacmel. After the fall of Pétion, he returned to Port-au-Prince as secretary to the Jacobin Billaud-Varennes, who, after having been deported to Cayenne, was awarded honorary citizenship in Haiti. Maître Coisnon died, poor and forgotten.

Dr. Dupuy had better luck. On boarding the British frigate

Bellerophon, which later carried Napoleon to Saint Helena, he surrendered voluntarily and was taken prisoner. After the murder of Dessalines, he returned to Haiti as agent of the English merchant firm Lloyd's & Co. and offered his services to King Christophe, Dessalines' successor. Christophe, who ruled the northern part of the island as an absolute monarch and needed money for his castle Sans-Souci, showed his gratitude for the credit Lloyd's had given him by opening the harbors of his kingdom to British ships and appointing Dupuy to the hereditary nobility. After King Christophe, surrounded in his palace by mutinous troops, had shot himself with a golden bullet, Dupuy helped the widowed queen to escape from the country and so gained possession of the considerable fortune she left behind her. He then put his political and economic experience at the disposal of President Boyer, who made him paymaster of the army and later finance minister. On his advice, Haiti carried on several wars with the neighboring Dominican Republic, which served chiefly to enrich Baron Dupuy, who lived to a high and prosperous old age and died at Cap Haitien. In the place of his motto LA VÉRITÉ SANS CRAINTE, his enemies had his tombstone incised with a lampoon: SI LES VERS CONNAISSAIENT TES FORFAITS, ILS RECULERAIENT D'ÉPOUVANTE DEVANT TON CADAVRE (If the worms knew your crimes, they would shrink in horror from your corpse). This was later removed at the expense of his descendants. *Krick? Krack!*

And what became of the other characters in our story?

General Rochambeau and his General Staff capitulated to Dessalines. Since England had again declared war on France, Dessalines bundled him off to the British fleet, which was cruising off Cap Haitien, or Cap Français, as it was then called. Rochambeau spent eight years as a prisoner of war in England and was killed on October 18, 1913, at the Battle of Leipzig. Since then no European soldier has trodden the soil of Haiti with hostile intent.

Toussaint L'Ouverture died on April 27, 1803, in a glacial, unheated cell at the Fort de Joux in the Jura Mountains, where he had been imprisoned by order of the First Consul. He sent several petitions to Napoleon, who never answered, though Toussaint was only asking for mercy for his wife and son; the Corsican's heart was of stone and he never relented. Toussaint was interrogated daily, and his jailers appropriated all his belongings, including his silver watch, yet he remained silent to the end and never revealed his political secrets or the whereabouts of his treasure. Four years after his death, a Prussian spy by the name of Kleist was locked up in the same cell at the Fort de Joux. There he wrote his celebrated novella *The Betrothal in San Domingo*, inspired, it has been said, by the ghost of Toussaint L'Ouverture.

Pauline Bonaparte accompanied her husband's mortal remains to Paris, where his ashes were interred in a marble sarcophagus in the Pantheon. After that she lived for several years in retirement at the Château de Malmaison. A mysterious ailment, which she was said to have contracted on the West Indian islands, gave rise to much malicious gossip. It was whispered that her dissolute life had brought her a venereal disease. The truth is that she was pregnant. Nine months after her last meeting with Vincent, she gave birth to a healthy boy who, because of his *café-au-lait* complexion, is not mentioned in the annals of the Bonaparte family. In memory of his sire, he was baptized Vincenzo. Pauline remarried and her illegitimate son took the name of his stepfather, Count Borghese. He grew up in a Capuchin monastery on the outskirts of Rome. His mother went to see him in secret, kept him supplied with money and whatever else he needed, and saw to it that he was given an education befitting his station. Pauline's beauty was admired to the end and immortalized by the sculptor Canova. The poet Lamartine, who visited her shortly before her death in Rome, likened her to a Grecian Aphrodite, with the rays of the setting sun playing over her marble bust.

After his mother's death, Vincenzo Borghese went to Haiti as a member of a French delegation sent to negotiate the terms of a peace treaty between France and its erstwhile colony, whose independence was now recognized. He settled in Port-au-Prince and married Dupuinette, an illegitimate daughter of Senator Dupuy; family tradition has it that Dupuinette's real name was Indépendance, since she was born on January 1, 1804, the date of the founding of the Republic of Haiti, and that she was actually Madame Dessalines' daughter by Maître Coisnon. If this is true, then by their union Vincenzo and Dupuinette not only set the seal on the old friendship of the doctor, the schoolmaster, and the colonel of engineers, but also established a blood bond between the Bonaparte and Dessalines families. *Krick? Krack!*

"But what part did you play in this confusing story?" I asked the cayman, who regularly disappeared under water and could only be brought to the surface by one more piece of cake. "If I've counted right, you were killed and hacked to pieces at least twice in the course of your story. And I'd also be interested to know: where did you hide Toussaint L'Ouverture's treasure?"

"I've often been asked that question," said the cayman with a bored, supercilious yawn, opening his jaws so wide that I saw the glint of his gold teeth. "Of course I know where the treasure is hidden, but you wouldn't expect me to tell a young whippersnapper like you, would you?

"And by the way," the cayman went on after a short pause, "even Europeans have caught on by now to the fact that if a West Indian cayman doesn't eat too much cake he'll probably live to be several hundred years old. A true cayman never dies—he has nine lives like a cat. The prehistoric reptile's memory is as insatiable as his stomach. It takes in infinitely more space and time than a human memory. One of these days I'll tell you some more true stories, but this will do for today."

With these words the cayman gave me to understand that he regarded our interview as terminated. Thereupon he withdrew into the somber depths—or shallows, if you will—of his pond. Nothing remained of him but an air bubble, which rose to the surface, expanded until its frail skin shone with all the colors of the rainbow, and at length burst without a sound.

THE WAGES OF UNDERDEVELOPMENT

*The dialogue between the rich countries of the
North and the poor countries of the South must be
conducted fairly and without prejudice; in particular, neither party must try to obtain unjustified
advantages at the expense of the other. . . .*
*(From the recommendations
of the North-South Commission)*

1. Conflict with Germany

URGENT

Port-au-Prince, September 23, 1897

Monsieur le Secrétaire d'Etat,

With reference to our conversation of the 21st inst. I have the honor to inform you that my compatriot Emil Lüders is still under arrest. Yesterday M. Lüders's attorney, Maître Edmond Lespinasse, filed an appeal against the decision of the Justice of the Peace. Failure to release M. Lüders to date represents a glaring infringement of the laws of your country.

I therefore request you to give the matter your personal attention, not only out of courtesy toward the German Embassy, but also out of respect for the laws of your country, which provide that an appeal has an immediate suspensive effect on a judgment of the first instance.

Though for the present refraining from any further comment on the proceedings—neither were M. Lüders's witnesses heard nor was it explained by what right the police burst into his dwelling—I take the liberty of pointing out that you yourself in your last annual report observed that, in the matter of appointments to your country's judiciary, a number of questionable if not disastrous decisions have been made. I therefore believe it to be in the best interest of your government to make certain that your laws are observed.

In the hope that M. Lüders will recover his freedom without delay, I assure you, etc.

COUNT SCHWERIN
Imperial German Resident Minister

Port-au-Prince, September 23, 1897

Monsieur le Comte,

I have the honor of acknowledging your letter of today's date, in which, referring to your conversation of the 21st inst., you inform me that M. Emil Lüders, despite the appeal filed by his attorney, is still in custody, and this, as you add, contrary to the provisions of Haitian law.

In this connection you express the hope that M. Lüders will be released forthwith.

Please believe me that the government of the Republic of Haiti would gladly avail itself of this opportunity to demonstrate its good will toward the Germans residing on its territory, and would be only too pleased, in line with the friendly relations prevailing between our countries, to give the Lüders case the outcome you desire.

Unfortunately, the pertinent legal provisions do not permit this. The fact that your compatriot has filed an appeal against the decision of the Justice of the Peace does not automatically allow his release. On the contrary, Art. 18 of the Law of September 19, 1836, provides that an appeal does not have suspensive effect if the sentence has been based on acts of violence as defined in Art. 402 of the Penal Code.

In this connection, you recall my remarks in the Annual Report for 1897 on the state of Haitian justice. I am glad to see that the German Embassy recognizes our government's efforts to have justice done to all; in this light, we should not be justified in anticipating the decisions of the competent court on the appeal filed by M. Lüders.

SOLON MÉNOS
Foreign Secretary

TO THE IMPERIAL GERMAN RESIDENT MINISTER

Port-au-Prince, September 28, 1897

I take the liberty of submitting to the Imperial German Resident Minister the following points, which, in view of my impaired health, I request you to take under urgent consideration. On September 22 the Justice of the Peace, on the strength of Art. 44 of the Law Concerning the Organization of the Municipal Police, sentenced me to a prison term, and on the following day I filed an appeal.

According to my attorney, Maître Lespinasse, who as a former minister of justice is well acquainted with the pertinent laws, these laws provide for my immediate release and guarantee my freedom until the competent court hands down its decision.

Accordingly, I ought to have been free since the morning of September 23—as Maître Lespinasse has explicitly stated in the presence of the German Resident Minister and other witnesses. It follows that I am being held illegally.

Since even under the most favorable circumstances several weeks are bound to pass before the decision is handed down, and since in the meantime I have fallen seriously ill, I request the Imperial German Resident Minister to obtain my immediate release on the basis of the appeal filed by my attorney.

On Saturday, September 25, I was transferred to the caretaker's lodge of the local prison. With heartfelt thanks to the German Legation for the sympathy it has shown me and the steps it has taken toward my release, I remain, etc.

EMIL LÜDERS

TO HIS EXCELLENCY
THE MINISTER OF FOREIGN AFFAIRS IN BERLIN

Port-au-Prince, October 1, 1897

I respectfully take the liberty of submitting the following facts to Your Excellency, based on a memorandum that I have this day communicated to the Resident Minister of the German Empire in Port-au-Prince (see enclosure).

Without wishing to repeat the details noted in the enclosure, I wish merely to observe that the German Resident Minister, Count Schwerin, who at my request attended the judicial proceedings, has to this day, one week after the trial, not received the written judicial opinion he requested.

I am a citizen of the German Empire. Your Excellency is no doubt aware that Germans living abroad are seldom sufficiently patriotic to send their children to Germany to grow up, attend school, and do their military service, so as to become true Germans.

In this respect, my family is a laudable exception. Though we have been living abroad for years, we have remained German at heart. I myself was brought up in Germany, volunteered in Berlin for one-year service in a cuirassier regiment of the Imperial Guard, after which I attended officers' training school in Deutz. My family is one of the best and most esteemed in Haiti and enjoys an excellent reputation in the German colony of Port-au-Prince.

I therefore feel justified in calling on my fatherland for support against an act of violence, a glaring injustice most damaging to my person and business interests. The laws of the Republic of Haiti provide that natives or foreigners may be arrested in their homes only in the presence of a justice of the peace. Although this provision is suspended for Haitian citizens when a state of siege is proclaimed, it remains valid for Germans even then.

The police who invaded my house violated the sanctity of the home, and if I had expelled them by force of arms, I would only have been exercising my legal right. Trusting in my special knowledge of this country and its people and wishing to avoid complications with the government, I was careful not to use force. Nevertheless, I was condemned without a hearing, solely on the strength of false statements by a few policemen, who were extremely prejudiced against me because I had complained about their conduct and they would have been severely punished if my complaint had found a hearing. Everyone in this country knows what to think of the allegations of a Haitian of the lower classes, whose chief characteristic aside from viciousness is undoubtedly duplicity. In this respect the Haitians outdo even the Arabs. No one is better placed than I to know that I committed none of the acts of violence I have been accused of. The court totally disregarded the fact that neither I nor any of the persons allegedly maltreated by me had the slightest bruise to show.

After the sentence was pronounced, I was immediately led away to prison. My house, my business, my entire inventory of cabs and horses were left without surveillance. If Your Excellency bears in mind that even under normal circumstances no one is safe from thieves in Haiti, you will be able to judge the losses I have incurred.

The fact that my family is one of the wealthiest and most prominent in the country makes it imperative that I obtain full satisfaction, because if the Haitians get the impression that one of the most respected and highest-placed Germans can be harassed with impunity, they will think, what with the prevailing hatred of foreigners, that they can get away with even worse mistreatment of other members of the German colony. Though the import and export trade in Port-au-Prince is almost entirely in German hands, and though our colony is the most influential of all the foreign colonies, the Haitians have a very low opinion of the protection given us by our government in cases of conflict, a state of affairs most distressing for us Germans and quite incompatible with our national dignity. It pains us to observe that the people here show a healthy respect for the English and the Americans, but think anything is permissible in their dealings with the Germans and the French. This has got to the point where well-intentioned friends have advised my father, who has an American business partner, to place himself under the protection of the American flag and so safeguard himself and his family from similar abuses.

Please do not infer from my addressing Your Excellency directly that the local legation refuses to help me—on the contrary, Count Schwerin, the new Resident Minister, has energetically espoused the interests of Germans living here and done everything possible to help me.

If in spite of all his efforts he has accomplished nothing up till now, it is due to the peculiar character of this country and its inhabitants. In cases of this kind, the Negro resorts to passive resistance and dilatory tactics. This enables the guilty parties to evade all responsibility for their misdeeds and, favored by the quick turnover of governments and ministers, pass it on to their

successors. But though the local authorities start with such ob-
structive tactics, they back down at once if they encounter resistance in the form of an unconditional ultimatum, based on the
right of the stronger. With this method the English, and to an
even greater degree the Americans, have had great success and
won for their compatriots a salutary respect that we Germans do
not yet enjoy in Haiti.

In conclusion, I should like once again to stress the fact that
all the Germans here are delighted with the great zeal with which
Count Schwerin, despite his limited possibilities, has taken my
case in hand. This, however, does not alter the fact that only
Your Excellency, with your wider scope, your greater experience,
and above all with the more effective powers at your disposal, is
in a position to obtain full satisfaction for me.

I remain etc., etc.

EMIL LÜDERS

Port-au-Prince, October 7, 1897

Monsieur le Secrétaire d'Etat,

I have the honor to call your attention to the fact that the judicial inquiry in the case of Emil Lüders was completed on September 30. Art. 166 of the Penal Code provides that the judgment
be pronounced *at the latest* at the session following the judicial
inquiry. The Port-au-Prince Civil Court sits every Tuesday and
Thursday. The session following September 30 would thus have
been held on the 5th of this month. But in its session of September 30 the Civil Court not only postponed publication of the judgment until October 8, but today adjourned once again until the
12th of this month, on the pretext that one of the judges was ill
yesterday.

Leaving the final appreciation of these facts to my government,
I beg you, Monsieur le Secrétaire d'Etat, etc.

COUNT SCHWERIN

TESTIMONY

FOREST JULIEN *[policeman]*: I was sitting in the Café de la Bourse
when I heard Benjamin (policeman) whistle for reinforcements.

Several police officers ran to his aid. They went to the hack stable to apprehend Dorléus (hack driver), but M. Lüders resisted the arrest by punching and kicking the police officers and hitting them with a stick.

SIMON FILS *[policeman]*: When I heard the whistle, I ran to the stable. When I got there, I saw M. Lüders assaulting two police officers. He knocked them down and was trampling them. Dorléus and two other individuals were also beating the police officers.

EUROPE FLEURY *[policeman]*: Lüders was so angry he was foaming at the mouth. He kicked the police officers and beat them with a club.

RICHARD MIOT *[Englishman, a friend of Lüders]*: I was standing on the Place Geffrard when I heard a noise from Lüders's stable. I went over. When I got there, I saw several policemen trying to arrest one of Lüders's employees. After stubborn resistance, the man was finally led away. Lüders went to the police station to file a complaint.

EMMANUEL JÄGER *[German, a friend of Lüders]*: I was standing outside Constantin Vieux's house, not far from Lüders's hack stable. From a distance I saw him in the middle of an excitedly gesticulating crowd. The trouble was about one of his hack drivers, whom the police were trying to arrest. M. Lüders was resisting the policeman. One of his arms was up in the air, and in the other he was holding a struggling policeman.

GEORGES LESPINASSE *[Frenchman, a friend of Lüders, married to a German woman]*: I was crossing the Place de la Paix when I heard police whistles being blown near a hack stable. I ran to the spot and saw Lüders resisting the arrest of a man who was hiding inside the stable. Lüders was furious. He was holding a stick. I can't say any more, because I wasn't there at the start.

EUGÈNE ROY *[friend of Lüders]*: I was talking to someone when I heard a big noise coming from the stable. I went over to see what was going on. Several police officers were tugging at a man who was clinging to a cab. Lüders had a stick in one hand; with the other he grabbed a policeman. Several policemen were knocked down in the free-for-all.

DAMIEN DELVA: Lüders chased the policeman out of the house with a club.

ANTONY WALLACE *[Englishman, groom]*: I was in the stable brushing one of the horses when I heard a noise. Three policemen were trying to arrest Dorléus, who was clinging to one of the cabs. M. Lüders was angry; he ordered the policemen to leave Dorléus alone.

ANTOINE OLIVIER *[one of Lüders's hack drivers]*: I don't know how it all started. When I heard the noise, I went running. Four policemen were arresting somebody. M. Lüders, for whom I work as a hack driver, was opposing the arrest. He was holding a riding whip.

THE DEFENDANT'S STATEMENT

I was sitting at my desk dictating a letter when I was startled by a noise from below. I went out on the stairs and saw two policemen fighting with my hack driver. He was washing a cab that was in the doorway, half in the stable and half outside—does that make any difference? They wanted to arrest him because he had allegedly stolen something from M. Fortunat, his former employer. I intervened, I admit it, and kicked the policemen out, because I need the man for my business and because the police have no right to burst into my premises.

I spoke roughly, yes, very roughly; I gave the policemen a piece of my mind. They blew their whistles; a mob came running; in fact, they invaded my premises. The police pulled my hack driver from one side; he resisted and other drivers came to his assistance, while I drove out the mob.

LIBERTY   · EQUALITY   FRATERNITY
IN THE NAME OF THE REPUBLIC

EXTRACT FROM THE MINUTES OF THE CIVIL COURT OF PORT-AU-PRINCE

The Civil Court of Port-au-Prince, convened in public session at the Palace of Justice, after hearing the complainants Maximilien

Prudent, Michel Marseille, Joseph Edouard; the witnesses Clermont Belmont, Europe Alexis Fleury, Simon Fils, Antoine Alexandre, Forest Julien, Richard Emmanuel Miot, Emmanuel Jäger, Jean-Baptiste Georges Bellevue Lespinasse, Eugène Roy, Paul Linné Miot, Damien Delva, Antony Wallace, and Antoine Olivier; the attorneys Edmond Lespinasse and Pascher Lespès; the defendants Emil Lüders and Dorléus Présumé; as well as the plea of State Attorney C. Innocent Michel Pierre, has arrived at the following judgment:

Citizen Maximilien Prudent, in his capacity as officer of the Port-au-Prince Police, received instructions from his superior, Sub-Inspector Antoine Alexandre, to arrest Dorléus Présumé, a hack driver in the employ of Emil Lüders, accused of stealing a silver spoon belonging to M. Décius Fortunat. In fulfillment of this order, said officer betook himself to the stables of the hack rental enterprise of M. Lüders, where he found the suspect and demanded in the name of the law that he follow him to the police station. Dorléus Présumé refused to comply with this demand, and resisted arrest by clinging to a cab that he had been engaged in washing. At this precise moment M. Lüders, who had been sitting in the upper story of his premises, appeared on the scene and tried to liberate his employee from the police. M. Lüders declared that he was a German citizen and that the police therefore had no right to harass his employees, grabbed the police officer by the collar, dragged him into the stable, threw him on the floor, and trod upon his abdomen, causing Maximilien Prudent to suffer grievous blood loss. Not yet satisfied, he beat the officer over the head with a club. In this Dorléus Présumé abetted his employer and helped him to rip from the complainant's jacket a banderole reading "Respect the Law."

Not content with this breach of the peace, Emil Lüders, effectively seconded by Dorléus Présumé, assaulted (1) Police Officer Michel Marseille with slaps on the face, kicks and blows on the jaw, (2) Police Officer Petit-Jean Louis Jean with punches whereby he damaged the jacket of his uniform and ripped off a banderole inscribed with the device "Respect the Law."

In view of the fact, emphasized by the State Prosecutor, that the Justice of the Peace of the Northern District of Port-au-Prince, in his capacity as Protector of the Peace, had no jurisdiction in this matter since it involved a public disturbance, and should, under Arts. 170, 173, and 256 of the Penal Code, have turned it over to the State Prosecutor, the judgment handed down by the court of first instance is annulled;

In view of the fact that, contrary to the assertion of the defendants, the police officers charged with arresting the hack driver did not enter his premises illegally, but, rather, as appears from the testimony, M. Lüders himself dragged Officer Maximilien Prudent into the stable for the purpose of assaulting him; and since in view of the foregoing we are dealing with a breach of the peace, committed (1) by M. Emil Lüders as principal and (2) by his hack driver Dorléus Présumé as his accomplice, who are judged guilty under Arts. 170, 177, 256, 44, and 45 of the Penal Code, which provide:

Art. 170: Every attack or resistance, by force or violence against officers or agents of the administrative or State Prosecutor's police while engaged in the enforcement of laws, orders, and injunctions issued by public authority, amounts to a felony or a misdemeanor of rebellion, depending on the circumstances.

Art. 173: If the rebellion was committed by one or two perpetrators, the punishment shall be imprisonment from six months to two years; if no arms were carried, from six days to six months.

Art. 256: When the wounds and blows do not cause any illness or disability, the punishment shall be imprisonment from one month to one year; if the blows were principally to the face, imprisonment from six months to two years.

Art. 44: Accessories to a felony or misdemeanor shall be sentenced to the same punishment as the principal except where otherwise provided by law.

Art. 45: The following persons shall be punished as accessories: any person who knowingly aids or abets the principal or principals in the preparation, promotion, or execution of the of-

fense, even if the crime conspired or instigated to be committed
has not actually been executed.

On these grounds the Court, after thorough consideration, an-
nuls the first-instance judgment of the Justice of the Peace of the
Northern District of Port-au-Prince of September 21, 1897, and
in the second instance sentences (1) M. Emil Lüders, age 26, merchant and director of a hack-rental enterprise, born and residing
in Port-au-Prince, and (2) his hack driver Dorléus Présumé, age
29, born in Pétionville and residing in Port-au-Prince; the former
as principal, who committed an act of unarmed rebellion against
Police Officers Maximilien Prudent, Joseph Edouard, and Petit-
Jean Louis Jean, upon whom he rained blows, which caused
bleeding on the faces of Officer Michel Marseille and Maximilien
Prudent; and the latter as an accessory, who effectively and inten-
tionally supported these illegal acts, each to one year's imprisonment, and under Art. 36 of the Penal Code both jointly to (1)
payment to the state of court costs; (2) payment to the plaintiffs
of 500 gourdes; (3) restitution of a banderole reading "Respect for
the Law" to Officer Joseph Edouard; and (4) payment of fees of
the defendants' counsel, Maître I. Vieux.

> Given by us
> INCIDENT GEORGES, Presiding Judge
> ANSELME, Associate
> MARCELIN, Second Associate
> in public session on October 14, 1897,
> in Port-au-Prince

EXCERPT FROM THE MINUTES OF THE CIVIL
COURT OF PORT-AU-PRINCE

This day, Thursday, October 14, 1897, at eleven o'clock in the
forenoon, before us, Paul Laraque, Secretary of the Civil Court
of Port-au-Prince, appeared: M. Emil Lüders, merchant and director of a hack-rental enterprise, resident in Port-au-Prince, and
he has, through his attorney, Maître Edmond Lespinasse, whom
he engaged to represent him, declared that he has herewith given

notice of his appeal from the judgment entered against him today, sentencing him to one year's imprisonment, to payment of a fine of 500 gourdes, and to the restitution of court costs.

> Signed:
>
> EMIL LÜDERS, Merchant
>
> EDMOND LESPINASSE, Attorney
>
> P. LARAQUE, Secretary to the Court

PRESS COMMENTS

As we learn from usually well-informed sources in Washington, new disorders are to be feared in the Negro Republic of Haiti.

Whereas the previous president firmly repressed all seditious stirrings by arresting or deporting suspects, his successor, Tirésias Augustin Simon Sam, does not seem capable of nipping sedition in the bud.

Corruption is to be seen on every hand, while the decline of industry and commerce makes for discontent among the lower classes.

Local businessmen are refusing to lend the government money, and, since the coffers of the state are empty, a revolution seems imminent. The government has been recruiting throughout the country and, with a view to keeping power, is concentrating hordes of ragged, starving soldiers in Port-au-Prince, the capital.

At the same time, the mayor is subjecting the European business community to arbitrary harassment and confiscating their merchandise to sell it for his own benefit. This has happened most recently to an American and to a German by the name of Obermeyer. The diplomatic representative of the German Empire has intervened in defense of Herr Obermeyer's business interests and is demanding appropriate financial compensation of the Haitian government.

(Vossische Zeitung, October 13, 1897)

NO RESPECT FOR THE GERMAN FLAG

It is sad for a German working on foreign soil to be forsaken by his own government. I know from a reliable source—and it is

no credit to our local diplomatic representation—that a number
of German citizens here have applied to the American consul for
protection, because from him they can expect more energetic and
effective defense of their interests. If, however, as our government chooses to do, one regards Haiti as a sovereign state to be
treated with kid gloves, white tie, and patent-leather shoes, Germany will never enjoy any prestige here.

This country cannot be handled with velvet paws—the only
language Haiti understands is that of a German drill sergeant.

Haiti is just a transplanted chunk of Africa. When you decide
to send us men like Leist and Peters, I'll be damned if they don't
finally respect us. The United States gets everything it wants.
Why? Because it settles diplomatic conflicts with a club, and because everyone in Haiti knows that if necessary an American warship will be offshore within three or four hours.

Our diplomats tear their hair out, write innumerable letters,
all as polite as can be, and get nowhere, because their instructions
from home are: "Red carpet, white tie, top hat, and never smash
the furniture."

When will there be a change?

A German who is being kicked around in Haiti
(*Das Echo*, Berlin, October 1897)

RESPECT FOR THE BLACK-WHITE-AND-RED FLAG IN HAITI?

We are living here under mob rule, but since 1892 we have not
seen a single German warship off the coast of Haiti, though, considering the insolence of this operetta republic, it is high time
Germany showed the flag.

What with the constant revolution, arson, and looting, the
property we have built up by the sweat of our brow keeps going
up in fire and smoke. Thanks to the intervention of their ambassadors, the subjects of other countries are always compensated in
the end for the losses they incur. Only we Germans stand here
empty-handed. Our diplomats let the niggers lead them around
by the nose; our demands for compensation are delayed until the
whole affair is forgotten. German subjects are arbitrarily arrested

and locked up without trial like tramps picked up off the street. Meanwhile, the niggers laugh up their sleeves at the way our ambassador bows and scrapes to free his compatriots from the clutches of the law. Englishmen, Americans, Frenchmen, and Spaniards are also unpopular here, because the niggers hate all white people, but they at least are respected, because their governments do something to make them respected. We Germans still have a long way to go.

(*Die Post*, Berlin, October 16, 1897)

TO THE SENATE OF THE FREE HANSEATIC CITY OF HAMBURG

Port-au-Prince, Haiti, October 17, 1897

We the undersigned Germans residing in Port-au-Prince take the liberty of addressing the following communication to the Senate:

The local German colony counts among its members the businessman Emil Lüders, citizen of Hamburg and son of Herr Theodor Lüders, likewise a citizen of Hamburg residing in Port-au-Prince, and partner in the commercial firm of J. Déjardin, Th. Lüders & Co.

On September 22 of this year, Herr Lüders went to the police station to file a complaint against certain police officers who, on the pretext of having to make an arrest, had illegally entered his premises. Thereupon he was accused by these same officers of rebellion against the state and sentenced by the Justice of the Peace, on the strength of Art. 44 of the Law on Maintenance of Public Order (Contemptuous and Violent Acts Against Persons Representing and Exercising Public Authority and Force), to a fine of 48 gourdes and one month in prison. He was apprehended on the spot and put in prison, where he filed an appeal through an attorney.

Since the legal steps taken by Maître Lespinasse, who is here regarded as the foremost authority in questions of law, brought no result, the German Resident Minister, having established that

Herr Lüders was being held illegally, in contravention of the laws of the land, intervened and demanded, first politely, then energetically, and in the end categorically, the immediate release of his compatriot. At present, eighteen days after his forcible arrest and seventeen days after the filing of his appeal, he is still in custody.

This intolerable situation is an offense against the honor and dignity of the German people and represents a threat both to our freedom and to our property.

The local Germans are a far-from-negligible factor in the economy of the country. We Germans are by far the largest and most important of the foreign colonies, and the lion's share of industry, commerce, and finance is in German hands. It is the sad truth, however, that we Germans are not nearly so well defended against official harassment as the Americans or the English, for example. Since in similar cases German subjects have not always benefited by the requisite protection or obtained appropriate compensation, the undersigned request the High Senate to bring its influence to bear with the imperial government with a view to winning satisfaction and full compensation for our compatriots. *Only if the perpetrators of such arbitrary acts are made to suffer their consequences shall we be spared such treatment in the future.* We are all the more in need of protection since the German Legation, though well intentioned, does not command the power to ensure our security. If an illegally arrested German has no other recourse than the cumbersome judicial machinery of Haiti, his very life is at risk, for no European can endure a protracted stay in a Haitian prison without serious danger to his health. Moreover, he cannot hope for fair treatment by the Haitian courts. Just as in the Orient religion permits a Mohammedan to bear false witness when dealing with an unbeliever, a state of affairs that has led foreign consulates to set up courts of their own, so race hatred leads Negroes to slander Europeans and leaves us defenseless in the face of the courts. If we address the Senate of the Free Hanseatic City of Hamburg in this matter, it is because a citizen of Hamburg is directly affected and because the majority of the business community here are from Hamburg or have business connections with this city. It follows from the foregoing that the life and health of Hamburg citizens are in danger. In the hope that the High Senate will examine our petition favorably and help to bring about a favorable solution we remain . . .

(Signed by all the Germans residing in Port-au-Prince)

Port-au-Prince, October 18, 1897

Monsieur le Comte,

His Excellency the President of the Republic has had the kindness to inform me that you presented yourself on your own initiative at the National Palace yesterday afternoon to notify him of a communication from your government concerning a German subject, M. Emil Lüders.

I feel obliged to point out that my department, to which you have been accredited by His Majesty the Emperor of Germany, has always been at pains to maintain relations of the utmost courtesy and friendship with the German Legation and with you personally, Monsieur le Comte, and was therefore quite unprepared for such a step on your part.

Be that as it may, I remain at your disposal as your natural intermediary, should you wish to request an audience with His Excellency the President of the Republic of Haiti. I shall always take an objective and impartial attitude toward whatever communications you may have to make to my department, and in particular those concerning M. Emil Lüders.

In conclusion, I venture to hope that you will recognize my desire, which I have often had occasion to express to you in the name of my government, to see the feeling of true sympathy that has long presided over our diplomatic and commercial relations expand in a manner increasingly favorable to the interests of our respective countries.

Accept, if you please, the assurance, etc.

SOLON MÉNOS

Port-au-Prince, October 18, 1897

Monsieur le Secrétaire d'Etat,

I have the honor to acknowledge receipt of your note of October 18.

Accept, if you please, etc.

COUNT SCHWERIN

TELEGRAMS

Solon Ménos to Edouard Pouget
Haitian Chargé d'Affaires in Berlin

Yesterday afternoon German ambassador suddenly called on President without requesting audience. Demanded immediate release Emil Lüders, German subject, imprisoned for public rebellion against police, also compensation and demotion of officers involved. Tell minister sentence delivered legally. Letters and documents follow. Regret incident provoked by German ambassador's haste on eve of expanding commercial relations between two countries. Accused has appealed sentence. Hope imperial government, better informed, will send new instructions.

Pouget to Ménos

Constructive interview. German ambassador instructed by Foreign Minister to inform President personally. Foreign Minister admits procedure unusual, but ambassador instructed to appeal to wisdom and evenhandedness of Haitian chief of state. Ministry promises not to approve procedure of German ambassador if contrary to diplomatic etiquette. Imperial government maintain demand for Lüders's release, since domicile violated and arrest made at police station, where Lüders gone voluntarily to ask hack driver's release. Foreign Minister regards appeal not as recognition of sentence but only as observance of juridical form.

MEETING OF THE PORT-AU-PRINCE COMMITTEE
ON JURISPRUDENCE, October 21, 1897

Present: Messrs. Thoby, Borno, Sylvain, Bonamy, Herard Roy, Maximilien Laforest, Saint-Rémy, Viard, Lafleur, Bouzon, J. L. Dominique. Chairman: M. Thomy

The chairman summarizes the reasons for the present session and gives the floor to the secretary, who proceeds as follows:

Gentlemen:

On September 21 the police court for the Northern District of Port-au-Prince sentenced M. Emil Lüders, a German subject, to one month's imprisonment and a fine of 48 gourdes for resisting arrest and for assault and battery on the persons of police officers.

M. Lüders filed an appeal with the Civil Court. At the sessions of September 28 and 30 the case was retried. On October 14, after examination of some fifteen witnesses, the court, finding in the attested facts the elements of a felony, sentenced M. Lüders to one year in prison and 500 gourdes in damages. The defendant immediately filed an appeal. But three days later, on October 17, before the higher court had even taken cognizance of the case, the German chargé d'affaires went unannounced to the Presidential Palace and presented the President of the Republic with an ultimatum, demanding the release of M. Lüders within twenty-four hours and the payment by the state treasury of substantial compensation for each day of imprisonment.

These, gentlemen, are the facts we have seen fit to submit to the Committee on Jurisprudence.

Was the judgment of the Civil Court fully justified by the principles of our jurisprudence or by judicial precedent? This is a doctrinal question which under other circumstances might have warranted discussion, but which is today without practical interest, since the conflict has been removed from the judicial sphere and relegated to the area of diplomacy.

The only question that concerns us is the following: in the present state of the proceedings, even if it is assumed that the Civil Court acted unwisely in increasing the sentence, was the intervention of the German government legally permissible?

To this question there is only one possible answer. The principles of international law allow of no doubt in the matter. Until all legal possibilities have been exhausted, there is no ground for speaking of injustice; there is no ground for abandoning judicial channels and demanding diplomatic intervention in a case that is still pending. What we expect of you, gentlemen, is therefore not a consultation but a protest.

LOUIS BORNO, GEORGES SYLVAIN

THE GERMAN QUARREL BEFORE THE
CHAMBER OF DEPUTIES

Yesterday morning the Cabinet addressed successively the Chamber and the Senate, presenting the government's view of the present conflict with Germany.

The Cabinet did not conceal the gravity of the matter. Rising to the situation, the ministers made it clear by what means the government was planning to safeguard our national dignity and defend the full rights of the Republic of Haiti. They gave every assurance that the government would show no weakness and shun no sacrifice needed to make our sovereign rights respected.

We, for our part, can only congratulate the deputies on their unanimous support of the government's decisions. Their noble attitude, which sounds a chord we thought our deputies had lost, the patriotic enthusiasm of the people, who are impatient to see the German warships—all this is comforting, for it proves that we have lost none of our pride and courage; it proves that government, Chamber, and people are in perfect agreement, all equally determined to forget our internal divisions and present a united front in these days of peril.

Yes, all this proves that patriotism is very much alive in Haiti. And if it is true that faith can move mountains, our patriotic faith will arm us for the fight. We shall know how to suffer and die . . . or conquer. Let the Germans come.

We are ready to die and to kill, first of all to kill. Not one of them will leave here alive. Not one.

They have cabled for the fleet. They expect to bombard our coast and seize our ships. They forget that our ships will scuttle themselves sooner than let themselves be captured. They forget that every shell fired at our capital will mean one massacred German, and first of all the German chargé d'affaires.

The government, it seems to us, must denounce the criminal behavior of the Germans to the civilized world. Let us make no mistake. At the present juncture, secrecy is no longer permissible. Down with secret diplomacy. Let the government's preparations for war be kept secret. Nothing else.

As for the negotiations—if negotiations are still possible—they must be public.

The government must not wait until German guns roar in our roadstead before proclaiming to the Haitian people and to the world that the German vulture is preparing to pounce on us.

If the Cabinet met in secret session yesterday, I imagine it was for reasons of wisdom and propriety. Hoping the German chargé d'affaires would be disavowed by the German Crown, the Cabinet, I presume, did not wish to exacerbate our quarrel with Germany through excessive publicity or to provoke our deputies to make speeches that might prevent the Germans from rectifying their mistakes. This was wise, no doubt. But the overseas cable functions, and if no disavowal arrives the German fleet will. And then the government will no longer need to make any announcement, for the terrible voice of the cannon will have spoken. And that must not be.

Therefore, no more secret sessions, no more secrecy. Let everything come out in the open.

We have confidence in our government, absolute confidence; but we want to know and we want to know immediately.

(R. P. FRÉDÉRIQUE in *L'Impartial*, October 21, 1897)

BULLETIN OF THE MINISTRY OF THE INTERIOR
OCTOBER 23, 1897

Without underestimating the patriotic sentiment that inspired the article "The German Quarrel Before the Chamber of Deputies," which appeared on October 21, 1897, in No. 7 of the newspaper *L'Impartial*, the Ministry of the Interior regrets that Monsieur Frédérique, political director of the newspaper and author of the article, should have voiced threats against Germany in general and the German chargé d'affaires in particular. Enlightened patriots, above all journalists, should know that the only way in which they can effectively support the government's policy is to set the people an example of calm and moderation, which does not preclude firmness and energy.

EDITORIAL COMMENT

This is not the time to examine the complaints of the German chargé d'affaires about the judgment of the Port-au-Prince Court of Appeals; for however well founded the principles invoked by Count Schwerin may be, they do not justify him in deviating from other, no less established principles in disregarding the rules and forms of diplomatic usage. To gain admittance to the President of the Republic, the chargé d'affaires of His Majesty the Emperor of Germany and King of Prussia should obviously have observed certain formalities, of which he cannot be unaware, but from which he apparently thought himself exempted on the premise that this was an affair concerning the relations of a powerful empire with a feeble nation.

Prince Bismarck, whose authority in this matter no one questions, teaches us "that an ambassador cannot claim the right to deal directly with a monarch without the intermediary of that monarch's ministers and cannot demand a personal interview with a sovereign." Now, this principle, which regulates the relations between ambassadors and chiefs of state, is all the more applicable to chargés d'affaires, the lowest rank on the diplomatic scale.

Little more than a quarter of a century ago, in Ems, His Majesty the King of Prussia refused to receive M. Benedetti, the French ambassador, who, on instructions from Napoleon III, had bypassed Foreign Minister Herr von Thiele and applied directly to King Wilhelm in an attempt to obtain a guarantee that Prussia would never support the candidacy of a Hohenzollern prince to the Spanish throne. And it was not so much the refusal of the King of Prussia to receive the French ambassador as Napoleon III's desire to bolster the morale of his army, which had shown a marked lukewarmness at the time of the imperial plebiscite, and to consolidate his dynasty through military glory, that decided the French Empire to declare war on Prussia.

Thus Count Schwerin has undoubtedly committed a grave breach of diplomatic etiquette. Moreover, his action offended the principle of national sovereignty, which accords every country on earth, regardless of its size and material power, unrestricted jurisdiction over its own territory. Just as the German Empire would never relinquish its right to judge a foreigner who had infringed its laws and endangered public order, it has no right to withdraw from local justice one of its citizens who has committed a felony on foreign soil.

We are not unaware that certain eccentricities have been attributed to Emperor Wilhelm; indeed, the European press is indignant about his last speech, in which the young emperor, reviving the old medieval theories of the divine right of kings, proclaims himself the Lord's anointed. Nevertheless, we find it hard to believe that he could have ordered Count Schwerin to fly in the face of hallowed diplomatic usages and that, to satisfy his thirst for military glory, he wishes to cross swords with our Republic. We believe he is destined for higher things and that to adorn his Caesar's brow, haunted by the specters of Charlemagne and Napoleon I, he dreams of other laurels than those he might gather on our hills, far from the glorious battlefields of old Europe.

Let us not lose our heads. Let us demand our rights with calm, firmness, and dignity. Extravagant gestures and warlike noises will not help us under the present circumstances. They have never brought worthwhile results; they can only whip up the passions and render all serious discussion impossible. Before unfurling the banner of national honor, let us wait until every basis for conciliation has been exhausted, until every honorable way out has been sealed off, until we have no other recourse than to avenge our outraged national dignity.

When we have reached this extremity, then it will be time to pass from words to actions, and the certainty of being in the right will arm us against the superior power of our enemies. Obedient to the voice of our fatherland and faithful to our national traditions, we shall know how to sacrifice our lives and show an astonished world how, entrenched behind our hills, we are able, like

Leonidas and his three hundred Spartans, to repulse the invaders, "though his multitudes darken the light of the sun."

Until then, let us be calm.

(THE EDITORS, *La Revue-Express*, October 23, 1897)

Legation of the United States
Port-au-Prince, Haiti, October 20, 1897

Honorable Solon Ménos
Secretary of State for Foreign Affairs
Port-au-Prince, Haiti
Sir,

Do me the favor, Mr. Minister, to release Mr. Emile Lüders, confined by the municipal authorities. In taking this initiatory step, it is with no intention on my part to interfere with your rules of law or enter in the grave complications that at present exist between your government and that of Germany in any way in this matter.

I assure you, Mr. Minister, in making this request, it is in view to relieve the present tension now existing, and to avoid that disorder and bloodshed that will be fatal to the interest of our American citizens resident and doing business upon your island.

I trust, Sir, you will be able to grant this request for the true benefit of all your Country as well as mine.

With my best wishes and assurance, Mr. Minister,

I am, sir,
Your obedient servant,
W. F. POWELL

Legation of the United States
Port-au-Prince, Haiti, October 21, 1897

Honorable Solon Ménos
Secretary of State for Foreign Affairs
Port-au-Prince, Haiti
Sir,

In accordance with a letter that I sent you this morning, that I trust you could see your way clear to release Mr. Emil Lüders,

my Government will consider it a friendly act in the interest of
an amicable adjustment to this whole matter, and I can assure
you, Mr. Minister, that Mr. Lüders will leave, if released, on the
Dutch Steamer for New York tomorrow. I trust, Mr. Minister,
that this will bring about his speedy release, then by relieving the
great tension existing, without any humiliation to your Government, being a friendly act on the part of your government to
mine.

With my personal assurance and esteem, Mr. Minister,

I am, Sir,

Your obedient servant,

W. F. POWELL

State Secretariat for Foreign Affairs
Port-au-Prince, October 22, 1897

To W. F. Powell
Mr. Minister,

I have the honor to acknowledge receipt of your two letters of
the 20th and 21st inst., on which, in the name of your government, you requested, purely as a friendly favor, the release of
M. Emil Lüders, now detained in the prison of this city.

His Excellency the President of the Republic and the Cabinet
fully recognize the motive that inspired your generous intervention, and I am instructed to communicate to you their sincere
thanks for the sympathy you have shown in these trying days for
a nation that is aware of its numerical weakness but wishes to
remain worthy of those to whom it owes its liberation and its
independence.

For this reason, inspired solely by the feelings of sincere
friendship prevailing between the Republic of Haiti and your great
and noble Republic, my government has decided to respond favorably to your magnanimous request, and I wish to assure you
that His Excellency the President of the Republic will this day
issue a decree pardoning M. Emil Lüders.

However, while taking note of your promise that the condemned man will leave the country immediately, I cannot omit to point out that my government reserves the right to issue an immediate order of expulsion and to forbid M. Lüders to re-enter this country, which he has renounced forever.

Accept, Mr. Minister, the assurance of my high esteem.

SOLON MÉNOS

LIBERTY   EQUALITY   FRATERNITY
IN THE NAME OF THE REPUBLIC
Decree
TIRÉSIAS AUGUSTIN SIMON SAM
President of Haiti

In consideration of Article 103 of the Constitution and the Law of September 26, 1860, concerning the exercise of the right to pardon and commute sentences,

In consideration of the dispatches of October 20 and 21 addressed to the Secretary of State for Foreign Affairs by the Honorable W. F. Powell, Ambassador Extraordinary and Minister Plenipotentiary of the United States of America,

Decrees as follows:

Article 1.

Full pardon is granted as of this day (the rights of any third parties being reserved) to M. Emil Lüders, sentenced by the Civil Court of Port-au-Prince on October 14 of this year.

Article 2. The present decree will be executed immediately by the Secretary of State for Justice.

Given at the National Palace of Port-au-Prince this 22nd day of October, 1897, the year 94 of Independence.

T. A. S. SAM

TELEGRAMS

To all diplomatic representatives of the Republic of Haiti

German delinquent pardoned request American Legation. Has left country.

SOLON MÉNOS
Secretary of State for Foreign Affairs

EDOUARD POUGET,
CHARGÉ D'AFFAIRES OF THE REPUBLIC OF HAITI IN BERLIN, TO THE
GERMAN MINISTER OF FOREIGN AFFAIRS

Berlin, October 24, 1897

The undersigned, chargé d'affaires *ad interim* of Haiti in Berlin and with the Holy See in Rome, has the honor to inform the Foreign Office of the German Empire that the Haitian Minister of Justice, at the request of the United States of America's Envoy Extraordinary and Minister Plenipotentiary, Mr. W. F. Powell, has proposed to the government that Emil Lüders, sentenced by the Civil Court, be pardoned. The Secretary of State for Foreign Affairs has charged the undersigned with informing the German Minister of Foreign Affairs that the prisoner has been released.

The government of Haiti has been glad to avail itself of this new opportunity to demonstrate its esteem for His Majesty the Emperor of Germany and King of Prussia, and to have confirmed the cordial relations existing between our two countries. The undersigned is pleased to note that the incident is thus closed.

With the assurance of his utmost respect.

ED. POUGET

2. Furor Teutonicus

Port-au-Prince, October 27, 1897

Monsieur le Secrétaire d'Etat,

In your letter published in *Le Moniteur* of the 23rd inst., you maintain that my dispatch of October 18 amounted to a definite refusal to enter into contact with your ministry; the local newspapers, *l'Impartial* and others, conclude that I have broken off relations with the government of Haiti.

I wish herewith to make it clear that as far as my *démarches* with His Excellency the President of Haiti are concerned, I am responsible exclusively to the German Imperial Government, and that, given my instructions, I could not have proceeded otherwise, for, as I see it, my government's orders are to be carried out and not discussed. But from the fact that I replied to your note of the 18th and that my reply does not contain a single word about wishing to break off relations, it may be inferred that our relations remain unchanged. I have received instructions from my government to communicate with you in the Lüders affair. Please be so kind as to set a time for an appointment.

> Accept if you please, etc.
> COUNT SCHWERIN

Port-au-Prince, October 28, 1897

Monsieur le Comte,

I take note of your assurance that you had no intention of breaking off relations with the government of Haiti and shall communicate the same to His Excellency the President of the Republic and to the Council of Secretaries of State.

With a view toward a final settlement of this matter, I accede

to the request contained in your letter and have the honor, Monsieur le Comte, to expect you in my office at ten o'clock in the forenoon of Friday, the 29th of this month.

> Accept, if you please, etc., etc.
> SOLON MÉNOS

Port-au-Prince, October 29, 1897

Monsieur le Secrétaire d'Etat,

With reference to our conversation of this morning, I have the honor to suggest, on my own initiative and pending the approval of my government, that the question of the indemnity to be accorded M. Emil Lüders be referred to Berlin, to be decided jointly by representatives of the Imperial Government of Germany and of the Republic of Haiti.

> Accept, if you please, etc.
> COUNT SCHWERIN

Port-au-Prince, October 30, 1897

Monsieur le Comte,

Compelling reasons related to the extraordinary events of the past week have impelled my government to entrust the final settlement of the questions arising from the sentencing of M. Lüders to the diplomatic representative of the Republic of Haiti in Berlin.

My government cannot so far disregard the authority of the Haitian courts as to indemnify a legally condemned person who, in accepting the pardon granted by said government, has withdrawn from the appeal that he himself initiated. It remains, on the contrary, convinced that any fair and scrupulous examination of the affair must be compatible with the principles of international law.

> Accept, if you please, etc.
> SOLON MÉNOS

Port-au-Prince, October 31, 1897

Monsieur le Secrétaire d'Etat,

I have received new instructions from my government, which informs me that the Haitian chargé d'affaires in Paris, alleging that Haiti is without diplomatic representation in Berlin, has asked the German ambassador, Count Münster, to communicate the opinion of the Haitian government on the Lüders case to the Imperial Government in Berlin.

To the best of my government's knowledge, Monsieur Pouget is the diplomatic representative of the Republic of Haiti in Berlin. My government therefore feels obliged to request you to send him, either through me or through the Haitian Legation in Berlin, all communications addressed to my government.

These communications cannot be transmitted to my government via London or Paris.

Accept, if you please, etc.
COUNT SCHWERIN

Port-au-Prince, November 3, 1897

Monsieur le Comte,

I have the honor to acknowledge receipt of your Note No. 576 of October 31.

In reply, I refer you to my Dispatch No. 80 of October 30.

Accept, if you please, etc.
SOLON MÉNOS

Port-au-Prince, November 5, 1897

Monsieur le Secrétaire d'Etat,

In acknowledging receipt of your Dispatch No. 81 of the 3rd inst. concerning the Lüders case, I have the honor to inform you that my government has agreed to the proposal I made you in my Letter No. 575 of October 29.

Accept, if you please, etc.
COUNT SCHWERIN

Port-au-Prince, November 9, 1897

Monsieur le Comte,

I have the honor to acknowledge receipt of your Dispatch No. 586 of November 5.

I take note of your communication concerning the ratification of the proposal contained in your Letter No. 575 of October 29.

Accept, if you please, etc.

SOLON MÉNOS

Port-au-Prince, November 10, 1897

Monsieur le Secrétaire d'Etat,

I have the honor to acknowledge receipt of your Note No. 88 of the 9th inst. and to inform you that my government conferred on the 6th inst. with the Haitian chargé d'affaires in Berlin. The Imperial Government of Germany called his attention to all the violations of law committed here in the Lüders case, and all the improper actions of the Haitian government since my interview with His Excellency the President of Haiti. My government demands an indemnity of twenty thousand American dollars for M. Lüders; in the event of a refusal, it will feel obliged to set warships in motion and to break off diplomatic relations between Germany and the Republic of Haiti. In view of the turn taken at my audience of October 17, my government also demands that the President accord me a courteous reception.

The foregoing is communicated by order of my government, and I must add that you have not to date officially notified me of M. Lüders's release.

While awaiting your reply, I wish to assure you, etc., etc,

COUNT SCHWERIN

Port-au-Prince, November 11, 1897

Monsieur le Comte,

I have the honor to acknowledge receipt of your Dispatch No. 604 of the 10th inst.

I must remind you that on October 29 you suggested that discussion of the question of the indemnity you saw fit to demand for M. Lüders be transferred to Berlin, and that negotiations should therefore be pursued between representatives of the Haitian government and of the Imperial Government of Germany.

On November 5 you informed me that your government had approved this proposal.

Obviously this communication implies the need for time enough to enable the Haitian chargé in Berlin to receive instructions from my department and thus to be in a position to refute the accusations that you have seen fit to put forward in this matter. It would seem quite unreasonable for the German Imperial Government to point out to M. Pouget "all the violations of law committed here" without waiting for M. Pouget to familiarize himself with the case.

Accordingly, I find myself obliged to ask you whether this new decision on the part of your government amounts to canceling the "approval" mentioned in your letter.

I should also like to know what "improper actions" you see fit to attribute to the Haitian government and at what moment you asked me for official notification of M. Lüders's release.

Pending a reply to these questions, I hope you will understand my unwillingness to discuss either the circumstances attending your audience of October 17, in connection with which you call the scrupulously correct conduct of His Excellency the President of the Republic into question, or the demand for an indemnity, which your government, anticipating the outcome of discussions whose utility had been agreed upon by both parties, puts forward quite arbitrarily.

My government, which, having no desire to prolong this deplorable affair, has thus far kept its righteous indignation under control, declines all responsibility for the calamities that would result from the arrival or action of German warships.

Accept, if you please, etc.
Solon Ménos

Port-au-Prince, November 12, 1897

Monsieur le Secrétaire d'Etat,

With reference to your Note No. 90 of the 11th inst., I wish to inform you that my dispatch of November 10 was fully consonant with my instructions from Berlin. I cannot answer your questions until my government, to whom I have just cabled the tenor of your note, gives me further orders.

I take the liberty of adding a purely personal observation—namely, that I fail to understand why Monsieur Pouget entered into negotiations with my government if he had not yet received instructions.

Accept, if you please, etc.
COUNT SCHWERIN

Port-au-Prince, November 15, 1897

Monsieur le Comte,

In acknowledging receipt of your Letter No. 610 of the 12th inst., I note that you are unable to answer the questions contained in my Dispatch No. 90 of November 11 without receiving further orders from your government, to which you have cabled.

As for your "personal observation," it strikes me as well founded, and I fail indeed to see how a conference can have taken place on November 6 concerning a question that your government did not decide to discuss until November 5, the day before.

Moreover, my department is convinced that the Haitian chargé d'affaires in Berlin could not have requested an interview on this subject before receiving either instructions or the documents of whose dispatch he has been apprised.

Accept, if you please, etc.
SOLON MÉNOS

PRESS COMMENTS

The Negro republic is in a state of political ferment that has resulted in the present conflict with Germany. But Haiti is only the tip of the iceberg: a similar fate threatens all European peoples of Latin or Germanic origin that have mixed with Negro or Indian blood and formed independent states. The higher the proportion of Negro blood, the greater the chaos. All Central and South America suffers from this political lawlessness, in which only the right of the stronger counts. Putsches and revolutions, violence and corruption are here the rule.

(Magdeburger Zeitung, November 5, 1897)

In its comments on the Lüders case, the Haitian press has the audacity to maintain that Count Schwerin has been bribed by local businessmen to take strenuous measures: "He has been promised an impressive baksheesh for his services in behalf of the business community." The daily *Impartial* writes: "If we continue to tolerate Germans in Haiti, then only as hostages, until the German government offers a public apology for the behavior of its diplomatic representative." One can scarcely conceive of anything more grotesque than this Negro republic, whose government, frightened at its own temerity, dissociates itself in the official *Le Moniteur* from the article in question.

(Germania, Berlin, November 7, 1897)

The conflict with Haiti has taken a surprising turn. . . . It appears that the government intends to demand an indemnity of 50,000 piasters from the Negro republic. Persons familiar with conditions in Haiti have pointed out that this sum is far too low to make an impression there. If Germany is too modest in its demands, the Haitians will never respect Germans as they do English or Americans.

As already reported, the training ships *Charlotte* and *Gneisenau* are expected off Port-au-Prince shortly. It is high time, for letters from Haiti speak of the natives' fanatical hatred of the seventy-odd members of the German colony. Germans are afraid to show themselves on the street unarmed, and they lock and bolt their doors at night.

(Berliner Tageblatt, November 7, 1897)

TELEGRAMS

Berlin, November 1, 1897

Edouard Pouget to Solon Ménos
    Berlin press, citing cable from Port-au-Prince, reports rupture

diplomatic relations and dispatch German warships to Haiti. Request information.

Port-au-Prince, November 2, 1897

Ménos to Pouget

Rupture diplomatic relations not confirmed. Nothing known here about dispatch German warships. German chargé here awaiting instructions from his government.

Berlin, November 10, 1897

Pouget to Ménos

Foreign Minister complains of attempt to make contact through German Embassy in Paris despite existence accredited Haitian chargé in Berlin. Unsolicited interference American Embassy brought more prestige to United States than to German Empire. Increase of penalty in second instance legally inadmissible. Pardon unaccepted because connected with compulsory deportation.

German government's position: police entered Lüders's premises without warrant; Lüders was maltreated during arrest; witnesses for the defense not heard; held too long in prison unhealthy for Europeans; former ambassador Luxburg vouches for defendant as honorable man without criminal record. German government therefore demands $20,000 compensation and courteous reception of chargé by President. I could answer all points immediately but await additional instructions. Recommend maintenance *status quo*.

Port-au-Prince, November 12, 1897

Ménos to Pouget

Conditions unacceptable. Further discussion necessary. Chargé arrogant. Recall indispensable. To cover up inadmissible behavior distorts and falsifies facts. Witness for defense heard in court. Defendant magnanimously pardoned, though not a European. Further information follows, salary being transferred.

PRESS COMMENT

Herr Emil Lüders, whose arrest has provoked a conflict between Germany and the Republic of Haiti, has been here since
Thursday. As reported by the *Berliner Neueste Nachrichten*, his first
visit was to Dr. Goering, the former Imperial Resident Minister
in Port-au-Prince, who is putting him in touch with the Foreign
Office, where he will be questioned. Dr. Goering, who spent five
years in Haiti and is thoroughly familiar with conditions there,
will be consulted in the present proceedings.

(*Vossische Zeitung*, November 14, 1897)

Port-au-Prince, November 20, 1897

Monsieur le Secrétaire d' Etat,

My government has just informed me that the Haitian chargé
d'affaires in Berlin has given it a copy of the judgment against
M. Emil Lüders and refused to comply with our demands. My
government instructs me to give you a summary of its final demands, which His Excellency Baron von Rotenhan, Undersecre-
tary in the Imperial-German Foreign Office, communicated orally
to M. Pouget yesterday:

(1) Payment of an indemnity of $20,000 to M. Lüders;

(2) A guarantee that M. Lüders will be permitted to return
freely to Haiti and reside there without danger;

(3) An official note to the Imperial-German Government from
your government apologizing for its conduct in the Lüders incident;

(4) Once the above-mentioned demands are met, the Imperial-
German Resident Minister is to be given a courteous reception by
His Excellency the President of Haiti.

You are requested, Monsieur le Secrétaire d'Etat, to send me
your government's answer without delay.

Accept, if you please, etc.

COUNT SCHWERIN

Port-au-Prince, November 22, 1897

Monsieur le Comte,

I have the honor to acknowledge receipt of your Dispatch No. 617 of November 20.

To enable my government to answer your communication, please let me know:

(1) Whether on the basis of the instructions you have received from Berlin your note signifies that your government has definitively abandoned all idea of a diplomatic solution to the Lüders case;

(2) What measures taken by my government the government of the German Empire feels obliged to complain of.

Looking forward to clarification of these two points, I bid you to accept, if you please, etc.

Solon Ménos

Port-au-Prince, November 23, 1897

Monsieur le Secrétaire d'Etat,

In acknowledging receipt of your note of the 23rd inst., I have the honor to inform you that I communicated my government's final demands in my Dispatch No. 617 of the 20th inst.

Should you still be in doubt as to the intentions of my government, I can only refer you to Monsieur Pouget, your chargé d'affaires in Berlin.

Accept, if you please, etc.
Count Schwerin

Port-au-Prince, November 24, 1897

Monsieur le Comte,

Recognizing your inability to explain your government's demands, I share your opinion that the Haitian chargé d'affaires in Berlin will be able to provide me with the information that is evidently not at your disposal.

Accept, if you please, etc.
Solon Ménos

TELEGRAMS

Berlin, November 22, 1897

Pouget to Ménos

Foreign Minister advises me off record to use my influence to
settle affair because high-level decision to send warships is irrevocable. He admits that he has not been instructed to allow time
for communication of documents. Reply to ultimatum pointless
since decision German government irrevocable. Request your last
word: are you or are you not prepared to pay indemnity? Cable
reply. New conference today. Arbitration rejected, since Chancellor must be consulted before acceptance. Will keep you informed. Maintain *status quo* until further notice. Still have hope.

Solon Ménos to Haitian chargés in London and Washington

German chargé insists on indemnity, safe conduct for the condemned man, public apology, courteous reception by the President. Humiliating conditions, unacceptable. Since Germany rejects
neutral arbitration, Haiti prefers destruction of its cities and war
of extermination. Inform Foreign Ministers.

INTERNATIONAL PRESS CORRESPONDENCE

As can well be imagined, the tone taken by the President of
Haiti has not been at all to the liking of the German government.
Its indignation at such insolence is only too understandable. This
provocative attitude has aroused extreme dissatisfaction in Berlin
government circles. Convinced that nothing can be gained except
by force, they are determined to use it to bring these savage stick-
lers for diplomatic protocol to their senses.

A good lesson can do them no harm, and one can only hope
that they get one. All these little governments of tropical and
equatorial republics need to be taught how to behave.

Will the arrival of a flotilla off Port-au-Prince bring them to
their senses, or will they oblige us to take drastic action?

An example must be set, and we shall be the first to applaud if these hotheads, who treat us Europeans as if we were in an enemy country, are made to see the light.

On the seventy-fifth anniversary of the Republic of Haiti, Victor Hugo wrote the grandiloquent sentence "How beautiful to behold, among the torches that light the pathways of mankind, one held by the hand of a black!" This species of torchbearer is not unknown to us: we often come across them in the vestibules of noble houses, bearing a candlestick in one hand and a silver tray for visiting cards in the other.

(La Revue Diplomatique, Paris, November 21, 1897)

The flotilla ordered to Port-au-Prince is believed to consist of the training ships *Charlotte* and *Gneisenau*, now cruising in the Indian Ocean, and the *Gefion*, at present being overhauled in the Kiel shipyards. Since the last-named ship cannot put to sea for several days, the government of Haiti still has time to think it over.

(Gazette de France, November 22, 1897)

According to the most recent reports, the United States is siding with Haiti. The conflict is threatening to assume dangerous proportions.

Europe has sufficient instruments of power to put the arrogant Yankees in their place. England, to be sure, has chosen to stand aside, possibly to let others raise the first outcry, but this should not lead us to suppose that the rest of Europe looks upon the matter with total indifference. The German naval demonstration on the coast of Haiti is an indication that no intelligent person can ignore.

(Le Figaro, November 23, 1897)

A storm is brewing in the Old World, and there's been a lot of saber rattling. Kaiser Billy the Little is launching his warships and stirring up water in the bathtub. He has bombarded and set fire to a New Guinea village, whose inhabitants had recently killed their German governor; he has landed troops in China and demanded an indemnity for the murder of two German missionaries. And now his indignation against Haiti over the arrest of an alleged German is evidenced by the high-handed conduct of the German Resident Minister, Count Schwerin. The individual in question had claimed Haitian citizenship until certain incidents made it seem advisable to register with the German Consulate. Finding himself in difficulty with the police, he called attention to his newly acquired German citizenship with a view toward evading arrest. In any case, he does not seem to have been a very commendable citizen.

The German minister seems to have demanded everything short of surrender of the island. But Uncle Sam stepped in as peacemaker, and the release of Mr. Lüders, due to the American minister, has probably averted serious trouble. Even the Germans have noticed that Mr. Lüders had been pulling the wool over the eyes of the Imperial Government. The man is now in Berlin, pressing his demand for an indemnity but apparently with little hope of success.

(*The Standard Union*, Brooklyn, November 20, 1897)

The statement of a Berlin daily, doubtless made for the gallery, that the arbiter in the dispute with Haiti would be German cannon lends special interest to the way in which this same arbiter has just settled a dispute between Germany and New Guinea. It is true that the Papuans do not possess a responsible government with which to negotiate—a circumstance often cited in justification of "punitive expeditions" such as the one that has just resulted in the burning of a native village. But Germany does regard the Haitian government as a responsible interlocutor, as evidenced by the presence of a German consul in Port-au-Prince. The grievances are similar. In the one case a German was deprived of his life, in the other of his liberty.

For a number of reasons, it will be interesting to see whether the same arbiter will be sent to the coasts of North America as to the South Sea Islands.

(*The New York Press*, November 21, 1897)

Kaiser Billy the Little of Germany has been playing the seawolf again, making a show of naval might against the tiny Republic of Haiti on behalf of one of its quarrelsome subjects, who adopted German nationality for the sole purpose of evading just punishment for breaking the laws of the land. It is gratifying to note, however, that the Empire does not as a whole sympathize with the Emperor. The German people know him only too well: he is an inflated clown, a bull in a china shop, an arrogant schemer. And the German Resident Minister in Haiti seems to be a man after Billy's heart. He has had the insolence and bad taste to barge into the President's residence to press his extortionate demands; by this violation of diplomatic usage he has forfeited the sympathy of the diplomatic representatives of all other countries.

(The Standard Union, November 22, 1897)

If Germany goes too far in the Lüders affair, the United States will have to step in. In any event, our government will offer its good offices if the situation threatens to take a violent turn.

Though the Germans seem to take pleasure in intimidating small countries, they are expected to show restraint in their treatment of Haiti.

If Germany backs up its demand for an indemnity by sending a punitive expedition to Haiti, the United States government will probably insist on assurance that such an expedition will remain within certain limits.

As for the Lüders affair, the German flag has not been insulted in any way. For one thing, Mr. Lüders's nationality is open to doubt. Mr. White, our ambassador in Berlin, can be relied on to defend this country's interests by proposing a fair and peaceful solution. To kick the present government of Haiti around would be to endanger the most conservative and reliable government the black republic has had for many years; it would endanger the prosperity and progress of Haiti, and thus represent a threat to American economic interests on that island.

(The New York Journal, November 24, 1897)

The German cruiser *Gefion*, commanded by Captain Follenius, is leaving Kiel for Haiti on December 10. Thanks to its speed, it is well suited to this mission. It can cover ten thousand knots without refueling and is fitted with modern rapid-fire guns. The Germans think it necessary to set an example lest the other republics of Central and South America should take a leaf out of Haiti's book.

The British government is believed to have proposed its good offices in the hope of averting coercive measures against the Republic of Haiti in the event that it refuses to meet the German demands. In Berlin, however, the incident is not regarded as important enough to justify outside arbitration.

(The Evening Standard, London, November 25, 1897)

Cables from Washington report that the Haitian government has asked the United States to arbitrate its conflict with Germany. It does not seem likely that Washington will intervene actively. The American government has decided, however, to send the cruiser *Marblehead*, now at anchor off Annapolis, to Port-au-Prince.

The moment this report became known, Prince Bismarck, the former chancellor, issued the following statement: "From a political standpoint, we deem it imperative that the German government take a firm stand against the arrogance of the Americans, especially when it is directed against Germany. No one in Germany has any thought of annexing Haiti, but we expect our government to demand compensation commensurate with the injury inflicted and to support this demand with adequate pressure."

(Hamburger Nachrichten, November 30, 1897)

In the course of an interview with Herr von Bülow, the Minister for Foreign Affairs, Mr. White, the American ambassador, obtained definite assurance that the German government would be moderate in its demands on Haiti in connection with the indemnity demanded by Herr Lüders. As proof of its good will and out of consideration for American interests in the region, the German government has reduced its demand to $20,000.

(North German Wire Service, Berlin, December 1, 1897)

Port-au-Prince, November 29, 1897

Monsieur le Secrétaire d'Etat,

I have the honor to inform you that I am about to leave for the Dominican Republic.

During my absence the legation secretary, M. Robert Stecher, will be in charge of the German Legation in Port-au-Prince.

Accept, if you please, etc.

COUNT SCHWERIN

Port-au-Prince, November 30, 1897

Monsieur le Comte,

I have the honor to acknowledge receipt of your Dispatch No. 633 of the 29th inst., in which you inform me of your impending departure for Santo Domingo.

I take note of this information and of the fact that M. Robert Stecher has been put in charge of the German Legation.

Accept, if you please, etc.

SOLON MÉNOS

TELEGRAMS

Berlin, December 2, 1897

Pouget to Ménos

Demands of German chargé d'affaires confirmed. Last night the Foreign Minister, citing friendly relations between German Empire and Haiti, informed me that if we persist in refusing to pay indemnity greater pressure will be exerted. Warships soon under way. American ambassador advised me this morning to avoid military complications by paying the sum demanded. Then further demands might be dropped or settled amicably.

December 2, 1897

Ménos to Léger, Haitian envoy in Washington

Two German frigates are leaving Saint Thomas today for Port-au-Prince. Inform State Department and ask if we can count on U.S. support if necessary.

Washington, December 3, 1897

Léger to Ménos

Germany assures U.S. government it is only planning a show of strength. Frigates are only training ships. Support probable if conquest intended.

COMMUNIQUÉ

The Cabinet informed Parliament of the latest demand of the German government in the Lüders case.

A naval demonstration in our coastal waters seems inevitable. But it seems unlikely that, contrary to all custom and principle, the German fleet should go to war over an affair that has not even been discussed by our diplomatic representatives. If this should happen and if danger threatens, the government will not hesitate to inform the public and sound the alarm. In the meantime, it calls on all citizens to remain calm and united, as is indispensable in a time of national emergency. Let all Haitians forget their petty quarrels and concentrate their thoughts on the self-sacrificing devotion that our country is entitled to expect of its sons.

The government is counting on your patriotism to make sure that public peace and order are not for one moment disturbed. That would be high treason, the worst of all crimes, a crime that is punished severely all over the world.

The government is keeping watch over the welfare of all its citizens and the dignity of the nation. The population must trust it to take the necessary measures. Even if we are attacked, let us not forget that the Republic must maintain its good relations with the neutral powers and guarantee the life and property of their nationals to the exclusion of damage resulting from enemy action, for which the aggressor must be held responsible.

F. L. CAUVIN
Secretary of the Interior and Police
Port-au-Prince, December 4, 1897

PRESS COMMENTS

The reading of the government communiqué was greeted on every street and square of the capital with lively applause.

The people of Haiti are facing up with dignity and joy to the unequal struggle that is being forced on them. It is a fine thing to see a young nation of only a million people stand firm against the might of the German emperor. And it is magnificent that our government does not fear to defend the national honor at the cost of whatever sacrifice.

The nation stands united. Fired by the spirit of the immortal heroes of 1804, we are ready to fight. Victory will be ours, for even if crushed, we shall achieve a moral victory over our cowardly aggressors, a victory far nobler than theirs.

(L'Impartial, December 5, 1897)

If Haiti refuses to meet the German demands, we shall take drastic action. First the coastal forts will be bombarded. Then, if the Haitian government persists in its negative attitude, our guns will be trained on the public buildings of the capital. In this connection, Herr von Bülow, the Foreign Minister, made the following statement to the Reichstag:

"Far from contenting ourselves with the release of Herr Lüders, we have demanded compensation for his arrest, an act contrary to all Haitian and international law. We hope the Haitian government meets our just and moderate demands, for on our side we have not only right but also the power to make it respected."

(Die Post, Berlin, December 5, 1897)

On board the German-Imperial Warship Charlotte
Port-au-Prince, December 6, 1897

Monsieur le Secrétaire d'Etat,

You have not given me a satisfactory answer to my note of November 20, which contained the final demands of the German-Imperial Government.

I have the honor to inform the government of the Republic of

Haiti that our relations are suspended until the ultimatum presented by Captain Thiele, commander of the German fleet in Haitian waters, is met.

Accept, if you please, etc.

Count Schwerin

ULTIMATUM

CAPTAIN THIELE, COMMANDER OF THE IMPERIAL GERMAN FLEET IN HAITIAN WATERS, TO T. A. S. SAM, PRESIDENT OF THE REPUBLIC OF HAITI

Port-au-Prince, December 6, 1897

In the name of H.M. the Emperor of Germany I call on you to provide the following before 1300 hours:

(1) Payment of an indemnity of $20,000 to M. Emil Lüders;

(2) Assurance that M. Lüders will be permitted to return to Haiti at any time and live there in full freedom;

(3) A letter to the Imperial-German Legation on board H.M.S. *Charlotte*, in which the Haitian government apologizes for its unacceptable behavior in this affair;

(4) A twenty-one-gun salute to the German flag from the admiral ship of the Haitian fleet, which will furl its flag on this occasion;

(5) After fulfillment of these conditions, courteous reception of the German chargé d'affaires by the President of Haiti.

THIELE

KOMMANDO
H.M.S. *Charlotte*
G.Bf. No.167

Port-au-Prince, December 6, 1897

To the Dean of the Diplomatic Corps in Port-au-Prince, Haiti
Monsieur Th. Meyer
Minister Extraordinary and Plenipotentiary
   of the French Republic
Monsieur,
   I have the honor to inform you that if by 1300 hours the government of Haiti has not met the demands I have addressed to it

in the name of H.M. the Emperor of Germany, I shall initiate punitive measures.

Because of the nearby fortifications, the life and property of neutral nationals would then be endangered, and I must ask you to notify all persons under your protection as well as nationals of friendly countries.

You are advised to show flags on legation buildings as conspicuously as possible. As far as conditions permit, I am prepared to give the nationals of friendly states protection on board my ships.

Half an hour before the inception of the punitive measures I shall fire a warning shot.

> CAPTAIN AUGUST THIELE
> Commander of the German naval forces in Haitian waters

MINUTES OF AN EMERGENCY MEETING
NATIONAL PALACE, PORT-AU-PRINCE
DECEMBER 6, 1897, 10:00 A.M.

THEODORE MEYER [*the French chargé d'affaires*]; *holds up the letter, takes out his watch*]: There's not a moment to lose. I have hundreds of French nationals to look after. How can I get them aboard the German ships in three and a half hours? It can't be done. It's absurd. The whole diplomatic corps must protest. We must appeal to the commander to suspend his ultimatum until all foreigners are safe.

PRESIDENT OF THE REPUBLIC: Exactly. We need more time. Time enough to debate each separate point in the ultimatum, consult the chambers of Parliament, work out a compromise to serve as a basis for negotiation. The Secretary of State for Foreign Affairs will take the necessary steps.

SOLON MÉNOS: I shall go at once to the American Legation and explain my government's position.

MEYER [*to Ménos in an undertone*]: If I were you, I'd resign. That would facilitate a settlement.

MÉNOS: I shall do nothing that might be interpreted as desertion. If my resignation can make the Germans withdraw their ultimatum, I won't hesitate for one moment. Please make that clear to the German commander. Have you drafted the protest of the diplomatic corps?

MEYER: No. A great power, which is not France, has cabled its representative not to sign it. Without unanimity there is no point in protesting.

AUDAIN [*the Liberian ambassador; aside to Ménos*]: That power, sir, is Great Britain. Lord Salisbury is doing his "splendid isolation" act again. The Cabinet of Saint James does not wish to alienate Germany, whose support it may want in its conflict with France over the Sudan.

A GRAY-BEARDED GENERAL OF THE HAITIAN ARMY: It would be madness to take up arms against an all-powerful enemy when we are not united, when everyone is intent on his private passions, his partisan hatreds. For such a task we would need perfect unity, a spirit of infinite self-sacrifice. If each of us distrusts his neighbor, if while German shells are raining down on our city we live in fear of being shot in the back, no serious resistance is possible; the outcome can only be defeat and anarchy. Have you read this morning's *Impartial*? Listen to this [*he opens the paper and reads aloud*]:

> It is every citizen's duty to show unconditional obedience to the military and political leaders the President of the Republic has entrusted with the defense of our country. But in time of crisis the people are sovereign: titles and ranks lose their meaning, we are all equal in the face of the enemy. Only one thing counts, and that is personal courage; every citizen and every soldier capable of distinguishing true from false heroism has the right to organize the defense of our country.

PRESIDENT: Monstrous. That's an incitement to anarchy. [*To the Minister of the Interior*] The whole issue must be confiscated.

MINISTER OF THE INTERIOR: Too late. It was sold out long ago. The people snapped it up. The army and police have thrown up sandbags and barricaded themselves in their barracks.

PRESIDENT [*with resignation*]: We are not a nation after all. We deserve no better.

A YOUNG OFFICER OF THE NATIONAL GUARD: It's disgraceful. . . .
German officers delivering an ultimatum and the people running
down to the harbor to help them land. No dismay, no indignation, as if they were doing the most natural thing in the world.
And now they've crept away to their holes to laugh and applaud
every cannonball, every shell that hits a Haitian house or ship.
By what right does Germany dare to insult our president and
demand apologies and gun salutes for a common criminal? And
by what right do they deny us the time needed to plan our defense, to launch our fleet, to open fire? Instead we must wait for
the Germans to train their guns on us, to sink our little fleet with
their heavily armed warships! They treat us like savages, and we
respond like the subjects of a civilized nation. It's a game with
loaded dice and we haven't a chance in the world. Under such
conditions it would be absurd to resist a great power that is sure
to crush us.

A SENATOR: All this because a hack driver stole a silver spoon.
And to think that all Count Schwerin demanded was to have
M. Lüders let out on bail. Here you have it in black and white.
[*He brandishes a letter.*] The President was kept in the dark. The
Foreign Minister never showed him the Count's letter or various
other documents. He alone is to blame.

VOICES IN THE CROWD: True! True!

MEYER [*aside to Ménos*]: If I were you, I'd offer my resignation.

MÉNOS: I shall go immediately to the American Legation and
inform Mr. Powell of the government's attitude.

CAUVIN, THE MINISTER OF THE INTERIOR: Watch your step. The
people are inflamed—they blame you for what has happened. I'm
giving you a police escort for your personal protection. [*To the
President*] I've just learned that the coastal batteries are not manned
and that the guns have not been put into position. A mutiny has
broken out in the army; the soldiers refuse to carry out orders.
Crowds are gathering in the streets.

PRESIDENT: We are paralyzed by our internal quarrels. Raise
the white flag on the roof of the government palace.

PRESS COMMENTS

Half past twelve. The white flag is going up on the Presidential Palace. The government has accepted the ultimatum, though under protest against the brute force it is powerless to resist.

The population is reacting with mixed feelings: on the one hand with shame and outrage over the humiliation, on the other with relief that the danger is past. One wonders why the government has waited until now to announce its decision, which must have been made some time ago. Our young men, fired by the memory of our nation's glorious past, can hardly control their righteous indignation. The older generation are worried about the survival of the government, to which the young men reply, "The Cabinet should resign."

Many a Haitian has tears in his eyes at the sight of the white flag flying over the Presidential Palace. And many a Haitian who only yesterday was condemning resistance as suicide now wishes with all his heart that the German guns had shot his house to pieces. "The man you see before you has just escaped death by the skin of his teeth." That kind is to be met with all over the world.

(L'Ami de l'Ordre, December 6, 1897 [evening edition])

Port-au-Prince, Sunday, December 5, 1897

This afternoon almost all the Germans who owe their livelihood to our hospitality have fled aboard two German merchant ships. And once again the ones with Haitian blood in their veins were in the biggest hurry.

(L'Impartial, December 6, 1897)

RECEIPT

I hereby acknowledge receipt from the President of the Republic of Haiti of $20,000 for M. Emil Lüders.

AUGUST THIELE
Commander of the German fleet
in Haitian waters

Port-au-Prince, December 6, 1897

Monsieur le Comte,

In fulfillment of one point in the ultimatum that Captain August Thiele, commander of the German fleet in Haitian waters, addressed this morning to His Excellency the President of the Republic, I hereby express, as demanded, my regret over "the conduct of the government of Haiti toward the government of H.M. the Emperor of Germany in the Lüders affair."

Accept, if you please, etc.
SOLON MÉNOS

Port-au-Prince, December 6, 1897

M. le Secrétaire d'Etat,

The government of Haiti has met all the demands contained in the ultimatum of Captain Thiele, commander of the German naval forces in Haitian waters. I therefore have the honor to inform you that I am resuming the suspended diplomatic relations with your country. May I ask you to let me know when His Excellency the President of the Republic will receive me in audience.

The Imperial-German warships *Charlotte* and *Stein* will remain at anchor for several days in Port-au-Prince Bay. Accordingly, His Excellency the President of the Republic of Haiti need only name the day and hour when he wishes to receive Commanders Thiele and Oelrichs. To enhance the solemnity of this reception, the commanders will be accompanied by their staff officers and a military escort.

In the event that the President wishes to visit the warships *Charlotte* and *Stein*, he will be received with all the honors due to a chief of state, a consummation which can only help to revive the cordial friendship between Germany and Haiti.

In order that I may inform the commanders in good time, would you please, Monsieur le Secrétaire d'Etat, acquaint me some days in advance with His Excellency's intentions with regard to the projected reception.

Accept, if you please, etc.
COUNT SCHWERIN

Port-au-Prince, December 7, 1897

Monsieur le Comte,

I have the honor to acknowledge receipt of your dispatch of this day.

His Excellency the President of the Republic, to whom I have submitted your request for an audience, has instructed me to inform you that he will receive you on Wednesday at ten o'clock. I shall not fail to inform you in good time of the President's decision concerning the other points raised in your dispatch.

Accept, if you please, etc.

SOLON MÉNOS

PROCLAMATION

TIRÉSIAS AUGUSTIN SIMON SAM
President of Haiti

Haitians:

The bulletin published in the *Official Gazette* has informed you concerning the first phase of the conflict between the German Empire and the Republic with regard to the case of Emil Lüders.

When M. Lüders was pardoned at the request of the United States Minister Plenipotentiary, this seemed to have put an end to the conflict. The German chargé d'affaires, however, was quick to revive it. At first he proposed direct negotiations in Berlin between the representative of the Republic and the German Cabinet. But this suggestion, though accepted by all and ratified by the German government, was soon implicitly withdrawn. It seemed reasonable to suppose that a meeting between the diplomats of our two countries would yield a just solution. Then yesterday morning two German frigates suddenly appeared off Port-au-Prince, carrying an ultimatum which we were given four hours to accept or reject.

The government's first thought was to offer armed resistance and let the German commanders carry out their threats. But since in its hour of need the Republic was reduced to its own meager resources and could hope for no more than moral support from abroad, we thought it wiser to spare our women and children the suffering that would inevitably have resulted from such an un-equal combat. Might triumphed over right.

Haitians:

For the second time since 1872 our country has been forced by its weakness and attendant circumstances to accept the demands of the German government. Shall it be said once again that we have learned nothing? Shall we let our sterile divisions, our internal conflicts, our repeated mistakes weaken us still further, forgetting that right and reason are of no avail to weak peoples? No, let us learn to benefit by our bitter experience. Let us not forget that there is strength in unity, that internal peace is essential to the progress of our country. Let us with all the ardor of our outraged patriotism reorganize and rebuild our state and lay the foundations for its future prosperity and power.

Given at the National Palace of Port-au-Prince on December 8, 1897, in the 94th year of our Independence.

T. A. S. SAM, President of the Republic

F. L. CAUVIN, Secretary of the Interior and Police

S. MARIUS, Secretary of the Army and Navy

S. MÉNOS, Secretary of Commerce, Finance, and Foreign Affairs

ARTEAUD, Secretary of Agriculture and Public Works

J. J. CHANCY, Secretary of Education

A. DRYER, Secretary of Justice and Public Worship

Port-au-Prince, December 8, 1897

Monsieur le Comte,

With reference to your Dispatch No. 116 of yesterday, I have the honor to inform you that His Excellency the President of the Republic will receive Captains Thiele and Oelrichs with their officers on Saturday morning at ten o'clock.

His Excellency regrets that he will not be able to return their visit in person and will therefore send a representative to their ships.

Accept, if you please, etc.

SOLON MÉNOS

THE HONORABLE SOLON MÉNOS
SECRETARY OF STATE, ETC.

Port-au-Prince, December 8, 1897

Sir,

I have just heard that it is His Excellency's intention to execute the editor of the *Impartial*. Will you be kind enough to see the President for me and express to him my request to spare this man's life? He has been a friend of his country, he has defended her to the best of his ability, though it may have been crudely, and should not be executed by those whom he has defended. I believe he has been a friend of the government. Let the government execute vengeance upon its foes—but not its friends. I do not know the man, have never seen him; therefore my interest in him is simply in the cause of humanity, and for his fearlessness in defending his country.

> I write this letter in haste to you.
> Accept my thanks.
> Your obedient servant,
> W. F. POWELL

PRESS COMMENTS

Port-au-Prince, December 8, 1897

It appears that Powell, the American chargé d'affaires in Port-au-Prince, had promised Ménos, who was still minister of foreign affairs at the time, to do everything in his power to spare Ménos from having to write a letter of apology and gave him his assurance that no naval guns would be fired. The Haitians were expecting American warships to arrive at any moment. Otherwise it would be hard to account for the Foreign Secretary's intransigence. Mr. Powell had inquired of Count Schwerin whether German warships were expected, and if so when and how many. A most improper question. Quite rightly, Count Schwerin replied that the German government's orders and instructions were the concern of the German Legation alone and of no one else.

A diplomatic merry-go-round ensued. England, the United States, and France were asked to send warships. And so they did, but several days too late. By then Germany had settled the affair to its own satisfaction. The foreign warships were of no use whatever.

Pierre Frédérique, editor of the chauvinist paper *L'Impartial*, which had published the crudest and most libelous attacks on Count Schwerin and the German colony, was arrested Wednesday and confined aboard a Haitian warship. The government's plan was to have him transferred with all dispatch from this vale of tears to a better world. But Monsieur Frédérique has many friends and relations. When his arrest became known, a panic resulted—a *couri*, as they call it here (because people start running in all directions). There was serious fear of revolution. So that same afternoon Count Schwerin drove to the Presidential Palace and asked the President not to punish the man on his account or that of the German colony. Saved by the skin of his teeth, an impertinent scoundrel was reborn.

The Count's action made a big impression on the honest Negroes, who still dream loyally of the honor and dignity of the nation and who, what with their hatred of mulatto trickery, feel a certain sympathy for whites. "It has been a cruel blow," say the Negroes at the end of this affair. "We have had to put up with this first blow for the sake of our homes and our families, because might is stronger than right. Now comes a second blow, a moral one that is even more bitter than the first: having to learn from a German gentleman what it means to be civilized and magnanimous."

The German Empire should leave a man like Count Schwerin in Haiti as its representative, or at least send a successor of similar stature.

(*Frankfurter Zeitung*, December 12, 1897)

Port-au-Prince, December 10, 1897
(By our special correspondent W. Katsch)

Count Schwerin and his wife left Haiti suddenly by a steamer of the Hamburg-America Line, for Saint Thomas, where our training ships were anchored. Meanwhile, the Haitian press was stirring up the populace with all sorts of rumors. In government circles the hysteria surpassed all bounds. On Saturday, December 4, when the news spread that our warships had been sighted, the urban population fled to the mountains or barricaded themselves in their homes.

On the same day, our legation received a dispatch from Count Schwerin, announcing that he would arrive in Port-au-Prince at 6:00 A.M. on Monday. While in Saint Thomas he had arranged that two ships of the Hamburg-America Line, the *Slavonia* and the *Galicia*, would take German residents and their families on board for their protection. On the recommendation of the German Legation, most German nationals did indeed board the ships. In town the excitement was at its height. Citizens were running around, armed to the teeth. No German could dream of venturing out of doors. On Saturday the government had issued a patriotic proclamation, dripping with blood and honor and concluding with a declaration to the effect that once the German warships arrived the government would take responsibility only for the subjects of neutral powers. We Germans, in other words, would be fair game.

Monday, at six o'clock sharp, the *Charlotte* and the *Stein* appeared with decks cleared and open gunports. They pulled into the harbor slowly, always keeping the same distance between them, a magnificent spectacle that thousands of Haitians witnessed in silence. In the middle of the harbor they dropped anchor. The four units of the Haitian fleet, two of which had been abandoned by their crews, had withdrawn behind the fortified island known as Fort Islet. Sailors were rushing around wildly on the decks of these small gunboats.

At about nine o'clock, four boats put out from the *Charlotte*, each mounted with a Maxim gun and flying a white flag in the bow and the German battle flag in the stern. Like arrows they sped over the water. When they reached the shore, an officer and a few sailors jumped out of the first boat. First came a sailor bearing a flag of truce, then the officer and his escort with mounted bayonets. The officer handed the port commandant a large envelope and said in his best French: *"Violà l'ultimatum pour le remettre tout-de-suite au Président d'Haiti. Donnez-moi un reçu. Vous avez du temps jusqu'à une heure. J'ai maintenant neuf heures."*

This plain language knocked the wind out of the port commandant. Stammering, he asked the officer to follow him to the Presidential Palace. "Not necessary," said the officer, turning on his heel. The boats returned immediately to the mother ship.

At the same time, letters containing the text of the ultimatum were sent to all the consulates in Port-au-Prince, informing the consuls that two German merchant ships were prepared to receive citizens of neutral powers on board and advising them to display their flags as visibly as possible.

A French Line steamer had been summoned by telegram. When it arrived early that day, its captain received a letter from Captain Thiele of the *Charlotte*. It read:

Monsieur le Capitaine,

At one o'clock I am going to sink the Haitian fleet. Please keep your ship as far as possible from the line of fire.

THIELE
Commander of the German forces
in Haitian waters

Meanwhile, some two dozen German landing craft were racing around the harbor, apparently for the fun of it, or so the Haitians thought. Actually, they were taking soundings. Later, I myself counted more than thirty-four small buoys. They consisted of two crossed bamboo poles weighted down by lead sinkers and showing little flags on top.

At the sight of all this activity, the purpose of which did not dawn on him until much later, the Haitian port commandant was so terrified that he drank himself into a stupor.

In less than an hour the ultimatum was known all over town. I thought it wise to board ship. The harbor was deserted. The *Stein* and the *Charlotte* had put about in such a way as to threaten the town with their rows of gleaming guns. The two Hamburg-America liners and the French steamer had anchored far out at sea. Aboard the French ship there were some 900 people of various nationalities. The Germans, along with some Haitian friends and a hundred or so Italians, had gathered on the deck of the liners *Slavonia* and *Galicia*. The Haitian government had four hours in which to make up its mind. At half past one a first shot was to be fired as a warning for the benefit of the consulates. At one o'clock the bombardment was to begin.

I was on board the *Slavonia;* the Americans had gathered in their legation, since their warship, the *Marblehead*, had not arrived in time.

At about ten o'clock a delegation from the diplomatic corps boarded the *Charlotte* to protest the short time allowed by the ultimatum. The French chargé demanded forty-eight hours, the Britisher likewise; the American wanted no less than four days.

"Gentlemen," the commander replied, "I am here by order of His Majesty the Emperor of Germany. My orders are to bombard the city if the ultimatum is not met by one o'clock. I will carry out those orders."

With that, the gentlemen were dismissed. By then the whole town was in arms. The populace didn't want to surrender: they wanted war. Such madness was not a sign of courage, but showed only that the Haitians are a lot of frivolous children, who never know when it's time to stop playing.

At eleven the port commandant took the President's answer to the *Charlotte*. The government declared its willingness to pay the sum demanded, but rejected the other conditions of the ultimatum. When the commandant saw that the ships' decks were being cleared for action, he was so terrified that he stumbled over a pile of ammunition. The warlike look on the sailors' faces convinced him that the Germans meant business. At twelve o'clock the two warships weighed anchor and maneuvered until they were less than half a mile from the town. The *Charlotte*'s mission was to sink the Haitian fleet; the *Stein* trained her guns on the Fort National and the Presidential Palace.

On board the *Slavonia* we were trembling with excitement. Most of us were following every movement on land and sea through binoculars or spyglasses. The *Charlotte* had got into a position where the fire of only one Haitian gunboat could touch her, and the whole enemy fleet was within range of the *Stein*'s guns. This complicated maneuver was made possible only by the above-mentioned soundings, for the bay is full of shoals and there are few channels wide and deep enough for ships of any size. The *Charlotte* was now only three hundred yards from the Haitian ships and had more than twenty guns trained on them.

At twelve noon a divine service was held on board one of the training ships. The celebrant drew attention to the gravity of the situation. At the end of the service the whole congregation joined in the Lord's Prayer. Then the cry rang out: "Man your posts!"

At 12:30 the first warning shot came thundering over the sea.

The excitement mounted from minute to minute. We all took out our watches and counted the seconds.

A terrifying silence reigned. The streets were deserted; only the port swarmed with soldiers. At exactly 12:56 a white flag went up on the Presidential Palace.

A thunder of cheers was heard from the *Slavonia*, to which the *Galicia* replied. The *Charlotte* and the *Stein* exchanged signals, and five minutes later the port commandant set out in a boat flying a white flag. He brought the President's answer: all conditions were accepted, but it would take time to raise the money and write the required letters.

Captain Thiele extended the deadline to three o'clock and demanded in pledge the surrender of the Haitian fleet. For this communication as well, the port commandant signed a receipt. Later, Captain Thiele sent a courier to announce that he would board the ships at four o'clock. At this the admiral, who was quite drunk, lost his head completely.

By three o'clock the $20,000 was on board; at three-thirty Count Schwerin was in possession of a letter of apology and a document annulling the judgment against Herr Lüders. At four Captain Thiele sent an officer to the admiral of the Haitian fleet with an order to honor the German flag with a twenty-one-gun salute.

This was done. The *Charlotte* answered the salute, and with that the incident was closed.

Though I, like all other Germans, would have wished to see Haiti punished even more severely for its misconduct, I was pleased at Germany's moral victory. In the event of hostilities, bloodshed would have been inevitable, and we would all have been heartbroken if a single German had been numbered among the victims.

On December 8 Count Schwerin was received by the President. The President drank to the health of the Emperor of Germany, and the Count to the health of the President. Tomorrow at ten a reception will be given for the German officers. And the President will be received on board the *Charlotte*.

On December 9 the *Marblehead*, the long-awaited American warship, finally arrived, and half an hour later a French warship dropped anchor. Today we expect one Italian and two British warships.

They are all too late.

Once again Germany has forestalled foreign interference through prompt action.

The people's anger has now turned against the government. Not a night passes without some attack on the Presidential Palace or the army. The shooting never stops. We Germans are glad that our warships are staying for the present and that the *Geier* will be arriving at the end of December for a stay of several months.

(*Die Post*, Berlin, December 14, 1897)

DOUBLE CAPITULATION: CHINA, HAITI

Two victories in one day, two moral triumphs in places as distant from each other as Peking and Port-au-Prince—such success would satisfy the most voracious appetite. All it took to obtain far-reaching concessions was a certain display of force, or, rather, of the intention to use force. The Negro republic has seen its mistake. To the original offense of maltreating a German national it had added the still greater one of opposing passive resistance to the legitimate demands of the German government. It was counting on help, or at least moral support, from Washington. President Tirésias Sam and his advisers imagined that the Monroe Doctrine, that flexible principle of international law which the Americans manipulate for their own convenience, would be applied to this case. Entrenched behind its big brother, the Negro republic imagined that it could defy the German Caesar and his legions with impunity.

It imagined wrong. The United States takes little interest in showing solidarity with Negro states. The race prejudice that has come down from the days of slavery is still strong enough in the American people and their political leaders that they can be counted on to turn a deaf ear to ebony-skinned petitioners.

The American Cabinet is realistic. They know the relation of forces in the world and are in no hurry to alienate Germany— which is not only a great empire but also the birthplace of many American citizens—just to please a Negro republic.

(Le Temps, Paris, December 13, 1897)

THE HAITIAN LESSON

Germany has given us a very disagreeable lesson with its action in Port-au-Prince. The Emperor is reported to have said that his training ships, though manned by cadets and young sailors, were quite capable of teaching the Haitians good manners. Their way of inculcating manners shows as much contempt for the foremost country in this hemisphere as it does for Haiti, and the American people are none too pleased about it.

It was wrong to let the German training ships get to Port-au-Prince first. If we had got our warships moving in time, it is doubtful whether the German commander would have rejected the diplomatic corps's request for an additional twenty-four hours. What men like Admiral Walker or Captain Evans or Commander Buckingham would have done under the circumstances is not open to doubt. As it was, the American residents of Port-au-Prince had to take refuge in the American Legation and wait for the bombardment that might well have killed them all.

When the American Resident Minister went aboard the German flagship, he was treated with contempt. That was regrettable but only to be expected. Unquestionably the Emperor, in giving the Haitian government only four hours to decide whether to crawl or be bombarded, meant to show his contempt for us no less than for the Haitian government. In other words, we were humiliated because we had no warships off Port-au-Prince at the time.

It is hard to dispel the suspicion that this absence was deliberate. It might be argued in favor of the Navy Department that a certain amount of time was needed to get the *Marblehead* ready to set out for Haiti. The plain truth is that it took long enough to have the *Marblehead* arrive several days after the crisis. And it would have been a simple matter to send to Haiti two or three of the ships that patrol our coastal waters to defend American interests and make those German commanders behave with moderation.

(The Washington Times, December 15, 1897)

"A GANG OF NIGGERS"

"They are a contemptible gang of niggers with a thin veneer of French culture. My training ships, though manned by cadets and youngsters, will teach them good manners."

Such were the choice words used by Emperor Wilhelm in commenting on the Haitian incident before the Reichstag.

The Emperor's cadets forced the Negro republic to apologize and pay ransom. The methods they used were pretty crude. But that's how it's done nowadays, so there is no ground for complaint.

The Emperor and his ministers did not think it beneath them to put through massive new credits for the navy thanks to the political passions whipped up by this trifling incident. That makes it a matter of internal policy, so here again there's no ground for complaint.

But the Germans have gone further. They have forced the President of Haiti to accord a "courteous reception" to their chargé d'affaires, Count Schwerin, who had insulted President Sam and was for that reason considered *persona non grata* in Haiti. This is outrageous, contrary to all international usage.

The German emperor has humiliated the Haitians and taught them a cruel lesson. But the fact is that the Negroes could give *him* a lesson in good manners. They have right on their side as long as he imposes on them a diplomatic representative who conducts himself like a bully and a scoundrel.

(The New York Times, December 15, 1897)

TO THE SECRETARY OF COMMERCE, FINANCE, AND FOREIGN AFFAIRS

Port-au-Prince, December 10, 1897,
in the 94th year of Independence

Monsieur le Secrétaire d'Etat,

At the suggestion of one of its members, the House of Representatives has resolved at today's session to question the government on Monday the 13th inst. about its handling of the German-Haitian conflict.

Enclosed please find the text of our question.

Accept, if you please, Monsieur le Secrétaire d'Etat, etc.

V. GUILLAUME
President of the House of Representatives

Port-au-Prince, December 11, 1897

Monsieur le Président,

The obstacles that the House of Representatives has persistently put in the way of any serious attempt at administrative reform oblige me to resign from my post as Secretary of State for Commerce, Finance, and Foreign Affairs.

In retiring to private life after futile efforts to advance the condition of this country, I take with me the comforting memory of the precious assistance Your Excellency has never failed to give me in my work.

Permit me on this occasion, Monsieur le Président, to assure you etc. etc.

SOLON MÉNOS

LIBERTY   EQUALITY   FRATERNITY
REPUBLIC OF HAITI
TIRÉSIAS AUGUSTIN SIMON SAM
President of Haiti

Port-au-Prince, December 13, 1897,
in the 94th year of Independence

Monsieur le Secrétaire d'Etat,

In reply to your letter of December 11 in which you tender your resignation, and in cognizance of the grounds motivating your decision, I regret to inform you that I accept it, though not for one moment doubting that your loyalty to the government and your feelings of friendship for me remain unchanged.

Allow me, dear friend and fellow citizen, to assure you of my unalterable devotion.

T. A. S. SAM

3. Unheroic Epilogue

ADMIRAL KILLICK, COMMANDER OF THE HAITIAN FLEET, TO W. KATSCH,
GERMAN MERCHANT IN PORT-AU-PRINCE

Port-au-Prince, October 10, 1898

Monsieur,

I have just read, quoted in *The Lüders Affair*, a pamphlet by
M. Solon Ménos, an article that appeared under your name in the
Berlin newspaper *Die Post*. In that article it is untruthfully alleged
that on December 6 of last year I "was so terrified" that I drank
myself into a stupor.

These words are an insult, for which you owe me reparation.

I am therefore sending you Messrs. A. Riboul and J. Barthe
with instructions either to obtain from you a formal retraction of
this statement to be published in the German and Haitian press,
or to challenge you to a duel.

I trust that you will not deny authorship of the article in question and will give me satisfaction without delay.

H. KILLICK

MEMORANDUM

Meeting at the home of Dr. Riboul, Dr. A. Riboul and
M. Joseph Barthe, representing M. Killick, and M. Ernst Stempel
and M. Detlev Heydebrand, representing M. Katsch, took note
of M. Killick's letter to M. Katsch, demanding either formal retraction of the libelous article published by M. Katsch in the Berlin press, or satisfaction on the field of honor.

After this letter was read, M. Katsch's representatives declared
that M. Katsch had heard the allegations appearing in the *Post*
article from third persons whom he would think it dishonorable

to name, and that he was therefore inclined to accord M. Killick the requested retraction.

At the suggestion of certain friends, M. Katsch was prepared to express his regret to M. Killick in the following terms:

"Since Messrs. Ernst Stempel and Detlev Heydebrand have heard from an authorized source that His Excellency the President of the Republic thinks the incident has gone far enough and wishes to see it closed, I consent, in deference to the chief of state, for whom I have the profoundest respect, to express regret at having written said article, based on information that I was unable to verify."

In reply to this communication, M. Killick instructed M. Barthe to inform Messrs. Stempel and Heydebrand that he desired reparation commensurate with the offense or satisfaction on the field of honor; otherwise, he would feel obliged to shoot down M. Katsch in the street, and he was quite capable of repairing his injured honor without help from the President of the Republic.

This oral statement was confirmed in the following letter.

TO MESSRS. RIBOUL AND BARTHE

Port-au-Prince, October 12, 1898

Messieurs,

I have given you full powers to make arrangements for the duel, but if despite your efforts you fail to obtain a satisfactory solution, I shall feel obliged to provoke my insulter, M. Katsch, at the first opportunity.

Accept, if you please, etc.

H. KILLICK

Despite the rudeness of this communication, M. Katsch's witnesses prefer not to insist on M. Katsch's right to represent himself as the insulted party, but to recognize M. Killick's claim to be the insulted party, and accordingly let a duel take place on his conditions:

(1) The distance will be of twenty-five thirty-two-inch paces.

(2) The duelists will exchange shots.

(3) Each duelist will arrive at the appointed spot accompanied by a medical doctor.

(4) Each duelist will be armed with a brace of pistols of his choice.

(5) The duel will be directed by an arbiter, who will have previously searched the combatants for hidden weapons and will determine the victor afterward.

(6) The respective positions of the duelists will be decided by lot.

(7) The duel will take place at 6:00 A.M. on Thursday, October 13, 1898, at the mouth of the Diquiny River.

(8) The party to arrive first will be under no obligation to wait more than half an hour for his adversary. At the end of that time, it will be officially established that the absent party has failed to defend his honor, unless *force majeure* can be established to the satisfaction of the seconds.

(9) A shot that misses its mark counts nevertheless.

(10) If both duelists miss, the duel must be repeated.

> Dr. A. Riboul
> J. Barthe
> Detlev von Heydebrand
> Ernst Stempel

Memorandum

The adversaries arrived on the field at the appointed hour, accompanied by their doctors and seconds.

After the distance was measured and the respective positions chosen by lot, Dr. Roche Grellier, having asked and obtained leave to speak, proposed to the contending parties that they call off their duel on humanitarian grounds and let bygones be bygones.

Dr. Riboul then turned to M. Killick and asked, "Monsieur l'Amiral, will you accept a statement by M. Katsch?"

"Yes."

Thereupon M. Heydebrand addressed Admiral Killick as follows: "M. l'Amiral, as you have agreed in principle to accept a statement by M. Katsch, I am empowered to say the following: 'M. Katsch regrets having written the article in question.' Does that satisfy you?" Reply: "Yes."

The adversaries shook hands and the incident was closed.

Given at Port-au-Prince, at the mouth of the Diquiny River, on October 13, 1898.

BOOK THREE

PASTIMES

OF

GERMAN EMIGRANTS

Ein Fichtenbaum steht einsam
Im Norden auf kahler Höh.
Ihn schläfert; mit weisser Decke
Umhüllen ihn Eis und Schnee.

Er träumt von einer Palme,
Die, fern im Morgenland,
Einsam und schweigend trauert
Auf brennender Felsenwand.

(HEINRICH HEINE)

[In a hemlock tree stands lonely
On a barren northern rise;
Its drowsy limbs are covered
With a blanket of snow and ice.

Dreaming, it sees a palm tree,
Far away in its eastern home,
Alone and silent, mourning
On a burning bluff of stone.]

Nature Morte

1

ON January 28, 1898, the Hamburg-America liner *Spreewald*, which had taken on coal at the Danish island of Saint Thomas and, in addition to its passengers, was carrying a cargo of boilers that would be unloaded in Curaçao to make room for a shipment of tropical hardwood, put into the harbor of Port-au-Prince. Among its passengers were my grandfather Louis Buch and his wife, Pauline, née von Drach and widow von Lilien, whose son by her first marriage had stayed behind with relatives in Berlin, where he was preparing for admission to the Lichterfelde Cadet School; the boy's father, a Prussian uhlan officer, Fritz von Lilien, had succumbed two years before to the late consequences of a war injury.

On entering the harbor, the *Spreewald* was welcomed with a twelve-gun salute by the warship *Geier*, which had been cruising in Port-au-Prince Bay since mid-December to protect the German residents of Haiti from possible attack by the native population.

"It's good," said Louis Buch to his wife, who was fanning herself with a silk scarf—the deck where they were standing was crowded with first-class passengers who were surveying the approaching coast through opera glasses and binoculars—"it's good to see our fatherland showing the flag and keeping its guns primed in these distant waters. Here, take a look." And he handed his wife the binoculars, having turned the focusing ring until the black-white-and-red flag on the German Legation, which had just been raised to welcome the German passengers, stood out clearly.

Louis Buch was a man in the prime of life. He was wearing a light summer suit of twill, or possibly drill, and a tropical helmet that shaded a face framed by an imposing beard; his amber-colored eyes still had the same vigorous sparkle as seven years before,

when he had bidden the fatherland good-bye forever to seek his
fortune in foreign parts. In so doing he may have been following
the example of a celebrated ancestor, the Prussian botanist Leo-
pold von Buch, who early in the previous century had investi-
gated the flora and fauna of the Canary Islands; or possibly he
was following in the footsteps of his elder brother Georg, who in
protest against Bismarck's antisocialist laws had emigrated to Bismarck, North Dakota, where he gained high repute as a Mormon
preacher and begot numerous children, who all answered to their
father's name, though, in keeping with the Mormon custom of
the time, they were not all the issue of one and the same mother.

In truth, it was a very different sort of drive that sent my
grandfather to the West Indies. One of his duties as a youthful
apprentice at the Lion Pharmacy in Weimar was to deliver a bottle of boric-acid lotion each Wednesday to the home of the composer Franz Liszt, who used it to treat the warts on his nose,
which were giving him more and more trouble with advancing
age and fame. One morning, when no one responded to my
grandfather's repeated ringing and knocking—the composer's cook
had gone to market and his manservant had been given the day
off—he opened the door and, clutching the bottle of boric-acid
lotion, climbed the narrow staircase. From within the drawing
room resounded impassioned chords that raised a storm in the
young man's blood, for he was not insensitive to music. Did he
dare disturb the world-famous composer at his work? My grandfather's employer, the court apothecary Bertuch, had instructed
him to get a receipt, for the composer was not noted among Weimar shopkeepers for regular payment of his bills. My grandfather
knocked at the door, first hesitantly, then more loudly; when that
brought no result, he plucked up his courage and pressed the door
handle, which had been wrought in the shape of a lion's paw.

For a moment he thought he must have come to the wrong
address and that this was the home, not of a composer but of a
big-game hunter. Inside the mahogany-paneled drawing room a
greenish dusk prevailed, as in a tropical jungle. The thick velvet
curtains were drawn, and in the slanting beams of light that shone

through, thousands of motes danced in time to the music. The entrance was guarded by a stuffed tiger, which bared its teeth as though preparing to pounce on the intruder, who involuntarily took a step backward. From the walls, horned animal skulls looked down at him out of empty eye sockets. A Moorish coffee set, two crossed damascene knives, and a smoking table with an inlaid ebony-and-ivory chess set completed the furnishings, which would have been better suited to the tent of a desert sheikh than to the home of a Weimar composer. But what captivated my grandfather most was a gilt globe supported by four bronze figures symbolizing the continents and the four principal races of mankind: a European with pith helmet and elephant gun, a turbaned Levantine, a Chinese with a pigtail and a pointed bamboo hat, and a half-naked woman who seemed to be a Negress or an Indian or a mixture of the two. Her dark eyes looked at my grandfather so penetratingly that he stood rooted to the spot. A painful sweetness invaded him, a promise of happiness that seemed to emanate from those black eyes.

A gruff order wrenched him out of his revery: "Don't just stand there. Turn the pages." Without a moment's hesitation my grandfather took his position behind the composer, whose silver mane rose and fell like foaming waves over the keyboard. While listening to the last chords of music, my grandfather resolved that, come what might, he would some day enfold the original of that bronze form in his arms.

When he had finished playing, the composer turned to my grandfather, whose intrusion he did not seem to take amiss. "I have the impression, young man," he said with a glance at the bronze figure, "that you have fallen in love with the little Creole girl. Isn't she pretty? The last French emperor made me a present of the globe shortly before abdicating. It is thought to have belonged to his great-aunt Pauline Bonaparte, who brought it back from the West Indies. Pretty, isn't she?" The composer stood up and took my grandfather to the door. "Get some wind in your lungs, young man," he said, daubing the warts on his nose with lotion. "The Hungarian *puszta* is still worth the trip, and for that matter the West Indies are not to be sneezed at. Who knows, some day perhaps you will hold a flesh-and-blood Creole girl in your arms. Life often takes strange turns, young man." With these words Franz Liszt bowed my grandfather out.

My grandfather never forgot the composer's words. He went to the World Exhibition in Paris, to the Industrial Exhibition in London, and to the Colonial Exhibition in Brussels, where he stood in line outside a cage full of Zulus. What fascinated him more than the wild dances of the Zulu warriors was a Zulu woman, clad only in a skirt of palm fronds, whose bare breasts hopped rhythmically as she pounded manioc in a wooden mortar. But even this sight was a poor substitute for the pair of black eyes he had glimpsed in the dusk of Franz Liszt's music room, which had haunted his thoughts by day and his dreams by night. Most likely it was the memory of those eyes that impelled my grandfather, after his years of apprenticeship in French Switzerland and Northern Italy, where he completed his training as an apothecary, to turn his back on Europe and venture the leap across the big pond to take over the management of the German pharmacy in Port-au-Prince, Haiti, in response to an advertisement put in the *Frankfurter Zeitung* by a certain Herr Stecher, acting for the firm of Lüders & Sons.

2

PAULINE sighed. The wind from the shore carried a sickening miasma, the touch of which on her sensitive skin made her shudder in spite of the heat. It was the pestilential breath of the mangrove swamps, a nauseating mixture of land and sea, of muck and brackish water, the dark depths of which swarmed with alligators that churned up the fetid bottom with their jagged tails, an obscene thought that aroused her in spite of herself. Pauline closed her eyes. She felt close to fainting. She had felt sick since the start of their trip, or, more precisely, since Hamburg, where she had boarded this ship, whose constant rolling turned her stomach. According to Dupuis, the ship's doctor, she suffered from *mal de mer*, a chronic ailment, which did not improve in the course of the long voyage but, on the contrary, got worse from day to day. In the English Channel, which, as usual at that time of year, was churned by winter storms that sent great breakers crashing down on the deck, she vomited for the first time; later on, while the *Spreewald* was pounding its way through the long Atlantic swell, she lay strapped in her bunk, trying in vain to fight down her nausea. Everything made her want to vomit: the smell of seaweed and lubricating oil, the sight of smoked eel and salmon on the breakfast table, the bursting of clay pigeons and the popping of champagne corks at the never-ending festivities of the first-class passengers, the misery of the emigrant families penned up in steerage, who spent most of their time staring into space like cattle going to slaughter, but now and then, catching sight of a first-class passenger, would shake a menacing fist. That class of people, her late husband used to say, would bring great evils to society; but those evils were nothing compared to the dangers awaiting her on the other side of the ocean. And that thought started a fresh wave of nausea.

Pauline had consented to the journey with a heavy heart, only for the sake of her newly wedded husband, who had left her no peace with his dreams of a better life in foreign parts. She almost regretted that, despite the bitter experience of her first marriage, she had accepted a second proposal. Nothing could cheer her, though her young husband had been touchingly attentive during the crossing. She locked herself in her cabin and stuffed cotton in her ears to shut out the noise of the engines, the groaning of the woodwork, the pounding of the waves. The thought that only a frail steel wall lay between her and an ocean of black water infested with sharks, krakens, and other sea monsters brought on new nausea.

The only ray of light was Dupuis, the ship's doctor, an educated Creole, who had studied medicine in Germany and showed no sign of his Negro blood. Sitting for hours at her bedside, he felt her pulse with his tapering fingers, whose tips had a yellowish tinge, and told her in nasal tones of the wonders that awaited her beyond the sea: mangoes and papayas, flowering bougainvillea and prickly bayahondas, pink flamingoes, green hummingbirds, and many other exotic plants and animals, the very names of which were unknown to her. In Vienna Dr. Dupuis had attended the lectures of one Sigmund Freud, a Jewish *Privatdozent*, and now he tried to apply what he had learned to Pauline's case. He came to the conclusion that she was suffering not only from *mal de mer* but also from a newly fashionable ailment called "hysteria," which had spread like an epidemic from its point of origin in Vienna over half of Europe. Its causes were to be sought in a traumatic experience deep in the patient's past.

After initial resistance—the mere thought made her blush for shame—she told Dr. Dupuis about the unpleasant symptoms she had experienced toward the end of her first husband's life, the true meaning of which had become clear to her only after his death. As a young lieutenant of uhlans, he had fought in the Franco-Prussian War and distinguished himself by leading a cavalry charge against a vastly superior number of French cuirassiers. He had suffered ever since from a mysterious ailment, attributable in the opinion of his doctors to a shell fragment that was wandering about in his intestines. Despite the doctor's efforts, his condition grew steadily worse; his joints became so swollen that he was unable to move without assistance. Eventually he was removed to the military hospital in Koblenz and subjected to a painful mercury cure, which, however, proved ineffectual. Pauline was inconsolable until she learned from an indiscreet night nurse that her husband was suffering, not from the consequences of a war injury but from an incurable venereal disease, contracted not in combat with the enemy but in a brothel behind the lines. In its final stage the disease had begun to affect his mind. On her next visit, when she reproached him for his conduct, he took his cavalry saber from under the bed and shook it in her face until overpowered by the orderlies, who came running in response to her screams and put him into a straitjacket.

When he died, she wished she could somehow suppress her

marriage and wash away the taint that would now cling to her forever; she hated herself for having been the victim of a debauchee who had infected her with the poison of venal love, which she had unknowingly passed on to her children. She had fallen into a deep depression, which had not lifted until she met my grandfather in Wiesbaden, where she had gone for the cure. His love had given her new self-confidence and for a time dispelled the shadows of the past. Though the doctors had given her a clean bill of health before her second marriage, she obstinately refused to sleep with her husband for fear of infecting him.

After this confession, interrupted by violent fits of weeping, she threw her arms around the doctor's brown neck and drew him down to her. Her breathing became spasmodic, faster and faster, and rose to a violent climax; after which she fell into a deep sleep. Next morning she felt newborn. Her turn for the better was generally attributed to the invigorating effect of the Azores' high-pressure zone, though in fact it resulted from Dr. Dupuis's revolutionary therapy. She appeared on deck with her husband and, sitting up in a deck chair, watched through binoculars the dolphins disporting themselves in the wake of the ship. Later, as the *Spreewald* crossed the calm Sargasso Sea, she strolled for hours alone on the promenade deck, and was not in the least dismayed when a flying fish fell onto the deck at her feet. At her husband's side, she took part in the boisterous festivities with which the first-class passengers celebrated the crossing of the Tropic of Cancer, and danced with the captain long after midnight. The next morning the air was loud with gulls, and islands, which from a distance resembled the seaweed islands of the Sargasso Sea, emerged from the water. Then pelicans came flying toward the ship, coconut shells sloshed about in the swell, and the wind carried the scent of tropical vegetation. An ocean-going yacht flying the Union Jack hove in sight as the islands receded on the horizon, soon replaced by sand spits crowned with palm trees, which formed a semicircle around a coral reef. Through a spyglass Pauline saw enormous sea turtles depositing their eggs in the hot sand of the lagoon. An American merchantman passed in the distance,

wigwagging his friendly identity. After passing the east coast of
Santo Domingo, the *Spreewald* headed for Saint Thomas to take
on coal. Pauline went ashore on her husband's arm. Despite the
ship's doctor's warnings, she let herself be tempted to taste the
milk of a fresh coconut; its slightly putrid taste reminded her of
the sulphur spring in Wiesbaden, where as a young girl she had
met her first husband.

Perhaps, thought Pauline as she breathed in the pestilential vapor of the mangrove swamps and watched the white houses of
Port-au-Prince coming slowly closer, perhaps the coconut milk,
like the water of the sulphur spring, contained a slow poison,
which was corroding her organs from within. She rested her head
on her husband's shoulder and felt that her legs were giving way.
But apparently she hadn't lost consciousness for long, for when
she opened her eyes she was in a lifeboat being rowed swiftly to
the shore. Black storm clouds were gathering over the bile-green
hills. Her head rested on her husband's lap; he was fanning her
with his pith helmet, while Dr. Dupuis was massaging her bare
feet. Behind the rising and falling prow of the boat, she saw the
rust- and mildew-corroded roofs of the waterfront quarter emerge
and disappear, as though the whole island were a bad dream, a
mirage, that would vanish when touched. Most of the passengers
going ashore would stroll briefly through the streets, from the
port to the Champ de Mars and the Presidential Palace, with a
short detour to the market, where they would hold their noses
and battle the buzzing flies, then pay the obligatory visit to the
Hotel Olofsson—Dr. Dupuis had warned them against native res-
taurants—and hurry back to the *Spreewald*, only too glad to escape
the heat, the dust, and the importunate guides, who were bent
on showing them the sights or the way to the nearest brothel.
Pauline was condemned to stay on this island. She felt like a de-
portee, arriving at her place of exile in the knowledge that she
would stay there till the end of her days. The old nausea rose to
her throat at the thought; perhaps it was also the rocking of the
lifeboat and the sweetish smell of the sweating black oarsmen in
front of her. As she bent over the gunwale to vomit, she looked

into the eyes, inflamed from prolonged contact with salt water, of a black boy who was clutching the bow of the boat with one hand and trying with the other to catch the copper coins that passengers, amid loud laughter, were tossing into the water. An oar hit him on the head, he went under, and Pauline saw the tail fin of a shark cutting through the water, which a moment later was tinged with red. Then the world went black before her eyes.

She dreamed she was a little girl playing in a sandbox. A gentleman wearing a white summer suit and a pith helmet, who seemed to be her father, picked her up and put her on a swing. Several times she shouted, "No, I don't want to swing," but he ignored her protests. As the swing went up in the air, she saw to her horror that the man in the white suit was not her father but her late husband; the face under the pith helmet was eaten away with leprosy. She cried out for help, but it was too late. The swing rose higher and higher and carried her over land and sea until her skirt puffed up in the wind like a parachute and she fell on a bile-green island. She landed in a mangrove thicket—softly, for the swampy ground braked her fall. The black water gurgling under her feet gave off a sweetish, musty smell. A cayman was wriggling under her skirt; she drew up her legs to escape its jagged tail and clung with her last strength to a slender aerial root, which gradually gave way under her weight, leaving her to the cayman's gaping jaws.

3

"It's nothing," said Dr. Dupuis, bending over the sick woman, who lay, surrounded by luggage, under an enormous ventilator in the lobby of the Hotel Olofsson. "A passing malaise. Madame is suffering from a particularly stubborn form of *mal de mer*, which persists on *terra firma*. In her case it is a symptom of nervous hysteria, caused by a traumatic shock connected with the death of her first husband. Put ice bags on her forehead and rub her hands and feet with cinchona bark—you are a pharmacist, I don't

have to tell you how it's done. The damp heat down here in town
is hard on Europeans; I'm sure a change of air would do your
wife a world of good. My house in Pétionville is at your disposal;
there's always a cool breeze up there in the hills. Madame will
recover in no time."

When Pauline regained consciousness, the doctor, who was
giving up his post on the *Spreewald* to take up medical practice in
Port-au-Prince, moved her to Pétionville. Meanwhile, my grandfather attended to the luggage. At the end of the jetty his future
partner, a German resident of Haiti by the name of Stecher, was
waiting for him. By bribing the customs officers, Herr Stecher
obtained clearance for the pharmaceuticals that my grandfather
had shipped from Hamburg three months before, and the cases
of precious medicines, which would ordinarily be subjected to
import duties, were passed through unopened. Only the Bechstein piano, which by then had been winched from the hold of
the *Spreewald*, aroused the customs officer's suspicion for some
unknown reason. He examined it from all sides, struck a few notes,
raised the lid, put his head inside as though searching for hidden
contraband, and lost his cap in the process. He was not placated
until my grandfather played Beethoven's *Moonlight* Sonata—rather
well, considering that the instrument was badly out of tune after
the long sea voyage.

The chests of pharmaceuticals as well as the piano were loaded
onto oxcarts drawn not by oxen but by sweating blacks. At their
destination, the Place Geffrard, an unpleasant surprise awaited
my grandfather. Where he had expected to find a pharmacy there
was only a ramshackle hack barn, which was being guarded by a
soldier with planted bayonet. A faded sign read: *Emile Lüders—
Location de voitures.* "My cousin Emil," said Herr Stecher, leading
my father across a yard clogged with weeds, "has authorized me
to rent you the land with its buildings and outbuildings on favorable terms. Unforeseen circumstances have forced him to leave
Haiti, and he has put me in charge of his affairs. Herr Lüders has
been the victim of political intrigue, designed to undermine the
traditionally good standing of the German colony in Haiti. He is

most favorable to your plan of founding a German pharmacy and hopes you will sell the natives large quantities of poison so as to cut down the indigenous population and make room for German immigration. Welcome to Haiti, *mon cher* Louis. And now to the Hotel Olofsson to celebrate your arrival."

The German colony spent the night drinking tropics-proof bock beer to my grandfather's arrival. In the morning he set to work. With the help of his future partner, who spurred the native workmen and artisans to greater effort with blows and curses, he demolished Lüders & Sons' erstwhile hack barn. On its foundations arose a two-story structure, with beams of the tropical hardwood known as *bois de fer*. The roof was of sturdy corrugated iron, the outer walls of whitewashed brick; the window and door frames were hewn from sandstone, which in those days was still used as ballast in deep-sea sailing ships, and the ground floor was paved with the same material; the inside walls were paneled with mahogany and fitted with shelves that reached up to the ceiling. Along one wall of what was to be the store, a local carpenter built a counter equipped with two brass rails, at chest and knee level, the one for tired customers to hold on to, the other to wipe their dirty shoes on—an innovation inspired by the bar of the Hotel Olofsson. The cash register, the latest Adler & Co. model, stood enthroned on a raised platform in one corner; every transaction released a mechanical bell tone. Beside it stood a brass spittoon, which only my grandfather was privileged to use. The stables were cleaned and made into storehouses. When all was in readiness, my grandfather with his own hands embellished the shop door with a brass plate notifying beggars and peddlers to keep out, and a little higher up fastened another sign with the inscription: *Pharmacie L. Buch—Produits Chimiques et Pharmaceutiques en Gros et en Détail*. Instead of the Buch family blazon, a beech tree with apothecary's scales and anchor, the Haitian artist who made the sign had depicted a palm tree topped with a Phrygian cap and flanked by two cannon, possibly with a view to discouraging unauthorized persons from entering the shop.

At the grand opening, which was celebrated just six weeks later,

Count Schwerin, the resident minister, who had just returned from home leave, had an opportunity to address the whole German colony as well as the international business community of Port-au-Prince. Sweating profusely in his white uhlan uniform and silver helmet adorned with a horse's tail, he cleared his throat with authority.

"Excellencies, *Damen und Herren, mesdames et messieurs*, ladies and gentlemen," he began.

"The immigration of Germans into Haiti is destined to transform this backward country and open up new pathways of civilization. Guided by the God-inspired leadership of our emperor and king, the German colony will disseminate ideas of progress and discipline, which have not up until now taken root in Haiti, and thus bring about a gradual change in the social, political, and economic conditions of this island.

"The Negro race cannot become fully civilized without the white man's help, because Negroes are not capable of developing on their own initiative, as is amply shown by the example of our protectorates in West and East Africa, where German effort has created flourishing communities where previously there was nothing but chaos and anarchy. Since Germany is now at the peak of European culture, and the German businessman is more competent than his English or French counterpart"—at this point the English and French diplomats present rose to their feet, uttered a few words of protest, and walked out—"the culturally inferior Negro can only benefit from being subjected to German discipline and German ideas.

"If the Negro or colored Haitians nevertheless fear German superiority and try to keep the Germans out of their island by means of restrictions unknown in civilized countries, they will thereby be pronouncing their own death sentence, for the iron law of ethnic development decrees that any people which fails to adopt the civilization of the culturally superior races it comes into contact with is doomed to extinction. The truth of this law is demonstrated by the fate of the Maoris of New Zealand, the aborigines of Australia, and the last of the Mohicans. With this in

mind, I bid you join me in toasting our imperial family and drinking to the economic success of the German pharmacy of Port-au-
Prince. May it enjoy many years of fruitful activity! *Prosit!*"

Except for a handful of Haitian chauvinists, who made a ridic-
ulous display of national pride, the guests all joined in the toast.
The polyphonic clinking of glasses was followed by several blasts
from the sirens of the German cruiser *Geier*, then anchored in the
roadstead—a demonstration of German precision and punctuality
that made a profound impression on the assembled businessmen,
diplomats, and officers.

4

ALTHOUGH my grandfather spared neither pains nor expense in his concern for Pauline's health, it did not improve. Every
morning before breakfast a black servant named Annaise, whom
Dr. Dupuis had engaged to care for her, rubbed her from head
to foot with cinchona bark. Pauline spent the morning in the
kitchen, watching Annaise at her work, in order to learn the language and get acquainted with the products of this strange country. But apart from the word *office*, which means "kitchen" in
Creole, she learned nothing. At noon she ate a light meal of rice
and cooked vegetables, followed by fresh fruit. In the heat of the
day, when life just about stopped in the house, she lay on her
bed bathed in sweat, listening through closed blinds to the chirp-
ing of the crickets. At five o'clock a cup of herb tea was served
her on the bougainvillea-entwined veranda; from there she cast
longing looks at the white steamships passing in and out of Port-
au-Prince Bay. Shimmering in the heat, the city lay spread out
below her. She could distinguish the cathedral, the snow-white
Presidential Palace, and the venerable cannon that flanked its entrance. As she watched the changing of the guard on the Champ
de Mars through her opera glasses, it seemed to her that she could
hear the muffled rolling of the drums. In the four months since
her arrival, she had not set foot in the city; the thought of the

heat and dust in the streets and the piercing cries of the hawkers, which she had heard in her delirium on her way through the town, had struck terror in her heart. And, to make matters worse, she learned through an indiscretion of her servant Annaise that the *Geier* would be leaving for Cuba in a few days. Pauline felt defenseless, at the mercy of this strange country. At night she tossed and turned for hours, and even when she finally fell asleep she was pursued by the beat of the drums, which rose up from the city until long after midnight. Her condition became more and more alarming; she suffered from nausea and vomiting. Dr. Dupuis's therapy was no more successful than the medicines her husband, whose duties kept him in town on workdays, brought with him on his weekend visits. She rejected all food; soon she was too weak to hold the frame of the embroidery she had been working on since leaving Europe, and the needles kept slipping out of her fingers.

Alarmed at her mistress's condition, Annaise, without consulting either the doctor or my grandfather, went to see the voodoo priestess Délira Délivrance, who, thanks to her familiarity with the old African gods, was able to cure all manner of ills. Annaise promised her a week's wages if only she would help her mistress. In a night of full moon—Pauline's husband was in the city and Dr. Dupuis had gone to Gonaïves on business—Maman Délira, as she was popularly known, appeared, accompanied by her *hounssis*, or assistants, who were dressed all in white in token of their virginity; she herself wore a long purple gown. The mambô set to work at once. While her *hounssis* swept Pauline's bedroom with palm fronds, she strewed corn meal over the threshold and sprinkled the room with aromatic essences to dispel all evil demons. Lighted candles, bottles of rum and lemon soda, and plates piled high with food were placed around the bed to tempt the gods, who found it hard to resist the smell of their favorite dishes: roasted ears of corn for Cousin Zaca, patron saint of the peasants; rice with black mushrooms for Baron Samedi, lord of the graveyards; boiled sea urchins, whose pink flesh is prized as an aphrodisiac in Haiti, for Mistress Erzulie, goddess of love; sugar-cane spirits and cigars for Papa Legba, lord of the thresholds and crossroads. Pauline lay impassive as in a trance. The *hounssis* picked her up, sat her down in a chair, and washed her feet with lukewarm water. Then Maman Délira doused her with cheap perfume and rubbed her feet with an ointment the composition of which she revealed to no one, not even to her intimates; it was said to contain the fat of an unborn kid and consecrated graveyard soil. The priestess mumbled Latin litanies, asking the Christian saints for permission to invoke the heathen gods. While the *hounssis* intoned a monotonous chant, she strewed corn meal on the floor to form a magic circle, at the center of which the patient, clad only in a nightgown and carrying a wax candle weighing several pounds, was made to kneel. Pauline trembled with terror and excitement, or perhaps she was shaken by chills and fever. The priestess bade Papa Legba open the gate separating the world of the living from the realm of spirits and the dead. The refrain of her chant was repeated in chorus by the *hounssis*:

> *Papa Legba, ouvri barriè pou' nous*
> *Atibon Legba, ouvri barriè-á pour nous*
> *Papa Legba, maît' trois carrefou'*
> *Maît' trois chemins, maît' trois rigoles*
> *Ouvri barriè-á pou' nous passer nan Guinée!*

> [Papa Legba, open the gate for us
> Atibon Legba, open the gate for us
> Papa Legba, lord of the three crossroads,
> Lord of the three pathways, lord of the three ditches
> Open the gate for us and lead us to Africa!]

A chicken, which Annaise had purchased at the market that morning, was brought in. The priestess seized it by the neck and swung it three times around her head, then quick as a flash bit its head off and sprinkled Pauline with the blood that spurted from its neck. Meanwhile, she murmured the following spell:

> *Au nom Maît' Grand Bois*
> *Au nom Maît' Carrefour*
> *Au nom Maît' Cimetière*

Au nom de Malolu
Au nom de Kadia-Bosu
Qui soldat Maît' Carrefour
Nan tous pays
Voici youne garde protection
Pour épargner malins esprits
Voici youne couvert qui préparé
Ce soir pour 'ous.

[In the name of the Lord of the Big Woods
In the name of the Lord of the Crossroads
In the name of the Lord of the Graveyards
In the name of Malolu
In the name of Kadia-Bosu
Who serves the Lord of the Crossroads
In all countries
This is a talisman
To ward off evil spirits
This is a sacrifice that I've prepared
This night for you.]

A gust of wind swept through the room and the candle went out. Pauline fell with a scream and lay writhing on the floor. The priestess whispered in her ear something that sounded like the twittering of birds, and Pauline answered in the same bird language; then the priestess lifted her carefully and led her to a chair. Pauline's belly rose and fell rhythmically, as though she were about to give birth; her eyes revolved in their sockets until only the whites showed. Then she fell into a deep sleep. As she lay inert, the priestess cut a lock of her hair and put it into a rum bottle along with some of Pauline's nail parings. After corking the bottle and sealing it with pitch, she buried it in the moonlight in a place known to her alone.

When Pauline awoke the next morning, she had no recollection of the night's events. She ate heartily and was able to leave her bed that same day. She recovered quickly and made such rapid progress in French that after a few weeks she was able to chat with Annaise.

5

AFTER his wife's recovery, which he attributed to the medicines he had prescribed, my grandfather, on the doctor's advice, rented a villa in the most fashionable part of Port-au-Prince, the heights overlooking the Presidential Palace, where there was always a cool breeze. The villa on the Chemin des Dalles, like a number of other properties in the area, belonged to the widow Dupuis, the doctor's mother. Though built entirely of wood in the colonial style of the day, with neo-Gothic turrets and oriels, the house was equipped with every modern comfort. There was even a swimming pool, in which my grandfather swam a few strokes every morning on rising. Before stepping into the water, which could not have been more than five feet deep, he invariably tied a rope around his waist and entrusted the end of it to his coachman Dorléus Présumé, whome he had "inherited," as it were, from the bankrupt Lüders estate. Pauline refused to bathe in the narrow pool, for fear of the soup turtles that were kept in it for the needs of the kitchen. Later on, a small cayman was added, which my grandfather had brought back from an excursion into the interior. At seven o'clock sharp the couple sat down to breakfast on the roofed veranda, shaded by a magnificent avocado tree. Coffee was served by a black "boy" in white livery.

After breakfast Pauline sat down at the piano, which had been placed in the drawing room amid exotic plants and was daily rubbed to a high polish by Annaise, and struck up *Für Elise*, while my grandfather took a weeks-old German newspaper and withdrew to the outhouse. This wooden structure, shaded by an ancient breadfruit tree, was his favorite retreat. Here, surrounded by buzzing flies, disturbed only very occasionally by the thunderous sound of a breadfruit falling on the tin roof, he perused the *Vossische Zeitung* or the *Kladderadatsch* and listened to the cackling of the chickens, the gobbling of the turkeys, or the bickering of the servants washing clothes, cooking, or putting coffee beans out to dry in the yard. The fragrance of the freshly roasted coffee combined with the sweetish sweat of the black women and the stink

of excrement to produce an inimitable aroma, which beguiled him
into spending more and more time in this peaceful spot. He never
left it until the piano inside the house fell silent. In response to
this signal, he tore his newspaper into squares, wiped himself,
pulled up his trousers and washed his hands. Next, placing first
one foot, then the other on the running board of his carriage, he
would let his coachman, Dorléus Présumé, shine his shoes before
he stepped into the carriage that he had likewise inherited from
the bankrupt stock of Lüders & Company. A few minutes later
he alit on the Place Geffrard. With his bamboo cane, known as
Cocomacaque, he would shoo away the clusters of beggars holding out gouty hands or artificially mutilated arm stumps at the
entrance of the pharmacy. Selecting one from among a jangling
bunch of keys, he opened the wrought-iron gate.

Meanwhile, Pauline would repair to the kitchen to inspect the
produce spread out on the tile floor, which peasant woman had
brought from the hills during the night in heavy baskets balanced
on their heads. In time she learned to differentiate the various
sorts of fruit and vegetables according to quality and origin: plump-
cheeked mangoes, the little ones from Jacmel and the larger, juicy
ones from the low-lying Cape; papayas that looked like scaly pine-
apples, and *chadettes*, pear-shaped grapefruit the size of a child's
head; green vegetable bananas and golden-yellow dessert bananas;
sweet *corossols*; sour *cachimans*; sweet-and-sour *queneppes*, which grow
in clusters and look like unripe cherries; wild strawberries from
Furcy; wild rice from the Artibonite valley; sweet potatoes and
manioc; beans of every shape and color; *djon-djon*, black mushrooms that were dried in the air; and *piment d'oiseaux*—small red
peppers so hot that after barely tasting one of them an officer of
the *Geier*, who boasted of having eaten the hottest foods imagin-
able in India and Ceylon, fell into a faint and had to be taken to
the hospital with internal burns. Sometimes the peasant women
also brought guinea fowl and wild pigeons, which they tied up
alive in bundles and suspended head-down from their waists, or
fat capons, turkeys, goats, and pigs, which they led on ropes and
which were fattened on corn for several weeks before being
slaughtered in the yard. Sometimes my grandfather's stick failed

to impress the beggars, for Haitian beggars are used to blows, and then he would toss them a handful of coppers. In extreme cases he might have to call the policeman, who stood with shouldered gun outside the Banque Royale du Canada next door, or, if that too failed, he would dispense medicinal alcohol, that infallible wonder drug, to the beggars.

After thus gaining admittance to his pharmacy, my grandfather took his customary seat behind the automatic cash register, from which he could conveniently observe his clerks, the comings and goings of the customers, and the movement of merchandise and cash. He employed half a dozen clerks, whom he himself had trained and who—though few were able to read or write—had quickly learned by heart the Latin names for many medicines. The native clientele usually asked for simple remedies, for which no prescription was required; these my grandfather prepared in the laboratory behind the salesroom. There was, for instance, the purgative Célomme, consisting of table salt, distilled water and, for men—*sel homme*—a strong dose of garlic; *sel femme*, its female counterpart, contained somewhat less garlic. In more stubborn cases, castor oil was indicated. For venereal diseases mercury ointment was prescribed, for yellow fever and malaria dried cinchona bark either in powder or in pills. My grandfather waited in person on foreign customers, European and North American businessmen, and members of the indigenous upper classes. He recommended the typhus and cholera vaccines recently developed by Dr. Robert Koch of the Charité Hospital in Berlin and on request sold painkillers containing large quantities of morphine and opium, with or without prescription. In this way he took in so much money that in barely six months he was able to repay every cent of the loan that the German Overseas Bank had accorded him for construction, and was also able to satisfy his creditor Emil Lüders, who through an intermediary had invested in my grandfather's business the $20,000 indemnity received from the Haitian government. Herr Stecher appeared only once a month, to collect the rent, which he and his dark-skinned concubine then proceeded to drink up at the Hotel Olofsson.

At ten in the morning the postman brought the daily mail,

consisting largely of pharmaceutical prospectuses, business letters, and cables relayed via Kingston or Havana, advising my
grandfather that a shipment of medicines was on its way from
Europe or the United States. Occasionally, however, there would
be a letter from his father in König im Odenwald, informing him
that a cloudburst had left the cellar flooded, or a picture postcard
from his brother Georg, who had by now moved from Bismarck,
North Dakota, to Salt Lake City, Utah, announcing the birth of
a nephew or niece.

My grandfather kept in touch with the leading international
manufacturers of pharmaceuticals, whose agents—Gluck in Paris
and Feingold in Frankfurt—were prepared to send him any desired quantity of any product he named and could be counted on
to send him letters of congratulation on his birthday and at the
start of every promising new business year. In return for their
congratulations he would send them orchids gathered on his botanical forays into the interior, and to make sure of their prompt
delivery he organized a special courier service. A hobby thus gave
rise to a flourishing enterprise, which was soon extended to other
tropical products—wild honey, precious woods, parrots, hummingbirds, and young caymans. My grandfather captured these
last in the swamps of the Etang Saumâtre and kept them in his
garden swimming pool until they were big enough to sell profit-
ably to the Berlin Zoo or to Hagenbeck's Wildlife Park in Ham-
burg-Stellingen.

The pharmacy, like most shops in the city, closed at noon. On
the dot of twelve my grandfather locked the cash register, lowered the blinds, bolted the wrought-iron gate, and stepped into
his waiting carriage. As often as not, live langoustes, which on
Pauline's instructions the coachman had bought in the market,
would be crawling about on the floor of the vehicle. There was
usually seafood for lunch—fresh oysters, boiled lobster, or my
grandfather's favorite dish, a fish weighing several pounds that
was known as *poisson neg'*, though it looked more like a red-faced
Irishman than a Negro. The leftovers would be fed to the cayman. At three o'clock sharp my grandfather went back to the

pharmacy, where he dozed at the cash desk until six—customers were rare in the stifling afternoons. Returned home, he would swim a few strokes in the pool while the cayman lay motionless on the bottom, watching him coldly out of yellow reptilian eyes. He would then sip a rum cocktail on the shady veranda and leaf through a pharmaceutical journal. For his wife's reading requirements he had subscribed to a French fashion magazine and a German house-and-garden publication.

After supper, consisting of the local chicken-and-rice dish, my grandfather would retire to his workroom, where he devoted himself to his double-entry bookkeeping and his botanical studies. He read the standard works of Ritter, Schomburgk, and Descourtilz on the flora of the Antilles, and examined and labeled the carefully dried and pressed plants gathered on his expeditions. He specialized in the ferns of the subtropical upland forests, more than a hundred species of which he described and classified over the years. Before going to bed, he would read his wife a chapter of Fritz Reuter's *Ut mine Stromtid* to practice his *Plattdeutsch*, command of which he thought indispensable for his dealings with Hanseatic merchants.

At eleven o'clock sharp my grandfather put out the light. He slept soundly and dreamlessly until the next morning, while Pauline tossed and turned under her mosquito net, haunted by the sound of the voodoo drums that rose up from the slums to blend with the howling of dogs baying at the haze-shrouded moon, creating a hideous cacophony. In her dreams she saw Mambô Délira Délivrance's bloodshot eyes above her and, reflected in them, the lighted candles and Pauline's own terror-stricken eyes. Pauline lay on the bare ground at the center of a geometric figure drawn with corn meal. The sinuous lines of the figure seemed to have their starting point in Pauline's womb, which formed the center of the magic circle. Her arms were chained to a pole adorned with fetishes, which supported the roof of the temple, and her legs were tied to two stakes driven into the ground. Through a narrow opening in the roof she could see what looked like the Southern Cross upside down; a rat was running along the ridgepole; her hair was standing on end and was silhouetted against the night sky. All around her were naked figures, shiny with sweat, rising and falling to the rhythm of the drums. Closer and closer they came, brandishing machetes, their faces distorted with hellish passion, while the music rose in an infernal crescendo. Then suddenly the drums fell silent, the priestess raised her arms, and with loud cries the crowd flung themselves on Pauline. Waking at this point in her dream, she was relieved to find that her husband lay quietly breathing beside her. She thrust back the mosquito netting, opened the window, took a swallow of distilled water from the carafe on her bedside table, and, as a new day dawned over the mountains to the east, tried in vain to make up for lost sleep.

Pauline's sleepless nights took their toll: her beauty paled like the nightshades that burst into bloom in the moonlight and fade before sunrise. During her first months in the tropics, Pauline's condition had steadily improved, but now the symptoms of her old melancholia recurred, and her attacks became more violent. Resuming the embroidery begun on shipboard, she wove new threads into her carpet of flowers, until the bright blossoms were caught in a tangled web of lianas. Nothing could cheer her; she spent whole afternoons sitting on the veranda, her eyes shaded by dark glasses. Half benumbed by the scent of the flowering bougainvillea, she would listen to the monotonous chant of the heavily guarded convicts, at work in the seering heat, building an emergency exit to the Presidential Palace, a quick way out for the President in case of revolution. Lucky President: he could escape, or if the conspirators failed he could have them court-martialed and shot. But Pauline was hopelessly caught; for her there was no escape into life and freedom. Nothing could shake her out of her lethargy, neither the loving attentions of her husband, who every morning brought a vase filled with freshly picked orchids to her bedside table, nor the efforts of her maid, Annaise, who put ice bags on her forehead, massaged her feet for hours, and sang her to sleep with Creole lullabies such as black nurses had sung a hundred years before to the white children entrusted to their care:

Quand cher zami moin va rivé
Mon fait li tout plein caresse.
Ah! plaisir là nou va goutté;
C'est plaisir qui duré sans cesse.
   Mais toujours tard
     Hélas! Hélas!
Cher zami moin pas vlé rivé.

Si zami moin pas vlé rivé
Bientôt mon va mouri tristesse
Ah! coeur a li pas doué blié
Lisa là li bélé maîtresse.
   Mais qui nouvelle?
     Hélas! Hélas!
Cher zami moin pas cor rivé!

Comment vous quitté moin comme ça!
Songez ami! n'a point comme moin
   Femme qui jolie!
Si comme moin gagné tout plein
   talents qui doux.
Si la vous va prend li; pas lé bon pour vous
Vous va regretté moin toujours.

[When my lover comes to me
I'll give him caresses a-plenty.
Ah, the pleasure we'll have
Will last forever.
   But it's getting late
     Alas! Alas!
My lover hasn't come.

If my lover doesn't come soon
I'll die of sadness.
Ah, why should his heart forget Lisa?
He called me his dearest love.
   But still no news!
     Alas! Alas!
My lover has still not come.

Why have you left me like this?
Just think, no other woman is
    As pretty!
If you find another as
    Affectionate as me,
And if you like her, take her. But that can't be.
You'll always miss me.]

Dr. Dupuis advised my grandfather to take his wife on a trip
to Europe; the change of air, he said, would do her good, and she
would be able to spend the Christmas holidays, which make Germans abroad so poignantly homesick, in the bosom of her family,
with no need to pretend that a palm was a fir tree. Ready for any
sacrifice when his wife's health was concerned, my grandfather
was quick to take passage on a Hamburg-America liner, and on
Saint Nicholas Day 1899 they set sail for Germany. Since he
always managed to combine business with pleasure, he took with
him a West Indian cayman, captured and raised by himself, which
had become so tame and trusting that it was sure to be welcome
in any zoo or circus. He entrusted the key to the pharmacy to his
partner, who had scarcely shown his face of late, a remissness
that my grandfather, who countenanced no meddling in his business affairs, had not minded in the least. It was all the same to
him if Herr Stecher chose to drink up the rent money with his
concubine at the Hotel Olofsson—that was his business and nobody else's.

6

THE crossing was uneventful. The Atlantic, which ordinarily
at that time of year was churned up by violent storms, lay smooth
as glass under a friendly December sun, and Pauline, free from
the usual symptoms of *mal de mer*, was suntanned and cheerful on
landing in Hamburg. After my grandfather had delivered a happy,
well-fed cayman—the first-class passengers had fed it cake all the
way over—to Hagenbeck's Wildlife Park, the couple went on by

train to Darmstadt. There Pauline at last had the pleasure of embracing her son, who was now a young man, irresistible to the ladies in his dashing cadet's uniform. Annaise, whom Pauline had taken along as a reward for her faithful services, could have gazed for hours at his Prussian-blue tunic; every morning she spat on the buttons and polished them until she could see her shining eyes reflected in the yellow metal. She made herself useful in the kitchen and household and, thanks to an innate gift for mimicry, learned German quickly; only the word for "parsley," *Petersilie*, remained beyond her powers. On Christmas Eve she sang, accompanied by Pauline on the piano, "O Tannenbaum," which my grandfather had taught her during the crossing, and beamed with joy when given her Christmas present, Dr. Hoffmann's *Struwwelpeter*. This, it was thought, would help her learn to read and write, and indeed she did study under the strict supervision of Pauline's son, Franz. She was especially fond of the story about tall Agrippa, who punished the bad boys for making fun of the poor blackamoor by dipping them in the inkwell until they were black; before long she knew it by heart and recited it to the delight of the German guests who flocked to my grandfather's house to admire his black cook.

After the holidays Pauline went to Wiesbaden for the cure. The fat Christmas goose with currant-and-chestnut stuffing, the Dresden Christmas loaf, the Aachen cookies and Lübeck marzipan proved too much for her stomach, which had grown accustomed to a light diet. The wooded, gently rolling hills that ringed the town, the bracing yet mild climate, the combination of brisk wintry air with the hot springs, whose salutary effect has been recognized since Roman times, soothed her overwrought nerves and restored her shaken health. In the morning, accompanied by Annaise—who shivered under her warm coat even when the thermometer rose to well above freezing—she walked across the market place to the spa and drank a glass of the lukewarm water, which tasted like a mixture of beef broth and bouillabaisse. Then she took a thermal bath, after which Annaise, under the doctor's supervision, packed her in hot mud and washed it off with cold water. After lunch, she went for a walk in the casino park with her husband, or with Annaise when he was away on business, and had tea at the Café Blum on Wilhelmstrasse, while her husband leafed through the *Frankfurter Zeitung* and Annaise warmed herself with a cup of hot chocolate. One afternoon—my grandfather had taken the morning train to Frankfurt to have lunch with a business associate—a fashionably dressed gentleman in a sable cape stepped into the café, bowed curtly but politely to Pauline and Annaise, and asked permission to sit at their table. Just as politely, Pauline refused, whereupon the gentleman muttered an apology and left the café. As Pauline learned from the waiter, the man was a Russian nobleman, adventurer, and womanizer, who was in Wiesbaden to indulge his passion for gambling. When he won at roulette, he gave the waiters at the café regal tips.

Three days later—in the meantime a new century had dawned amid popping champagne corks and cheers for the Emperor and his family—she read a short item in the society column of the *Frankfurter Zeitung* that made her blood run cold. During the night of December 31, Baron S., after gambling away everything he owned and even pawning his fur coat, had shot himself in his suite at the Wiesbaden Kurhotel with a six-shooter revolver. The sound had been drowned out by the deafening fireworks that had been going off all over town, and it was not until the following morning that the blood-soaked body had been discovered by a pageboy. In reality, however, as could be gathered from a letter of farewell found in the dead man's room, the prince had been driven to suicide, not by his gambling debts but by his unrequited love for a lady whose identity, for fear of endangering her marital happiness, he had not revealed. The lady's name, said the article, was known to the police, who, needless to say, were observing the strictest discretion.

After this fateful encounter, which augured no good for the new year, Pauline felt the symptoms of her old ailment returning, though the doctor at the spa assured her that she was well enough to travel and to face the tropical climate. It was in this state that she started on the journey from Hamburg to Haiti—which, unlike the eastward voyage, proved extremely trying.

On entering the North Sea from the Elbe, the ship met with a storm so severe that the captain was obliged to put into Wilhelmshaven and wait for a change in the weather. On the way into Jade Bay, the steamer almost collided with a warship that was coming out; maneuvering to avoid it, the passenger ship damaged its steering gear and had to be towed into the harbor, listing heavily. Time-consuming repairs would be needed before it could go on. The first-class passengers were taken by train to Amsterdam, where they boarded the *Lusitania*, a New York–bound packet boat of the Royal Dutch Steamship Line.

Another ill-starred voyage. In the Bay of Biscay, the *Lusitania* ran into rough weather. Towering waves damaged the superstructure and washed two lifeboats overboard. Pauline had felt unwell before setting out, and her condition grew worse as the ship carried her farther from her home and beloved son. She felt that she was leaving Europe forever. Overwhelmed with seasickness, she shut herself up in her cabin and let no one come near her, not even the ship's doctor or her husband, who paced the corridor wringing his hands and beseeching her to open the door.

For the first time since leaving Haiti, she heard the drums in a dream. She was lying on her back; her outspread legs were tied to two stakes driven into the ground; her hands were chained to a fetish-decorated pole that supported the roof of the temple. The Southern Cross had vanished behind clouds; bats flew in and out through a narrow opening, attached themselves to the ridgepole head-down, and looked at Pauline out of glittering eyes. The priestess led in a white billy goat, while the *hounssis* intoned a solemn chant and the crowd repeated the refrain in chorus. The horns of the sacrificial goat were wreathed in garlands, and it was clothed in a purple robe that reached down to the ground. An acrid goat smell rose to Pauline's nostrils, the goat's beard tickled her belly, and the obscene contact aroused her against her will. She closed her eyes in disgust and felt the goat's panting breath. Egged on by the shouts of the onlookers, he bucked faster and faster. And then, tingling with excitement, he stopped. Spittle dripped down on her from his beard. When she opened her eyes, she saw that the he-goat had the face of her first husband, of Dr.

Dupuis, and of the mysterious stranger who had spoken to her at the café: his name was Baron Samedi. The priestess cut the goat's throat with a knife; warm blood spurted over Pauline's naked belly. When the goat had lost all its blood, her labor pains began. She screamed, heaved, and brought forth a diabolical hybrid such as she had seen on a porch of the Strassburg Cathedral, with the hoofs and horns of a he-goat and the scaly tail of a cayman. At the sight of the monster she had brought into the world, her head reeled; she lost her balance and fell into a well so deep that the sound of her body hitting the water went unheard and she sank like lead into its endless night.

While Pauline, tortured by nightmares, was tossing and turning in her berth, the *Lusitania* was plowing through the Sargasso Sea. Moonlit clouds hid the Southern Cross from view. The ship glided through a milky haze. Schools of fish, playing in the bow wave, glittered in the slanting beams of light that poured from the portholes. From hour to hour the thermometer rose and the barometer fell. The heat in the cabins was unbearable; the first-class passengers gathered in the dining room to celebrate the crossing of the tropic. At midnight the first mate reported ball lightning over the smokestack. A deafening peal of thunder was heard, and a cyclone lashed the water into towering waves that fell crashing onto the deck. The smokestacks snapped like matchsticks. The passengers, who were just raising their glasses in a toast to Father Neptune, were flung through the salon like billiard balls, amid dancing plates and cups. Tables and chairs broke loose from their moorings and hopped about as if they had put on legs; every dish in the galley was smashed.

When the steward opened Pauline's cabin with his passkey in the morning, she lay dead. Only the whites of her eyes could be seen. A wave had crashed through the porthole; every lurch of the ship showered her with salt spray. It was impossible to determine whether Pauline had been killed by an accident or had died of some illness. The ship's doctor, who examined the body, could establish no cause of death. The body was taken to the smoking room and placed in a zinc bathtub and filled with ice. My grandfather shut himself up in his cabin and refused to see anyone,

even the ship's chaplain, who wished to bring him words of comfort. Wrapped in a blanket, Annaise kept watch day and night by
the dead woman's side.

Though the ice was constantly renewed, the body soon began
to rot in the tropical heat. A smell of death and decay hung over
the damaged ship, which was forced to reduce its speed. While
the smokestack was being repaired, a dying albatross came to light;
caught in the rigging, it had suffocated in the oily smoke, which
had turned the normally snow-white bird pitch-black. The superstitious sailors, taking the death of the albatross as an evil omen,
thought the dead woman had already brought enough misfortune
on the ship and its crew and wanted to have her buried at sea.
The stokers went on strike and had to be driven back to work at
pistol point.

When the *Lusitania* arrived at Port-au-Prince several days later,
Annaise, who had sat up day and night beside Pauline's body,
was so chilled that she had to be taken to the hospital. Pauline
was buried that same day, but even the great mounds of flowers
could not drown out the smell of decay that rose from the closed
coffin. The members of the German colony, who accompanied
the dead woman to her last resting place, held their handkerchiefs
to their noses as my grandfather, with tears in his eyes, took leave
of his wife. The only German absent from the funeral was Herr
Stecher, my grandfather's partner. One night, while Pauline was
wrestling with death on the high seas, he had dug up the garden
of the Dupuis house, looking for treasure. All he had found was
a bottle containing nail parings and a lock of hair; in his rage and
disappointment, he had smashed the bottle with his spade. That
same moment, Pauline had died a violent death on the high seas,
hundreds of miles away.

7

AT this point the author begs leave to interrupt his narrative
and describe the embroidery that Pauline had begun on first leaving Europe, which she finished on the morning of the day of her

death. On this square of silk, bordered in the colors of the German Empire and the Republic of Haiti, Pauline had depicted in bright thread everything that had caught her imagination during her two years on the island, in good times and bad, in sickness and in health.

What had begun as a German still life with apples, pears, and nuts ended as a *nature morte*, a desolate mangrove swamp, in the dark depths of which a voracious cayman lurked in wait for unsuspecting victims. Not life but death seemed to rule over this dreary landscape. Even in the luxuriant colors of the flowers and fruit the seeds of death were discernible. A bluebottle was getting ready to dine on the sweet flesh of a red-cheeked apple. Under its glowing, golden-yellow surface a pear was rotting away; a wasp had pierced its skin and was avidly drinking the fermenting juice; all that protruded from the pear was the wasp's black-and-yellow-striped abdomen, prolonged by its poisonous sting, pointed upward to ward off enemies. Beneath its radiant surface, the seemingly paradisiacal jungle with its glittering butterflies and intricately woven carpet of flowers concealed invisible perils. The calyxes of carnivorous plants opened like hungry lips, waiting to swallow the hummingbirds that hovered motionless in mid-air, sucking their deadly nectar; a hissing jaguar, its spotted fur deceptively adapted to the sun-drenched foliage, crouched ready to leap in the branches of a great mapou tree, over whose smooth trunk a gigantic anaconda glided soundlessly toward the unsuspecting young antelope drinking from the stream. The black mangrove swamp swarmed with obscene vermin. A hairy bird spider had caught a scorpion in its deadly net; the scorpion was wriggling in a vain effort to strike the spider with its sting. A fiery-red hermit crab had dug a buried tortoise egg out of the sand and was drinking the yolk, having broken the shell with its powerful claw. Deep in the morass the skeletons of Spanish fighting men were moldering in their rusty armor marked with the sign of the cross. In the upper right-hand corner, spitted on the prickles of a holly tree, the Prussian imperial eagle was dying; around it were piled empty coconut shells that looked like burst cannonballs. With the help of a magnifying glass one could see that the bristling beard of the jaguar resembled my grandfather's Wilhelminian mustache, while the cayman's scaly skull suggested the leprous face of Pauline's first husband; the giant anaconda had the black eyes of Mambô Délira Délivrance, and the gazelle threatened by the jaguar had the timid look of Pauline. But let's not interpret the picture. After all, it was only harmless needlework, the pastime of an ailing woman exiled to an alien coast.

What became of the embroidery is uncertain. Some say Annaise laid the silk square over her dead mistress's folded hands and that it was buried with her. Others claim that toward the end of the 1940s it was bequeathed to the historical museum of Port-au-Prince, along with others of my grandfather's possessions. There, so they say, it was displayed in a vitrine until it was confiscated by Papa Doc's secret police, along with everything else in the museum, and vanished forever in the catacombs of the Presidential Palace. When Pauline's grave in the Cimetière National of Port-au-Prince was recently opened at the behest of her heirs, the coffin was empty except for some dried flowers, which instantly crumbled into dust. From the open grave leapt a billy goat, which butted the gravediggers and jumped over the cemetery wall, leaving behind it such a stench of goat that the visitors to the cemetery had to hold their noses. *Krick? Krack!*

The Adventures of a Cola Nut

1

O N his return to Haiti, my grandfather found everything changed. A hurricane had devastated the island and destroyed most of the harvest. Hungry peasants from the interior had plundered Port-au-Prince and ransacked the Presidential Palace. It had cost the army under the aged general Pierre Nord Alexis heavy losses to drive them out of the capital. My grandfather's house on the Chemin des Dalles had not been spared. Books and furniture had been stolen or used for firewood; only the Bechstein piano, like a rock in a tempest, had weathered the popular fury. Herr Stecher, my grandfather's partner, along with the deposed president's entourage, had fled to Jamaica and applied for political asylum. Before leaving, he had sold the pharmacy with all its furnishings and stock, and deposited the proceeds in his bank.

Another man might have been discouraged by two such cruel blows. My grandfather, however, who always saw the bright side of the most hopeless situations, decided to indulge a long-cherished wish, which his wife's delicate health had hitherto caused him to shelve. Along with Dr. Dupuis, who was working on an archaeological study of the culture of the Carib Indians who had inhabited Haiti before the conquest, he set out on a botanical foray into the interior. For safety's sake they attached themselves to a punitive expedition led by General Nord Alexis against the rebellious peasants, who had withdrawn to the mountains after pillaging the capital. The two friends rode at the head of the troops, side by side with the aged general, who had been fighting these rebels for a generation with varied success and knew the rugged

interior like the back of his hand. When they turned in their sad-
dles, they saw behind them the sweating columns of native soldiers, marching barefoot over the stony ground, their heads covered
not with caps or helmets but with tin cans, which also served as
cookpots. Their uniforms were in tatters and their armament consisted of rusty rifles dating back to the American Civil War and
an ancient Spanish mortar, which looked as if it had come to
Haiti aboard Columbus's flagship, the *Santa Maria*, and lain on
the bottom of the sea ever since. This antediluvian monstrosity
was carried on an oxcart, which also served as a gun carriage,
drawn by four naked blacks. The soldiers had been issued no
food for days, and their diet on the march consisted of prickly
pears, which gave them stomach cramps and diarrhea. Drinking
water was strictly rationed and restricted to horses and officers;
the rank and file drank contaminated water from ponds and puddles. Cholera broke out among the undernourished men, their
bellies swelled to monstrous proportions, and many had to be left
behind.

Even before starting out, the aged general had complained of a
queasy feeling. It grew steadily worse despite the quinine tablets
my grandfather gave him; he slumped in his saddle, pressing his
hand to his belly, and his ordinarily dark-brown face took on a
greenish hue. The general rode a Spanish stallion, while my
grandfather and Dr. Dupuis shared the stout back of a mule. They
also had a number of pack asses with them, on which they had
loaded their scientific equipment, spades, specimen containers, and
a barrel of rum, which served to quench their thirst, disinfect
wounds, and preserve specimens. My grandfather was planning
to use the barrel on the way back to house a cayman that Professor Grzimek had ordered for the Frankfurt Zoo. Once the soldiers
had found out what was in the barrel, my grandfather had to keep
an eye open all night and occasionally fire his Krupp repeating
rifle into the air as a warning to would-be marauders. Now and
then the doctor relieved him of his sentry duty. The small advance guard rode along the dry bed of the Artibonite River, which
was ordinarily in full flood at that time of year. What had once

been a luxuriant green plain, covered with cane fields and bamboo groves, had become a desert shimmering in the heat. The dust stuck to the lips of the thirsty men and gritted between their teeth.

"This time," said the general, "we'll teach the rebels a lesson they'll never forget, because they won't have time to." Raising his binoculars to his eyes, he searched the surrounding hilltops. Two eagles were circling overhead; in their bird's-eye view the marching army looked like a snake crawling through the desert. "I admit, we haven't got the most modern equipment," the general went on, looking enviously at my grandfather's Krupp repeating rifle, "but when it comes to fighting spirit, my grenadiers are the equal of any modern army, not to mention those illiterate peasants, who know nothing of military strategy and tactics."

The general had not finished speaking when my grandfather fired two shots. The eagles fell dead at his feat, but then, as though my grandfather's shots had given the enemy entrenched behind the riverbank the signal to attack, rifle fire was heard from all directions. The soldiers threw down their guns and fled with wild screams, while the general, whose face had turned ashen, took cover behind a clump of cactuses and ordered his artillerymen to load the mortar. No sooner had the mortar been put into position than a dispatch rider, whose horse had bolted during the volley of rifle fire, came running up to the general and informed him that it had all been a false alarm: because of the extreme heat my grandfather's shots had sparked off a chain reaction in a sandbox tree, whose seed capsules had exploded with a sound like rifle fire.

"I'm afraid I'm too old for soldiering," said the general, coming out from his clump of cactuses and wiping the sweat from his forehead. "Seventy years are no joke," he said. "My senses would never have tricked me like that in my younger days. Let's have a swig of your rum, my dear Louis. If anything should happen to me on this campaign, I want you and Dr. Dupuis to take command."

When my grandfather tried to give the general his drink, he discovered to his dismay that a bullet fired by mistake during the momentary panic had pierced the rum barrel. Its precious contents were trickling irretrievably away. While he was trying vainly to plug the hole, the general, intoxicated by the rum fumes, fell to the ground in a faint. The doctor was bending over to feel the general's pulse when a deafening thunderclap was heard, followed by an underground rumbling as of distant gunfire. Awakened by the noise, the general opened his eyes. Was it an earthquake? Or had the hostile Dominican Republic equipped the rebels with modern artillery? The general had no time to answer these questions, for in that moment a flash flood came roaring over the dry riverbed. The foaming waves drove before them an avalanche of rock and underbrush, uprooted trees and peasant huts, occupants and all. In a matter of seconds the surrounding plain became a watery waste, and in its muddy waves the entire Eighth Field Army perished, leaving not the slightest trace in history. Only an occasional officer's sword or soldier's cookpot that had been caught in the prickly arms of a cactus or the thorny branches of a sandbox tree emerged here and there from the water. A rifle butt hit my grandfather on the head, and the world went black before his eyes.

In his dream, he was wandering through a jungle dimly lit by glowworms. Deep within it, on a bed of water lilies, a naked water nymph was waiting for him. Her hair was powdered with gold dust, and she was combing it with a silver comb. Her eyes were as deep and dark as the black water into which she drew him in an embrace of overpowering sweetness, from which he would never have awakened if his shirt collar hadn't got caught on a forked branch and held him above water.

When he opened his eyes, what he was holding in his arms was not a naked water nymph but the empty rum barrel, which was still giving off heady alcohol fumes. His rear end was aflame. The flood had thrown him, along with the barrel he was clutching, into the open arms of a cactus, whose prickly embrace had saved his life. Clogged with mud and vegetation, his repeating rifle was hanging from his shoulder. The painful lump on his forehead was where the stock had hit him. Otherwise, apart from the prickles in his behind, which he was acutely aware of every time he moved, he was unhurt. The flood had receded as quickly as it had come, and only a few mud puddles bore witness to the cataclysm that had engulfed a whole army. The entire plain, as far as the eye could see, was covered with mud. Already ravens and vultures had made themselves at home on the swollen bellies of dead horses and asses, which emerged from the mud like islands. Two steps away, he distinguished the barrel of the mortar, half buried in the muck; its broken wheels spun with a rasping sound when the wind caught the spokes, and at a little distance, framed by neatly aligned bayonets sticking out of the mud, the general's cap floated like a boat on a puddle lashed by falling rain. Using his repeating rifle as a pole, my grandfather fished the cap out of the water, with the intention of giving it as a memento to the general's widow on his return to the capital. Just then he heard a terrified neighing and saw, close above him, in the branches of a sandbox tree, the spotted belly of a mule, lashing out with its hind legs at a cayman that had got hold of its tail and was trying to pull it into the water. On the mule's back sat the trembling doctor, who welcomed my grandfather as a savior. With a shot from his repeating rifle, which disgorged more mud and vegetation than lead, he drove the rapacious monster away, and a moment later, with the help of a lasso, he freed the doctor from his awkward situation.

The friends' first thought, after congratulating each other on their miraculous rescue, was for the rum barrel, which was not quite empty; a little rum, they thought, would come in handy on the return journey. After plugging the bullet hole with the seed pod of a sandbox tree and fishing their luggage out of various ponds, they resumed their journey. They could not return directly to the capital, for the flood had made the roads impassable, nor did it seem advisable: they feared that, being the sole survivors, they would be held responsible for the destruction of the Eighth Army. After saddling their mule, they therefore took a narrow path leading to the mountains, where their mount soon had solid ground under its hoofs. The fruitful island lay stretched out at their feet under a sky as pure as when Columbus first landed on this coast. Only here and there could smoke be seen rising, but from the distance it was hard to tell whether a wood was being cleared, stubble burned, or a peaceful village razed. The sun had passed the zenith and was inclining toward the western horizon. The friends unsaddled their mule and fastened their hammocks to the wide-spreading branches of a monkey-bread tree, the fruit of which supplied them with a simple but tasty supper. With a swig from the rum barrel they bade the parting day good night, wrapped themselves in their mosquito netting, and slept soundly until morning.

My grandfather was up and about before sunrise. With butterfly net and specimen container, he explored the countryside while the doctor lay snoring in his hammock. Myriad dew drops glittered on the emerald-green grass, and a chorus of mountain parrots was greeting the rising sun. My grandfather was disentangling an orchid from a hanging liana when he glimpsed nearby a shimmering gold butterfly, reeling, drunk with love, from flower to flower. Eager to capture this rare specimen of *Botys reginalis* of the Pyralididae family for his collection, my grandfather followed the butterfly, which seemed to hover motionless, its wings fluttering, but evaded him every time he prepared to throw his net over it, so luring him deeper and deeper into the forest. When he finally noticed that the elusive butterfly had led him astray, it was too late. Throwing his butterfly net away, he sank exhausted to the forest floor.

He heard a splashing of water from not far away and, shifting an overhanging branch, he caught sight of a waterfall. In its spray the slanting beams of the sun painted concentric rainbows, whose iridescent light made him think of a stained-glass window in a Gothic cathedral. Under the arching rainbow sat a nude woman running a silver comb through her flowing hair. My grandfather's first impulse was to go away discreetly, but the young woman had already seen him. With a silent glance she bade him follow her. Behind the curtain of spray lay the entrance to a cave faintly lit by glowworms, which, as my grandfather recognized on closer scrutiny, were butterflies of the Pyralididae family, unloading the gold dust they had gathered in the mountains. The good fairy—for that's what she was—took my grandfather by the hand and led him through secret passages with clusters of bats clinging to their walls, to an underground treasure room, where the gold was smelted in a volcanic smithy and wrought into ornaments, goblets and statues that reminded my grandfather of Aztec idols: infants and old men, hunchbacks and parturient women, who instead of human faces had the beaks of parrots, the claws and fangs of caymans and jaguars.

The fairy told my grandfather he had nothing to fear. "The common people," she said, "call me Maman Zimbie, because I make my home in springs and ponds. They think if anyone looks me in the eye I'll pull them into the water. But that's superstitious nonsense. My real name is Anacoana, and I'm the queen of the Taino Indians, who lived here before the Spaniards came. For five hundred years I've been waiting here in the mountains for the foreign conquerors, who brought misery to my people, to go away. I've chosen you to keep my race from dying out."

With these words, she drew him down on her bed of water lilies and lianas, and he didn't leave it for seven years. My grandfather begot seven sons on Anacoana and gave them the names of the seven mountains of the Siebengebirge. The seven sons made their homes in seven valleys and founded seven settlements, whose inhabitants to this day answer to the names of the seven mountains. Ethnologists account for this phenomenon by saying that their fathers worked on the Port-au-Prince waterfront and named their children after the German ships they loaded and unloaded.

The seven years passed like a dream. My grandfather would gladly have stayed on in Anacoana's cave, where he wanted for nothing, but after the birth of her seven sons she had no further use for him and sent him home, making him swear not to breathe a word about what he had seen and heard in her underground realm. When he asked for some of her gold as a parting gift, she explained that she had already made him a priceless present: the pod with which he had plugged the leak in his barrel was more precious than gold; it was not the pod of a sandbox tree, but a cola nut, the miraculous fruit that had enabled the priests of the Taino Indians to talk with the gods. My grandfather, she said, had only to grate a bit of the nut and mix the resulting powder with water and rum. He was a made man, provided he reveal the secret of this magic potion to no one.

My grandfather was quick to act on her advice. He had no sooner crossed the waterfall and returned to their campsite, where the doctor still lay snoring in his hammock—it seems that not seven years but only seven minutes had passed—than he put the good fairy's recipe to the test. Lying on his back beside the rum barrel, he pulled the stopper and let the dark-brown liquid, which had fermented overnight, run out into his mouth. The result was staggering: after the very first swallow he felt blissfully refreshed and euphoric, at once drunk and sober. He would gladly have drained the whole barrel in one draft. Instead, however, he decided to strike while the iron was hot and exploit his discovery without delay. Quietly, so as not to wake the doctor, with whom he would otherwise have had to share the profits, he stood up, saddled the mule, and started rolling the barrel down the mountain. He was in such a hurry that the mule could hardly keep up with him.

When he got to Port-au-Prince, the scene left him speechless with amazement. The streets sparkled in the sunlight as if there had never been a flood; the houses were decked with flags and streamers. The whole population was on the streets. An arch of triumph had been erected on the Champ de Mars, and, rolling his barrel, my grandfather passed through it amid lively applause, followed by his faithful mule carrying his butterfly net and specimen container. The President of the Republic, wearing his tricolored sash of office, came to meet my grandfather with open arms and bade him a fraternal welcome. Then at last my grandfather realized what had happened: the good fairy's prophecy had come true sooner than he could have hoped, for the new president was none other than the aged general. The flood, which had engulfed his whole army, had carried him directly to the capital and the summit of power. A foaming wave, which he had ridden like a charger, had set him down on the steps of the Government Palace, where at that very hour the National Assembly was meeting to elect a new president. After the general, dripping wet and covered with mud from head to foot, reported that his army— under his own able leadership—had been destroyed to the last man after inflicting a crushing defeat on the enemy, the Assembly elected him, unanimously and by acclamation, president of the Republic for life. My grandfather handed the general his mislaid cap, which is still on display at the Historical Museum of Port-au-Prince, and was rewarded with an appropriate decoration. In return for his observance of strict silence about the recent campaign, the President appointed him purveyor extraordinary of pharmaceuticals to the army and gave him an unrestricted license to manufacture a cooling beverage that was later, under the trademark Coca-Cola, to conquer the world.

2

UNDER the regime of President Nord Alexis, my grandfather's affairs prospered beyond his wildest dreams. In Europe and North America he bought for a song medicines that had been taken off the market there because of undesirable side effects and sold them at exorbitant prices to the Haitian army and government. In the erstwhile hack stable of Lüders & Company, he installed a distillery in which he bottled an elixir, composed in the main of essence of cola nuts diluted with water from the stores of the Fire Department. As for the secret recipe, he secured it in a safe-deposit box at the Banque Royale du Canada. The tasty beverage, with a label featuring the mustachioed portrait of President Nord Alexis, found ready takers. In return for this free publicity, the President had it served, mixed with rum, at receptions for the diplomatic corps. Especially in the United States, the new drink became all the rage. Blacks liked it for its dark color, whites because in addition to quenching thirst it provided an excellent base for cocktails; teetotalers inscribed it on their banner because it contained no alcohol. Only the European consumers of whisky, wine, and beer had their doubts.

To make his happiness complete, my grandfather, at the end of the customary period of mourning, married a girl twenty years younger than he, a daughter of the widow Dupuis, whose black eyes and bronze skin reminded him of the good fairy to whom he owed his good fortune. That was how—foreigners were not allowed to acquire land in Haiti—he came to own the house on the Chemin des Dalles, which belonged to the widow Dupuis, as well as the adjoining lot, where he built a hothouse for the orchids and a pool for the caymans that he supplied to exotic plant and animal dealers all over the world. In the seven years of Nord Alexis's presidency my grandfather begot seven children, three of whom died soon after birth. He named the survivors, two boys and two girls, after the princes and princesses of the German royal family. They grew up in the care of their nurse, Annaise, and at the age of seven were sent to school in Germany. Only once was my father's connubial bliss troubled: when Annaise found on the doorstep a bottle containing a message from Dr. Dupuis, who he thought had perished in the mountains, announcing his forthcoming return to claim his inheritance. But, hearing nothing further from him, my grandfather ignored the warning.

The aged general ruled the country severely but justly. Since he could neither read nor write and spoke no French, he surrounded himself with knowledgeable advisers, headed by my grandfather. He stimulated the sluggish economy by decreeing tax benefits for foreign investors, granted multinational concerns concessions for the installation of street lighting and of telegraph and telephone lines, and commissioned a German consortium to build a railroad line along the coast to transport sugar. When the forcibly recruited peasants walked off the job, he had a few hundred of them shot, which cured the survivors of their disinclination to work. When the President appeared in the streets of his capital, either on horseback or in his carriage escorted by elite troops, every citizen, white or black, male or female, young or old, had

to stop in his tracks, doff his hat, and lower his eyes; in his presence not only spitting and throat clearing, but smoking and loud
talking were forbidden and in flagrant cases punishable by death.
Public executions were held on Sundays after church on the Champ
de Mars; all the school classes of Port-au-Prince were required to
be present. Afterward the aged general delivered an hour-long
sermon, which the captive audience was obliged to stand through,
silent and bareheaded in the crushing heat. The success of these
methods is not open to doubt. A few political hotheads left the
country or joined the guerrillas, led, it was believed, by a certain
Dr. Dupuis, who were operating in the interior, but by and large
the population went about their labors without grumbling. Foreign investors were rewarded by ample profits, which, like the
President and his ministers, they transferred to Swiss bank accounts. Small wonder that the diplomatic representatives of the
leading industrial countries sent their governments glowing reports, stressing the excellent conditions for investment and holding up Haiti as a shining example to other countries of Latin
America.

3

B U T all good things must end. At three o'clock in the morning on August 8, 1912, the people of Port-au-Prince were awakened by a deafening explosion, the blast from which flung my
grandfather and his wife out of bed. During the night the rebel
army had come down from the mountains and blown the Presidential Palace to smithereens with an enormous charge of dynamite. More than two hundred members of the National Guard
were found dead in the ruins. The President survived the explosion because at the time he was questioning political prisoners in
the cellar. The rebels lynched him and dragged his body through
the streets of the capital. It was so mutilated that only the mustache clinging to a scrap of upper lip made him recognizable.
  Calamities seldom come singly: my grandmother fractured her

hip falling out of bed and was unable to move unaided. And that was not all; my grandfather's house on the Chemin des Dalles was confiscated and, since it was near the Government Palace and had a telephone, made the headquarters of the provisional revolutionary government. My grandparents and their four small children were obliged to live in the back room of the pharmacy. My grandfather distributed generous bribes in an effort to put order into the revolutionary chaos, but nothing came of it. Dr. Dupuis, who held a leading position in the rebel army, was obstinately deaf to economic considerations. From 1912 to 1915, presidents changed more quickly than the seasons. Since the German government had its hands full with the world war, my grandfather turned to the American naval attaché, a certain Major Beach, and pleaded for armed intervention, in the name of the international business community of Haiti. The major, himself a shrewd businessman, expressed his willingness to help, on condition that my grandfather make over to him the license to manufacture his wonder drink. With a heavy heart my grandfather consented, removed the secret recipe from the safe-deposit box at the Banque Royale du Canada, and handed it over. Thereupon the major sent the State Department a long cable, explaining that only military intervention could put a stop to the chaos that was engulfing Haiti and keep the country free for foreign investors. On July 28, 1915, five hundred U.S. marines commanded by Rear Admiral Caperton landed from the destroyer *Washington*, occupied the Presidential Palace, the post office, and police headquarters, and raised the Stars and Stripes in place of the Haitian flag. In a communiqué written in French, the rear admiral assured the people that the occupation was only a temporary measure, needed for the protection of foreign legations and their international personnel. At the same time, the gunboat *Jason* put another hundred marines ashore on the west coast, while the cruiser *Nashville*, arriving from Guantanamo, the U.S. naval base in Cuba, bombarded the capital of the northern province, where the rebel army were entrenched. The next morning Admiral Caperton, who had studied at the Sorbonne, and Major Beach paid courtesy calls on the arch-

bishop of Port-au-Prince and the dean of the Senate. Impressed
by the admiral's fluent French, the excellencies signed an appeal
prepared in advance by the State Department, calling on the army
and population to keep calm and put their full trust in the occupying forces. In his first official act as U.S. high commissioner
for Haiti, Admiral Caperton dissolved Parliament and deposed
the government. After putting Americans in command of the army
and police force, he then appointed Dartiguenave, a veteran dip-
lomat who had been accredited to Washington for years, president of a puppet government, whose ministers he personally
selected. The National Bank of Haiti was placed under American
trusteeship, and the U.S. dollar became the national currency.
All laws restricting the business activities of foreigners were re-
pealed. With his own hand the President of the United States
wrote a new constitution for Haiti, which opened up the country
to American capital and made it a *de facto* colony of the United
States.

4

I n the twenty years that followed, the country experienced an
unprecedented economic boom. Roads and bridges were built,
power and telephone lines installed, health care and compulsory
education introduced. American mission schools and hospitals
sprang up all over the country. My grandfather played a key role
in the development of the health services. In exchange for his
cola-drink license, he was authorized to supply the new hospitals
with pharmaceuticals. By importing Odol mouthwash, which the
hygiene-minded Americans required for the treatment of their
halitosis, and aspirin and quinine for the treatment of migraine
and malaria, he made handsome profits, which enabled him to
travel the newly built highways in a Ford car driven by his chauffeur, Dorléus Présumé.

Unfortunately, the policies of the occupying power did not meet
with undivided approval. Illiterate peasants, incited by Red

agents—the Russian Revolution had taken place in the meantime—obstructed the North American work of civilization. Many
refused to work, slipped out of the villages in the dead of night,
and joined the rebels in the mountains. From strikes to social un-
rest, and from there to armed insurrection, are only short steps.
The rebels—known as Cacos—blew up bridges, blocked roads and
trails, and, encouraged by initial success, went so far as to infiltrate the capital in broad daylight, robbing banks and post offices,
only to disappear without trace in the bustling market square or
the winding streets and alleys of the waterfront. The leader of
these criminal bands, a certain Charlemagne Péralte, for whose
capture dead or alive a high reward was offered, had for years
been defying his pursuers, inflicting heavy losses on the forces of
occupation by making attacks on isolated army posts and police
stations. The superstitious people worshipped him as a saint; some
said he was in touch with the spirits of the revolutionary heroes
Christophe and Toussaint L'Ouverture. One of his ancestors was
said to have been General Dessalines' aide-de-camp and to have
fought against the French. In reality, he was one Dr. Dupuis,
who had studied medicine in Vienna and there come into super-
ficial contact with socialist ideas. To satisfy his pathological am-
bition and avenge himself on the government, which because of
his voodoo methods had taken away his license to practice medicine, he had deserted to the rebels and, thanks to his superior
intelligence, soon risen to a leading position. From time to time
he sent my grandfather secret messages through his cook Annaise,
asking for medicines that he needed for his sick and wounded; in
return he sent money and instructed his soldiers to leave my
grandfather's house and pharmacy alone.

   In July 1918, the Republic of Haiti, under American pressure,
declared war on Germany. My grandfather's pharmacy was confiscated as alien property. He and his family were quartered in
the Hotel Olofsson, which had been temporarily turned into an
internment camp, and obliged to report to the police daily. Even
his Ford was taken away. When my grandfather complained to
Major Beach, who in the meantime had been promoted from na-

val attaché to assistant high commissioner, the major was sympa-
thetic. "The State Department might ask the Haitian government
to reconsider the sanctions taken against your business," said the
major, pacing the floor in a cloud of Odol. "It is true that from
the standpoint of international law the Republic of Haiti enjoys
full sovereignty, but I'm sure the President of this small country
won't disregard the request of a big friendly nation if you, my
dear friend, can see your way clear to cooperating with our fighting forces. It has not escaped our notice, *mon cher ami*, that you
are in secret contact with a certain Dr. Dupuis, alias Charlemagne
Péralte, to whom, through middlemen, you convey medicines for
the treatment of his wounded soldiers. That, my friend, is high
treason. I could have you court-martialed and shot. But never
fear, *lieber Freund*"—at those words the major rested a hand on
my grandfather's shoulder—"we Americans aren't monsters, we're
businessmen. Our principle is, live and let die. All I ask of you
is a personal favor. Lead me to the headquarters of Charlemagne
Péralte tonight, and tomorrow your pharmacy and Ford car will
be returned to you. Needless to say, we won't touch a hair of
your friend's head. I only want to talk to him and propose a truce.
I give you my word as an officer and a gentleman."

That afternoon my grandfather sent his cook Annaise into the
mountains with a handwritten message, asking the commander of
the rebel army for an immediate interview, explaining that he had
something urgently important to tell him. At midnight, accompanied only by the major, who had blackened his face with coal,
he made his way to the mountains over a secret path that Annaise
had marked with corn meal. At their feet lay the sleeping city
and the dark waters of Port-au-Prince Bay, over which fishing-
boat lanterns flitted back and forth like glowworms. The friends
passed several sentries, whose suspicions my grandfather lulled
by whispering the agreed password: "*La liberté ou la mort.*"

Shortly before reaching their goal, they heard muffled voices
from a pitch-black gully, and the smoke of a charcoal fire rose to
their nostrils. A moment later, two blacks, who could not be seen
in the darkness, barred their way and threatened the major with

their bush knives—their suspicions had been aroused by the over-powering smell of Odol he gave off. Only when my grandfather gave the password and explained that his companion had liberated the mouthwash in a raid on an American munitions dump and was using it for camouflage were they allowed into the camp.

The doctor was sitting by the campfire with a group of his officers. He rose to meet my grandfather, who approached him with open arms. Dressed like a plain peasant, the doctor was barefoot, wearing a straw hat and carrying a bag made of bast. The walking stick with which he had been poking the fire was his only weapon. My grandfather embraced him—more than seven years had passed since the parting of their ways. Meanwhile, the major stepped discreetly into the background. Unseen and un-heard, he released the safety catch of his automatic and fired until the magazine was empty. The legendary guerrilla leader, who had hoodwinked the United States army and navy for years, collapsed in a sea of blood. The brim of his hat caught fire and shone like a halo. My grandfather threw himself on his friend to smother the flames.

The shots were the signal for the marines posted in the sur-rounding hills to stage a blinding and deafening display of fire-works with grenade throwers, tracer bullets, and machine-gun fire. Taking advantage of the general confusion, the major removed my grandfather from the line of fire, and together they vanished into the darkness. It all went so quickly that the enemy, surprised in their sleep, had no time to organize a coherent defense. By the time they realized what had happened, it was too late. The U. S. marines, who had learned their trade in the bush wars of Cuba and the Philippines, took no prisoners. By order of Major Beach, the rebel commander's body, crawling with flies, was nailed to a door and put on display: that would show the superstitious pop-ulation what an inglorious end he had met. When the corpse be-gan to stink, it was embedded in a block of cement and dropped into deep water from the deck of the U.S.S. *Susquehanna*, so as to prevent the populace from making a martyr of Charlemagne Pé-ralte and trying to awaken the dead by black magic.

5

WITH the end of armed resistance, normalization made swift strides. Martial law was lifted and a transitional civilian government set up. Thus Haiti was prepared step by step for independence, a learning process that went on for fifteen years. That was the time it took for the whole island to be disinfected, electrified, and motorized and the population ripened for self-government. The marines would have stayed another fifteen years if public opinion at home, stirred up by sensational press reports of alleged massacres of civilians, hadn't clamored more and more vociferously for their withdrawal. The newly elected President Roosevelt bowed to the pressure of the streets. In July 1934, after personally visiting the island, he ordered immediate evacuation— a grave mistake, as later became evident.

On the eve of the historical day when the Stars and Stripes was to be furled and the last marine was to leave the island, Major Beach, who in the meantime had become U.S. high commissioner on Haiti and, on the eve of being pensioned, promoted to the rank of colonel, sent for my grandfather. "My dear Lewis," he said, "I don't have to tell you how glad I am to get out of this lousy nigger country. We've done a good job in the last twenty years, you and I, and neither of us has any call to complain about the other, because we've always been guided by the principle of mutual advantage. You, my dear Lewis, have feathered your nest, and I've helped you to market the otherwise unsalable products of this rotten, no-good island. Together we've pacified and liberated the country. We've built roads, drained swamps, put up schools and hospitals. The hookworm and the anopheles mosquito have been exterminated, the yellow fever and cholera that used to depopulate whole districts are practically unknown today, and a campaign of inoculation against tuberculosis is making giant strides. Only syphilis has defied our efforts, but with the help of the modern medicines provided by you, we're coming to grips with the last and most resistant families of bacteria. Only one thing is still lacking to crown our ambitious program of civilizing this island, and without it all the rest is incomplete: the voodoo cult, that festering abscess on the face of America, must be exterminated root and branch. I say this not only as a soldier of God, who knows his Bible as well as his army regulations—I'm a fundamentalist, you see, and in my opinion every comma of the Holy Scriptures is as binding as a command from a superior officer—I also speak as a member of the white race. It is our God-given duty to save the sinful souls of these black devils from the heathen idols they brought over from Africa on the slave ships and still worship. Their rites, I'm told, involve not only sexual orgies but also cannibalistic feasts." With these words the major smacked his lips, as though the thought of such gourmet delights made his mouth water. "As you see," he continued after a short pause, "I know a thing or two about the niggers here, even if they parley fransay and pride themselves on their fine manners. I know what I'm saying, because when I was a kid I used to play basketball with the nigger bastards on our block. What I'm going to tell you now is strictly confidential. You are not to breathe a word about it—that's an order—not to anyone, Lewis; have I made myself clear? All right. I have reason to believe that the leaders of the voodoo sect have condemned me to death *in absentia*, as they say in Latin, because my hygiene and social-welfare program has cut the grass from under their feet. They've put out a *ouangan*, a voodoo curse, with my name on it. I don't have to tell you how those things work: two crossed sticks on your doorstep, a few drops of chicken's blood in your cocktail glass, a handful of graveyard soil in your toilet bowl—and the damage is irreparable. Seriously, Lewis, what I'm telling you is top secret—not even my mother knows abut it—but I haven't been feeling at all well lately."

With these words the major clutched at his heart. "It's not the heat or the food here. The heat doesn't bother me—I always have a fan running in my room—and, as you know, in twenty years I haven't eaten a single mango or papaya or one mouthful of meat or fish, not one animal or vegetable product of this filthy country. My only nourishment has been the pecan cookies my mother sends me from Virginia—in germ-proof packages, I don't have to tell

you. But in spite of all that, I haven't been feeling well. Between
you and me, I think they're trying to poison me, though I never
drink anything but iced Coca-Cola. Never any hard liquor, just a
little rum cocktail now and then."

Again the major clutched his heart. His complexion, ordinarily
a wholesome pink, had taken on a dark-red, almost purple hue.
My grandfather unbuttoned the major's tunic and fanned him with
a napkin. "Thank you," said the major, apparently relieved. "It's
nothing. Only a passing malaise. Tomorrow I'll be leaving this
God-forsaken country. I'll go home to Virginia, and forget about
all this hocus-pocus. But if, unlikely as it seems, you hear that
I've died a natural or an unnatural death, then, dear Lewis, pray
for me and make sure that not a single one of the devil worship-
pers on this revolting island lives to see the next day dawn. And
now let's drink to the success of our crusade against superstition.
Chin chin! I don't need to tell *you*, my dear Lewis, that except
for a shot of rum this refreshing drink made from essence of cola
nuts doesn't contain a drop of alcohol."

Ice cubes tinkled promisingly as the major raised his glass. After
clinking glasses with my grandfather, the major emptied his at
one gulp. He clutched his throat, turned blue, then green, then
ashen, and fell dead to the floor. There he lay in a pool of melted
ice, which soon evaporated in the tropical heat.

As the autopsy performed in the United States showed, Major
Beach had been killed not by a voodoo curse, but by excessive
consumption of Coca-Cola: the effect of cola extract, caffeine, and
phosphoric acid, combined with a vitamin shortage and steady
consumption of hard liquor, had undermined his health. It was
also found that diabetes and poor circulation resulting from an
occupational lack of exercise had further impaired his resistance
to the trying tropical climate.

6

THE story of my grandfather would be incomplete without an
account of the events that took place in his presence near Saut

d'Eau during the summer of 1930 and provided the national and international press, as well as specialized ethnological journals, with material for sensational revelations and learned disquisitions. Although his account is subjectively colored and, because it was written under the immediate impact of the events, does not in every point bear close scrutiny, I nevertheless regard it as a historical document and quote it here as I found it among my grandfather's papers. The reader alone can judge its credibility. My grandfather's account begins:

In July 1930 my brother Georg paid me a visit. Half a century ago, in protest against Bismarck's antisocialist laws, he had emigrated to Bismarck, North Dakota, where he gained high repute as a Mormon preacher. We had not seen each other since, though we corresponded regularly over the years and kept each other informed about marriages, deaths, the birth of children and grandchildren, and other events of family interest. My brother George—as I shall call him from now on because even when he was little we called him "Schorsch" and later on he took to writing his name in its English form—had come to Port-au-Prince aboard the cruiser *Susquehanna* along with a Senate commission sent by President Hoover to study the possibility of gradually granting Haiti its independence—because Haiti had turned out to be a bottomless barrel, which consumed more dollars than it earned for American investors. My brother George was not traveling for his private pleasure. One day, while he was preaching hellfire to the workers at a Chicago meat-packing plant, an angel of the Lord had appeared to him in the form of a white bull and, before the butcher's ax descended, had commanded my brother, in the name of the Lord, to go among the heathen of Haiti and convert them to the Mormon faith. At first my brother, in an access of weakness and pusillanimity, had doubted whether the angel had really meant *him*, for he was past seventy and hardly equal to the hardships of so long a journey. But the white steam that rose heavenward from the bull's bleeding heart like the smoke of Aaron's sacrifice overcame all fainthearted doubts. When he announced the glad tidings to his home congregation, they took up a collection for him; the Council of Twelve Apostles not only approved the crusade against superstition, as the project was officially termed, but also contributed a check, which was used for the purchase of Mormon Bibles, crosses, and gasoline with which to burn heathen idols.

"My son!" Thus unctuously did my brother, whom I had last seen as a blond-haired youth, but whose locks had turned to silver long before he descended the gangplank from the *Susquehanna*, address me. "My son, Jehovah has sent me here to proclaim the truth of our Lord Jesus Christ and of his Prophet Mormon—which in the year 1827 Joseph Smith received from God's hand on seven brass tablets—to a people living in shameful sin and ignorance. The end of the world is nigh, but there is still time to repent; all the people on earth—and you too, Louis, my son—must be converted to the faith of the Latter-Day Saints and learn to observe the commandments of the Book of Mormon: to abjure tobacco and alcoholic beverages, to donate a tenth of your income and your labor to the Mormon Church, and to forswear all lewdness in thought as well as deed." With these words my brother gave me a penetrating look.

"I'm glad, dear brother," I replied, while leading him to my car— a 1927 Ford at the time. My chauffeur, Dorléus Présumé, doffed his cap in greeting. "I'm glad, dear brother, to see you so hale and hearty after all these years. I have the impression that you are still the same old Schorsch, except that in those days your missionary zeal was devoted to the Social Democratic faith of Ferdinand Lassalle, whereas today it is to the Latter-Day Saints, which, if not more convincing, seems at least to be more profitable, to judge by your impressive luggage."

After telling my chauffeur to stow my brother's bags in the back of the car, I went on. "I shall try to make your stay with us as pleasant as possible, and you can count on my help and advice, in case you want my advice. But one thing I ask you: stop calling me your son. I'm not your son but your brother. And don't try to convert me, because I'm a hopeless case. My prophet is not Joseph Smith but Charles Darwin, and my Bible is not the Book of Mormon but *The Origin of Species*. All you need to do is take a good look at one of our blacks, and you'll be forced to recognize that man is descended not from God but from the ape. My driver here is the living proof of it— *n'est-ce pas, Dorléus?*"

"*Oui, Monsieur,*" muttered the driver, whose receding forehead behind the windshield really did look rather apelike just then.

"You are sinning against the children of God," said my brother, unable to conceal his distaste for my opinions. "The Negroes and all other colored peoples are the descendants of Laman the son of Lehi. They forsook the true teachings of Nephi and were therefore stricken with spiritual blindness by our Prophet Mormon. As punishment for their sins, God made their skins black, brown, yellow, or red, and condemned them to eternal barbarism, from which they can be redeemed only by conversion to the true faith."

"In at least one respect," I put in facetiously, "our blacks are no different from you Mormons: they practiced polygamy long before it was invented by your prophet Joseph Smith. But never mind, dear George. In a few days, on July 15, the adepts of voodoo will be gathering beside the Saut d'Eau waterfall to sacrifice to their idols and implore the African gods for their blessing. That will give you ample opportunity to test your missionary powers; if you can persuade a single one of those black devils to renounce tobacco, rum, and women, I will renounce Darwin for Joseph Smith."

Since my brother saw no need to get acclimatized or even roughly acquainted with the language, manners, and customs of this strange country, we started bright and early the next morning in a truck piled high with Mormon Bibles and driven by Dorléus Présumé. Holding that sinners should be converted not by the sword but by God's word alone, my brother had declined the armed escort offered by General Russell, the U.S. high commissioner. The man of God rode in the lead, straddling the radiator. Like Jesus on his way into Jerusalem, he waved palm branches in token of blessing, and proclaimed the Gospel of the Prophet Mormon in a voice of thunder. The words of his sermon were jumbled by the roar of the engine, and the English-language Bible was a book with seven seals to the illiterate blacks, but the old man's snow-white hair and the zeal with which he sprinkled holy water, drove evil spirits out of houses and temples, and set fire to wooden fetishes, had its effect on the superstitious natives, who poured from all directions to see the crazy *blanc*. The children in particular rushed out to join the crusade and submitted gladly to conversion for the sake of a Hershey bar or a few Chiclets.

We had almost reached our destination when, in crossing the Artibonite River, which was not very high at that time of year, the truck got stuck in the mud. So many people tried to push it that it turned over and lost its cargo: a flood of Bibles slid into the river, forming an island of books, which were slowly carried away—one by one, as it were—by the sluggish current. My brother was undismayed. After all, the Bibles hadn't sunk into the mud but were being driven seaward by the viscous waters, and would carry the Gospel of the Prophet to the ends of the earth. Fortified by this sign from God, he resumed his interrupted crusade with fresh courage.

The news of the miracles my brother had performed en route had preceded our little expedition to Saut d'Eau, where the adepts of voodoo had gathered, as they did each year on this day, to bathe in the sacred waterfall and hold converse with the gods. An eagerly awaited feature of this occasion was a *mangé yam*, a ceremony comparable to the Lord's Supper, at which the most famous *hougan* of Haiti, Dieudonné Saint Léger, would demonstrate his magic powers by bringing an enormous kettle full of rice and vegetables to the boil without fire. At dusk, when my brother made his entry into Saut d'Eau, the preparations for the *mangé yam* were in full swing. The faithful were gathered around a giant mapou tree, which, because of its imposing size and venerable age, was revered as the home of the gods and hung with fetishes, ranging from empty bottles wrapped in cotton cloth and containing magic messages, to freshly sacrificed cocks and even hegoats suspended head down from the thick branches. Several dozen women were busy cleaning and cutting up great mounds of vegetables—peas, beans, carrots, onions, eggplants, and yams—which, along with rice and ears of Indian corn, were then ladled into an enormous copper kettle, the contents of which would have sufficed to feed ten thousand. This kettle, supported by a rusty tripod, had been placed in the middle of a stone fireplace which, as I personally convinced myself, contained neither wood nor coal nor any other solid or liquid fuel.

When the kettle was full to the brim, the *hougan*, a black giant with a purple cloth over his head, stood up and spread his arms to impose silence on the multitude. He drew geometric figures around the fireplace with white beans and black beans, meanwhile mumbling an endless litany. I understood snatches of it: Legba Atibon, Loco Atisson, Aizan Velequiété, Ela Agassou, Ela Agoué Ta-Royo, Ela Boussou, Ela Acassa, Ela Erzulie Fréda, Ela Ogoun Badagris, Ela Ogoun Ferraille, Ela Ogoun Shango, Ela Baron Carrefour, Ela Baron La Croix, Ela Baron Cimetière, Ela Guédé Nibo, Ela Maman Zimbie, Ela Nation Wangol', Ela Nation Ibo, Ela Nation Sinegal, Ela Papa Brisé, Ela Contes Loas Petros, Ela Contes Bocors, Ela Houngeniçons, Ela

Laplaces, Ela Porte-Drapeaux, Ela Hounssis Canzos Bossales, Ela Hounfort. The drums began to beat—first the small *rada* drums (*Boulatier*), then the gourd rattles (*Asson*), finally the big drum dedicated to the god Damballah (*Assôtor*). The *hounssis* danced in a circle around the fireplace, waving their head scarves to drive away the smoke, which rose from the fireplace though there was no flame to be seen.

Suddenly my brother, who had been reading his Bible aloud the whole time to fortify himself against all this diabolical mischief, stepped forward firmly and advanced on the cooking pot, from within which a telltale bubbling could be heard. In his upraised arms he carried a cross; its shadow, enormously magnified by the setting sun, fell across the heathen and their cult site. The drums stopped. With a strength I would not have expected in a man of his age, he seized the copper pot—it must have weighed several hundred pounds—in both hands, lifted it, and overturned it. As he did so, he shouted in stentorian tones the historic words that Martin Luther on the Wartburg had flung at the devil along with his inkwell: "APAGE SATANAS! Get thee behind me, Satan!"

And then an amazing thing happened. The drums started in again and my brother began to dance. He hopped about to the rhythm of the drums like a dervish, he danced every dance that had ever been danced in Europe or America—waltz, polka, cha-cha, samba, rumba, tango, shimmy, Charleston, foxtrot; he even executed the complicated rhythms of the *yan-valu*, which only the adepts of voodoo can dance, and certain eyewitnesses go so far as to claim that that night under the mapou tree he performed dances that were not invented until years later—the twist, hully-gully, bamba, pogo, and even the duck dance—until the drums stopped and he fell exhausted to the ground. This must have happened about midnight, because when I looked at his hands in the pale light of the moon they were charred black, as though branded with a hot iron.

But my brother George would not have been my brother George, and what's more he would have been a poor missionary, if after this first setback he had given up and deserted his flock. At daybreak he was up to his waist in water, making motions of benediction—unless he was merely dipping his burned fingers in the cool water. And behold, this time his missionary zeal bore fruit: the Lord's blessing rested visibly upon him. Standing in a temple formed by several intersecting rainbows, he baptized the natives, men and women, young and old, who, as in the days of John the Baptist, fell over one another in their eagerness to be immersed in flowing water by the white man of God. The spirit of God had come over him. He prayed aloud and thanked the Lord for the signs and wonders accomplished through him, my brother George; he sprinkled holy water left and right, up and down, east and west, north and south, each drop a pure crystal reflecting a thousand suns. He baptized the whole earth, the black and brown, the yellow and red peoples living in sin and ignorance, who had not yet heard of the Prophet Mormon and his apostle Joseph Smith, but whom he at last had saved from perdition. And, to crown his missionary triumph, he stepped out of the water, an awe-inspiring sage, the droplets glistening like pearls in his silvery beard, a man of God as in the Good Book. He stepped out of the water and attacked the root of the heathen tree, where the spirit of evil was lodged. He picked up the heavy ax with his blackened hands, which were still giving off smoke—in that moment he felt no pain, only triumph, heavenly rejoicing, hosannah! He swung the ax like Boniface when he cut down the sacred oak of the Frisians. Down with you, down with Yggdrasil, the world ash tree, *à bas Mapou maudit*. The ax struck the tree with a deep muffled sound, like a distant thunderclap, a Chinese gong, or a death knell—a few of those present even claim to have seen lightning, though that I absolutely deny. There was no lightning, but—and with this I approach the end of my story—from that moment on my brother George was never seen again. He had vanished into thin air. Nothing was left of him but his black hat floating on the water, getting closer and closer to the waterfall, which finally carried it down into the abyss. And though the gendarmes searched the region systematically the following day, sounding the bottom of the river with poles, firing cannon to make the body rise to the surface, my brother's remains were never found. But the rusty blade of the ax is still in the bark of the tree, which is still festooned with fetishes, bright strips of cotton, empty rum bottles containing magic messages, freshly sacrificed roosters and he-goats dangling head down from the tree's thick branches.

The recollection of this memorable event is still alive in Haiti; parents tell children, grandparents tell grandchildren about it to teach them to revere and obey the gods of Africa. After the missionary's departure, the story goes, his spirit moved into a sacrificial white ox who, as the ax descended, reportedly bellowed loudly and clearly: "APAGE SATANAS." And it seems that several gold teeth were found in the ox's mouth. Others maintain that the missionary turned into a 1927 Ford, which haunts deserted street corners in the midnight hours and runs over—or, rather, assaults—belated revelers. In the trunk of the car, which is always traveling around without a driver, the police are said to have found a sack full of skulls and Mormon Bibles. *Krick? Krack!*

With these words my grandfather concludes his report, and here for the present I let his story rest.

My Honor Is Loyalty

You must be a white man if you'd rather face this pitch-black night than a black woman.

(HEINRICH VON KLEIST,
The Betrothal in San Domingo)

1

ON January 28, 1938, on its way from Santo Domingo, the battleship *Schleswig-Holstein*, which had been converted into a training ship, dropped anchor off Port-au-Prince, capital of the black republic of Haiti. The purpose of the call was to renew and consolidate the traditional friendship between the two countries; indeed, the time was ripe for such a visit, for it was just three years since the departure of the last contingent of American troops, who had been occupying the island for almost twenty years. After a short stay in Haiti, President Roosevelt had come to the conclusion that the continued presence of American soldiers on the hopelessly mismanaged island was neither politically nor financially justifiable. Moreover, the morale of the U.S. marines stationed there had been so undermined by malaria, syphilis, and sensation-mongering stories about alleged massacres of the civilian population that it became necessary to withdraw them in all haste. But there was still another reason why a visit from the German navy seemed advisable at this particular time. While the Stars and Stripes was being furled and the blue-and-red Haitian flag was being raised on the island, the German army had occupied the Rhineland, thus wiping off the map the last traces of the shameful Treaty of Versailles. Under the resolute leadership of the new chancellor, Adolf Hitler, the German nation, humiliated by the

Allied victors after the First World War and enslaved by economic depression, rose like a phoenix from the ashes.

Captain Thiele therefore decided to celebrate the fifth anniversary of the National Socialist seizure of power with a sumptuous
reception on board his ship. He planned to invite not only the
leaders of the German colony of Port-au-Prince, but also the
members of the diplomatic corps and the highest-ranking officers
of the Haitian army and government. The crew of the *Schleswig-
Holstein* were eagerly looking forward to this break in the daily
monotony of shipboard life. Every sailor from ship's cook to first
mate went about his work with unprecedented zeal, and the steel-
gray battleship with its immaculate superstructure—the only dark
spots on it were the muzzles of the guns—sparkled like a damascene blade in the sun.

Ensign Gustav von R., the captain's aide-de-camp, was looking
forward with particular impatience to the impending celebration;
quite apart from the official occasion—the anniversary of the national renewal—he had a private reason for rejoicing. The ensign
was expecting to take advantage of the social function to announce
his engagement to a ravishing German girl, with whom he had
fallen head over heels in love on his first day of shore leave. They
had met at a reception given by the German Club of Port-au-
Prince in honor of Captain Thiele and his officers. It was love at
first sight. Struck speechless, the ensign had stared at the young
woman over foaming beer glasses and plates piled high with sau-
sages and potato salad, and she had returned his gaze unblush-
ingly. He was fascinated by her black eyes, her bronze skin, set
off to excellent advantage by her sleeveless evening dress, and by
her long silken hair with only a rose for ornament, while she gazed,
equally spellbound, at his meticulously pressed white dress uniform with its silver braid flashing in the lights of the hall. They
had stood motionless in the crowd around the cold buffet, inca-
pable of saying a word. At length a black waiter came up to them
with a silver tray. It was then that the young woman broke the
silence. Raising her champagne glass and looking the young ensign full in the face, she drank his health. In speaking, she re-

vealed two rows of snow-white teeth, the sight of which almost robbed him of his reason. That same evening, while the chairman of the German Club, an exporter by the name of Streitwolf, was welcoming the guests from the homeland in a speech interrupted by frequent applause, the two young people, in whispers, plighted their troth. Late in the night, while a group of drunken sailors were bellowing the "Horst-Wessel Song" and a civilian in a brown uniform was asking for contributions to Winter Aid, the National Socialist welfare fund, the lovers strolled hand in hand beneath the subtropical sky, and the ensign learned that Toni—for that was the exotic-looking young woman's name—was the daughter of the German pharmacist of Port-au-Prince. She had returned only a few weeks earlier from Switzerland, where she had completed a course of study to prepare her to take over her father's pharmacy in partnership with her brother.

Haunted by the seductive images of that night, the ensign had been waiting impatiently for his next shore leave, when he would ask the pharmacist for Toni's hand. And even more passionately he was longing, after the privations of the long sea voyage, to hold his beloved in his arms.

Two days later the occasion finally presented itself. While the crew of the *Schleswig-Holstein* were taking the waterfront bars by storm (despite Captain Thiele's order-of-the-day forbidding all fraternization with the natives, not to mention sexual intercourse with the nigger whores), the ensign, beset by ragged beggars and gesticulating tourist guides eager to show him the sights or take him to the nearest brothel, fought his way to a taxi. It was some time before he came to terms with the driver, who seemed to know no civilized language and demanded an exorbitant sum, a two-digit figure in dollars which he daubed with his index finger on the filthy windshield of his ramshackle Ford. Only when the ensign offered him instead his silver cigarette case with his initials engraved on it did the driver agree to take him to Pétionville, where the aged pharmacist was living in a comfortable country house on the slopes overlooking the town. The driver stepped on the gas, the motor roared, and the taxi shot into the city's jumbled traffic, consisting chiefly of hooting motorcars, clattering horse-drawn cabs, squeaking oxcarts carrying clusters of humans in addition to their cargo of sugar cane or bananas. After crossing the Champ de Mars just as the guard was being changed, the taxi chugged up the steep hill leading to the residential quarter of town, where foreign merchants and members of the native upper crust had built their villas.

In Lalue, halfway to Pétionville, the old Ford slowed down. The engine began to stutter and finally gave up. Cursing, the driver got out and rolled up his sleeves. His head disappeared under the hood. As a crowd gathered, the ensign kept his seat inside the car and lit a cigarette. After the third cigarette the driver informed him that he could go no farther: his engine was shot and there was no garage for miles around. The ensign handed him his silver cigarette case and, sweating in the blazing noonday sun, proceeded on foot up the steeply rising road. A chattering crowd of black children poured out of the huts along the road and followed him, pointing their fingers at him as though they had never seen a white man before. Gustav had great difficulty in defending himself against his annoying retinue. Some threw stones at him; others ran their dirty fingers over his freshly cleaned uniform; some even laid hands on his shoelaces.

The ensign was glad when he came to a barracks gate marked with the legend *L'Union fait la force*. A sentry drove the children away with his whistle and showed Gustav the way to the German pharmacist's home, which was not far off. While waiting outside the wrought-iron gate entwined with bougainvillea, Gustav noticed, to his annoyance, that one of the little rascals along the way had made off with his shoelaces. A barefoot black servant opened the gate. "*Vous désirez, monsieur?*" Instead of answering, the ensign presented his visiting card. The servant vanished into the garden and soon came back, this time in shoes, to let him in. He led the ensign along a neatly swept gravel path bordered by shade trees, past a snow-white villa, which with its Gothic turrets and oriels reminded him of his parents' house in Grunewald, to a greenhouse hidden behind banana plants. The heavy scent of the damp, sultry air that poured from the half-open door almost took his breath away. When he went in, it was some time before his eyes grew accustomed to the green half-light, filtered through tropical vegetation. In the farthermost corner, surrounded by broad-leafed potted plants, a white-haired old man with a tanned, leathery skin was sitting at a wobbly mahogany table covered with dried and pressed flowers. With the help of a bamboo cane he rose to meet the ensign and held out a gouty hand.

"Isn't it lovely?" said the old man, whose voice sounded a lot more youthful than his appearance would have led one to expect. "Isn't it lovely? Everything you see here is my doing. For more than twenty years I've been studying the flora of the West Indies—only the indigenous flora, mind you; I'm not in the least interested in any of the cultivated plants introduced by man, coffee, tea, sugar cane, cotton, and so on. My great passion is orchids, which I myself breed here in my greenhouse. Since coming to this island forty years ago, I've collected and classified more than eighty species and subspecies; my scientific findings are recorded in the Botanical Institute of Uppsala. I correspond regularly with its director, my honored friend Professor Solander. Unfortunately he is not in the best of health; he was supposed to pay me a visit this summer, but he has had to call it off. A lifetime is much too short for the study of tropical flora and fauna. Did you know that we have four different climatic zones here in Haiti? The hot, damp coastal region with its mangrove swamps, the dry savannas of the interior with their cactuses and agaves, and the high and medium mountain zones, where Ritter and Descourtilz counted more species of ferns than in all the temperate zones of the earth together. And do you know the secret of the photosynthesis with which nature works all these wonders? With just a bit of water and sunshine. But I haven't offered you anything to drink yet—you must be dying of thirst in this heat. Have a rum cocktail; the doctor has put me strictly on the wagon, but I enjoy seeing my guests drink."

After sitting down in a proffered wicker chair and taking a sip of the iced drink served him on a silver tray by a black houseboy, the ensign said gravely, "I've come to ask you for your daughter's hand." His heart pounded as he made this little speech, which he had composed in the taxi. To his astonishment the old man seemed quite unmoved and merely asked him to repeat what he had said. "I would like to ask you for your daughter's hand."

"True enough," said the old man, "my hearing isn't what it used to be, but my eyes are as sharp as they were fifty years ago. Tell me, young man, is there anything wrong with your legs?" Gustav shook his head, but the old man was far from satisfied. "Just let me see you take a few steps," he said. Gustav took a few steps and the old man cried out, "Just as I thought. You drag your left leg. I'm sorry to disappoint you, young man, but I can't consider you for a son-in-law with that sort of physical defect."

"I assure you there's nothing wrong with my leg," said Gustav, blushing. "It's just that someone stole my shoelaces on my way here."

"Well," said the old man, relieved, "if that's all it is . . ." He stood up with the help of his stick and embraced the ensign. "If you're as sound of limb as I am, you may lead my daughter to the altar, provided she'll have you and you promise to treat her properly. In the meantime, my houseboy will get you new shoelaces. But you haven't even touched your drink. *Prost*, son-in-law. To our health!"

On the way down the gravel path to the house, where he planned to pay his respects to his future mother-in-law, the ensign heard loud laughter coming from a bamboo grove. He turned off into the bushes and proceeded on tiptoe. Bending aside an overhanging branch that cut off his view, he saw Toni, clad only in a bath towel that she had wound around her waist like a sari, kneeling on the edge of a marble pool. Her feet were in the water, in the dark depths of which, amid water lilies and goldfish, lurked a cayman, looking coldly at her out of its yellow reptilian eyes. The pool was shaded by a magnificent flamboyant; at every gust of wind, a dense cloud of golden-yellow petals came tumbling from its crown to drift like Chinese junks on the surface of the water. Head tilted back and eyes closed, Toni was running a sil-

ver comb through her silky hair, which fell in black waves over
the edge of the pool. Meanwhile, as though lost in a dream, she
murmured a poem against a musical background of plashing water
and twittering hummingbirds. It seemed to the ensign that he had
never heard so lovely a poem:

> I gaze bemused into the sky-blue air
> Framed in the forest leaves' green-golden glow.
> I breathe the heady fragrance of a rare
> Flower which the breeze a little while ago
> Sent flying into my expectant hand.

From deep in the pool the cayman responded in a sonorous bass:

> I rest my carcass in this woodland pool
> Its waters lovingly caress my flanks.
> A roof of foliage keeps it darkly cool
> In this most hospitable of wildlife tanks.
> My life, I tend to think, is simply grand.

With this duet there mingled the nasal singing of the old nurse
Annaise, who was washing clothes in the yard:

> *Angélica, Angélica,*
> *chita caille maman ou.*
> *Ça qui pas connaît' laver passer*
> *chita caille maman ou,*
> *ça qui pas connaît' laver passer*
> *reter cailla maman.*

> [Angelica, Angelica,
> Stay home with your mother.
> If you don't know how to wash and iron yet
> better stay home with your mother.
> If you don't know how to wash and iron yet
> better stay home with your mother.]

A golden butterfly flitted past the ensign and settled in his fian-cée's lap, which it powdered with golden-yellow pollen. Inspired by the sight, Gustav improvised the following lines:

> Drunk with the sun, a gilded butterfly
> Reels through the dark, fruit-laden mango trees.
> No deeper, more alluring wish have I
> Than here to live and love and lie at ease
> Dreaming beneath the limpid tropic sky.

As though to conclude the singing contest, a bird named Malfini, hidden in the crown of a palm tree, croaked the refrain of the washerwoman's song: "*Angélica, Angélica, chita caille maman ou.*"

Toni gathered her towel around her as the ensign stepped out of his hiding place. "Pierre," she cried, running to meet him.

"Who's Pierre?" asked Gustav, unable to suppress a note of displeasure.

"Oh, Gustav." A slight irritation was discernible in the young woman's eyes, but it passed as quickly as the shadow of a cloud. "I didn't expect you so soon. Pierre Roumel is a childhood friend. We played in the sandbox together when we were little. We're expecting him back any day from Paris, where his poems have swept the literary salons off their feet. But don't worry—you have nothing to fear from him."

After showing him through the house and garden and persuad-ing him to stay to dinner, Toni introduced her fiancé to his future mother-in-law, who was sitting in the kitchen in a wheelchair, supervising the servants at their work. She was wearing a flow-ered dress and holding a rosary. Her hands were covered with dark spots and felt as smooth as parchment. Though she was mar-ried to a German and had been to Baden-Baden a number of times for the cure, her German vocabulary consisted only of *Schwein* and *Kartoffeln*—"pig" and "potatoes." She seemed to confuse the ensign with a distant relative who had been a page at the Em-peror's court and had visited Haiti before the world war.

After dinner, the pharmacist insisted on escorting his guest to the garden gate. "What you see there," said the old man, as his chauffeur opened the door of his ancient but resplendent Oldsmobile, in which the tropical firmament was reflected, "is a rare variety of nightshade. Its vegetative activity is quiescent during the day and attains its climax about midnight." With his stick he pointed at a cactus blossom that had opened wide in the silvery moonlight and gave off an aromatic bittersweet fragrance. "By dawn tomorrow it will have closed. Good-bye, young man. On your next visit I shall show you my collection of orchids."

2

SHORTLY before midnight the ensign returned safe and sound to the *Schleswig-Holstein*. A number of drunken sailors who had outstayed their shore leave had been brought back by the shore patrol and locked up in the brig to sober up. Lieutenant Lüning, the ship's medical officer, had his hands full all night administering prophylactic injections to sailors who, in contravention of the commander's express orders, had spent the evening in Negro bars and brothels. "This island is a pesthouse," said the doctor to the ensign, who was helping him with the injections. "All nigger women have syphilis. But with them, thanks to the biological resistance of their bastardized race, the disease assumes an atypical form. Every Aryan male who squanders his precious seed on such women gets infected with their insidious poison, thus inflicting irreparable damage on the genetic heritage of his people. In this way the Jew, ably seconded by the germ-carrying nigger, is undermining the foundations of German overseas culture. And," Dr. Lüning concluded, thrusting his scalpel deep into the buttock of a sailor, who screeched with pain as yellowish pus spurted from a lanced boil, "there is only one remedy."

Next day, as soon as he was off duty, the ensign hurried to the German pharmacy, situated in the center of town, not far from the port, to replenish the *Schleswig-Holstein*'s depleted stores of malaria and syphilis vaccines and, while he was at it, to pay his fiancée a visit. When he came in, Toni was sitting in a swivel chair behind the cash register, chatting with a toothless old black woman who wanted a certain medicine but had forgotten what it was called. Though Gustav could not understand Creole and Toni had to interpret, he found it hard to keep from laughing.

TONI: *Bonjour, Madame. Qu'est-ce que vous désirez?*

OLD WOMAN: *Est-ti?* (Beg pardon?)

TONI: *Ça ou gagné?* (What's your trouble?)

OLD WOMAN [*with a sigh*]: *M'malade, oui.* (Sick, very sick.)

TONI: *Ça ou senti nan corps à ou?* (Where does it hurt?)

OLD WOMAN: *M'gagné saisissement.* (I've got cramps.)

TONI: *Ça ou senti encore?* (What else is wrong?)

OLD WOMAN: *M'gagné vent qui monté nan tête à moin!* (I've got wind, it goes up into my head!)

TONI: *Ça encore?* (What else?)

OLD WOMAN: *Lait à moin tourné, li ba'm youne veine foulée.* (My milk has clotted and stopped up a vein.)

TONI: *Est-ce ou senti la fièvre?* (Do you feel feverish?)

OLD WOMAN: *Est-ti?* (Beg pardon?)

TONI: *Ou senti youne heure fraite et youne heure chaud?* (Do you feel hot and cold by turns?)

OLD WOMAN [*with enthusiasm*]: *Ouiii!* (Oh yes!)

TONI [*with a slight shiver*]: *Est-ce ou tremblé?* (Do you shiver?)

OLD WOMAN [*nodding*]: *Si fait.* (Definitely.)

TONI: *Dipi quiquand ou senti ça?* (How long have you felt this way?)

OLD WOMAN: *M'senti ça quelques jours, oui.* (For a few days.)

TONI: [*suspiciously*]: *Ou est-ce ou senti ça dipi quelques années?* (Or for a few years?)

OLD WOMAN: *Oui, papa.* (Yes, Papa.)

TONI: *Ou seulement dipi quelques semaines?* (Or only for a few weeks?)

OLD WOMAN: *Oui, maman.* (Yes, Mama.)

TONI [*sternly*]: *Couté! Dipi quiquand ou senti ça?* (Listen here! How long have you been feeling this way?)

OLD WOMAN: *Pas connaît'.* (I don't know.)

TONI [*with a sigh*]: *Qui l'âge ou gagné?* (How old are you?)

OLD WOMAN: *Vingt ans, oui.* (Twenty.)

TONI: *Et combien pitites ou fait'?* (And how many children have you had?)

OLD WOMAN: *Quatorze, maman. Yo gagné pitites yo même.* (Fourteen, Mama. They've had children themselves.)

TONI: *Sous qui président ou fait'?* (Under what president were you born?)

OLD WOMAN: *Président Salnave, oui.* (Under President Salnave.)

TONI [*leafs through a list of the presidents of Haiti*]: *Ou gagné soixante-dix ans donc!* (That makes you seventy!)

OLD WOMAN: *Oui, papa.* (Yes, Papa.)

The conversation ended with Toni's feeding the old woman a tablespoonful of castor oil. Toni then led the ensign through the pharmacy to a shed where, along with empty bottles and a rusty still, an improvised wooden airplane was propped up on blocks. "It's a copy of a Fieseler Storch," she informed him. "My brother wants to fly the Atlantic with it, like Lindbergh. He's in the Dominican Republic now, but before going he worked on it day and night. All he thinks about is flying." She glanced at the clock. "It's almost six," she said. "Time to shut up shop and have a drink." When she had sent the clerks home, she and Gustav took the day's receipts to the bank. Then the two of them went strolling on the shore promenade. The *Schleswig-Holstein* was bobbing up and down at the wharf. Screaming gulls circled around the steel-gray gun turrets; the swastika flag hung limp, and the setting sun bathed the battleship in a sea of blood. While Gustav stood silent, overpowered by the sight, Toni pressed close to him and whispered a poem in his ear:

> Riotous ocean, breaking on cliffs,
> Radiant wilderness flooded with light,
> Flaming red blossoms amid darkling leaves,
> Usher in evening's festive display;
> Dusky-dark forest but sun on the heights—
> Heavenly island, how lovely you are!

"Who wrote that?" Gustav asked, drawing Toni close.

"My favorite poet," she whispered, stroking the military smoothness of his neck with her fingertips. "His name is Pierre Roumel. I translated it."

Toni suggested dinner at the Hotel Olofsson, followed by a swim in the hotel pool, but, mindful of the doctor's admonition and fearful of what the highly seasoned food would do to his digestion, he declined with thanks.

3

On returning to his cabin that night, the ensign found a note ordering him to report to the officers' mess at an ungodly hour the next morning. When he entered the mess hall, Captain Thiele, Lieutenant Lüning in the brown uniform of the party, and a swarthy gentleman in civilian clothes were waiting for him. All three rose when he came in.

"I don't have to introduce Dr. Lüning to you," said the captain, who was pacing the floor with his hands behind his back, blowing nervous puffs of smoke that seemed, like Indian smoke signals, to convey some secret message. "Today, as you can see by his uniform, he is not here in his capacity as medical officer, but as a National Socialist indoctrination officer, charged with watching over the spiritual health of my men. The other gentleman is a military attaché at the Dominican Embassy in Port-au-Prince. His name is of no importance; let's call him Señor Gomez." At those words, "Señor Gomez" bowed politely in the captain's direction. "As one might gather from his civilian dress, Señor Gomez is here incognito—as a private observer, so to speak. The reason for his presence will be explained in a moment by Dr. Lüning. It goes without saying that everything you hear from this moment on is top secret. Go ahead, Dr. Lüning."

Dr. Lüning rose from his brown leather armchair. Legs firmly planted, hands clasped over his belt buckle, he glared at the ensign. "Why," he bellowed, "why, when there are thousands of

strapping German girls at home in the Reich, does it have to be
that particular woman?"

"I don't know what you're driving at, Dr. Lüning." The ensign's face had gone scarlet.

"Lieutenant Lüning to you, if you please."

"Yes, sir, lieutenant, sir."

"You know exactly what I'm driving at," said Dr. Lüning a
little more calmly, taking long strides across the room. "We are
perfectly informed. When you joined the army you swore alle-
giance to the Führer, you swore to sacrifice everything to folk and
fatherland—yes, everything, at all times, with no ifs and buts.
Am I right?"

"Yes, sir!" The ensign clicked his heels.

"Ever heard of the Nuremberg Laws?"

"Yes, sir."

"And what, if I may ask, is the substance of these laws?" Dr.
Lüning came closer and glared at the ensign over the leather pommel of his riding whip.

"Protection of the German people and German honor, sir. To
prohibit mixed marriages and extramarital intercourse between Jews
on the one hand and Aryans or, more specifically, Germans on
the other."

"Excellent. So that is known to you. And yet on your first
shore leave in this Kaffir kraal you have the effrontery to take up
with a nigger whore." The doctor's riding whip hissed through
the air in accompaniment to his words. The ensign went pale. He
turned as though pleading for help to the captain, who stood with
folded arms by the porthole, looking out at a passing fishing boat
manned by half-naked blacks; there was no help to be expected
from that quarter.

"I beg your pardon, sir," said the ensign hoarsely. "There must
be some mistake. My fiancée comes of a good German family."

"A splendid family!" Dr. Lüning thundered. "I've made in-
quiries. This is what the German consul tells me." He took an
envelope from his breast pocket. "Your fiancée's mother is a nigger bitch, a Creole of the third or fourth generation, allegedly of

French descent, but what does that mean? Racially inferior in every respect, totally nigger-Jew contaminated; it could take centuries for that kind of thing to get Mendeled out. Incidentally, your fiancée's father is distantly related to our supreme party judge. So what? There's no saying how much alien blood some of our party members have in their veins."

"Sir," said the ensign firmly, looking the doctor full in the face, "I love the girl. We mean to announce our engagement at tonight's shipboard reception and to marry before the year is out."

"To produce nigger babies who will have to be exterminated at the taxpayers' expense, like the French bastards the Gestapo had to kill in the Rhineland. A fine how-do-you-do! If you want a nigger whore, go to a whorehouse like the men and come to me for a shot afterward." Dr. Lüning arrested his pacing directly under the portrait of Hitler and brandished his riding whip as though conducting an invisible orchestra. The ensign went up to him and twisted the riding whip out of his hand. "This is outrageous," he said. "You have insulted my fiancée and so offended my honor as an officer. I demand immediate satisfaction!"

"Gentlemen!" said the captain, stepping between them. "Please moderate your tone. Lieutenant Lüning may have erred in his choice of words, but this matter is a lot more serious than you seem to think, Ensign. Señor Gomez will . . ."

Señor Gomez stubbed out his cigarette—at which he had been absently puffing the whole while, as though the conversation were no concern of his—cleared his throat, and began in perfect German: "My supreme commander, His Excellency Generalissimo Rafael Leonidas Trujillo, has commissioned me, by way of rendering service to a friendly nation, to acquaint you with the following facts." Here he drew a sealed envelope from his pocket and opened it with a stiletto. "I am sure you have heard about the recent strike in the cane fields of Santo Domingo. It reduced our sugar production to next to nothing. The Dominican sugar harvest always attracts a considerable number of illegal immigrants from Haiti, undesirable elements who infiltrate the country at night. As might be expected, these include numerous communists and criminals. The conspiracy behind the strike was headed by a terrorist known as Carlos, who crept into our country disguised as a tourist. This individual studied medicine and ethnology in Zurich, Geneva, and Paris and speaks German fluently; he writes French poetry, which he reads in literary salons and publishes in communist periodicals. I don't have to tell you gentlemen that from a literary point of view the stuff is worthless. His real name"—Señor Gomez leafed through his papers—"is Roumel, Pierre Roumel, but in Comintern circles he is known as Cobra. He was trained as a secret agent in Soviet Russia; for a time he operated as a courier between Moscow and Madrid, crossing borders with the help of forged diplomatic passports. This Roumel alias Carlos alias Cobra"—Señor Gomez looked up from his papers—"has been engaged to your fiancée for two and a half years. I thought that might interest you."

After pausing to let his words sink in, Señor Gomez gave the ensign an inquisitorial look over the rims of his dark glasses. "Unfortunately," he went on, "we were obliged, in crushing the strike, to call in the regular army, because the police and militia had proved inadequate. People were killed—twenty thousand, according to the Hearst press; the actual figure must have been higher. The Haitians were wiped out." Señor Gomez took off his sunglasses and wiped a grain of dust from one of the lenses. "Unfortunately—and here I come to the end of my little speech—Roumel was not among the dead. You, young man, will help us put him out of action."

The captain glanced at the clock. "To make our position perfectly clear," he said, giving the hopelessly bewildered ensign a friendly tap on the back, "this is an order, for the execution of which you will be personally responsible to me. Once you've completed your mission, I shall put you in for promotion. To all intents and purposes you are already a lieutenant. Lieutenant Lüning will instruct you in the details of the projected operation. *Heil Hitler!*"

4

AT that very hour—the Caribbean Sea was still in darkness, but the first streaks of dawning light were appearing over the mountains in the east—a small fishing boat put into a rocky cove to the north of Port-au-Prince. The three men who got out seemed to have made a poor catch: where one might have expected lobsters or sea turtles, all they had to show was a number of canvas-wrapped fish which, to judge by their size and weight, must have been sharks or swordfish. These were loaded into a truck that had been waiting by the roadside, its engine running. Two of the men climbed into the cab, while the third wrapped himself in a tarpaulin and stretched out among the fish in back. The truck drove off with a jolt. As the driver was lighting a match, having offered his companion a cigarette, his face could be seen for a moment. It seemed to be lighter in color than that of his neighbor.

"They call me L'Amour," he said. "My real name is beside the point."

"Member or sympathizer?" asked the other distrustfully.

"Sympathizer. But you can trust me—I'm an old friend of Roumel's."

"Trust is all very well, but it's better to be on the safe side," said the other with a laugh. Only the glow of his cigarette could be seen in the darkness. "They call me La Mort. I've been underground so long I've forgotten my real name. We communists are living corpses, zombies. Am I right, L'Amour?"

"Comrade La Mort is always right," said the other, leaning forward. His face had a greenish glow in the light of the dashboard. "In the last strike we lost our best fighters, honest democrats and communists. The fascist army attacked unarmed workers, women and children, with machine guns. They slaughtered us Haitians like dogs."

"What about Roumel?"

"We slipped him through the enemy lines and smuggled him across the border at night. He's OK. Watch it—police patrol."

With a screeching of brakes the truck came to a stop, inches from a sandbag barrier. A machine gun on top of the sandbags was pointed straight at the windshield, behind which there was no one to be seen but the driver. "Halt. Don't move. Identity check. Who are you? Where are you going?" The driver handed the soldier his identity card. "I see, *la pharmacie allemande*. My mother used to buy calomel from your father." The soldier sounded a bit friendlier than before. "I'll have to check your load. What are you carrying?"

"Just a few fish. For the pharmacy—for making fish oil."

The soldier lifted the tarp and looked into the wide-open mouth of a hammerhead shark with its razor-sharp teeth. He recoiled in fright. "It's OK, *m'sieur*, you can go on. Excuse me for stopping you. But there are communists afoot tonight. They're planning something big. You wouldn't by chance know a certain Pierre Roumel?"

Half an hour later the truck stopped in the inner court of the pharmacy. The sky had turned red over the mountains in the east. A man disentangled himself from the pile of fish inside the truck, a man whose face at that very hour was being distributed all over the island on countless "Wanted" notices. His sensitive, almost feminine features suggested a poet rather than a revolutionary. While L'Amour and La Mort unloaded the truck, Toni threw herself into the stowaway's arms.

"Is the plane ready?" he asked.

"Everything's ready. The marriage plans are in full swing."

"You've done a good job. I'll bring you and your brother up for membership."

Roumel looked at his watch. "The sun will be rising in a few minutes. We don't have much time." The sharks were taken to a nearby shed and hung up on hooks. Their bellies were slit open, revealing blood-soaked cloths. When these were unwrapped, out came rifles, tommy guns, hand grenades, and ammunition belts, all made in the Spanish Republic; there were also a few sticks of dynamite, which were passed from hand to hand as cautiously as if they had been raw eggs. The weapons were distributed to men who came in singly or in groups: communist longshoremen, unemployed men from the outlying slums, landless peasants who had proved themselves in the struggle against the North American occupation. They took their weapons in silence and then Roumel made a short speech:

"You have only a few minutes in which to make yourselves invisible. You all know what you've got to do. Wait for the sound of the bombs; that will be the signal to attack. We will occupy the key positions, Presidential Palace, post office, ministries, banks, army and police barracks—our agents are everywhere. We can't have any individual, unorganized actions. No one must attack on his own initiative. All for the party, the party for all, that's our motto. Our victories are the victories of all the workers in the world, our defeats are their defeats. If we beat fascism here, we will beat it in Europe. And never forget: Unflinching loyalty to the Soviet Union, the first country to build socialism, from whose triumphs we draw our strength. And love of Stalin, that shining star in the night of imperialism that has fallen on our hemisphere. We must show ourselves worthy of our great ancestors. Now let us repeat their oath: We swear to die on the ruins of a free country rather than endure the disgrace of tyranny any longer. *La liberté ou la mort!*"

"*La liberté ou la mort,*" murmured those present in chorus. Then, one after another, they went out into the dingy morning light and vanished without trace in the jumbled streets of the waterfront quarter.

5

AT five o'clock the ensign called for his fiancée at the pharmacy. He had promised to take her to the movies. Then, at the shipboard reception that night, they would announce their engagement. Toni was a movie fan. As a child she had gone every Saturday, hand in hand with her nurse, Annaise, to a matinée in a converted cockfight arena. Annaise always brought a basket full of sandwiches and lemonade for them to refresh themselves with during the show. Toni had laughed with delight when Charlie Chaplin rolled up his shoelaces on his fork and had screamed for help as Jean Harlow lay chained to the railroad tracks waiting for the locomotive to come and run her over; she had covered her eyes when Bela Lugosi bared his bloody vampire's teeth, and trembled all over when Boris Karloff, bandaged like a mummy, climbed out of the pharaoh's tomb.

She liked horror movies best. And though she had seen any number of bodies dissected in anatomy class without the slightest fear or revulsion, she still believed in the horror stories with which Annaise had lulled her to sleep in her childhood—stories about red-eyed demons called *zobop* or *vlanbindingues*, which lurk in wait at lonely crossroads for defenseless wayfarers, or werewolves, which tap on windows at night, wanting to come in and suck the blood of sleeping children.

When Gustav arrived at the pharmacy shortly before closing time, Toni was busy gutting a ten-foot hammerhead shark. "A fisherman brought it this morning," she explained, plunging her arm between two rows of razor-sharp teeth and into the monster's hammer-shaped gullet. "Let's see what surprises its stomach has to offer. I feel something." Out from the shark's belly she pulled a blood-smeared gasmask. The ensign turned away in disgust. "What's on at the movies?" he asked. "*Frankenstein*," she said, washing the blood and slime off her hands. "A talking picture with Boris Karloff."

The feature had already begun when they got there, and the house was packed despite the repeated storm warnings on the radio. Coming from Cuba, Hurricane Betsy was nearing the coast of Florida. The ensign squirmed in his bumpy seat. He felt ill-at-ease among all these vociferous, sweaty blacks; their sweetish smell made him sick to his stomach, and he found it hard to concentrate on the picture.

A murmur runs through the audience when, under a full moon, Dr. Frankenstein cuts down a corpse from the gallows and loads it into his carriage drawn by black horses. Like Baron Samedi, lord of the graveyards, he is wearing an old-fashioned tail coat and a top hat. Toni is evidently as superstitious as the people around them, for when the fateful blunder occurs, when the jar containing the brilliant scientist's brain falls off the shelf and Dr. Frankenstein unknowingly implants the criminal brain of the murderer in the dead man's head, she snuggles up to the ensign's shoulder for comfort. Through his uniform jacket he feels her heart pounding. A flash strikes the lightning rod on Dr. Frankenstein's house and descends hissing and roaring on the monster as he lies fettered and bandaged from head to foot on the operating table. The monster, who seems to have superhuman strength, sits up with a shattering jolt and bursts his bonds. After jumping off the operating table, he lumbers through the laboratory, undeterred by the furious lightning flashes. The hunchbacked assistant appears with a lighted torch and tries to bar his way, but the monster thrusts him aside with a blow of his fist and lumbers out of the house. Outside, he is dazzled by the lightning flashes, which throw his shadow, magnified to gigantic proportions, over the Bavarian landscape faithfully reproduced by Hollywood. In a frenzy, the monster tears off his bandages, revealing Boris Karloff's skull, held together by screws. When Dr. Frankenstein realizes what he has done and foresees the crimes the monster he has created will commit, he faints with horror. Toni presses still closer to the ensign; with her right hand, she clutches the hilt of his officer's dagger, on the blade of which the words MY HONOR IS LOYALTY are incised in Gothic letters. In the meantime, Boris Karloff sets fire to the cell of the blind hermit, who for a time pacified him with his violin. Now his lumbering steps are nearing the riverbank where a little girl is picking flowers. The storm has blown over. The sun is shining. The little girl looks up and holds out a daisy to the monster. She shows no sign of fear. The monster raises the flower to his nose; a blissful smile crosses his face; then he bends down. It is not clear whether he is going to help the girl pick flowers or strangle her and throw the little corpse into the river. The audience is quiet now. They even seem to have stopped breathing. Toni shuts her eyes and buries her face in the ensign's lap to keep from seeing the monster kill the little girl. On her lips she feels the cool hilt of the officer's dagger. The metal has a bitter taste.

Unfortunately, the ensign never found out what happens next, whether the monster helps the chid to pick flowers or murders her, for at that point the film broke. Evidently the projectionist had trouble mending the break, for the hall remained in darkness for several minutes. Maybe the current had gone off. Shouts of protest, a shuffling of chairs. Then steps were heard, as though someone had gone out to complain to the management. After a while the manager appeared and expressed his regrets. A technical mishap, he said, an act of *force majeure*. It seemed that Hurricane Betsy, which had featured hour after hour in the weather bulletins of the U.S. Coast Guard, had blown down the power lines, and all Port-au-Prince was in darkness, but the picture would be shown again and it went without saying that all admission tickets would be honored. When at last the doors were flung open, the seat beside Toni was empty. All that remained of the ensign was a wet spot on the back of his seat, which she had overlooked in the darkness.

Toni rushed out and wandered aimlessly through the streets, which were crowded with jeeps and trucks carrying armed soldiers. Ambulances with blue lights and blaring sirens were darting about. Natural catastrophe or revolution? Possibly both at once. The hurricane had uprooted numerous trees, carried roofs away, and cut a swath of death and devastation through the city. Fires could not be put out, because the Fire Department had secretly sold its reserves of water to swimming-pool owners. Toni ran to the harbor and stopped total strangers: had anyone seen her fiancé? She wanted help and had no one to turn to.

The storm-roiled sea had turned leaden. The *Schleswig-Holstein* had put about; its guns were pointed menacingly at the great smoke cloud enveloping the city. Oily smoke poured from a gaping hole in the ship's side, just above the water line.

The storm had blown in the door of the pharmacy and swept the bottles off the shelves. The inside of the shop was a heap of broken glass, as though looters had been at work. As Toni left the pharmacy, a policeman with drawn pistol barred her way and demanded her papers. Under questioning at the police station, she got tangled up in contradictions. She claimed she had left her handbag at the movies, but she couldn't remember the name of the film. Was it *Dr. Caligari* or *Dr. Mabuse?* In the end, however, the manager of the movie house, alerted by the police, brought the missing handbag to the police station, and Toni was allowed to go home. No one saw her take a scrap of paper from her handbag, crumple it, and throw it into the gutter. On it someone had scribbled in pencil these unintelligible words: *Nous nous reverrons—dans un autre monde.* Evidently the writer had been in such a hurry that he forgot to sign his name.

6

THOUGH all the border crossings were closed and all ships entering or leaving Port-au-Prince were closely watched, Pierre Roumel was not caught. Some said he had fled to Cuba in a rubber dinghy; others that a private single-engine plane had taken him out of the country, but that is unlikely, for in that same night the wooden fuselage in the shed behind the pharmacy was chopped into kindling by an army patrol. The government, which at that time had no air force at its disposal, may have feared an air raid on the Presidential Palace.

Three years later—in the meantime the government had fallen and a new president been elected—Pierre Roumel returned to Haiti and, in recognition of his services, was appointed ambassador to Mexico. There, at the suggestion of the author Anna Seghers, a refugee from Nazi Germany, he wrote a novel, but he did not live to see its worldwide success: he died in 1945 of complications resulting from the tuberculosis he had contracted in prison. Others claim that President Lescot, feeling threatened by Roumel's popularity among the students and workers, had had him murdered.

As for the ensign, nothing more was ever heard of him. What

seems most likely is that after leaving the movie house he was crushed by a collapsing building. Years later, a rusty officer's dagger was found in the belly of a hammerhead shark caught in the harbor. On its blade were inscribed the words MY HONOR IS LOYALTY. But that proves nothing, because in the meantime the Second World War had broken out and the dagger might just as well have belonged to a member of the crew of a German submarine sunk off the Haitian coast. In another version of our story, the ensign manages to make his way through the raging hurricane to the *Schleswig-Holstein*; after the war, with the help of some old navy buddies, he starts a scrap-iron business specializing in dismantling retired battleships, becomes the richest shipbuilder in the Federal Republic, retires to the Bahamas after a resounding billion-mark bankruptcy scandal, and there spends his declining years dreaming of his youthful love in Haiti.

Movements in the Air

1

THIS is the story of my uncle Guillaume, whose real name was different but who never used it, because he had no use for the Emperor he was named after and in general, for reasons that will soon become apparent, set little store by his German descent. So let's just call him Uncle G. The story begins in August 1914 aboard a ship of the Hamburg-America Line. As it is negotiating the English Channel, a Zeppelin flies over. Some leaflets dropped from its gondola drift down on the ship's deck. Uncle G., who, though only six, is able to read and write but knows no German, picks one up and hands it to his father, whose sunburned face goes pale as he reads it. "*Ce n' est rien*," he mutters, while smoothing the paper out and slipping it into his wallet as though it were a historical document, a valuable banknote, or a rare postage stamp, "*ce n' est rien*." And when the son seems dissatisfied with this observation, the father mumbles the name of a city, Sarajevo or something of the sort, which my Uncle G. has never heard of, while the Zeppelin changes its lumbering course and, pursued by a British biplane, falls in flames a few miles away. Pieces of wreckage with survivors clinging to them are picked up by lifeboats, and an hour later a pillar of smoke can be seen against the blood-red setting sun on the western horizon. That moment engraved itself indelibly on my Uncle G.'s mind, and from then on he had a *burning* interest in Zeppelins.

I could have his story start earlier—in the fall of 1910, for instance, with Uncle G., in the arms of his nurse Annaise, staring at the overcast sky of Port-au-Prince. What is expected is not the rainy season, *la saison des pluies*, but Halley's comet. Masses are

being said in the churches and drums are being beaten in the
voodoo temples to avert the cataclysm prophesied by the astrolo-
gers. Or a year later, in the green hills around Pétionville, when
Uncle G. sends up a kite, which gets tangled up in an aerial battle
with another, fiery-red kite, the tail of which is studded with bits
of glass, and plummets down on a distant hill, whither the inconsolable Uncle G. follows it.

Or that summer afternoon in the same year when the people
of Port-au-Prince flock to the Champ de Mars and point black,
brown, and yellow fingers at the blue sky, where a cigar-shaped
airship glides down and drops anchor on the roof of the Presidential Palace. A mailbag is lowered on a rope, a receipt in due form
is hoisted up, and the airship, saluted by shots from the palace
guard and shouts from the crowd, rises into the cloudless sky.
This same afternoon it will descend on Santo Domingo, capital
of the Dominican Republic, and deliver another mailbag.

My story might begin with any of these memorable events. My
Uncle G.'s aeronautical interests could be traced back to any of
them.

But let us dwell for another moment on that afternoon in August 1914, which a fellow traveler, possibly at my grandfather's
request, recorded with his antiquated camera. In the yellowed
family photo my uncle G. can be seen in a sailor suit, hand in
hand with his father in twill, or possibly drill, I can't say for sure.
They are standing beside a lifeboat bearing the faded letters HAPAG
LLOYD. Far away, in the sky, one seems to see a shadowy movement, which could be billows of smoke, flocks of birds, or a falling Zeppelin.

Our story, without having properly begun, ends half a century
later at Miami International Airport, where Uncle G., in orange
overalls marked with the emblem of an American oil company,
Exxon or Texaco, is saying good-bye to my father (dark-blue suit
and diplomatic dispatch case) before squeezing himself into the
cockpit of a plane that he himself had knocked together along the
lines of a single-engine Cessna, before disappearing forever in the
Bermuda triangle. This historical moment too is immortalized, in

a picture taken by me, a greenish Polaroid photo with blurred contours. The only part that came out really clearly is the shark's teeth painted on the nose of the plane and under them the inscription *Plaisirs de l'éternité*. But suppose I tell the story from the beginning.

In September 1914, when Uncle G. landed in Bremerhaven, he was amazed at the black-white-and-red flags flying from every window and the endless columns of men in field-gray or navy-blue wherever he went with his father. What amazed him even more was his own breath, which was as white as a vapor trail. This spectacle recurred morning after morning; he feasted his eyes on it until the day when he was taken to the hospital with pneumonia. There he dreamed of flaming Zeppelins plummeting into the ocean, while his father talked in whispers with the nurse, who gave him a spoonful of a horrid-tasting liquid morning and evening, each time muttering unintelligible syllables in a foreign language: COD-LI-VER-OIL. When he was discharged from the hospital six weeks later, the white smoke he had seen coming out of his mouth every morning had spread all over the country: a milky-white sea of fog, from which only the church steeples emerged. Along with streets and houses, it had also swallowed up his father, who had gone back to Haiti on a Hamburg-America liner. The *Lusitania* had not yet been sunk: the submarines were still sparing passenger ships. From then on the only signs of life from his father were letters and checks drawn on the Banque Royale du Canada, sent punctually from Port-au-Prince to Darmstadt on the first of each month, until July 1918, when the Republic of Haiti declared war on the German Empire. But I'm getting ahead of my story.

2

WHERE am I and why am I writing all this?

Where I am I wish I were not, and I'm not where I would like to be. I'm not sitting on the terrace of the Hotel Ibo Lélé, looking out at the glittering bay of Port-au-Prince, with a glass of ice water and a dish of cut papaya, in whose butter-yellow flesh the black seeds shine like grains of caviar; and no barefoot waiter is bringing a rum cocktail on a silver tray. I'm sitting under soot-blackened rafters in the attic of a Lower Saxon farmhouse; the house is silently going under in the gentle March rain that has darkened the sky for days and soaked the stubble fields. There are still no storks in sight, not to mention sun. Will this winter never end? It's night, and instead of the electrifying rhythm of the *rada* drums, only the rattle of my electric typewriter comes to my ears, a choppy staccato broken by pauses for thought, minutes of silence that grow longer and longer, traversed just now by a car; the beam of its headlights glides over the whitewashed wall, on which no emerald-green lizard darts or lies motionless with pulsating heart or looks at me out of cold, glittering reptilian eyes; no hummingbird hovers with whirring wings in mid-air, sucking nectar from the open calyx of an orchid; instead, the neighbor's cat creeps unseen around the house, a field mouse scurries under the rotten floorboards, and a screech owl screeches in the bare branches of the oak tree across the road, where begin the woods that are inexorably turning into a garbage dump. A beat-up mattress, its rusty spring bedded in putrid grassweed with green tips of real grass sprouting from it, crumpled cellophane, unread instructions for the use of sperm-killing condoms, coated with protective ointment; first and second nature, First, Second, and Third World stratified and intermingled—at a depth of five feet the metal detector locates a burst gun barrel or live ammunition from the First Second Third World War; plenty of history here, battered cooking utensils, a leaky messkit, a hopelessly entangled gasmask, better steer clear of it.

Who am I? And why am I writing all this? My name is not Sanchez Artigas Salagnac Bustamonte Larrea, my name is not Artus Portus d'Artagnan; I've forgotten the name of the fourth musketeer, or were there only three? My name is not Christophe Dessalines Pétion Toussaint L'Ouverture Soulouque Roumain Alexis Papa or Baby Doc; I am who I am not and never will be Legba Ogoun Ferraille Erzulie Fréda Maman Zimbie Cousin Zaca

Baron Samedi Maître Carrefour Compère Général Soleil. I am writing what was not and never happened as I tell it, the story of a man who really lived but whose real name I may not give here.

In the photo before me on the desk, Uncle G. is wearing *Lederhosen* with horn buttons, much too wide, much too long, reaching from his chest to his knees, and woolen stockings that look as if they must have been disgustingly scratchy—how do I know all this after more than fifty years?—and brilliantly polished laced boots with hooks and eyes that need to be threaded and unthreaded morning and evening, a complicated task on which, from start to regulation bows, eight-ten-twelve-year-old Uncle G. spends hours, minutes, and in the end only seconds. That may account for the dumb-defiant look he gives the photographer who snaps him with unseen camera: click, but no birdie in sight, only the photographer's shadow across the picture. There stands Uncle G. in laced boots by the box hedge that might also be a garden wall—one can't be sure in the dark photo. He has assumed an obstinate, almost military attitude. With clenched teeth, clenched fists, vertical crease in forehead, exclamation points between the eyes, he looks you full in the face: a picture of forced adaptation. It's plain that his collar button is cutting off his breath. The only flaw in this portrait of perfect training is the great tuft of hair rising like a tropical ocean wave. In another second the wave will break, the surf will crash down, submerge box hedge, house, and garden in salt foam, and carry them away, inhabitants and all. That wave will carry little Uncle G. across the North Sea, across the Bay of Biscay and the Sargasso Sea, to Port-au-Prince Bay, into the arms of his nurse, Annaise, who is washing clothes on the beach. Into his mouth she pops a piece of sugar cane, a caramel, or, if nothing else is available, her lavender nipple, which sends sweet milk flowing into his stomach. But nothing of the sort happens: the tuft of hair stands congealed, a frozen wave over his forehead, the box hedge, the rabbit hutch which I forgot to mention because in the picture it's nothing more than a black spot—all that stays right where it is, a scratched phonograph record that plays the same snatch of melody over and over.

We see him next in 1919. As stipulated in the Treaty of Ver-

sailles, French troops occupy the Rhineland, among them a Senegalese regiment that distinguished itself by special bravery in the
Battle of the Marne and has been sent to the Rhineland as a reward, or, rather, as punishment for the local population, who
have kept faith to the end with their emperor, who is now chop-
ping wood in a Dutch castle, a suitable pastime for a deposed
monarch. Between Cologne and Koblenz the first meetings occur,
brief embraces in the shadow of high barracks walls or in the
bushes beside some railroad line over which a train carrying rep-
arations in kind is rolling westward. The cold Rhine maiden from
Cologne, whose flesh isn't cold at all, and the black man from
Dakar, whose skin under the light isn't black at all, are far from
suspecting that the fruit of their union, which sees the light of
day nine months later, as light-brown as the *café au lait* in which
the soldier dunks his breakfast bread, far from being welcomed as
a love child, a symbol of friendship between nations, will be re-
viled as a bastard, a crime against the race, a life unworthy to
live, and seventeen years later, by the Führer's order, efficiently
carried out by the Gestapo, will be taken off a Rhine steamer—
whistling a tune, the kinky-haired Hans or Jean is scrubbing its
deck—by two men in leather coats, or that later, in the gray of
dawn, he will be trucked along with other kinky heads to the
Westerwald for a free vacation in a hospital for respiratory diseases, the director of which six weeks later will send the boy's
mother a message of official regret informing her that her son has
unexpectedly died of tuberculosis and that his ashes are being
mailed COD. And when the mother protests to the priest and the
mayor, disturbing the peace with unwarranted allegations and ir-
responsible rumors, she is officially advised to wear her mourning
discreetly and maintain a politic reserve, because if she doesn't
unspecified consequences are to be feared. By then little Jean's or
Hans's father has disappeared without trace from the Dakar
waterfront, where in the meantime he has begotten another half-
dozen children. The case can therefore be regarded as closed, and
even forty years later, when taken up by a news magazine specializing in National Socialist crimes, it attracts little attention. It

happened too long ago, and this particular brand of injustice affected too few people as compared with the victims of subsequent
events.

3

B U T let's get back to the beginning of our story, which still
hasn't got very far. Little Uncle G.'s father has entrusted him to
the care of cranky Aunt Miechen, the embittered widow of the
food chemist Dr. Best, who died of cholera while serving as medical officer to the German garrison in Budapest. This old-maidish
governess, smelling of rancid butter ("the vagina requires an acid
environment, to keep the lactoprotein bacteria in levorotatory motion"), a fanatical Protestant, anti-Semite, and anti-Catholic ("the
Pope's just another Jew"), avenges herself for the disregard shown
her by the male sex, on the boy, whose father has been shameless
enough to take up with a nigger woman in the West Indies and,
not satisfied with getting the black hussy with child, goes and
marries her—Aunt Miechen avenges herself for the hardships of
her manless existence by repressing every sexual stirring in little
Uncle G. At night she makes him wear a chastity belt, an iron-
and-leather contraption purporting to keep him from touching his
genitals. Every night before he goes to sleep his aunt checks his
hands, which must be properly crossed over his blanket. He is
obliged to lie on his back; no other position is permissible—this
to prevent involuntary emissions of sperm, which induce tuberculosis of the spine and softening of the brain. During the day he
has to wear a corset to promote the upright posture that distinguishes Nordic-culture peoples from the members of degenerate
races, and steel shin guards, with which he metes out dreaded
kicks when a schoolmate ventures to tease him about the color of
his skin: A COAL-PITCH-RAVEN-BLACK-A-MOOR WENT WALKING JUST
OUTSIDE THE DOOR. THE SUN BEAT DOWN UPON THE FELLA SO HE
UNFOLDED HIS UMBRELLA.
When an older student—by now Uncle G. is in his first year

of secondary school—inspects his fingertips and calls him "nigger" because of the yellow half-moons on his nails, Uncle G. thrashes out in blind rage and keeps it up until the older boy spits blood and the Latin teacher supervising the recreation period separates the combatants with a blast from his whistle: two hours' detention. "Never again," says Uncle G. fifty years later in Miami, where we're sitting face to face on the veranda of the bungalow he has built with his own hands, "never again did any of my schoolmates dare to insult me." He compensates for his differentness, which most of the people around him affect not to notice, with prowess in sports. He is an excellent athlete, makes the school hockey team, takes riding and fencing lessons twice a week, and does knee bends and pushups every morning to the point of exhaustion. Already of an age to attract ladies when working as a ball boy at the tennis club, he is consistently made to look the other way when the goat, which is tied to a stake in the garden, is being milked.

Milk is in short supply during the world war, and the checks on the Banque Royale du Canada haven't been coming lately; the sailors are mutinying in Kiel and marching through the streets with red flags, but at Aunt Miechen's in Stuttgart the clock has stopped. Here petticoats are still UNMENTIONABLES, as in the days of Queen Victoria, and there is no word to designate what happens in the shed when the billy goat comes to "visit" the nanny goat and nothing comes out but a frightened bleating accompanied by a penetrating smell that throws Aunt Miechen into an inexplicable state of excitement. As punishment for peeping through a crack, Uncle G., who by then is in the third year of secondary school, is locked up in the dark coal cellar, from which his aunt, stricken with remorse, soon frees him. Heaving great sighs, she hugs him, kisses him, and gropes about between his legs in search of some object she evidently hopes or fears to find there.

Shortly before the end of the war, something happens on Uncle G.'s way home from school that imprints itself as deeply on his memory as the experience recorded in the first pages of our account. Sweating under the weight of his schoolbag, he stops to peer at the sunny sky over Darmstadt, where a French "Spad" pursuit plane is circling around a German "Taube." Suddenly he hears a distant rustling, suggesting the music of the spheres or the *Freischütz* Overture, which Aunt Miechen sometimes plays on the phonograph on Sundays; while he is still wondering where the sound came from, a rain of steel splinters falls around him and disappears irretrievably in the soft, sun-warmed asphalt, from which, as from a puddle lashed by hailstones, little bubbles arise. When he gets home, he finds one of these razor-sharp steel nails in his schoolbag. He carries it about with him as a talisman from that day on.

In the meantime, the red flags have come to Darmstadt, and the performance of the Festival Symphony, the difficult cello part of which Uncle G. has been rehearsing with the school orchestra, is called off, because, to everyone's surprise, the reigning archduke Ernst Ludwig, whose portrait hangs beside the Emperor's in the classroom, has abdicated on the eve of his fiftieth birthday. Gray columns of soldiers undefeated in the field wander through the streets; schoolboys offer them their sugar-syrup sandwiches in return for a belt buckle or a cartridge case. Then Prussian and Bavarian Free Corps move in, putting an end to the red nightmare, and the black-white-and-red student caps, introduced by one of the first decisions of the revolutionary student council, are waved to salute the Republic and Friedrich Ebert, its first president.

4

I WILL not obstruct the flow of time; on the contrary, I'm going to speed it up, because I'm eager to end my story, which is made up entirely of beginnings, loose threads that don't show a regular pattern when taken together, don't add up to a carpet with geometric designs, but only to a tangled skein, which I shall try to disentangle before the reader's eyes.

In the following year, while the slowly growing Uncle G. ad-

vances from the third to the fourth to the fifth class of secondary
school, time accelerates as never before. History, which only yesterday was jogging along at the pace of a rural jitney, goes racing
through the landscape at the speed of an express train. The news-
reels show rhythmically chug-chug-chugging locomotives spew-
ing steam and sparks, pulling with backward-turning wheels into
provincial stations, where smoke-beclouded gentlemen alight in
tailcoats and top hats and make history by arriving late or early,
punctually or unpunctually. Flags and hats are waved to welcome
them; broad shoulders carry them through the streets in triumph.
But before the new era, rung in by salutes from the battleship
Aurora, can get off to a proper start, it comes to an end. The
locomotive of revolution, which was going strong only a short
while ago, ends up in the dustbin of history. Halfway between
Moscow and Paris, history's engine breaks down; in a forest near
Compiègne, in a plush-upholstered saloon car, the high contract-
ing parties sign an armistice that puts the next world war on the
agenda. Lenin, who only yesterday crossed Germany in a sealed
train, suffers a stroke, while Trotsky, who only yesterday was
hunting counterrevolutionary partisans in an armored train, is reduced to hunting pheasants. Behind his back, Stalin looks around
for a suitable widow for Lenin; the sight of a corpse fished out of
the Landwehr Canal in Berlin inspires a pleiad of Expressionist
poets to revive the Ophelia motif. In Munich, Eisner is murdered
and Leviné shot, while Ernst Toller in his prison cell feeds the
sparrows and an anonymous housepainter in Landsberg prison
writes a best-seller, the mass sales of which result in mass deaths.
Mussolini's Blackshirts march on Rome, the Black Reichswehr
stages secret shooting parties in Russia, the coastal waters of Brazil are blackened with coffee, and on the Berlin black market a
pound of black bread costs a million marks. Kafka dies in a sana-
torium near Vienna, Mayakovski commits suicide in Moscow, and
Brecht writes *The Threepenny Opera*, while in Shanghai the Kuo-
mintang massacres communists; Lindbergh crosses the Atlantic in
solo flight and on returning to New York finds his son missing,
Sacco and Vanzetti are lodged in death row, while Einstein preaches
eternal peace to the League of Nations, Heisenberg computes

quantum leaps, and Charlie Chaplin eats soft-boiled shoes with spaghetti shoelaces on the side.

Meanwhile, Uncle G., unimpressed by what's happening in the world around him, folds checked or lined paper into darts, which fly back and forth between the front and back rows during classes, and after school hours are swept away by the cleaning woman. His models are not Lenin Trotsky Stalin Liebknecht Luxemburg, or Ebert Noske Scheidemann Hindenburg Hitler, or even Brecht Kafka Toller Curie Planck Einstein, though now we're getting warmer. His models are Blériot Lilienthal Lindbergh Wright Richthofen; with burning cheeks he reads about the pioneering feats of the polar fliers Byrd and Nobile, dreams about the heroic deeds of the aces Ball and Udet, who sent the blood of English pilots raining down from the sky, yet kept themselves clean and pure of heart, and attends an air show, at which he falls in love with a sun-tanned lady stunt flier, who whooshes past his wondering eyes as she flies upside-down within little more than reaching distance of the grandstand. But once again I'm getting ahead of myself.

Before we get to that point, our hero's interest in aviation will have to evolve through certain phases, such as Darwin described in connection with the evolution of the species—the finches, for instance. The paper darts evolve into gliders made of plywood and canvas, which glide for hours in an upwind over the hills of the Odenwald, until, caught in a fall wind, they wobble slowly downward or plummet into the nearest treetop. Since repairing these model planes, which crumple like houses of cards at every crash landing, proves too costly and bothersome in the long run, Uncle G. experiments in Aunt Miechen's goatshed (which he has converted into an aeronautical workshop), with gas-filled balloons and airships, which in unsupervised moments go soaring over the roofs of Darmstadt, and solid-fueled rockets, which take off from an improvised launching pad and shoot, hissing and whistling, into the night sky, until the premature explosion of his secret stock of gunpowder ravages his tuft of hair and comes close to costing him his eyesight.

5

AFTER the air show, which I locate in and over a converted
soccer field, Uncle G. joins the line of fans waiting to ask the
suntanned stunt flier, who is no longer upside-down in the sky
but has both feet planted firmly on the ground, for an autograph.
"Haiti," she says dreamily, while signing a postcard addressed to
Uncle G.'s parents in Port-au-Prince. "Isn't that in the South Seas?"
"You must be thinking of Tahiti," says Uncle G., shifting his
weight from a stationary leg clad in checked knickerbockers to a
free-moving leg likewise sheathed in checked knickerbockers.
"That's in the South Seas. Haiti is a West Indian island in the
Caribbean; with your little Messerschmitt you can easily get there
in forty-eight hours, if you don't run out of gas on the way."

This makes it clear why Uncle G., instead of spending the
weekend as he should be, studying for his final exams, is sitting
in the stands with the suntanned stunt flier, a rising star in the
firmament of German aviation. Their heads are so close that from
a distance it may look like a lovers' tryst, but if you come nearer
you'll hear that those heads are talking about trans-Atlantic air
routes. The suntanned stunt flier, whose name I am not authorized to mention, though it will soon be named in a breath with
the most famous flying aces, is looking for a copilot and knowledgeable companion for a projected flight via the Cape Verde Islands to Brazil and on to Argentina; on the way—as stipulated in
her contract with a Berlin illustrated magazine—she will visit
German settlements, thus combining business with pleasure, a
pioneering flight with publicity for the cultural mission of the
German settlers in foreign parts.

The young man seems to be just what she wants; he comes
from a German family with business connections on every continent and speaks several languages; he is as thoroughly besotted
with aviation as she is and is willing to drop everything for a
chance to fly. Moreover, despite his exotic complexion, he's not a
bad looker, and best of all, he has a dollar account in a Canadian
bank. Uncle G. has neglected to tell his prospective boss that he
is under twenty and still in secondary school.

After the show she takes him to the hangar, where, with a knowing air, he inspects her blue-and-white Messerschmitt M-23 B. While he sits in the pilot seat caressing the joy stick, which responds to the slightest pressure, and turns the dashboard buttons, she tells him about her emergency landing in the southern Sahara, her stay among the Songhais, who had never seen a white man, let along a white woman in an airplane, and who had to be cajoled with a rhinoceros whip into carrying her and her little Messerschmitt on their shoulders to the nearest oasis.

In the weeks that follow, Uncle G. turns up in the gossip columns as the constant companion of the suntanned stunt flier. It's hard to tell, writes the *Berliner Zeitung am Mittag*, whether he is more taken with her prowess as a flier or with her feminine charms. Uncle G. is invited to every major air show between Riem and Staaken, Langenhagen and Echterdingen. He learns to swing the propeller of the little Messerschmitt without cutting his head off, to oil and grease the eighty-horsepower engine, and to check the pressure gauge and tachometer. Everyone likes the bright young fellow, who makes himself useful around the airfield in any number of ways. Ritter von Greim, an unemployed flying ace, instructs him free of charge in the rudiments of aerodynamics, while ex-champion Udet takes him under his wing and teaches him what every copilot should know: "Strap yourself in good—you wouldn't want to fall out when you loop the loop—and don't leave any junk lying around the cockpit, or you'll have it flying around your ears. OK, now, good luck!" Already, in his mind's eye Uncle G. sees himself in the back seat of the little Messerschmitt, flying over the Andes and the Amazon, the pampas and the llanos, before him the short blond hairs on the suntanned flier's neck, while on the ground below industrious German settlers, surrounded by happily waving natives, brandish black-white-and-red flags.

But things turn out very differently; once again reality beats fantasy by several plane lengths.

6

THE time has come; the great moment is at hand; the plane stands ready on the runway. Uncle G. sits firmly strapped to the back seat, with a thermos bottle full of coffee and an unfolded map on his knees. The propeller is swung, the eighty-horsepower engine of the Messerschmitt M-23 B starts with a roar, an even hum fills the air as the plane rolls slowly to the takeoff line, takes a run like a broadjumper, and hops off the ground. They're off to a good start. Now in a single sentence I could catapult the plane and its two occupants across the Rhine, the Alps, the Po valley. And there come the seven hills of Rome. Escorted by two Italian biplanes, the little Messerschmitt honors the Colosseum with an overflight and lands at Fiumicino Airport, where the pilot, whose period has come on during the flight, repairs to the ladies' room and her copilot delivers the tailcoat ordered from Berlin by Il Duce, who is to wear it that same evening when the Pope receives him at Castel Gandolfo. And onward via Naples on the right and Sicily on the left to Bizerte, where French pursuit planes force the Messerschmitt to land; then, after all is explained and the requisite visas are issued, via Oran and Fez to Agadir, and from there, after a last fueling stop at a desert airfield, on to the Cape Verde Islands, where the intrepid fliers are treated to cold beer, frankfurters, and potato salad on board a Hamburg-America liner anchored in the harbor—a boon after grinding desert sand between their teeth for twenty-four hours. I won't record the further stations of their flight across the South Atlantic, but return instead to Staaken, where the fully fueled plane, before starting on its westward adventure, describes a farewell circuit over the airfield and then, instead of heading for the western horizon, behind which lies the ocean, suddenly starts to wobble, then takes a nose dive in the direction of the grandstand, behind which a number of press photographers take cover. Sweeping just over the heads of the onlookers, who scatter in all directions, it grazes the roof of the airport building with one wing, shaving off an antenna, and plunges into a plowed field with a thud that can be heard in the center of the town. The scene is veiled in oily smoke. From the burning wreck, which breaks in half under the impact, the ambulance men extricate two soot-blackened figures who, except for the tips of their tongues, which the bumpy landing has made them bite off, seem to have nothing wrong with them.

7

THUS Uncle G.'s leap across the Big Pond, after so promising a start, bogs quite literally down in the bogs of central Germany. At this point in our story, we hear again from morose Aunt Miechen. She sends to Port-au-Prince an envelope full of clippings concerning her charge and gets an answer by return mail. Uncle G., who has been dismissed from school for unauthorized absence, is sent to boarding school in the Odenwald, where he passes his final examinations. He is then sent to Weimar to serve, as his father did, as an apprentice at the Lion Pharmacy. He soon learns that apprenticeship is no joke. Three times daily he sweeps the premises; he rubs the brass plate over the door, showing a lion rampant with apothecary's scales in his mouth, to a high polish, weighs camomile and senna, and once a month delivers a bottle of boric-acid lotion to the widow of Franz Liszt, with which for thirty years she has been treating the warts on her nose without discernible success.

In his free time Uncle G. busies himself testing condoms. He slips one over his stiffened member as graphically shown in the instructions, then, after it has proved serviceable, washes it, hangs it up to dry, and repackages it for interested customers. One morning during his breakfast break—he has forgotten to lock the toilet from inside—the pharmacist's wife surprises him at his hobby. Since her husband is out and not expected back until noon—he advises Frick, the newly appointed Thuringian minister of public education, on matters of public health and racial hygiene—she gives her apprentice a hand with his testing. They enjoy the work and engage in it whenever possible, sometimes as many as five

times a day, so as to make absolutely sure that not a single un-
tested condom is put on the market. On Sunday, while her husband, who belongs to an SA troop, is running himself ragged on
maneuvers, she accompanies her apprentice on expeditions through
the Weimar area. They combine business with pleasure, body
building with higher education, by testing condoms in the garden
of Goethe's cottage or the park of Schloss Belvedere. Or they
saunter up the Ettersberg hand in hand and bed down in the
sunlit grassy clearing; not a breath of wind stirs the box trees
above them; even the forest birds keep silent for fear of disturbing
the lovers. Afterward, Uncle G. blows up the tested condoms
and tosses them, with instructions attached, into the sun-drenched
sky, to be borne by the wind over the mountains and forests of
Thuringia, which at that time was still rightly termed the green
heart of Germany. All that summer, my uncle G.'s life was a
German idyll, the Weimar pharmacist's wife supplying the prose
and the Thuringian forest the poetry.

But then brown clouds rose on the horizon and darkened the
sun. While the lovers were tasting the ultimate happiness in the
shade of an ancestral oak, in the bark of which Goethe carved his
initials 120 years ago, an SA honor guard led by Public Education
Minister Frick was parading on the Frauenplan, outside Goethe's
house in homage to the greatest German of all time, determined,
after the overwhelming electoral victory of the National Socialists
(1931), to cleanse Goethe's memory of the un-German filth with
which un-German asphalt literati, first and foremost that obscene
hack Thomas Mann, had befouled it. Was it accident or malicious
intent? At that very moment Uncle G., sitting in the branches of
Goethe's oak, sends up a whole squadron of condoms, which the
south wind carries from the Ettersberg to the center of town.
There they descend on the SA company, which has drawn up in
formation to salute the flag. Attention! Drum roll. And while the
solemn motto "Our honor is loyalty" resounds from hundreds of
throats, a dark cloud rises in the sky; from it descend dozens of
blown-up condoms, which deflate with a hissing sound and wrap
themselves like washrags around the shoulder straps, collars, and

belt buckles of the parading storm troopers. One of the condoms lands on the visor of Public Education Minister Frick's cap just as he is stepping forward with arm upraised to salute the swastika flag. Numbing fear spreads through the crowd and finds release in laughter—ridicule kills—but before this insight can find its voice a shrill whistle blows, followed by the command "Up and at 'em!" Whereupon the SA combat troop, tested in countless brawls, fling themselves, in plain sight of the police, on the passers-by, among them social-democratic and communist workers who will later be called to account for the disturbance.

To top it all, one of the condoms, which up until then had never given ground for complaint, failed, for exactly nine months later the pharmacist's wife gave birth to a son who, in view of his *café-au-lait* complexion, could not possibly have been begotten by her husband. Offered the choice between divorcing and sending her bastard to an orphan asylum, she chose the second alternative, which five years later led to the discreet elimination of a living creature classified as unworthy to live, of whose existence the natural father was never made aware.

8

I n the meantime, a new era has dawned, even more heroic than the one that expired in November 1918, and since the rulers of the new Reich reckon their term of office in thousands of years, Uncle G. prefers to turn his back on the Old World and take passage on a Dutch ship bound for the West Indies. His decision to move on was influenced most of all by the words that Paul Klee, the teacher at the Bauhaus to whom he had submitted some designs for nonrigid airships, has said to him as he was leaving Dessau: "There are regions where other laws apply, for which we must find new symbols, corresponding to freer movement and a more mobile medium. In the air there are other possibilities of movement than on earth."

While the *Batavia*, carrying numerous refugees from Germany, is plowing through the Bay of Biscay, Uncle G. makes the acquaintance of a young woman who, like him, has resolved to emigrate because the racial makeup of her forebears doesn't fall in with the ideas of the new rulers. The name of the young woman with the finely cut features, who spends most of her time in a deck chair reading, is Anna Feingold. A goldsmith by profession, she was honored, after the first showing of her works, with the city of Nuremberg's Dürer Prize. Her father, a Jewish art dealer, has stayed behind in Germany, convinced as he is that National Socialism is no more than a passing episode. His daughter does not agree with his optimistic prognosis. "German history," she says, standing at the rail with Uncle G. and looking out over the sluggish Sargasso Sea, "German history can boast a phenomenon unknown to any other nation." And after a pause during which Uncle G. gives her a light, she goes on: "You see, we've shared the restorations of other modern nations without sharing their revolutions. Our development has been arrested, first because other peoples dared to make revolutions and second because other nations suffered counterrevolutions: in the first instance because our masters were afraid and in the second because our masters were not afraid. Only once have we and our leaders found ourselves in the company of freedom: on the day of its funeral."

"That is contemptible cultural Bolshevism," said a voice trembling with agitation, as a dark figure stepped from the shadow of the smokestack. "Millions of people parrot that Jewish nonsense, though nature refutes it at every turn. Every animal . . ." The stranger paused to blow his nose with a checked handkerchief, then continued: "Every animal mates with its own species—titmouse with titmouse, chaffinch with chaffinch, field mouse with field mouse, house mouse with house mouse, stork with stork, and wolf with wolf. Instinctively every animal strives for racial purity, and the consequence of this instinct, common to all nature, is that every race has its own unalterable character, which distinguishes it from every other race."

"But," Uncle G. interrupted blandly, "what about crosses between different animal species—between wolf and dog, for instance? The product is the German shepherd, a bastard which, though not excessively bright, is remarkable for its sense of duty and unconditional obedience."

The stranger was not put off by this argument. "A fox will always be a fox. You'll never find a fox belying its nature by harboring tender feelings toward geese, for instance, any more than you'll find a cat with a soft spot for mice. The struggle for daily sustenance weeds out the weak and sickly. The battle of the male for the female restricts the right to reproduce to the healthiest specimens. And no more than a hyena will desist from carrion will a Marxist desist from treason against the fatherland."

When the stranger had finished his speech, he was astonished to find himself standing alone at the rail; the Southern Cross had vanished behind brown clouds, and his interlocutors had retired discreetly to their cabins.

As it transpired in the light of day, Herr Streitwolf—for that was the stranger's name—came from a German family that had been resident in Haiti for several generations. He seemed to have black blood in his veins; at all events his coppery-red hair and shiny pig's eyes indicated a bastardized race. Despite his warlike speeches, he had no luck at all when it came to shooting clay pigeons. It was rumored that the National Socialist Overseas Organization had sent him to Haiti to give the German Club of Port-au-Prince a good shaking up, to promulgate the racial principles of the new rulers, and to pursue the long-term aim of liquidating the black population and making Haiti the first overseas Gau of the Third Reich. He had several dozen brown uniforms in his luggage. Their effect on the impressionable native population, it was foreseen, would be backed up by visits from German warships and exhibits of German manufactured goods. Not so much on political as on aesthetic grounds, Uncle G. avoided all communication with the Nazi agent. Young Streitwolf gave off an unpleasant smell that made him think of unwashed socks.

9

MONSIEUR BOUC, as the natives called him, did not at first recognize his son among the passengers who came ashore from the *Batavia*. Instead, he enthusiastically shook the hand of young Streitwolf, who strode down the gangplank and greeted him with "*Heil Hitler!*"

The old man, who was very hard of hearing, put his hand to his ear. "Beg pardon?"

"*Heil Hitler!*" the SA man bellowed, clicking his heels.

But again Monsieur Bouc failed to understand, and the "German greeting" had to be shouted in his ear again before he replied with a friendly "Good morning."

The old pharmacist still wore the same twill, or drill, as when he had arrived in Haiti thirty-five years before; his bushy mustache had to be "styled" now and then with a curling iron, and his broad-brimmed hat was of a type that had been fashionable while the Panama Canal was being built. In walking, he supported himself on Cocomacaque, a stick that he himself had carved. "I needed it," he explained to his son on their way to the waiting car, "to gain the respect of the native population. There's no other way. *Dat is all so, as dat nu ledder is*" ("It can't be helped, but that's how it is"), a *Plattdeutsch* saying he had learned from Fritz Reuter, his favorite author, and would mumble on every suitable or unsuitable occasion.

His way of life had changed little in three and a half decades. At 7:00 A.M. his chauffeur, Dorléus Présumé, would drive him at a snail's pace to the pharmacy, which gave him time to doff his hat to every friend or acquaintance who crossed his path—"*Bonjour, madame; bonjour, monsieur; comment va la santé, comment vont les affaires, et les enfants?*"—until a concert of horns from the cars waiting behind him put an end to the conversation. After dispersing, with the help of Cocomacaque, the swarms of cripples who besieged the entrance to the pharmacy, he would take up his post on the swivel chair by the cash register, whence he surveyed the comings and goings of the customers; in the afternoon hours he would doze off over his work, and it would take the tinkling of the cash register to wake him. After business hours he would rest on the veranda, in his rocking chair, drink his rum cocktail, pick up a weeks-old issue of the *Frankfurter Zeitung*, and immerse himself in the crossword puzzle, which he seldom succeeded in completing. Before going to bed, he would put on his mustache holder and read a page of Fritz Reuter's *Ut mine Stromtid* in a hollow, sepulchral voice; despite constant practice over half a century, he had not learned to pronounce *Plattdeutsch* properly.

At first cock crow he would creep across the yard in his nightshirt and shut himself up in the outhouse, which as usual was swarming with flies, just as the birds were beginning to clamor in the branches of the breadfruit tree overhead. Here he felt more at home than in the newfangled "sanitary installation" built in accordance with U.S.-army specifications, that he had had installed in the house. Instead of swimming in his own pool as he had formerly done, he had his chauffeur drive him on Sundays to a sulphur spring on the coast, known as Source Puante. There, having undressed in a wooden cabin, he would plunge his gouty limbs into the bile-green spring concealed behind a dense clump of cactuses. After his bath he would sit by the roadside, enjoy the picnic he had brought along, feed his leftovers to children and dogs, and feel reborn.

Madame Bouc refused to accompany her husband on these Sunday excursions. Twenty years earlier, she had been thrown out of bed by the blast of an explosion in the nearby Government Palace; since then she had been sitting in a wheelchair and had never left the house on the Chemin des Dalles. The peasant women who came down from the mountains at night, balancing baskets of fruit and vegetables on their heads, went to her room early in the morning and spread their wares on the tile floor in front of her; sometimes they even brought a grunting pig or a gobbling turkey. Madame Bouc spent the morning with the servants in the kitchen. Here she had her bath—that is to say, her aged servant, Annaise, threw a bucket of water over her. Later, her wheelchair would be rolled out into the yard, where, half dazed by the aroma

of the great mounds of oranges and coffee beans, she would dry
her hair. From a distance one might have supposed her to be
chatting with the lizards that were sunning themselves on the warm
stones. The beads of her rosary moved through her coffee-brown
hands, and her lavender lips mumbled soundless prayers. A tremor
went through her frail body at the sight of her son who had gone
away twenty years before; she threw her thin arms around his
shoulders, tried in vain to stand up, and sank back helplessly in
the wheelchair. "*Enfin*," she murmured with a sigh, retrieving her
rosary. "*Je suis contente de te revoir.*"

Uncle G. set to work with feverish zeal. He had brought all
sorts of projects from the Old World, and he tried to carry them
out. But his enthusiasm soon flagged, for it was only too obvious
that his father set small store by such ultramodern medicines as
the penicillin recently developed by Sir Alexander Fleming and
wanted no truck with systematic bookkeeping. More and more,
Uncle G. withdraws from the pharmacy. He sets up a workshop
in the shed behind the house, where in his leisure hours, surrounded by retorts and empty bottles, he knocks together an un-
gainly structure of bamboo and balsa wood, which looks like the
skeleton of an archaeopteryx, that long-extinct bird whose stubby
wings enabled it to glide but not yet to fly. No stranger is admitted to the workshop, and not even Uncle G.'s closest friends are
initiated into his plans. Monsieur Bouc worries about his son's
eccentricity. Instead of participating in social events at the German Club, where the brown uniforms introduced by Streitwolf
have in the meantime become socially acceptable, Uncle G. attends political rallies organized by radical students under the leadership of a young poet named Pierre Roumel, to protest the
American occupation of the island. And instead of contributing
to the Winter Aid welfare fund needed for the construction of the
new German superhighways, he collects money for the support
of some communist refugees who have founded a Jewish-
Bolshevist cultural association in Mexico. He writes long letters
to the secretary of the association, whose acquaintance he made
on board the *Batavia*, though there are plenty of nice German

girls at the club who would be only too glad to dance with him
and whose parents would have no objection whatever to a marriage with the son of the German pharmacist. And even the charms
of the dark-skinned beauties, who ogle him with their eyes and
hips, leave him cold when he deigns to notice them.

10

PASSING over the next few years, we meet Uncle G. again
on December 7, 1941, by which time he is several years older.
Early that morning, while listening to the short-wave radio in the
back room of the pharmacy, he hears that the Japanese air force
has bombed Pearl Harbor. The following morning the President
of Haiti declares war on the Emperor of Japan. What Japanese
nationals can be found in Haitian territory are interned and their
property is confiscated. There follow days and nights of anxious
waiting, in which the whole family listens spellbound to reports
from the Atlantic and Pacific theaters of war, from Russia and
North Africa. And then, on December 12, little Haiti, following
the example of its big brother in Washington, declares war on the
Axis powers, Germany and Italy. A German submarine is sighted
in Port-au-Prince Bay. It makes its getaway after sinking a Haitian coast-guard cutter. That same evening, shortly after closing
time, a Military Police jeep stops outside the pharmacy on the
Place Geffrard. An officer alights, followed by two noncoms. They
set seals on the shop. The pharmacy and its entire inventory,
including its accounts with the Banque Royale du Canada, are
confiscated as alien property.

Every effort is made to keep the bad news from old Monsieur
Bouc. He is over eighty and so hard of hearing that he understands little of what is said in his presence. He goes about from
morning to night mumbling his pet *Plattdeutsch* dictum. Moreover, he is so tortured by gout that he seldom leaves the house to
see what's going on in the pharmacy; he lets his son take care of
all that. But, as usual with the hard of hearing, he has a way of

hearing the very things he's not supposed to. And the servants' whisperings arouse his suspicions; a certain buzzing in his ears tells him that someone is talking about him behind his back. He summons the chauffeur and demands to be driven to town. At first Dorléus, he too an old man by now, pretends to have pains in his back; then he says the old Ford has engine trouble and has been sent to the garage for repairs. But in the end, when threatened with Cocomacaque, he admits, crossing himself and trembling like a leaf, that the Ford has been confiscated by the police. The old man, who for the second time in his life feels cheated out of the fruits of his labors, and to make matters worse systematically deceived and circumvented by his family, collapses after beating Dorléus unmercifully with his stick. Foaming at the mouth, he falls to the ground. A stroke. The left half of his body is paralyzed, but he still has strength enough in his right arm to grab the doctor, who has bent over him with a hypodermic, and choke him till he goes blue in the face. The old man has gone out of his mind. He shouts unintelligible words; his bellowing is heard out in the street, where a crowd gathers. He calls for a notary, he wants to disinherit his family, he reaches under the skirt of the nurse who comes in to empty his chamberpot, and dies with a blissful smile on his lips, after muttering for the last time: "*Dat is all so, as dat nu ledder is.*"

11

T H E funeral was a quiet affair. Responding to the call of the distant fatherland, most members of the German colony had sailed home and rallied to the colors. Only a few of the old settlers had remained on the island, feeble old men, who hobbled behind the coffin, thinking in their hearts that they too would soon be going to their last rest. Hats in hand, sweating in their black suits, they stood beside the open grave as the coffin was slowly lowered. A Catholic server—since Haiti's entrance into the war, the Protestant minister had been forbidden to perform religious offices—

sprinkled holy water and murmured Latin mumbo-jumbo. Dr. Eckmann, a personal friend of the deceased, made a short speech extolling his botanical investigations and quoting his *Plattdeutsch* dictum with a South German accent. A chorus of old men sang *"Ich hatt' einen Kameraden"*—softly, for fear their singing might be interpreted as a patriotic demonstration. One after another, the mourners expressed their sympathy to the widow in the wheelchair, who showed no sign of emotion. And then the funeral was over. The last thing Uncle G. saw on leaving the Cimetière National was the gravediggers, dressed in dirty rags and covered with powdered lime, who lurked like hungry hyenas in the shadow of the cemetery wall and stuck out their violet tongues at him before spitting on their hands and starting to fill in the grave. They were said to be in league with Baron Samedi, lord of the graveyards, and to celebrate cannibalistic orgies at night in the Cimetière National.

Uncle G. couldn't get to sleep that night. Tossing and turning under his mosquito net, he heard the drum beats that rose from the slums, calling the faithful to the *hounforts*, the voodoo temples. He could clearly distinguish the bass voice of Assôtor, the big drum dedicated to the thundergod Damballah, from the shrill descant of the *rada* drums. He heard the irresistible rhythm, which crept into people's legs and turned them into whirling dervishes. At midnight he got up; an invisible force drove him out into the street, where he joined the crowds of people pouring out of the houses. All together, rich and poor, masters and servants, followed the drums into the center of town. No one asked Uncle G. who he was or where he came from; no one was put off by his striped pajamas.

His mother was dancing at the head of the crowd, as light-footed as a young girl, followed by her servant Annaise, who had tied a blood-red scarf around her head and was waving a flag covered with Masonic symbols. Singing and dancing, the procession crossed the Champ de Mars and came to a halt outside the Presidential Palace. The President of the Republic came out and, followed by his guard, took the lead of the procession. He was wearing a black tailcoat and top hat, resplendent patent-leather shoes, white spats, and white gloves, and was twirling a sword in the manner of a drum major. Under the gleaming medals on his chest, the contours of a woman's bosom were discernible. Coming to the closed gate of the Cimetière National, he halted, stamped his feet in a rage, and cried out to the accompaniment of a muffled drum roll, *"Papa Legba, Maît' Carrefour, Maît' Quatre Chemins, Maît' Trois Cimetières—ouvrez barrière-a!"* Whereupon the rusty gate swung open with a squeak. Beside the open grave lay the heavy oak coffin in which Uncle G.'s father had been buried the day before. The wood of the coffin began to work; the lid opened with a loud groan. There lay Uncle G.'s father, his eyes closed, his face framed by a silk cushion, just as he had been laid to rest. The President rubbed salt under the dead man's nose and commanded him to stand up. When the body failed to move, the President stamped his foot and repeated his litany to the accompaniment of a martial drum roll: *"Papa Legba, Maît' Carrefour, Maît' Quatre Chemins, Maît' Trois Cimetières—ouvrez barrière-a!"*

A tremor ran through the dead man's body, and up he sat with a jolt. He sat bolt upright in the coffin, with sunken chin and firmly closed eyes. When the President commanded the departed to give some sign of life, the eyelids opened, the lower jaw moved, and the corpse began to speak in an unknown language, which Uncle G. had never heard but every word of which he understood. Possibly *Plattdeutsch* or Pig Latin. His family, said the deceased in a toneless voice, wanted to kill him; they had shut him up in a wooden box and were letting him rot alive. It was hot and stuffy in the box and stank disgustingly; he was hideously thirsty; he hadn't washed in days and hadn't been given anything to drink; the smell of his rotting body was more than he could bear. The President stuck a cigar in the dead man's mouth and gave him a light. Annaise doused him with cologne and poured rum into his mouth, which trickled down over his starched shirt front. He was beginning to feel better, he said; the only fly in the ointment was the presence of his son, who had given him nothing but worry in his lifetime and had come tonight to murder him—

and he glared accusingly at Uncle G. out of his glassy dead eyes. Uncle G. tried to run away, but the crowd wouldn't part to let him through; the people closed around him, pushing him toward the open grave. Meanwhile Annaise sang a song and the crowd took up the refrain.

> *M'mandé-ou couteau*
> *M'mandé-ou machette*
> *M'mandé-ou népée-a*
> *Pou' m'fini ac li.*
> *Saignez, saignez, saignez!*
>
> [Give me your knife
> Give me your machete
> Give me your sword
> To kill him with.
> Bleed, bleed, bleed!]

Uncle G.'s hair stood on end. With both hands he clutched the hilt of the saber the President handed him and drove the blade into the dead man's chest. Blackish blood gushed out. The dead man's eyes turned in their sockets till only the whites could be seen, and the body sank back into the coffin. The lid fell into place with a loud thud, and in the same moment Uncle G., bathed in sweat, started up from his bed. The morning sun shone in through the cracks in the shade, painting bright curlicues on the rumpled bedspread. The smell of freshly roasted coffee pouring in from outside dispersed the ghosts of the night.

12

THREE days later, Uncle G. was arrested without explanation and thrown into a dark cell, where he remained for twenty-four hours without food or drink. The duty officer brought him pencil and paper and told him to save the authorities trouble by writing a confession. When he refused, the officer hit him across the fingers with a ruler until they were too bloody and swollen to hold a pencil. Uncle G. had no idea what crime he was accused of until the police showed him the plans for the glider, the skeleton of which had been discovered in the shed behind the pharmacy. He was suspected of being a Nazi agent and planning to bomb the Presidential Palace. He was easily able to clear himself by citing respected character witnesses. One of those who testified in his favor was the writer Pierre Roumel, who in the meantime had been promoted to Cabinet rank.

Uncle G. was then transferred to the Fort National, where other enemy aliens were interned—ostensibly for their own protection. The *"commandeuse"* of the fort, Madame Max Adolphe, was a favorite with the President; rumor had it that she celebrated black masses in the cellars of the palace, at which enemies of the regime were put to death. Madame Max Adolphe's only white features were her teeth and the whites of her eyes. She wore a black tailor-made uniform, dark sunglasses, and gleaming black boots that she would tap with the pommel of her riding whip while speaking to lend emphasis to her words. When she was bored or out of sorts, she would exercise her whip on the back of a subordinate or the buttocks of a prisoner. She left the internal administration of the camp to young Streitwolf, who had stuck to his war-essential post in Haiti rather than volunteer for front-line duty in the homeland. He marched around the fort in a brown uniform, harassed his fellow prisoners, and, loudly clicking his heels and raising his right hand in the Hitler salute, reported the slightest irregularity to the *commandeuse*. In return, he was admitted at all times to her private quarters, until one night she threw him out with the observation: "The only manly thing about you is your pants."

In search of a new lover, Madame Max Adolphe, wearing her usual dark glasses, passed the prisoners in review. Her gaze fell on Uncle G. She commanded him to step forward, felt his inguinal muscles, examined his teeth, and ordered him to do two dozen knee bends and pushups. Evidently satisfied with the demonstration, she summoned him to her office, offered him a cigarette, and invited him to visit her after dark. When he declined the invitation, he was relegated to an underground cell, crawling with rats and roaches. Only the sympathy of a beautiful unknown woman, who squeezed her milk-swollen breasts through the bars of his cell, saved him from dying of thirst. Uncle G. claimed later on that this was his nurse, Annaise, who had gained admittance to the fort by bribing a sentry, but that is unlikely, for Annaise was well past sixty and her milk had dried up long before.

After midnight his cell door opened and a black hand pulled him into the open, across the pitch-dark barracks yard, and into the bedroom of the *commandeuse*, who, clad only in her riding boots, was kneeling on the floor with her torso stretched across her bed. She pointed at a whip that was hanging on a nail. Her bare back shone like black silk, and the temptation was too much for Uncle G. All night long the whip swished and smacked; all night the *commandeuse* whimpered and moaned. And the sounds penetrated to the casemates, where the internees were tossing and turning in their bunks.

13

AT the end of March 1942 the internees were loaded onto an American troop ship and taken to Florida. There, up to their knees in mud, beleaguered by clouds of mosquitoes and bossed by the descendants of black slaves, they were made to plant rice and drain mangrove swamps. When the German government protested this outrageous treatment of Aryans and backed up its protest by sending a submarine, which shelled the hotels of Miami Beach and left deep craters in the carefully manicured grass of a golf course, the internees were moved inland. After a days-long trip through the waving wheatfields and rustling cornfields of the Middle West, they reached their destination, Bismarck, North Dakota, where they were welcomed with open arms and a banquet by the ship's cook of the *Bremen*, which, finding itself in New York harbor when the United States entered the war, had been seized with all on board. Thanks to the unaccustomed abundance of food, the internees put on so much weight that escape became unthinkable. Their families at home, living on barley soup and skim milk, wouldn't have recognized them.

To combat un-German obesity, gymnastics and sports contests were organized, as were amateur performances of classical plays, calculated to impress the barbarous Americans with the enormous superiority of German culture. Because of his olive complexion, Uncle G. was given the roles of Franz Mohr in Schiller's *The Robbers* and of Mephisto in Goethe's *Faust*. In his free time he made airplanes out of plywood and canvas to carry secret messages to his relatives in Bismarck. One of his messages reached its addressee, who, however, instead of schnapps or cigarettes, sent only Bibles to the camp: like all Mormons, he looked upon liquor and tobacco as snares of the devil.

While General Paulus is capitulating in Stalingrad and Rommel in North Africa, and Eisenhower is getting ready for the Normandy landing, the belligerent powers, through neutral intermediaries, negotiate an exchange of prisoners. The list drawn up by Count Bernadotte includes the name of my uncle G., who protests that, though holding a German passport, he is a Haitian citizen because his mother was an authentic Haitian; her skin, despite the regular use of soap and water, has lost none of its original color. His petition is rejected, or perhaps merely disregarded. He is condemned to exchange American fleshpots for German stewpots, and in August 1943 a ship flying the flag of the Swedish Red Cross lands him in Hamburg.

During the previous night, Allied bombers have subjected the residential quarters of the city to a massive air raid. An enormous smoke cloud fills the sky, and with every gust of wind a gray rain of ashes descends on the burned-out ruins. Wrecking teams in striped pajamas are clearing away the rubble, intermingled with survivors searching for relatives or belongings. Though it has been expressly stipulated that no exchanged prisoner should serve in the armed forces, Uncle G., who under questioning lays claim to some knowledge of rocketry, is assigned to a special unit of the

Waffen-SS, in Peenemünde, which is developing, under the direction of a certain Wernher von Braun, a miracle weapon which the High Command hopes will reverse the fortunes of war.

Uncle G., who had gone about his earlier aeronautical experiments with heaven-storming enthusiasm, takes only a halfhearted interest in his new assignment. He is negligent in the performance of his duties, leaves secret papers lying around, shares his food ration with the Polish and French prisoners working under him, and says "Good morning" instead of "*Heil Hitler.*" His boots are not polished bright, his black uniform jacket is not buttoned properly; the SS rune sits askew on his collar, and the death's-head emblem is absent from his cap. All in all, he looks more like a hippie who has donned a uniform on Mardi Gras than a member of an elite troop, whose motto, "Our honor is loyalty," implies iron discipline and unconditional obedience. Though Rottenführer Streitwolf, his company commander, reports every lapse of military discipline to higher quarters, Uncle G. goes unpunished, thanks to the protection of Wernher von Braun, who attaches more importance to imagination and technical know-how than to military punctilio. But when Uncle G. refuses to wear the Iron Cross that is conferred on every member of the special unit after the V 1 rocket is fired successfully on London, Streitwolf's denunciations can no longer be ignored. At his trial by court-martial, Uncle G. explains that he prefers to keep his Iron Cross in his locker for fear of its rusting in the damp air. The SS judge gives him an Iron Cross Second Class as a substitute for his rust-prone Iron Cross First Class. When this one too remains unworn, both decorations are canceled. He is discharged from the special unit and sent to Buchenwald as a concentration-camp guard. A punitive and probationary assignment.

I don't know whether Uncle G. ever did any guarding in Buchenwald. There are three versions of the story, two heroic, one unheroic. According to Version No. 1, Uncle G. showed even less zeal as an SS man in Buchenwald than he had in Peenemünde and tried to palliate the suffering of the inmates under his control by sharing his bread ration with them and slipping them chocolate and cigarettes whenever possible. In this way, he gained the confidence of the illegal prisoners' organization and smuggled secret messages out of the camp, including blueprints, sketches, and photographs, thanks to which the Allies were accurately informed about the internal organization of the camp, the situation of SS barracks, inmates' barracks, shot-in-the-neck room, crematorium, and so on.

All went well until one morning when his immediate superior, Rottenführer Streitwolf, surprised him sitting in the branches of Goethe's oak tree, which happened to be in the middle of the camp, blowing up condoms and releasing them—with attached instruction tags on which he had scribbled demoralizing slogans—into a sunlit wintry sky. By order of Commander Pister he was shorn of both rank and hair in the presence of his entire unit, given twenty-five lashes, and converted from guard to inmate. The illegal prisoners' organization took him under its wing as a "political" and protected him from the chicanery of the kapos and the vengeance of his former comrades. Armed with a homemade pistol, which is still exhibited in the Buchenwald Museum, Uncle G. is believed to have taken part in the uprising in which the prisoners liberated themselves in the morning hours of April 11, 1945, shortly before the American troops got there.

If only for chronological reasons, this version is impossible. The celebrated Goethe oak, which the notorious Obersturmbann-führer Koch had left standing for reasons of piety when the woods on the Ettersberg were cleared, was cut down during the last winter of the war and used as fuel for the crematorium. It seems more likely that Uncle G. never embarked on his duties at Buchenwald. No sooner had he arrived there than he was sent to escort a shipment of prisoners to the Moselle, where airplane engines were being built in a munitions plant owned and operated by the SS. As the train was passing through a tunnel, the prisoners overpowered their guards and exchanged their striped pajamas for black SS uniforms. Only Uncle G., who is believed to have taken a hand in the revolt, was allowed to keep his uniform. With the armored train and its guards as hostages, the prisoners are thought to have crossed the West Wall in the course of the Ardennes offensive.

This version strikes me as too adventurous. Uncle G. was no more cowardly than the next man, but he was also no hero. What seems more likely is that he quite unheroically deserted his company by ducking into the bushes by the side of the road, hid during the day in woods and vineyards, and under cover of darkness crossed the border into France. He claims to have fêted the capitulation in Paris with oysters and champagne, though, as every child knows, May is not an oyster month and after the Allies' victory parade there wasn't a drop of champagne to be found in Paris.

14

I n June 1945 Uncle G. set out for Port-au-Prince on a freighter sailing under Panamanian flag. His second stay in Germany, like his first, had ended in flight. He took French leave, left by the back door. Once and for all, he had his belly full of the Greater German Reich and its rulers. He was a victim of *force majeure*, a product of historical circumstances, not a hero, more like a footnote to history. But one thing is certain: he was the only SS man in Buchenwald whose mother was black and who might far more appropriately have worn the striped pajamas of the inmates than the black uniform of the SS.

His involuntary trip to Europe has so aged him that his friends scarcely recognize him when he lands in Port-au-Prince. He looks like an extinct volcano, a repentant sinner on Ash Wednesday; only his eyes show a spark of the old fire. Grown taciturn and morose, he seems to have shelved his high-flown plans. His one aim in life is now to get married, establish a family, and enjoy the simple pleasures out of which the war cheated his generation. But there is a lot to do first. The pharmacy is in bad shape. The greater part of the furnishings and stock have been damaged or stolen, the cellar is crawling with rats, half the roof has been eaten by termites, bats fly in and out of the unglassed windows, the name plate sits crookedly over the door, the paint has peeled off, and the calligraphic inscription—*Pharmacie L. Buch*—*Produits Chimiques et Pharmaceutiques*—*en Gros et en Détail*—has paled and become illegible. The beggars and cripples who once besieged the entrance have moved elsewhere, giving way to hungry dogs lacking an eye, an ear, a paw or two. Since there is little hope of financial compensation—the competent ministry has postponed its decision indefinitely—Uncle G. leases the more-or-less restored premises to a furniture importer, who uses them to store imported French beds, which have become wildly fashionable in Port-au-Prince. Uncle G. retires to the tumbledown shed in the back yard and lives there like a hermit amid the rusty machines formerly used to bottle essence of cola nuts. In good weather he takes American GIs, who are recovering in the Caribbean from the horrors of war in the South Pacific, for rides in a glass-bottom boat that he himself has built, pointing out the sights through the bulletproof glass: swarms of many-colored fish, coral, sea anemones, and so on. "See that shark over there," he says in his best English. "It's REAL." As he starts the motor up again, the blood-group tattoo under his left shoulder becomes visible for an instant; in case the reader hasn't noticed, Uncle G. is lefthanded.

15

I PASS over a number of years in the course of which he marries, begets children, builds a house inspired by the Weimar Bauhaus, hence free from the tyranny of the right angle. After work he sits with his wife on the veranda, looking out over Port-au-Prince Bay, whose blue is dotted with white sails, thoughtfully sipping a rum cocktail that he has mixed from Barbancourt rum, the juice of three fresh-squeezed oranges or limes, several heaping tablespoonfuls of sugar, and plenty of shaved ice—as an optional refinement a dash of grenadine and two squirts of bitters may be added. With this drink, the excellence of which I am prepared to vouch for, the story of Uncle G. might end, if on September 22, 1957, a new savior of Haiti had not stepped forward to guide the island, devastated by Hurricane Hazel, to a grandiose and unprecedented future. HAITI—C'EST MOI! JE N'AI D'ENNEMIS QUE CEUX DE LA PATRIE! This time it's not a loudmouthed housepainter who wants to repaint the whole globe, but a simple country doctor, affectionately addressed as Papa Doc by his patients, though they died like flies under his hands. His name is Dr. François Duvalier, and his models are Jesus Christ Hitler Stalin Mao Tse-tung Nasser N'Krumah and Kemal Ataturk. Unlike his forerunners, who favored lighter colors, the new housepainter works exclusively in black, black like the night he brings down on his country—the nights in Haiti are blacker than anywhere else—a night from which his victims never awaken. During the day, the self-appointed president for life keeps to his palace, hiding his eyes behind dark glasses, as fearful of light as an owl; at night, under cover of darkness, he sends out his secret army after prey.

Inevitably a squad of Tontons Macoute break into the shed behind the former pharmacy one night and once again chop Uncle G.'s almost finished plane to kindling. He is obliged to slip away on a fishing boat that takes him to Miami Beach, where he wades ashore in the gray of dawn, with no other belongings than the shirt on his back and, in his head, the plans for his airplane. He applies for American citizenship—Wernher von Braun vouches for him by telex from Texas—sends for his family, and opens a carpentry shop. He specializes in doors—doors are needed everywhere and Uncle G. makes sturdy ones, reliably mortised and glued, that can be slammed or wrenched open without disintegrating into their components. Simple wooden doors for illegal immigrants from Haiti, thrown up dead or alive on the Florida beaches, or luxury portals for millionaires, with silver fittings and mahogany veneer, which open and close soundlessly in response to a pressed button.

But Uncle G., at the expense of his hard-earned savings, fashions the finest door for himself, a winged door to the beyond,

chockful of the most modern electronic instruments. I saw this
sinfully expensive object with my own eyes, chocked up on the
lawn of his modest bungalow in Miami Beach, swathed, like a
monument waiting to be unveiled, in a plastic tarp. Just then Uncle G. was busy fastening the name plate to his "door." With a
deft stroke he apposed his signature to the calligraphic sign, *Plaisirs de l'Eternité*. How literally these words were meant my father
and I didn't realize when we bade Uncle G. good-bye at the Miami
International Airport, unless it was the Miami Domestic Airport.
Nor did Uncle G.'s wife and children suspect the destination of
his flight. Maybe he was going to visit his sister in Beverly Hills
or attend a class reunion in Darmstadt. Or could he have been
planning an assassination, a flaming signal that would burn his
name once and for all into the annals of the twentieth century?
The date points in that direction: November 22, 1967, the lucky
day of his deadly enemy Papa Doc, the date on which he had
seized power ten years before, and on which six years later he
would murder his adversary John F. Kennedy with a *ouangan*, a
deadly voodoo curse, as was whispered at the time in Haiti. While
on the streets of Berlin and New York the passers-by burst into
tears, champagne bottles were uncorked in Haiti's Presidential
Palace.

What were Uncle G.'s plans? And what was in the firmly tied
bundle that with my help he heaved into the hold of his plane?
Leaflets to drop on the teeming streets of Port-au-Prince or a bomb
for the Presidential Palace? Both were possible. But before we
find out for sure, we see him taking leave of his wife and children,
we see him squeezing into the cockpit of his plane and giving the
thumbs-up sign, meaning that all is well on board. We see the
plan, on instructions from the tower, taxiing to the starting position; we see it accelerating, lifting off, and, framed in waving
handkerchiefs, flying out over the Atlantic, into the rising sun.

That evening the international news agencies receive a telex to
the effect that a single-engine plane of unknown origin had dropped
leaflets with antigovernment slogans on Port-au-Prince and released a bomb over the Presidential Palace—which, however,

missed, though it slightly injured a member of the palace guard. Since then no news of Uncle G. and not a trace of his plane, the *Emeraude*. Possibly the plane was hit by one of the anti-aircraft guns stationed in front of the palace, or forced by a pursuit plane to land on the Aéroport François Duvalier, where Uncle G., under the expert supervision of a certain Streitwolf, was tortured to death by the Tontons Macoute; or he may have been taken to Fort Dimanche and entrusted to the care of Madame Max Adolphe, who amused herself with him for one night before relegating her faithless lover to a pit filled with quicklime. Or perhaps the *Emeraude* landed in the Savanne Zombi behind the Seven Mountains, and perhaps its pilot joined the Jeune Haiti guerrilla group, operating in the border region between Haiti and the Dominican Republic, on the head of whose commander, a certain Plaisir Eternité, Papa Doc set a price. Furious that this partisan leader kept tricking his pursuers by turning himself into a stray dog, Papa Doc seems in his last government decree to have ordered the murder of all the stray dogs in Haiti. *Krick? Krack!*

Or else—and for aesthetic reasons I prefer this version of the end of my story—Uncle G. simply flew away, in the traces of Saint-Exupery, flew over the sea and toward the sun, until, coming too close to it, he burned his wings and, somewhere in the Bermuda Triangle, plummeted into the ocean, which sent up a shower of foam as when Icarus fell, before taking him to its watery bosom irrevocably, once and for all.